Many a French/English teacher, **Emma Darcy** changed
careers to computer programming before the happy demands
of marriage and motherhood. Very much a people person, and
always interested in relationships, she finds the world of
romance fiction a thrilling one and the challenge of creating
her own cast of characters very addictive.

Chantelle Shaw enjoyed a happy childhood making up stories
in her head. Always an avid reader, Chantelle discovered Mills
& Boon as a teenager and during the times when her children
refused to sleep, she would pace the floor with a baby in one
hand and a book in the other! Twenty years later she decided
to write one of her own. Writing takes up most of Chantelle's
spare time, but she also enjoys gardening and walking. She
doesn't find domestic chores so pleasurable!

Seduced by the Boss

KATE HARDY
EMMA DARCY
CHANTELLE SHAW

Printed and bound in Spain
by CPI, Barcelona

MILLS & BOON

First Published in Great Britain 2019
by Mills & Boon, an imprint of HarperCollins*Publishers*
1 London Bridge Street, London, SE1 9GF

SEDUCED BY THE BOSS © 2019 Harlequin Books S. A.

Billionaire, Boss...Bridegroom? © 2016 Pamela Brooks
His Boardroom Mistress © 2003 Emma Darcy
Acquired by Her Greek Boss © 2017 Chantelle Shaw

ISBN: 978-0-263-27941-2

1019

BILLIONAIRE, BOSS...
BRIDEGROOM?

KATE HARDY

For Charlotte Mursell and Sheila Hodgson—
with love and thanks for letting me
have so much fun with this story. x

CHAPTER ONE

I'm coming to get you, Bella texted swiftly. Hold on.

For once, it looked as if she was going to be the rescuer instead of the rescuee. With her new job to boost her confidence, she thought she might just be able to handle it. For once she would be the sister who was calm, collected and totally together instead of the flaky, ditzy one who always made a mess of things and needed to be bailed out of a sticky situation.

She glanced around and saw a black cab waiting at the kerbside. Relieved, she rushed up to it and jumped in.

'Can you take me to the Bramerton Hotel in Kensington, please?' she asked the cabbie.

There was a dry cough from beside her, and she whipped her head round to discover that there was already a passenger sitting in the back seat.

She'd been so focused on getting to Grace that she hadn't even noticed the other passenger when she'd climbed into the taxi.

'I'm so sorry,' she said. 'I didn't mean to be rude. Look, I realise that you were here first, and technically I ought to leave right now and let you get on with your journey, but I really do need to get to the Bramerton as quickly as possible. Would you mind finding another taxi and...and...?' She waved a desperate hand at him. 'Look, I'll pay for your cab.' It'd mean extending her overdraft yet again, but what were a few more pounds if it meant that she could return the favour for once and help Grace? Besides, she was about to start a new job. Next month, her cash-flow situation would be a bit better.

'Actually, I'm heading towards Kensington myself,' he said. 'I'll drop you off at the Bramerton.'

Relief flooded through Bella. She'd found the modern equivalent of a knight on a white charger: a man in a black cab. She wouldn't have to let her sister down. 'Thank you. Thank you so much.' She gave in to the impulse, leaned forward and kissed him soundly on the cheek. 'You have no idea how much I appreciate this.'

'What's so urgent?' he asked as the taxi drove off.

'It's a family thing,' she said. It wasn't her place to tell anyone about her sister's situation, let alone tell a complete stranger.

'Uh-huh.' He paused. 'Did I see you just come out of Insurgo Records?'

She looked at him, surprised. The man looked like a businessman on his way home from a late meeting, and he was hardly the target market for an independent record label—even though Insurgo's artists were a real mixture, from folk singer-songwriters to punk and indie bands, with a few oddities thrown in. 'Yes,' she said.

'Are you one of their acts?'

In her black jeans and matching plain T-shirt, teamed with a shiny platinum-blonde bob, Bella knew that she probably looked as much like an indie musician as she did a graphic designer. 'No,' she said.

But the man had been kind enough to let her share his taxi, so she didn't want to be rude to him. Besides, making small talk might distract her enough to stop her worrying about whatever had sent her normally cool and capable big sister into meltdown. She smiled at him. 'Actually, I'm a graphic designer, and I'm starting work at Insurgo next week.'

'Are you, now?'

Something about the way he drawled the words made alarm bells ring in the back of her head. But he was a total stranger. She was making something out of nothing. 'Yes, and I'm really looking forward to it,' she said with a bright smile. 'I'll be designing website graphics, album covers and band merch. Actually, I'm still trying to get my head round the fact that I've just been offered my dream job.' In an ideal world she would've preferred to have Insurgo as a client rather than as her employer, but working for someone full-time again meant that she'd have a regular income for a while—and right now she needed a regular income rather more than she needed her freedom.

'You don't know who I am, do you?' he asked.

'Other than a stranger who's been kind enough to let me share his taxi? No,' she admitted.

'Allow me to introduce myself,' he said, leaning forward out of the shadows and holding out his hand.

Bella caught her breath. He was gorgeous. Dark hair that was brushed back from his face, cornflower-blue eyes, and the kind of jawline that would've made him a hit in any perfume ad. She really had to resist the urge to reach out and trail her fingertips down his clean-shaven cheek. And that mouth. Almost pouting, the sexiest mouth she'd seen in a while.

Almost in a daze, she shook his hand, noting how firm his handshake was. And she studiously ignored the fact that her palm was tingling; after the way Kirk had let her down, she was officially off men. Even if this one was very easy on the eye and was wearing a beautifully cut designer suit, what looked like a handmade white shirt, a silk tie and highly polished Italian shoes.

No involvement.

Full stop.

Because she was never going to let anyone make her feel as foolish and useless as Kirk had made her feel, ever again.

'Hugh Moncrieff,' he said, and he waited for the penny to drop.

It took five seconds.

'Hugh Moncrieff—as in *Insurgo's* Hugh Moncrieff?' Bella asked in horror.

'That would be me,' he said. And he looked as if he was enjoying her reaction.

He was her new boss? 'But—you can't be.' Even though it would explain why he'd asked her if she was one of the artists; he must've thought that his second-in-command had signed her up in his absence.

'Why not?'

'Because you—you—' She gestured to his suit. 'You don't look like an indie record label owner. You look like a stockbroker.'

'The bank always likes the company's MD to wear a suit,' he said mildly. 'If I'd turned up to the meeting in ripped jeans and an avant-garde T-shirt, with funky hair, they'd have seen me as less of a professional and more of a risk.'

The bank? That nasty feeling got a lot worse. If he'd been to the bank for a meeting, all dressed up, at this time on a Friday evening, did that mean the company was in trouble and her job would be over before it had even started?

Her fears must've shown on her face, because he said, 'It's our annual review, and I went for a drink with a business contact afterwards. Don't look so worried. So you're my new graphic designer?'

'Bella Faraday,' she said. 'And I'm very good at what I do.'

'I expect you are, or Tarquin wouldn't have hired you,' he said dryly.

'So what are you doing in a taxi, when you own a record label? Why don't you have your own car, or a limo or something to drive you around?' The question was out before she could stop herself and she groaned inwardly. Way to go, Bella, she thought. Just grill your new boss, two minutes after you insulted him by saying he didn't look like the owner of an indie record label. Carry on like this and you'll be picking up your cards on Monday morning instead of starting your job.

So much for never letting herself feel foolish again. Right now she felt like a prize idiot.

'That's an easy one.' He smiled. 'My car happens to be in the local garage, having something fixed. I'd rather put my money into the business than waste it by hiring a flashy limo to do little more than wait around for me all day. Hence the taxi.'

Bella could feel the colour swishing through her cheeks. 'I'm sorry. It's not my place to question you. Look, um, please ask the cabbie to pull over and drop me off, and I'll get out of your way and find myself another taxi.'

'You said it was urgent—a family thing.'

'It is.'

'Then let me get you to the hotel. Tarquin obviously

overran with the interviews and made you late in the first place, so it's Insurgo's fault.'

'No, it's not,' she said. It wasn't anyone's fault. But right at that moment she was more worried about Grace than about making a good impression on her new boss, so she'd accept the offer. 'But thank you for the lift. I really appreciate this.'

'No problem.'

She texted Grace swiftly.

In taxi now. Wait for me in Reception.

Finally the taxi driver pulled up outside the Bramerton Hotel.

'Thank you again, Mr Moncrieff,' she said politely. 'How much do I owe you for the cab fare?'

'Nothing. You're practically on my way,' he said.

'Thank you. Really. And I'll work late every night next week to make up for it,' she said, and left the taxi before she could say anything else stupid.

When she walked into the reception area, Grace was waiting there, white-faced and silent. And there was no sign of Howard. Why wasn't Grace's fiancé waiting with her? Had something happened to Howard? No, of course not, or Grace would've said something in her texts. Not just that single word: Help, followed by rejecting Bella's call and sending a second text: Can't talk now. And now Bella was seriously worried. What on earth had happened?

But Grace had been right about one thing. They couldn't talk about it here. Not with Howard's parents' golden wedding anniversary going on in one of the function rooms. Whatever it was, Bella had her sister's back. And they were leaving. Now.

'Come on. Let's get out of here,' Bella said softly, put her arm round Grace and led her out of the hotel.

Back in the street, she looked around for a taxi.

Then she realised that the taxi that had dropped her off was still waiting at the kerb, exactly where she'd left it. And Hugh Moncrieff was still there too, though he'd moved seats so that his back was to the cabbie. He wound the window down and beckoned them over. 'Can I give you a lift somewhere?'

'But—' she began.

'Everything's clearly not OK,' he said softly, looking at Grace, 'so I'll drop you and…your sister, I presume?' At her nod, he continued, 'I'll drop you where you need to go. What's the address?'

Bella definitely didn't want to leave Grace alone tonight, and her own flat wasn't big enough for two. Biting her lip, she gave him Grace's address. 'Thank you so much,' she said. 'We both really appreciate this. Especially as you didn't have to wait.'

'No problem.'

She helped Grace into the car. Grace still hadn't said a word. Worried, Bella took her hand and squeezed it; but Grace didn't return the pressure. And this time nobody seemed disposed to make any small talk. With every second, Bella felt more and more awkward.

Then, just as the taxi turned into Grace's road, Grace threw up. All over Hugh's posh Italian shoes and suit trousers.

'I'm so sorry,' she mumbled.

She looked almost as mortified as Bella felt—and Bella had no idea what to say. What could you say when your sister threw up over your new boss? Apart from an equally apologetic, 'I'm so sorry.'

Hugh brushed it aside. 'These things happen. Do you need help getting her indoors?'

'Thank you, but no—I think you've done more than enough to help us, this evening.' Bella took a deep breath. 'Look, I'll pay for valeting the taxi and I'll pick up the bill for dry-cleaning your suit and replacing your shoes.'

'We'll sort it out later,' he said. 'Are you sure you can manage?'

'I'm sure,' Bella fibbed. At least she had Grace's spare door key, so actually getting into the flat wouldn't be a problem. 'And thank you. And sorry. And—'

'Just get your sister safely inside,' Hugh cut in. 'We'll sort out everything later.'

'Thank you. And I'm sorry,' Bella whispered again, and helped Grace out of the taxi.

This really wasn't how Hugh had expected to spend a Friday evening. Or how he'd expected to meet the newest member of his team.

The poor woman had looked horrified when her sister threw up everywhere.

Did Bella often rescue her sister like that? he wondered. Funny, the other woman had been dressed so soberly, in a navy linen dress and sensible shoes. Looking at them together, most people would've guessed that the younger woman was the one who partied too hard and would be most likely to throw up in the back of a taxi and need looking after.

Or maybe Bella's sister hadn't been drunk. Maybe

she'd been ill. But then surely Bella would've said that her sister was ill, or even called an ambulance?

But it was none of his business. He should just take a step back and ignore it.

'I'm sorry about all that,' he said to the driver. 'If you can drop me home, I'll pay for the cost of valeting the taxi and lost fares.' He gave the driver the address.

Though he still couldn't get Bella Faraday out of his head. Especially the moment when she'd kissed his cheek; it had felt as if he'd been galvanised. And then, when she'd shaken his hand, every nerve-end had been aware of the feel of her skin against his.

Hugh was definitely attracted to her. More attracted than he'd been towards anyone in a very long time.

But.

After the whole fiasco with Jessie, he'd learned his lesson well. Hugh would never, ever mix work and pleasure again. As Tarquin had just hired Bella as their new graphic artist, it meant that she came firmly under the category of work. So he'd have to just ignore the pull of attraction in future and treat her just the same as he did every single one of his colleagues—by keeping her at a professional distance.

Even if she did have the sexiest mouth and sparkliest eyes he'd ever seen.

No involvement.

No risks.

This time, he'd stick to the rules.

'I'm so sorry I was sick everywhere,' Grace said once they were sitting down inside her flat.

Bella frowned. 'Didn't you eat anything to line your

stomach before you started knocking back whatever it was that made you throw up?'

'Champagne. No,' Grace said miserably. 'My stomach was tied in too many knots to eat.'

And Grace hardly ever drank. It wasn't a good combination. Not to mention really worrying—what had been so bad that Grace had had to get drunk? She took a deep breath. First things first. She needed to get Grace sober. 'Right. First of all you're having water—lots and lots of water,' Bella said. Then she looked through Grace's cupboards. Please let there be something that she could actually cook. Or, failing that, cereal to soak up all that champagne.

Then she spied the box of porridge oats. Perfect. Even she could follow the instructions on the box and make porridge in the microwave.

While the porridge was cooking, she took a banana from Grace's fruit bowl and chopped it up. She added it to the finished cereal and put the bowl in front of Grace, who immediately pushed it away.

'I can't.'

'Eat it,' Bella said firmly. 'Your electrolytes are all over the place and bananas are great for sorting that out, and oats will help because they're bland carbs which will raise your blood sugar without upsetting your stomach.'

'How do you know all this stuff?' Grace asked, looking bemused.

Bella smiled. 'Remember I dated a doctor a couple of years back? He gave me the lowdown on the best food to eat for a hangover.'

'I'm sorry,' Grace said again. 'Was the taxi driver very angry?'

'Don't worry,' Bella said airily. 'My boss is sorting it.'

Grace did a double-take. 'Your *boss*?'

'Uh-huh.' Bella flashed her sister a grin. 'Guess what? I got the job.'

'I—oh, my God. Are you telling me that I just threw up over your boss before you even started the job?' Grace asked, looking horrified as Bella's words sank in. 'Oh, no. I'll talk to him and explain, so he doesn't sack you or—'

'Gracie, it's fine,' Bella cut in.

'It's not fine at all! I've messed things up for you. Look. I'll pay for the dry-cleaning.'

Bella smiled. 'I already told him I'd do that, and I said I'd pay for valeting the taxi as well.'

'My mess, my bill,' Grace said. 'I'll pay.'

'Gracie, just shut up and eat your porridge. I don't want to hear another word from you, young lady, until that bowl is empty.'

'You sound like Mum,' Grace muttered.

'Good,' Bella retorted. Usually Grace was the one who sounded like their mother and Bella was the one hanging her head in shame.

She made Grace eat every scrap and drink two more glasses of water before she resumed her interrogation. 'Right. Now tell me—what happened?'

'I can't marry Howard.'

It was the last thing Bella had been expecting. Her older sister had been engaged for the last four years. OK, so Howard was a bit on the boring side, and his parents were nightmares—Bella had dubbed them Mr Toad and Mrs Concrete Hair with good reason—but if Grace loved him then Bella was prepared to be as sweet as she could be to them. 'What? Why not? Don't you love him any more?' And then a nasty thought struck her. 'Is there someone else?'

'Of course there isn't anyone else.' Grace shook her head. 'I wouldn't do that to him.'

'Not deliberately, no, but you can't help who you fall in love with,' Bella said. She'd fallen for Mr Wrong enough times, and Kirk had shattered her trust for good. She'd never trust another man with her heart again, no matter how attractive he was. It had taken her six months to rebuild her life—and she was still angry with herself for being so naïve and trusting. Why hadn't she been able to see that he was stringing her along?

'I love Howard, but I'm not in love with him,' Grace said. 'There's a difference.'

'I know.' Bella squeezed her hand. 'And it's a big difference. A deal-breaking difference.'

'He's never made me feel breathless and dizzy, as if he'd swept me off my feet.'

Not surprising: Howard was cautious and sensible. Which wasn't a bad thing, Bella thought, but the occasional bit of spontaneity wouldn't have hurt. And it might have made her sister's world complete—which clearly hadn't happened. On paper, Grace and Howard were the perfect match—both sensible and cautious—but there was a little thing called chemistry. Without that, life would be miserable. 'You can't spend the rest of your life with someone who doesn't make your world light up.'

Grace bit her lip. 'I think you're about the only person who'd understand that. Mum's going to be so disappointed in me.'

'No, she's not, and neither is Dad—they both want you to be happy, and if marrying Howard wouldn't make you happy then you definitely shouldn't marry him,' Bella said firmly.

'I'm not sure if he was in love with me, either,' Grace said.

'Of course he was—you're gorgeous and you're clever and you're nice. What's not to love?' Bella demanded, cross on her sister's behalf.

'I think we both loved each other,' Grace said softly, 'but not *enough*. I mean, we've been engaged for ever— who stays engaged for four years in this day and age?'

'A couple who's saving up the deposit for a house?' Bella suggested.

'Apart from the fact that we already have enough money for that between us, you know what I mean—if we'd really wanted to be together, we'd have got married years ago rather than waiting. We don't even live together,' Grace pointed out.

'Mainly because Cynthia of the Eagle Eyes and Concrete Hair wouldn't let her little boy shack up with someone,' Bella said. 'Is that why you got drunk tonight?'

'No. That was the cartoon you drew for me,' Grace said. 'Fifty Shades of Beige.'

Bella winced. 'Sorry. I meant it as a joke, to make you laugh and relax a bit. I knew you weren't looking forward to the golden wedding party.'

'But it was so accurate, Bel,' Grace said. 'I was the only woman there not dressed in beige.'

Bella couldn't help laughing. 'Ouch. I didn't think it'd be quite that bad.'

'Oh, it was,' Grace said feelingly. 'I really didn't belong there. I drank three glasses of champagne straight down to give me courage and I didn't even feel them, Bel.'

Which was really un-Grace-like. She always stopped

after one glass. Sensible, reliable Grace who looked after everyone else and was usually the one mopping up, not the one throwing up.

'I was just numb. And that's when I realised,' Grace said, 'that I was walking into a life I didn't actually want. In fifty years' time, I don't want to be sensible Grace Sutton, whose heart has never once skipped a beat, and whose mother-in-law directed the whole of her marriage.'

'If anyone could live until well past the age of a hundred, marbles intact and with an iron fist, it'd be Mrs Concrete Hair,' Bella said feelingly. 'You've done the right thing, Gracie. It's much better to call a halt now than to wait until after you married Howard and then have all the mess of a divorce to go through.'

'Really?' Grace didn't look convinced. She looked guilty and miserable and worried.

'Really,' Bella said firmly, 'and Mum and Dad will back you, too.'

'I just feel that I've let everyone down—all the work that's gone into arranging the wedding.' Grace swallowed. 'Not to mention the money.'

'But you haven't let anyone down,' Bella said. 'Well, except you should have told me all this a *lot* sooner, because I'm your sister and of course I'm going to support you. I hate to think that you've been miserable all these months when I could've listened to you and made you feel better. You're doing the right thing, Gracie. And cancelling the wedding won't be that hard.' This was slightly surreal; it felt almost as if she and Grace had swapped places and it was her turn to be the sensible, super-organised one instead of the one who needed rescuing. 'Just give me a list of the names and contact details of the people you've invited and your suppliers, and I'll ring them all and explain the wedding's off.'

'I can't make you do that!' Grace protested.

'You're not making me do it. I'm offering. That's what sisters are for.' She took a deep breath. 'Have you told Howard?' Was that why her no-longer-future brother-in-law had been so conspicuously absent?

'No. I'm going to do that tomorrow.'

A nasty thought struck Bella. 'Does he actually know you've left the party?'

Grace nodded and winced. 'I told him I had a migraine and was going home.'

'And he didn't even offer to take you home? That's atrocious!'

'How could he leave? It's his parents' golden wedding anniversary party.'

'OK, so he probably had to stay there with the Gruesome Twosome,' Bella allowed, 'but he still should've made sure you were all right first and at least arranged a taxi to take you home.'

'I'm sure he would've done, but I told him you were coming to collect me,' Grace explained.

'Hmm,' Bella said, though she wasn't mollified. What on earth was wrong with the man? Howard had been Grace's fiancé for four years and he hadn't even made sure that she got home safely when she'd told him she felt ill—whereas Hugh Moncrieff, a man Bella had met only a few minutes ago, had not only come to the rescue, he'd offered to help them indoors. So her new boss had a good heart as well as a gorgeous face.

Not that she should be thinking about that right now. Or ever, for that matter. Even if she wasn't officially off men, her boss was completely off limits. She needed this job, to get her finances back on an even keel. 'So what are you going to tell Howard tomorrow?' she asked.

'The truth—that I can't marry him.' Grace closed her eyes for a moment. 'And that means I'll lose my job and my home, too, Bel. No way can I go back to work at Sutton's, not when I've just split up with the boss's son—and in the circumstances I can hardly ask them to give me a reference to work anywhere else. Plus I've already given my landlord notice on my flat. I know he's already found my replacement and signed a contract, so I can't ask him just to ignore my notice and renew my lease.' She blew out a breath. 'I've really burned my bridges, Bel—and who knows how long it'll take me to find another flat?'

'You don't have to. Come and stay with me,' Bella said immediately.

Grace hugged her. 'I love you, sweetheart, and thank you for the offer, but your flat's barely big enough for one person. You don't have room for me to stay. I'll ask round my friends—one of them will put me up until I can find somewhere—and I'll sign on with a temp agency. If I explain the situation, I'm sure they'll understand about the problem with references and help me to find a way round it.'

This sounded more like her level-headed older sister, Bella thought. Planning. Being sensible. The oats were clearly soaking up what remained of the champagne. 'It'll all work out, Gracie. You know what Mum always says: when one door closes, another opens.'

'I know,' Grace said.

'I was going to take you out for sushi and champagne tomorrow, to celebrate my job—because I wouldn't have got it without you—but we can take a rain check on that, because I'm guessing you won't want to see champagne again for months.'

'Definitely not.' Grace winced. 'And you might've lost the job, because of me.'

'Of course I haven't. I'll talk my boss round,' Bella said, sounding slightly more confident than she actually felt. 'Go and have a shower, clean your teeth, get in your PJs, and then we're going to snuggle under a throw on your sofa and watch a re-run of *Friends*.'

'I love you, Bel,' Grace said. 'You're the best sister I could ever ask for.'

Even though they were total opposites, Bella thought. And, weirdly, tonight, it felt more as if she was Grace and Grace was her.

'You came straight to rescue me without asking any questions,' Grace said.

'Of course I did! You've done it often enough for me,' Bella said. 'And you're the best sister I could ever ask for, too, and I love you to bits—even when I don't understand you. Now go and get yourself sorted out. I'm going to raid your fridge because I'm starving, and I'm sleeping on your sofa tonight. Tomorrow, you can talk to Howard and we'll make that list and work through it together. And then things will start to look better. You'll see.' She hugged her sister. 'Nothing fazes a Faraday girl, right?'

'Right,' Grace said. 'Nothing fazes a Faraday girl.'

CHAPTER TWO

ON MONDAY MORNING, Bella left her flat at what felt like the crack of dawn. For the last couple of years, she'd been able to set her own working hours—meaning that she could sleep in until ten a.m. and work until late, which suited her body clock better—but she knew that she needed to make a good impression on her first day at Insurgo. Particularly given what had happened at her first meeting with the boss. She couldn't afford to put a single foot wrong from now on, not if she wanted to keep her job and get her finances back on track.

And getting up early would take her mind off what had been a truly lousy weekend. Seeing Grace—the person she'd always looked up to as a tower of strength, someone who knew exactly what to do to sort out any given situation—fall apart had shocked Bella deeply. Right now Grace was in the almost same position that Bella had been in six months ago: recovering from a wrecked relationship, worrying about her job and her home and her finances, and feeling as if the sun would never rise again.

OK, so Grace had been the dumper rather than the dumpee, in this case, and she hadn't lost her best friend and the contents of her bank account as well as her partner; but it was still going to be a huge change in Grace's life. Even though it had definitely been the right decision.

Privately, Bella thought her sister had had a lucky escape. Howard was a nice enough guy, but he was completely under his mother's thumb. Marrying him would've basically meant having the rest of her life run by Cynthia of the Eagle Eyes and Concrete Hair, the most cold and judgemental woman that Bella had ever met. And finding another job might just mean that Grace's new employer would appreciate her and give her the promotion she deserved. At Sutton's, Grace had been totally taken for granted. They'd expected her to work way more than her fair share of hours, under the guise of being 'almost family', but they hadn't actually given her any of the privileges of being 'almost family'.

Howard had barely raised a single argument when Grace had gone to see him on the Saturday morning and called off the wedding. So he clearly hadn't loved Grace enough to fight for her. And Bella thought her sister deserved a lot better than a man who was nice enough but didn't have a backbone and would never stand up for her.

Today was a new chapter in both their lives. And hopefully this one would be better for both of them.

Bella paused outside the Insurgo Records building. The basement was a recording studio and practice rooms that local bands could book as well as being used by the Insurgo artists; the ground floor and mezzanine comprised a seriously upmarket café—the sort that offered coffee made in a way that looked more as if it was some kind of laboratory experiment than a hot drink, but apparently brought out the floral notes in the coffee; and the top two floors were the record label's actual offices.

'All righty. Welcome to your new life,' she told herself, and went inside.

She was the first member of staff to arrive in the office after Tarquin, Hugh's second-in-command—to her
relief, Hugh didn't seem to be there yet—and Tarquin
handed her a design brief, a portable CD player and a
pair of headphones. 'Welcome to Insurgo, Bella,' he said
with a smile. 'We're doing a limited edition of coloured
vinyl for Lacey's third single. She's one of our singer-
songwriters. I've given you a rundown here of our target
market, her career history, and the PR schedule. What I
need you to do is have a listen to the album—the song
we're releasing is the fourth track on the CD—and come
up with some ideas for the vinyl cover and a promo T-
shirt, based on what you hear. Or if you have ideas for
other promo items, bring them along. If you'd like to have
a second listen in one of the studios rather than working on headphones, just yell and I'll sort it out. And then
maybe we can talk about it, later this afternoon?'

'That sounds fine,' Bella said, smiling back. She was
being thrown in at the deep end, but she'd always thrived
on that. And this was her chance to shine and prove they'd
made the right decision in hiring her.

'This is your desk, over here,' he said, and ushered
her over to a desk by the window with a drawing board
and a computer. 'As soon as Shelley—our admin guru—
comes in, we'll get you set up with a password and user-
name. The meeting room's on the floor above, along with
Hugh's office, the staff kitchen and the toilets. I'm over
there in the corner, and I'll get everyone else to come over
and introduce themselves as they come in.'

'That's great,' Bella said, trying to damp down the
sudden flood of nervousness. She was good with people.

She knew she'd find her place in the pack and quickly work out how to get the best from the people she worked with. She always did. But these first few hours in a new role were always crucial.

'Is there anything else you need before you start?' he asked.

Yes, but she couldn't exactly explain why she needed to see the boss without making things awkward. But she'd just thought of the perfect excuse to go up to the next floor. Hopefully Hugh wasn't in yet, so she could leave the neatly wrapped parcel in her bag on his desk. Or, if he was at his desk, hopefully he'd be alone and she could snatch two minutes to apologise to him in person while the kettle boiled. She smiled. 'How about I make us both a coffee?'

'Excellent idea. Thank you.' Tarquin smiled back. 'Mine's black, no sugar. I'm afraid it's pretty basic stuff in the staff kitchen—tea, instant coffee and hot chocolate—but help yourself to whatever you want. If you'd rather have something fancier, you do get a staff discount downstairs at the café.'

'That's good to know. And instant does me just fine. At this time of the morning, any coffee works,' Bella said with a smile.

To her relief, she discovered that Hugh's office was empty. So she wouldn't have to confront him quite yet, then. There was a pile of post set neatly in the middle of his immaculate desk; she left the package and accompanying card on top of it. Then she boiled the kettle and made herself and Tarquin a mug of coffee before heading downstairs to her desk and making a start on the design briefs. And please, please, let Hugh Moncrieff accept her apology.

* * *

Hugh wasn't in the best of moods when he drove his car into the tiny car park behind the record label offices. His shoes had just about recovered from their ordeal on Friday night, and his dry cleaner had said that there would be no problem with his suit. But he hadn't been able to get Bella Faraday out of his head.

Worse still had been the slew of texts and emails and answering machine messages over the weekend from his mother, his brothers and their partners, all reminding him that his brother Nigel's engagement party was coming up and they couldn't wait to see him. Which meant that Hugh was in for another bout of familial nagging. Why was he still messing about with his record label? When was he going to treat it as the hobby it ought to be and get himself a proper job?

He knew what the subtext meant: he was the baby of the family, so they'd let him have his dream and do his degree in music instead of economics. Now he was thirty, they all thought it was about time he gave up his financially risky business and joined the long-established family stockbroking firm instead. Which was why Bella's comment about him looking like a stockbroker had really touched a raw nerve on Friday night.

He happened to like his life in London, thank you very much. He loved what he did at Insurgo—finding promising new talent and polishing their rough material just enough to make them commercially viable without taking away the creative spark that had caught his ear in the first place. Insurgo had made a name for itself as an independent label producing quality sound, from rock through to singer-songwriters, with a sprinkling of oddities who wouldn't fit anywhere else. Hugh was proud of what he did. He didn't want to give it up and be a stock-broker like his older brothers Julian, Nigel and Alistair.

But the question that drove him really crazy was when his family asked when he intended to find a nice girl and settle down. That wasn't going to happen any time soon. Jessie had cured him of that particular pipe dream. He knew his family meant well, but couldn't they see that they were still prodding a bruise?

His business, his heart and his music had all taken a battering. And finding a new, suitable girlfriend wasn't going to repair any of the damage. Sheer hard work and some quiet support from his best friends had rescued his business, but nowadays his heart was permanently off limits. And the music that had once flowed from his fingers and filled his head had gone for good. He didn't write songs any more. He just produced them—and he kept a professional distance from his artists.

He ran through a few excuses in his head. None of them worked. Even being in a full body cast wouldn't get him a free pass. He was just going to have to turn up, smile sweetly at everyone, and metaphorically stick his fingers in his ears and say 'la-la-la' every time his career or his love life was mentioned. Which he knew from ex-perience would be about every seven minutes, on average.

He collected a double espresso from the café on the ground floor—on a morning like this one, a mug of the instant stuff in the staff kitchen just wasn't going to cut it—and stomped up to his office, completely bypass-ing the team. What he needed right now was music. Loud enough to drown out the world and drown out his thoughts. A few minutes with headphones on, and he might be human enough again to face his team without biting their heads off even more than he normally would on a Monday morning.

And then he stopped dead.

On top of the post he'd been expecting to see, there was a neatly wrapped parcel and a thick cream envelope. It wasn't his birthday, and the parcel didn't look like a promo item. It was the wrong shape for a CD or vinyl, and in any case most unsigned artists pitching to him tended to email him with a link to a digital file on the internet.

Intrigued, he untied the ribbon and unwrapped the shiny paper from the parcel to discover a box of seriously good chocolates.

Whoever had sent them had excellent taste. But who were they from and why?

He opened the envelope. Inside was a hand-drawn card: a line-drawing of a mournful-looking rabbit with a speech bubble saying 'Sorry'. Despite his bad mood, he felt the corner of his mouth twitch. Whoever had sent this was saying they knew he wasn't a happy bunny—and Hugh had a very soft spot for terrible puns.

He opened the card to find out who'd sent it, and a wad of banknotes fell out.

What?

Why on earth would someone be giving him cash?

He scanned the inside swiftly. The writing was beautifully neat and regular, slightly angular and spiky—the sort you'd see on hand-drawn labels in an art gallery or upmarket bookshop.

Dear Mr Moncrieff
Thank you for rescuing us on Friday night and I'm
very sorry for the inconvenience we caused you.

*I hope the enclosed will cover the cost of valeting
the taxi, dry-cleaning your suit and replacing your
shoes. Please let me know if there's still a shortfall
and I will make it up.*
Yours sincerely
Bella Faraday

He blinked. She'd said something on Friday evening about reimbursing him, but he really hadn't been expecting this. Since the parcel and the card had been hand-delivered, that meant that their new graphic designer must already be at her desk. Most of his team didn't show their faces in the office until nearly ten, so she was super-early on her first day.

And, although he appreciated the gesture, it really wasn't necessary. His shoes had survived and the rest of it hadn't cost that much. He really ought to return the money.

He picked up his phone and dialled his second-in-command's extension. 'Can you send Ms Faraday up?'

'Good morning to you, Tarquin, my friend,' Tarquin said dryly. 'How are you? Did you have a nice weekend? What's new with you?'

Hugh sighed. 'Don't give me a hard time, Tarq.'

'Get out of the wrong side of bed, did we? Tsk. Must be Monday morning.'

Hugh knew he shouldn't take out his mood on his best friend and business partner. Particularly as Tarquin dealt with all the stuff Hugh didn't enjoy, and with extremely good grace, so Hugh could concentrate on the overall strategy of the label and actually producing the music. 'I'm sorry. All right. Good morning, Tarquin. How are you? Did you have a nice weekend?'

'That's better. Good, and yes, thank you. I'll send her up. And be nice, sweet-cheeks—apart from the fact that it's her first day, not everyone's as vile as you are on Monday mornings.'

'Yeah, yeah,' Hugh said, but he was smiling as he put the phone down again.

Bella was leaning back in her chair, eyes closed, listening to the music. Lacey, the singer, had a really haunting voice, and the song was underpinned by an acoustic guitar and a cello. The whole thing was gorgeous, and it made Bella think of mountains, deep Scottish lochs, forests and fairies. Maybe she could design something with mist, and perhaps a pine forest, and...

She yelped as she felt the tap on her shoulder; reacting swiftly, she sat bolt upright, opened her eyes and pulled off the headphones.

Tarquin was standing next to her, his face full of remorse. 'Sorry, Bella. I didn't mean to give you a heart attack.'

Bella's heart was galloping away. 'You did give me a bit of a fright,' she said. 'I was listening to the CD—it's really good.'

'Yeah, we think so, too.' He smiled. 'Lacey's a bit of a character. She always performs barefoot.'

'Like a fairy.' The words were out before Bella could stop them. 'Sorry. Ignore me. Did you want something?'

'Yes. Hugh just called down. Can you go up to his office?'

Uh-oh. This must mean that Hugh had seen her parcel and her card. And she had absolutely no idea what his reaction was going to be. 'Um, sure,' she said.

'Don't look so worried. The boss knows it's your first

day, so he probably just wants to say hello and welcome you to Insurgo,' Tarquin said kindly.

Bella wasn't so sure. If that was the case, why hadn't Hugh come down to the open-plan office? She had a nasty feeling that she wasn't going to be hearing a welcome speech but a 'goodbye and never darken our doorstep again' speech. Clearly the parcel she'd left on her new boss's desk hadn't been anywhere near enough of an apology.

Her fears must have shown on her face because Tarquin said, 'His bark's worse than his bite. He just isn't a Monday morning person, that's all. Whatever he says, don't take it to heart, OK? Everyone else in the office will tell you the same—and if he does say something horrible to you, he'll come and apologise to you in the afternoon when he's human again. It's just how he is.'

'Right,' Bella said, forcing a smile she didn't feel. 'I'll, um, be back in a minute, then?' She switched off the music, scribbled the word 'mist' on a pad to remind herself what she'd been thinking about, and then headed for Hugh's office, her stomach churning. Hesitantly, she rapped on the closed door.

'Come in,' he said, sounding brusque.

Tarquin obviously hadn't been joking when he'd said that the boss wasn't a Monday morning person.

And then her jaw almost dropped when she walked in. The last time she'd seen Hugh Moncrieff, he'd been clean-shaven and wearing a formal suit. Today, he was wearing black jeans and a black T-shirt with the Insurgo Records logo on it, and his dark hair looked as if he'd dragged his fingers through it instead of combing it. Teamed with the shadow of stubble on his face, it made him look as if he'd just got out of bed. He should've looked scruffy and faintly disgusting. But the whole package made him seem younger and much more approachable—not to mention sexy as hell—and her mouth went dry. Oh, help. She really had to remember that he was the boss, not just another one of the team. That made him totally off limits. And, besides, she didn't want to risk her heart again. Which gave her a double reason not to act on the desire flickering through her—even if he was the most gorgeous man she'd ever met.

He indicated the box of chocolates sitting on his desk. 'Why?'

Hugh was clearly a man of few words when it came to work. Or maybe it was his Monday morning-itis. 'Why the gift? Or why chocolates?' she asked.

'Both.'

'The gift is to say thank you, because you went way beyond the call of duty on Friday night. They're chocolates, because I can hardly buy a man flowers,' she said. 'Did I give you enough money to cover everything, or do I still owe you?'

He handed her the envelope, which felt thick enough to contain most—if not all—of the money she'd enclosed with the card. 'My shoes survived, and the taxi and dry-cleaning bill weren't much,' he said.

She knew that wasn't true. The taxi firm would've charged him for valeting the cab and for lost earnings while the cab was out of action, being cleaned. 'I'd rather you kept it,' she said, putting the envelope back on his desk. 'To cover the inconvenience.'

'No need,' he said firmly. 'Is your sister OK? She looked terrible.'

Bella was grateful he hadn't mentioned the 'incident'. 'Grace barely even drinks, normally,' she said, not wanting him to think badly of her sister. 'Friday was totally out of character for her. She's the sensible and together one who sorts everything out; I'm the flaky and unreli—' She stopped mid-word, realising what she was about to blurt out. 'Not when it comes to my job, obviously. I'm very together where my work is concerned,' she added swiftly.

'But in your personal life you're flaky and unreliable?' he asked.

'Not unreliable, even—just the one who opens her mouth without thinking things through,' she said ruefully. 'As you've just heard.'

'But you rescued your sister when she needed your help,' he said softly. 'That definitely counts in your favour. Is she OK?'

'She will be,' Bella said. 'I've never known her to drink three glasses of champagne in a row, let alone on an empty stomach. I think that's why... Well. What happened, happened,' she finished, squirming slightly.

'Thank you for the chocolates. They're appreciated,' he said. 'And you have good taste.'

'I have good taste in a lot of things.' And then, when she saw the momentary flicker in those amazing blue eyes, she wished the words unsaid. 'I wasn't flirting with you,' she added quickly.

His expression said, *much*. 'Take the money,' he said. 'I don't need it. Use it to take your sister out to dinner or something.'

'Just no champagne, right?'

This time, he smiled. 'Right. Welcome to Insurgo, Ms Faraday.'

'Thank you, Mr Moncrieff.' Formality was good. It put distance between them. And it would stop her getting crazy ideas about a man with a mouth that promised sin and eyes that promised pleasure. Ideas she most definitely couldn't let herself act upon.

'Are you settling in all right?' he asked.

'Yes. Tarquin's given me my first brief and I'm working on it now. The limited edition single.' She paused. 'He said it was coloured vinyl. I have to admit, I don't know that much about how records are physically made. Can the vinyl be any colour you like?'

'Yes.'

'So you could do clear vinyl with little wisps of mist running through it?'

He looked surprised. 'Yes. Would that tie in with your design?'

'It's what the music makes me think of. Obviously it's just an idea at this stage,' she said swiftly, not wanting to put him off. 'I'll do some rough mock-ups of three or four ideas, and then I'm discussing them with Tarquin this afternoon.'

'Good. I look forward to seeing what you come up with.'

She blinked, surprised. 'You're going to be in the meeting as well?'

'Not that one,' he said. 'But when you and Tarquin have agreed which one to work on, then you come and convince me.'

'Challenge accepted.' The words were out before she could stop them. Oh, for pity's sake. This wasn't about a challenge. This was about...about...

Why had her brain suddenly turned to soup?

He smiled, then, and it felt as if the room had lit up. Which was even more worrying. She didn't want to start feeling like this about anyone, especially not her new boss.

'I think I'm going to enjoy working with you, Bella Faraday.'

There was a faint trace of huskiness in his voice that sent a thrill right through her. This was bad. She could actually imagine him saying other things to her in that gorgeous voice. Things that would turn her into a complete puddle of hormones.

No.

This was *work*. She was really going to have to keep reminding herself that her relationship with Hugh Moncrieff was strictly business. Maybe she'd ask her friend Nalini to put a temporary henna tattoo on her hand saying 'work'—written in Hindi script, so Bella would know exactly what it meant but anyone else would think it was just a pretty design. The last thing she needed was for anyone to guess how attracted she was to her new boss.

'Good,' she said. 'I'll get back to it, then.' She gave him what she hoped was a cool, capable smile, and forced herself to walk coolly and calmly out of his office. One foot in front of the other. One step at a time. She could run once that door was closed behind her.

She'd just reached the doorway when he said softly, 'Bella. I think you've forgotten something.'

Oh, help. She had to suppress the surge of lust. 'What's that?' Oh, great. And her voice *would* have to be squeaky. She took a deep breath and turned to face him.

He waved the envelope at her.

'Keep it.'

He coughed. 'As your boss, I'm pulling rank.'

If she was stubborn over this, she could lose her job. If she took the money back, she'd be in his debt.

Caught between a rock and a hard place. Or maybe

there was a way out. 'Then I'll donate it to charity,' she said. 'I'm sure you can suggest a suitable one.'

'Bella, this isn't a war,' he said softly, and she felt horrible.

'Sorry. It's just... I don't want to be in your debt. And I don't mean just you—I mean in *anyone's* debt,' she clarified.

'The dry-cleaning bill wasn't much, and the taxi firm is one I use a lot so they were pretty accommodating. And,' he added, 'I'm not exactly a church mouse.'

'Church mouse?' she asked, not following. Then she remembered the proverbial phrase. 'Oh. Of course.'

'Take the money,' he said softly, 'and it's all forgotten. As far as I'm concerned—and everyone else at Insurgo, for that matter—today's the first day we've met. And I'm notorious in the office for not being a Monday morning person. Nobody usually talks to me until lunchtime on Mondays because I'm so horrible.'

That made her feel better. 'Thank you,' she said, and took the envelope.

'Have a nice day,' he said, and that smile made her feel warm all over.

'You, too,' she said. But this time she lost her cool and fled before she could drop herself in it any more.

CHAPTER THREE

EVEN THE IDEA was crazy.

Asking Bella was completely out of the question. She was practically a stranger; and she worked for him. Two huge reasons why Hugh knew that he should put this whole thing out of his mind.

Hugh paced up and down his living room. The problem was, now the idea was in his head, it had taken root. And he knew why. He could tell himself that asking Bella to play the role of his unsuitable new girlfriend was simply because she was vivacious enough to make it convincing. It was true enough. But he knew that the real reason was a little more complicated than that. Spending the weekend together in Oxford would give them a chance to get to know each other better. See where things took them.

Crazy. Stupid. Insane.

He knew better than to mix work and pleasure. Last time he'd done it, the whole thing had gone so badly wrong that he'd nearly lost Insurgo—letting down his business partner and the people who depended on them for their jobs. Only the fact that Roland, his other best friend, had bought into the business as a sleeping partner had saved him from having to shut the business down.

He'd worked stupid hours and he'd managed to stabilise everything, but he would never take that kind of risk again.

Strictly speaking, he knew this wasn't quite that kind of risk. Bella wasn't Jessie. She was part of the team, not one of his artists. She'd signed a contract with him rather than making a verbal agreement she could back out of because it would be her word against his. Getting to know Bella wasn't going to put Insurgo at risk.

But it still made him antsy. Since Jessie, he'd promised himself he wouldn't trust anyone with the battered remains of his heart. He'd keep an emotional distance. So why couldn't he get Bella Faraday out of his head? Why did he keep remembering that frisson of awareness when she'd kissed his cheek in the taxi? Why did her smile make him feel as if the room lit up?

And, more importantly, what was he going to do about it?

By Thursday morning, Bella felt as if she'd been working at Insurgo for ever. The rest of the team turned out to be total sweethearts, and they all shared a love of music, cinema and art. Everyone pitched in with ideas and suggestions, and nobody minded if theirs was passed over for a better one. And she absolutely loved working there.

The previous afternoon, they'd had a discussion in the office about which song fitted them, so that evening she'd made little name-cards for everyone's desk with a quick caricature of them and the title of 'their' song in place of their name.

It seemed mean to leave Hugh out just because he was upstairs rather than in the open-plan office with everyone else, so she made a card for him as well. 'I Don't Like Mondays' fitted him to a T, she thought.

That morning, as the rest of the team filtered in to the office and saw the name-cards on their desks, there was much hilarity.

Then Hugh walked into the office—clearly not in a good mood, again—and Bella rather wished she hadn't done a name-card for him after all.

'Ms Faraday—a word?' It was more of a command than a question, and his expression was completely impassive.

'Yes, Mr Moncrieff,' she said, and followed him meekly up to his office.

Even though he didn't say a word to her on the way up, she had a pretty good idea what this was about. He hadn't been amused at all by his name-card.

'I'm sorry,' she said as soon as he closed the door. 'We were messing about yesterday—' Then she stopped as she realised how incriminating her words were. 'Over lunch, that is,' she said swiftly, hoping that she'd saved the situation. She didn't want to get her new colleagues into trouble. 'We were talking about the song title that could be used instead of your name to describe you, and I drew the cards last night at home. It was just a bit of fun and I didn't mean anything by it.'

'You picked an appropriate one for me,' he said.

Though every single day seemed to be Monday, where his mood was concerned. He really wasn't a morning person. She winced. 'Sorry. Are you very cross with me?'

'No—and, just for the record, I don't mind a bit of messing about in the office. It helps creativity, and I know everyone on the team puts the hours in. As long as the job gets done on time and within budget, I don't actually care *how* it's done.'

'Then why did you want to see me?' Bella asked, now completely mystified. If he wasn't about to haul her over the coals for unprofessional behaviour, then what?

'Your hair.'

She frowned. 'What's wrong with it?'

'You were blonde, yesterday. Platinum blonde.'

'Ye-es.' She still didn't follow.

'And today your hair's red.'

A tiny bit brighter red than she'd intended, because she'd been so busy making the name-cards the previous evening that she'd left the dye in for a few minutes longer than she should've done, but she liked it. 'Yes.' Where was he going with this? 'Is there a problem with my hair colour?' she asked carefully.

'No, not at all.'

She really didn't understand. 'Then why did you call me into your office?'

'Do you have a boyfriend?'

Apart from the fact that you weren't supposed to answer a question with a question, what did that have to do with anything? She frowned. 'You're not supposed to ask me things like that. My relationship status has nothing to do with my job.'

'I know. I'm not asking you as your employer.'

She caught her breath. Did that mean he was asking her out?

No, of course not. That was totally ridiculous. Just because she had a secret crush on him, it didn't mean that her feelings were in any way returned. And in any case her boss was the last man she'd ever date. It would cause way too many problems, and she really couldn't afford to give up her new job. There was no guarantee that the receivers dealing with her former client would give her any of the money owing to her, because she'd be way down the pecking order in the list of creditors. And, with Kirk having cleaned out their joint bank account so she no longer had any savings to her name, she was stuck. 'Why do you want to know?' she asked, trying hard to sound polite rather than aggressive.

'Because I need you to do something for me, and I need to know whether I'm going to have to have a conversation with an overprotective boyfriend first.'

She was still none the wiser. 'Now you've really got me worried.'

He raked a hand through his hair. 'Bella, don't be difficult.'

That was rich, coming from him, she thought. Hugh Moncrieff was the walking definition of difficult. He was also the walking definition of sexy, but she had to keep a lid on that thought.

'Can you just answer the question?' he asked. 'Are you single or not?'

'I'm absolutely single,' she said crisply, 'and I intend to stay that way.' Just so it'd be totally clear that she wasn't trying to flirt with him—or anything else.

'Good.' He gave her a sweet, sweet smile. One that made a lot of warning bells ring in her head. 'Bella, remember when I helped you out last Friday night?'

The warning bells got louder. 'Ye-es.'

'Good.' He paused. 'I need a favour.'

So much for him saying that they'd forget what had happened. Clearly there were strings attached, after all. How *disappointing*. 'What sort of favour?' she asked carefully.

'I need you to be my date for a family event.'

That was the last thing she'd expected. Had she misheard? 'To be what?' she asked.

'My date for a family event,' he repeated.

That was what she thought he'd said. The words 'date' and 'Hugh Moncrieff' were a dangerous combination. 'Why?'

'A more pertinent question, in the circumstances, is "when?",' he said dryly.

OK. She'd play it his way. 'When?' she asked sweetly.

'Next weekend.'

What? 'As in tomorrow or as in next Friday?'

'As in a week on Saturday,' he clarified.

Talk about lack of notice. Did he think that she didn't have a social life? 'Where?'

'Oxfordshire.'

'Right.' She stared at him. 'So let me get this straight. You want me to go to a family do with you in Oxfordshire and pretend to be your girlfriend.'

'Yes.'

She folded her arms. 'Now I think "why" might be pertinent. And I think I deserve a proper answer.'

'If you want to know the truth, it's because you,' he said, 'will annoy my family.'

She looked at him through narrowed eyes. 'That's not very nice—to me or to them.' And it made her feel as if he was using her. Just like Kirk had. Even though Hugh was being upfront about it rather than pretending he loved her, the way Kirk had, it still stung.

'Given that you told me you were flaky and unreliable in your personal life, I think that's a fair assessment.'

He had a point. Just. 'It's still not very nice,' she said.

'I didn't expect you to go all Mary Poppins on me,' he drawled.

She resisted the urge to slap him or to say something rude. Just. 'That's because you don't know me very well. What do you want to achieve?'

He frowned. 'I don't know what you mean.'

'You said you want to annoy your family. What do you really want to happen?'

When he still looked blank, she sighed. 'Look, you're at point A and you clearly want to be at point B. What do you need to do to get from A to B, and is having a fake girlfriend really the most effective way to do it?'

He raised his eyebrows. 'That's a bit sensible.'

'Coming from me, you mean?' She rolled her eyes. 'It doesn't come from me, actually. It's the way my sister looks at things.'

'Your sister Grace? As in the woman who downed three glasses of champagne on an empty stomach…?' he said, with mischievous emphasis.

She put her hands on her hips and glared at him. 'Don't you dare be rude about my sister,' she warned. 'I already told you: that was really unlike her. It was due to special circumstances—and don't bother asking what they were, because I'm not going to tell you. It's none of your business.'

'Absolutely,' he said, disarming her. 'Actually, I like the way you stand up for your sister. And you have a point.'

'So why you do want to annoy your family?' she asked.

'This,' he said, 'is even more confidential than anything commercial I talk to you about.'

'That's *obvious*,' she said, rolling her eyes at him.

'You're my boss, so anything you say to me in this room stays in this room unless you say otherwise.'

'Thank you,' he said. 'Since you ask, the reason is because I'm sick and tired of them nagging me to settle down. So if I turn up to my brother's engagement party with someone who looks completely unsuitable, maybe they'll shut up and get off my case.'

She digested this slowly. He was saying she was unsuitable because of her hair? 'So basically you're asking me to play the kooky wild child. You want me to turn up with a mad hair colour, wearing ridiculous shoes and a skirt that's more like a belt?'

'What you wear is entirely up to you,' he said. Then he looked thoughtful. 'But, as you mentioned it first, yes, I think you probably have the chutzpah to carry off that kind of outfit.'

She still couldn't quite work out if he was insulting her or praising her. Instead, she asked the other thing that was puzzling her. Well, apart from the fact that he was single. Even though he tended to be grumpy in the mornings in the office, she knew he had a good heart. He'd rescued her and Grace when they'd needed help, even though at the time they'd been complete strangers—and at the time it hadn't felt as if there were any strings. Plus he had beautiful eyes and an even more beautiful mouth. The kind that made you want to find out what it felt like to be kissed by it.

She shook herself. That was something she shouldn't be thinking about. 'So why does your family want you to settle down?'

When he didn't answer, she pointed out, 'If you ask me to design something for you, then I need a brief to know what your target market is and what you want the design to achieve. I need to understand *why* before I can design something to suit. This is the same sort of thing. If I don't understand why you want me to play someone unsuitable, I'm not going to be able to deliver the goods, am I?'

'So you'll do it?'

'I didn't say that. I still reserve the right to say no.' If saying no was actually an option. Would her job depend on this? 'But if you tell me why and I agree with your reasoning, then I might consider it.' She spread her hands. 'Anything you tell me is confidential. But I would also like to point out that I do have a social life, actually, and I did have plans for the weekend.'

'I'm sorry.' He raked a hand through his hair, suddenly looking vulnerable. Which was almost enough to make her agree to help him, regardless of his motives.

Weird.

Hugh Moncrieff was old enough and tough enough to look after himself. You didn't get to be the successful owner of an independent record label if you were a pushover. He didn't need looking after by anyone. But that expression in his eyes had touched a chord with her. It reminded her of the look in Grace's eyes when she'd confessed that she didn't fit in with Howard's family and didn't think she ever could. That she'd felt trapped and miserable.

Was that how Hugh felt about his own family?

And why did she suddenly want to rescue him, when she was usually the one who had to be rescued?

'Of course you have a social life,' he said. 'And I don't expect you to say "how high" every time I ask you to jump.'

'Good,' she said. 'I'm glad that's clear.'

He gave her a wry smile. 'And I know I'm out of order, asking you to play a part.'

'It does make me feel a bit used,' she admitted.

'I don't mean it quite like that. I need help to deal with a tricky situation.'

'Just like I did—and you helped me, so it makes sense that I should return the favour.' Put like that, she thought, his request was much more reasonable.

'If it's possible for you to change your plans for the weekend and you do agree to help me by being my date, just be yourself. That'll do nicely.'

'Because I'm unsuitable?' she asked. Just when she'd started to feel OK about it, he'd made her feel bad again. Stupid. 'That's a bit insulting.'

'That isn't actually what I meant. You're confident,' he said. 'You're direct. You don't play games.'

'But you're asking me to play a game. Well, play a part,' she corrected herself. 'Which is pretty much the same thing.'

'I guess. I don't mean to insult you, Bella. I apologise.'

'Apology accepted.' She paused. 'So why do you need a date?'

He sighed. 'I'm the youngest of four boys. The other three are all stockbrokers in the firm started by my great-grandfather. My family would very much like me to toe the line and follow suit.'

She winced. 'Ouch. That's what I called you on Friday. I said you looked like a stockbroker.'

'I'm not one, and I never want to be one,' he said softly. 'Don't get me wrong. I'm not saying that it's a bad career—just that it's not right for me. My brothers love what they do, and that's fine. I'd support them to the hilt, but

I don't want to join them.' He gave her another of those wry smiles. 'That's why the label has its name.'

'Got you. Insurgo's Latin for "to rebel".' She wrinkled her nose. 'And, no, I didn't go to the sort of school that taught Latin. I looked it up on the internet. The only Latin I know is *"lorem ipsum"*—the stuff used as filler text in a design rough, and that's not really proper Latin.'

He smiled back. 'Actually, *"lorem ipsum"* is a mash-up of Cicero's *De finibus bonorum et malorum.*'

'Trust *you* to know that.' The words came out before she could stop them.

He laughed. 'I'm afraid I did go to the kind of school that taught Latin.' He dragged his hand through his hair. 'I love what I do, Bella. I like hearing artists play me raw songs—and then a different arrangement flowers in my head, and I can see exactly what they need to do to make it a hit without losing their original voice. I've never wanted to do anything else but produce music that I love—music that makes the world a better place. But my family worries about me, because the music business isn't exactly stable. Insurgo's doing well—well enough for some much bigger labels to have offered to buy me out, though I've always refused because I'm not going to sell out my artists like that—but I'm still at the mercy of the markets. We've managed to weather a few storms, but all it takes is one wrong decision that loses the business a lot of money, or for a couple of my biggest customers to go bankrupt and not pay me, and we could go under.'

'Tell me about it,' she said feelingly.

'I knew you'd get that bit. You've been there,' he said.

So either Tarquin had told him that she'd once had her own business, or he'd read her résumé. Or maybe both.

'Small businesses fail all the time,' she said, 'and I kept mine going for two years. If my best client hadn't gone bankrupt, owing me the equivalent of three months' salary, I'd still be a freelance designer now. But when one door closes another opens—and now I have a job I like here.'

'I take it back about being Mary Poppins,' he said. 'You're Pollyanna.'

'I'm just me,' she told him firmly, 'not a stereotype. But, yes, I believe in looking for the good in life.' She whistled the chorus from 'Always Look on the Bright Side of Life' and smiled.

'It's a good philosophy,' he said.

'You're right—you're perfectly capable of being a stockbroker, but it'd make you miserable. You're doing what you love,' she said. 'And there's nothing wrong with that. Why doesn't your family see that?'

He sighed. 'They have this little box ready for me. I'm supposed to fit in with a sensible job, a sensible wife, and two point four children or whatever it's meant to be nowadays. A *pied-à-terre* in London for me during the week, and an ancient pile in the countryside for the family, where the kids can grow up until we send them to boarding school.'

Was he describing what his own childhood had been like? 'I guess I'm lucky,' she said. 'All my parents and my sister want is for me to be happy and fulfilled.'

'Are you?' he asked.

She nodded. 'Are *you*?'

'Yes.' But she noticed that he didn't meet her eye. So did that mean he wasn't? And what, she wondered, was missing from his life?

Not that there was any point in asking. She was pretty

sure he'd stonewall her. Getting the information so far had been like pulling teeth.

'OK. So you want me to pretend to be your girlfriend, to show your family that you have no intention of meeting any of the criteria to fit that little box they've made for you. You already have a job they don't approve of, so what you need is an outrageous girlfriend to horrify them even more. That will be the icing on the cake, if you'll excuse me mixing my metaphors,' she said, hoping that she'd summed up the situation without missing anything.

'That's pretty much it.' He paused. 'So will you do it?'

'It's one way to get from A to B,' she said. 'But I think a much better one would be to sit down with your family and talk to them. Make them see how much you love Insurgo. Show them your passion for it. Play them the raw stuff, and then the final version with all the changes you suggested, so they can hear exactly what you do. Then they'll understand and be happy just to let you do it.'

'Maybe,' he said. 'But, even if they listened to me about my job, that's only half the problem dealt with. There's still the sensible wife they want me to have.'

She shrugged. 'You could always tell them you'd like a sensible husband.'

He grinned. 'You mean, ask Tarquin to pretend that he's my life partner as well as my business partner? I think Rupert—his other half—might have something to say about that.' Then his smile faded. 'I don't want a sensible wife. Or husband, for that matter.'

'What do you want?' she asked.

What did he want?

Never to have his heart broken again.

Which meant no more serious relationships. And it

had suited him just fine over the few months, dating casually and making sure that all his girlfriends knew that a diamond ring and a change of name were never going to be on offer. That he was looking for fun, not for for ever. And most of the time he didn't even bother with that. He concentrated on work. Though it wasn't quite the work of his heart any more. Not since he'd stopped writing music.

'What I want right now,' he said, 'is to get through Nigel's engagement party without being nagged about my choice of career or lifestyle.'

'You know that's not going to happen,' she said. 'That's the thing about families. They're interested in what you do, so of course they're going to ask questions and give their opinions, whether you ask for them or not. It's part and parcel of family life.'

Clearly she didn't mind about that as much as he did. Then again, she'd said that her family just wanted her to be happy. And she'd gone straight to her sister's rescue last week; he had a feeling that Grace would've come straight to Bella's rescue, too, if the positions had been reversed. His brothers certainly weren't batting his corner. They thought he ought to give in and join them in the family business.

She shrugged. 'So. Realistically, what's the best you can hope for?'

'That an outrageous girlfriend will distract them enough to stop them nagging me about when I'm going to settle down. Just for the weekend,' he added, wanting to make it clear that this wasn't a long-term thing.

'Weekend? I thought you said it was a party?'

'It's a weekend thing,' he explained.

She looked shocked. 'You're telling me that this engagement party is going to last for a whole *weekend*? Wow. I thought that my friends and I could party pretty hard, but we're all amateurs compared to that!'

'It's not that big a deal,' he said. 'We turn up for afternoon tea and cake on Saturday with the older relatives, and then we have a cocktail party in the evening. It's black tie, by the way.'

She looked thoughtful. 'So you want me to wear an unsuitable dress to the tea party bit, and something even more outrageous for the evening do rather than a proper little black dress.'

Oh, good. She understood and she wasn't going to give him a hard time about it. 'That would do very nicely.'

'And then what?'

'Um, we stay overnight— but you'll have your own room, don't worry. I'm not expecting you to share with me or anything,' he added swiftly. 'We'll have breakfast in the morning, go for a walk, stay for Sunday lunch because Ma will insist—except that'll be just my brothers and their partners and us, plus maybe an aunt and uncle or two—and *then* we can go home.'

'A whole weekend,' she repeated.

'The food will be excellent,' he said. 'And there will be pink champagne.' And then a nasty thought hit him. 'Unless last weekend put you off champagne?'

She rolled her eyes at him. 'That's mean. I already told you, my sister doesn't normally drink more than one glass. Last weekend was exceptional circumstances.'

'I apologise. Again.'

'Apology accepted, but I have a three strikes and you're out rule,' she warned. 'Do it again and I'll stand on your foot. In spike heels. I might be only five feet four, but I'm heavier than I look.'

'Got it.' The more time Hugh spent with Bella, the more he liked her. She made him feel different—she brought back the crazy, spontaneous part of him that he'd kept locked away since Jessie. Which was dangerous. Maybe he should call this whole thing off. For safety's sake.

'So what colour do you want my hair to be?' she said, cutting into his thoughts.

'Any colour you like. It's your hair.'

She smiled. 'Good answer. You're learning.'

'I'll pay for your frocks,' he said, 'and your shoes, and whatever else you want. Just tell me how much you need.'

'It's very tempting to say yes and drag you off to the fashion department in Selfridges with your credit card,' she said, 'but I guess it'd be more believable if I wore a charity shop find.' She paused. 'Or am I playing a gold-digger who expects you to bankroll her fashion habit?'

'I don't think you'd be a believable gold digger, because you're too independent,' he said. Again, so unlike Jessie, who'd always had an eye on the main chance. Except he'd been so in love with her that he hadn't seen it at the time. With Bella, what you saw was what you got—and that was refreshing. It tempted him to relax the rules where she was concerned. Part of him thought this was a bad idea; but part of him was intrigued enough to want to know where this could take them. 'A charity shop find would be good, but I meant it about paying for your clothes and what have you. Just get anything you need and I'll pick up the bill. You shouldn't be out of pocket when you're doing me a favour.'

'OK. I'll make sure I get receipts for everything. So I need outfits for a tea party, a cocktail party, breakfast, a walk and lunch.' She raised an eyebrow. 'I hope your car has room for a lot of luggage.'

'The brasher the better—and add that to your shopping list,' he said with a grin. 'And thank you. I think I'm actually going to enjoy this now.'

'Is it really going to be so bad, spending time with your family?' she asked.

And now she'd wrong-footed him again. He wrinkled his nose. 'I love them, but they don't see me for who I am. They don't listen to me. They want me to fit in their nice little box. That's the thing I find hardest to deal with.'

'So my job is to be their wake-up call. To make them see that by pushing you so hard, they're actually making you run just as hard in the other direction. Whereas, if they leave you be, you might just come up with a compromise that will keep you all happy.'

'I'm beginning to think that you should swap places with me and be head of strategy at Insurgo,' he said.

'Hardly.' She scoffed. 'I was working on design principles.'

'They work for strategy, too.' He paused. 'Thank you. I think I'm in your debt.'

'Strictly speaking,' she said, 'and, as you pointed out, I was in yours—you rescued Grace and me when we needed help. This is my chance to return the favour. And then we're quits—right?'

'Quits,' he agreed. 'That sounds good to me.' He reached over to shake her hand, then rather wished he hadn't when his palm started tingling. He really shouldn't start thinking about Bella in that way. He'd learned from Jessie that business and love didn't mix, and he didn't want to repeat his mistake. He was attracted to Bella—she was gorgeous and vibrant and she would make any man look more than twice—but he really shouldn't take this any further. They were going to keep this strictly professional. 'I'll let you get back to whatever you were working on,' he said. 'And thank you.'

'Last thing,' she said. 'What about an engagement present?'

'It's all taken care of. And the card.'

'How much do I owe—?' she began.

'It's all taken care of,' he repeated, cutting in. 'Really. I don't expect you to pay a penny towards this.'

'Can I at least take your mother some flowers, as we're staying at your parents' place?'

He frowned. 'That's very *suitable* behaviour, Bella.'

'Actually, it's common courtesy to take a present for your hostess,' she corrected. 'I don't mind people thinking I'm an airhead and unsuitable, but I *do* mind them thinking I'm rude and selfish. So. Flowers or chocolates?'

'She's a chocolate fiend. Dark. But you don't have to—'

'Yes, I do,' she cut in. 'Or the deal's off.'

And hadn't he asked her to help him partly because she was so outspoken and independent? 'OK,' he said.

'Good. And now I'm going back to what you pay me to do,' she said, and sashayed out of the room. As much as you could sashay in jeans and flat canvas shoes.

But the images in his head wouldn't shift all day. The curve of her backside. The confident, brisk way she moved. That spark of merriment in her blue, blue eyes. The curve of her mouth.

How would her mouth feel against his? Would she make his lips tingle as much as his skin? And how would it feel to lose himself inside her?

There suddenly wasn't enough air in the room. He

walked over to the window, opened it and shoved his head out. Maybe the noise from the traffic would clear his head.

It didn't.

'Get a grip, Moncrieff,' he warned himself.

This was strictly business. Letting his imagination loose was a seriously bad idea. He wasn't going to let himself think about what it would be like to touch Bella. To kiss her. To hold her close. This pretend girlfriend business was just to get him off the hook with his family. And, the more he kept telling himself that, the quicker he'd start to believe it.

CHAPTER FOUR

'ARE YOU SURE this is a good idea, Bel?' Grace asked.

'Going to Oxfordshire and pretending to be Hugh's unsuitable girlfriend? Possibly not,' Bella admitted. 'I did tell him I thought it'd be a better idea to be straight with his family and get them to see his passion for his work. But he's adamant that this is the best way to get them off his back—and I guess they're his family, so he should know the best way to handle them.'

'I don't mean just that,' Grace said gently. 'I mean getting involved in your boss's personal life.'

'I'm not getting involved in his personal life,' Bella insisted. 'Apart from the fact that I'm officially off men for good, I'm just doing this as a favour.'

Grace winced. 'To make up for me throwing up over him in the taxi?'

'No,' said Bella firmly. 'No.' Though he had hinted at it. Which had made it easier for Bella to say yes. Not that she wanted Grace to worry about it, so she kept that information to herself. 'He just needs someone to help him make his family back off. And I kind of fit the bill.'

'So you're going to a posh afternoon tea party wearing a skin-tight leopard-print dress,' Grace said.

'Yup. And I've got tiny, tiny shorts and high-heeled

mules for the country walk the next day. And, best of all, for the cocktail party... Meet my alternative to the little black dress.' Bella produced the curtains she'd found in one of the charity shops, flapped one with a flourish and draped it over one shoulder. 'Ta-da!'

Grace blinked. 'You're wearing a *curtain* to a cock-tail party?'

'Not quite—it's going to be a proper dress. Only I'm making it from a curtain instead of from normal dress fabric. Em said she'd come round tomorrow, measure me, and we'll cut it out and run it up together.' Bella grinned. 'This is where going to art school comes into its own. I know loads of people who can help. I just thought, what could be gaudier and more unsuitable for a black tie cock-tail party than a mini-dress made out of a curtain?'

Grace eyed the orange flowers. 'Um. Very nineteen-sixties.'

Bella's grin broadened. 'And it's so *The Sound of Music*, don't you think?' She draped the curtain over the back of her sofa, pulled Grace to her feet, and danced her sister around the tiny living room, all the while singing, 'How Do You Solve a Problem Like Maria?' but substi-tuting her own name in the song.

'You're impossible,' Grace said, but she was laughing.

'I'm a genius. And I've just had another great idea. We can have takeaway pizza tonight and watch *The Sound of Music* together. I love that film so much. And we can sing "Do Re Mi" in harmony—I'll even let you pick your part.'

Grace hugged her. 'I know what you're doing, Bel. You're trying to distract me. But I'm OK. Really. The hard bit was last weekend and breaking up with Howard. The temp agency's found me some work, I've got a couple of weeks to find a new flat before I have to move out of mine, and you've been the best sister and most brilliant support anyone could ask for. My new life starts now, and it's going to be just fine.'

'I still worry about you,' Bella said. She didn't quite dare ask if this was how Grace felt about her, most of the time. Grace had had to rescue her often enough from some scrape or other.

'I'm fine,' Grace reassured her again. 'But, yes, we can order a pizza and watch a film tonight. That sounds good.' She took a deep breath. 'And if this engagement party goes horribly wrong next weekend, just ring me and I'll drive straight down to get you, OK? It's only an hour and a bit from London to Oxford.'

'It won't go wrong,' Bella said. 'I'm just playing a part. Even if I wasn't officially off men, Hugh Moncrieff is the most unsuitable man in the world for me. He's my boss, and dating him would make everything way too complicated.'

'So why,' Grace asked, 'are my big sister antennae suddenly twitching like mad?'

'Force of habit,' Bella said with a smile. 'But nothing's going to go wrong.'

The following weekend, Bella's confidence in that statement had evaporated.

Had she gone too far with her outfit?

What if Hugh's family had a blazing row with him over her unsuitability and it ruined the engagement party? That really wouldn't be fair on Hugh's brother and his fiancée.

Maybe she ought to pack some suitable clothes as well, in case she needed to change at the last minute. Or borrow Grace's car so she could make a quick getaway if she needed to, rather than letting Hugh drive her down to Oxfordshire. Or maybe she should just make sure her mobile phone was fully charged and she'd got the number of a reliable local taxi firm.

Plus she and Hugh hadn't set any real ground rules. What did playing his unsuitable girlfriend actually mean? Holding hands, draping herself over him—or even kissing him?

The idea of kissing Hugh sent her into a flat spin.

He was her boss. She shouldn't even flirt with him, let alone entertain ideas about kissing him. Even if he was the most attractive man she'd met in years. Kissing was totally off the agenda.

So why, why, why couldn't she get the idea out of her head?

Her stomach was in knots by the time her doorbell rang, just after lunch.

When she answered the door, Hugh was standing there, wearing one of his business suits. He looked utterly gorgeous—and Bella felt completely out of place in her outrageous get-up. Particularly when his eyes widened in apparent shock as he took in what she was wearing: a tight leopard-skin mini-dress with a wide shiny belt cinched round her waist and spindly high heels, a chunky bead necklace, and she'd styled her hair so her normally sleek bob was in wild curls.

'This is a bit too much, isn't it?' she asked, indicating her outfit.

'It's, um, *interesting*,' he said. 'Very eighties. Especially the hair.'

In other words, he hated it. She'd gone way over the top. There was cutesy retro, and there was a total mess.

She'd clearly crossed the admittedly narrow line between the two. She took a deep breath. 'Sorry. Give me ten minutes and I'll change.'

He caught her hand. 'No, Bella, you're perfect as you are.'

A shiver ran through her at the feel of his skin against hers. She had to remind herself sharply that she was doing this as a favour to him—acting the part of his unsuitable girlfriend—and that was all. Any attraction she felt towards him was totally inappropriate and needed to be squashed. Like yesterday.

'Are you sure this isn't too much?' she asked, doubt still crawling through her. 'Are you quite, *quite* sure it wouldn't be better to switch to Plan B?'

'Which is?'

'Go to the party on your own and tell your family how much you love Insurgo, that you're perfectly happy being single and that you don't need a romantic partner to feel that your life's complete.'

'I could, but they wouldn't listen, so it has to be Plan A,' he said softly. 'And I want you to know how much I appreciate this, Bella. I don't know anyone else who could've carried this off.'

'Really?'

'Really. I'm not flannelling you.'

She could hear the sincerity in his voice. He really thought that she could do this. And to have someone believing her on a personal level, someone other than her family... That made her feel better about herself than she had in a long time.

'I'm truly grateful,' he said. 'Now, where's your luggage?'

She picked up her large, bright pink suitcase and

faked a confidence she didn't quite feel. 'OK. I'm ready. Let's go.'

His car was gorgeous—sleek and low-slung, with leather seats that were amazingly comfortable—and she wasn't surprised to discover that he had a really good sound system, too. She was happy enough to listen to music until they were out of London and on the motorway, and then she turned to him.

'Can I ask you some questions?'

'Sure you can ask,' he said, sounding as if he reserved the right not to answer.

'We'll start with your family,' she said. 'Even an unsuitable airhead girlfriend would know who she was going to visit. I know you're the youngest of four boys, and we're going to your brother Nigel's engagement party somewhere in Oxfordshire. Everyone else in your family is a stockbroker. And that's *all* I know. Do you not think that I might need to know everyone's names, at the very least?'

'I guess,' he said. His voice was totally expressionless, so she had no idea what was going through his head. 'OK. My parents are Oliver and Elizabeth. Pa's recently retired and spends half of his day on the golf course. Ma's in the WI and does charity work. My brothers—Julian's the oldest, married to Poppy, and they have a baby girl, Sophia. Alistair's the next and he's married to Harriet. Nigel's about to get engaged to Victoria, and they're getting married at Christmas. I'm the youngest, and I'm taking my new girlfriend Bella Faraday to meet the folks. Anything else?'

'Yes. Ground rules. What does playing your girlfriend actually mean?' she asked. 'Holding your hand? Draping myself artfully over you?'

He blew out a breath. 'I hadn't thought that far ahead, to be honest. I suppose they'd expect us to hold hands. And for me to dance with you at the cocktail party. Which is a point. Can you dance?'

She couldn't help smiling because he'd set up her answer so beautifully. And, with any luck, it would make him laugh and relax a bit, too. 'Would that be with or without a pole, Mr Moncrieff?'

As she'd hoped, he laughed. 'Without.'

'I don't really tend to go clubbing,' she said. 'But I go to a dance aerobics class, so I can move in time to music.'

'That's good enough for me.'

But he hadn't answered her question fully. 'Anything else?' she asked.

He frowned. 'Such as?'

'Normally, people who are dating tend to, um, kiss each other,' she said. 'Especially when dancing and parties are involved.'

'Ah. Yes. Kissing.'

The car suddenly felt way too small. And was it her imagination, or had the temperature just shot up by ten degrees?

'Chaste kissing would be acceptable,' he said.

Right at that moment, she didn't feel very chaste. And she wished she hadn't brought up the subject, because she could just imagine what it would be like to kiss Hugh Moncrieff. To cup his face in her hands and brush her lips against his, teasing at first, and then letting him deepen the kiss. Matching him touch for touch, bite for bite, until they were both dizzy with desire and he carried her off to his bed...

'Bella?'

'What?' She'd been so lost in her fantasy that she

hadn't heard him say anything to her. She felt colour flood into her cheeks.

'I said, are you OK with that?'

No. It was way too risky.

But she'd agreed to play his unsuitable girlfriend. And she was the one who'd brought up the question of kissing in the first place.

'I guess,' she said, trying to sound cool and calm and completely unbothered. 'Next question.'

'Hit me with it,' he said dryly.

'Why are you single?'

He blew out a breath. 'You're very direct. Why are *you* single?'

Because she'd put her trust in the wrong people. 'I asked you first.'

He shrugged. 'I was seeing someone and it didn't work out.'

That was obviously the need-to-know version of the story, she thought. She didn't think Hugh was the type to be a selfish love rat—someone like that wouldn't have come to her and Grace's rescue when they'd needed help, the other week—so she assumed that he hadn't been the one to end the relationship. Had his ex broken his heart? But there was no point in asking him. She knew he'd stonewall her.

'You?' he asked.

'You summed it up for me, too. I was seeing someone and it didn't work out,' she said. She didn't want to tell him the whole messy story. More precisely, she didn't want him knowing that she was so naïve and had such poor judgement in relationships. Her best friend and her live-in boyfriend. Just how had she managed to keep

her eyes so firmly closed to what was really going on
between them?

'Was it recent?' he asked.

'Six months ago,' she said. 'And you?'

'A year.'

'And you haven't met anyone else since?' That surprised her. When he wasn't being grumpy in the office,
Hugh was good company. And he was very easy on the
eye. Surely he had women lining up for him in droves?

'I've been too busy concentrating on my business.'
He paused. 'You?'

'The same.' Except it hadn't just been her romantic
relationship that had crashed. Kirk had dumped her for
the woman Bella had believed was her best friend since
sixth form, taking that support away from her, too. And
Kirk had quietly cleaned out their joint bank account, the
morning he dumped her—which was why Bella hadn't
had her normal safety cushion of the equivalent of three
months' salary when her best client went bust, and why
her finances were in such a mess now.

And there had been next to nothing she could do about
it, because the money had been in their joint names. She'd
talked to the bank, but they'd said that any signatory to
a joint account had the right to withdraw however much
money they liked, no matter how much they'd actually
put in.

Bella would never make that mistake again. And she
was really glad that she'd listened to Grace's advice and
put her tax money to one side in a different account rather
than keeping it with her 'salary', or she'd be in debt to
the Inland Revenue as well.

'Let's just say I'm tired of always dating Mr Wrong
and I'm happier being single,' she said.

'Works for me. Any more questions?'

He was definitely in his Monday morning office mode now. Grumpy and difficult. She decided that any other questions could wait. 'I guess we've covered the basics.'

'Good. If you don't mind, I'd better concentrate on my driving.'

Given that they were going to his family home, he probably knew the route blindfold, so Bella was pretty sure that this was just his way of avoiding any more questions. And she supposed he had a point. She knew enough to play her role. Asking him anything else would be intrusive, wouldn't it? She let him concentrate on his driving and fiddled quietly with her phone, until he turned off the main road and drove them through narrower country roads to the outskirts of a village.

'Here we are, then,' he said as he turned into a driveway. The fences on either side were in perfect repair, and huge lime trees lined the fences and cast dappled shade on the driveway.

Bella had known that Hugh was from a posh background, but she hadn't realised just how posh. At the end of the half-a-mile-long driveway was the most beautiful house she'd ever seen: an Elizabethan manor house built from mellow Cotswold stone, with floor-to-ceiling sash windows on the ground floor, mullioned windows on the top floor, wisteria climbing the walls which wasn't in bloom yet but would look stunning in a couple of weeks, and a wide front door with a spider-web fanlight above it.

'That's gorgeous,' she said. 'And I've got this weird sense of déjà vu—I know I've never been here before, but somehow I feel as if I have.'

'You've probably seen the house on TV,' he said. 'It's been used as a location for a few period dramas.'

Before she had the chance to ask which ones, he parked on the gravelled area outside the house.

'I see my brothers are already here,' he said.

There were two sports cars similar to Hugh's parked outside the house, along with a Range Rover, a Daimler and a Bentley. It felt almost as if she was walking into one of the period dramas he'd mentioned. And it was a million miles away from her own background. Was she really going to be able to pull this off?

'The grandparents and the aunts are here, too, by the looks of it,' he said. 'We might as well go in and say hello. There probably isn't enough time to give you a proper guided tour of the house before tea's served, but I promise I'll do it tomorrow. Ma's probably in the kitchen fussing about. She said afternoon tea would be in the dining room and the cocktail party tonight's in the ballroom.'

'Your parents have a ballroom?' She smiled to hide the panic that trickled through her. 'That's very Jane Austen.'

'It's probably been in one of the Austen adaptations. I can't really remember,' he said with a shrug. 'Which sounds terribly snooty, but it isn't meant to be.'

'Of course not.' Bella had the feeling that he was much more nervous about this than he looked, and somehow that made her feel a little less nervous. A little less alone.

'Imagine the kind of house parties they had back in Austen's time,' he said. 'I'd be off fishing or hunting with my brothers, or playing cards and drinking. But the women in the house party wouldn't be allowed to do much more than read or play the piano. They'd be under constant scrutiny, and there were all the intricate manners...' He shuddered. 'I hate that kind of stuff. I'm glad it's not like that now.'

'Isn't it?' she asked softly—because that bit about constant scrutiny and manners sounded personal.

'No.'

'It was for my sister.' The words were out before she could stop them.

He looked at her. 'How?'

'I…' She sighed. 'OK. You're unlikely to meet her again, but if you do and you tell her you know why she drank all that champagne that night I might have to kill you.'

'Noted. What happened?' he asked, sounding curious.

'She was at the golden wedding anniversary party for her fiancé's parents. Let's just say that Cynthia of the Concrete Hair—'

He blinked. 'Who?'

'Howard's mother. You know the sort of woman I mean. Everything's all about appearances and she's so polished that her hair is set like concrete.' Bella waved a dismissive hand. 'And she watches you like a hawk and judges you—usually unfairly.'

'Yes, I've come across people like that,' he said.

'So I think Gracie finally realised that if she went ahead and married Howard, her life was going to be seriously miserable.' She grimaced. 'She tried to blot it out by drinking champagne. It didn't work. So, for the first time ever, I was the sister who did the rescuing—with a lot of help from you.' She bit her lip. 'The wedding was meant to be next weekend.'

'So Grace was a runaway bride?' He looked surprised.

'No. She didn't jilt Howard at the altar—she'd never do anything that mean. But they'd been engaged for four years and he never swept her off her feet, not *once*.'

'Being swept off your feet is overrated,' Hugh said. 'You're more likely to fall into a puddle of slurry.'

'Slurry?' she asked, not understanding.

He grinned. 'You're definitely a townie, then. Slurry is liquid manure. Used as fertiliser on fields.'

She pulled a face. 'That's vile.'

'Exactly how it smells. You always know when it's muck-spreading season.'

'It's not muck-spreading season now, is it?'

He laughed. 'No.'

'Good.' She took a deep breath. 'Righty. Time to play my part, I guess. Ditzy and unsuitable girlfriend with a terrible taste in clothes—that's me, right?'

'Right. And thank you for saving my bacon. I appreciate this. Even if it might not seem that way.'

He took their bags from the car and they went into the house. Bella noticed the sweeping staircase coming into the hallway and the Regency striped paper on the walls; the house really was gorgeous, and she itched to explore, though she knew it would be rude to ask.

Three dogs came rushing down the hallway to meet them, their tails a wagging blur.

'I forgot to warn you about the mutts,' he said. 'Sorry. Are you OK with dogs?'

'Very OK. I grew up with a dog,' she said, and bent down to make a fuss of the chocolate Labrador, Westie and Cocker Spaniel.

'This lot are Lennie the lab, Wilf the Westie and Sukie the spaniel,' he introduced them.

The dogs wriggled and shoved each other and tried to get closer to Bella. 'They're lovely,' she said, laughing. 'Hello, you ravening beasties. I'm sorry, I don't have any treats for you because I wasn't expecting to meet you, but

I can rub your ears and scratch your backs for you, and I'll play ball with you for a bit if you want.'

'Do that and they'll pester you for the whole weekend,' Hugh warned.

She smiled up at him. 'And that's a problem, how?'

A woman who looked so much like Hugh that she had to be his mother came into the hallway and hugged him. 'Darling, I'm so glad you could make it.'

OK, so now she had to be Miss Ditzy. Breathe, Bella reminded herself, and stay in character. She stood up and gave her best attempt at a goofy smile.

'Bella, this is my mother, Elizabeth Moncrieff,' Hugh said.

'Libby will do nicely,' Hugh's mother said. 'We don't stand on ceremony in this house.'

'Ma, this is my friend Bella Faraday,' Hugh continued. 'Like the scientist?'

Libby had perfect manners, Bella thought, and didn't even look the remotest bit fazed by Bella's outlandish dress. 'Yes, like the scientist,' she agreed, before remembering that she was supposed to be playing the part of someone who would probably never have heard of Michael Faraday, let alone known who he was.

'I'll just show Bella up to her room,' Hugh said hastily.

'She's in the Blue Room, next to yours. I hope that's all right?'

'Thank you, Mrs Mon—' Bella began.

'Libby,' Hugh's mother reminded her.

'Libby.' Bella opened her bag and took out the beautifully wrapped package of dark chocolates she'd bought earlier. 'And these are for you, to say thank you for having me.'

'How lovely.' Libby went pink. 'And I recognise that

packaging. These are my absolute favourites. That's very kind of you.'

'My pleasure. I'm glad you like them,' Bella said. 'Don't let Hugh anywhere near them. He's a chocolate fiend. But I guess, as his mum, you already know that.'

'Oh, I do,' Libby said feelingly.

'Let's go and put our things upstairs,' Hugh said.

'Come down when you're ready. Everyone will be in the dining room,' Libby said. 'And it's a pleasure to meet you, Bella.'

Bella followed Hugh up the sweeping staircase and all the way to the end of a corridor.

The Blue Room was enormous. It was very plain, with cream walls and a polished wooden floor with a navy rug in the centre, but what really caught Bella's attention was the ancient wooden four-poster bed. She'd always wanted to sleep in a bed like that. 'This is amazing,' she said.

'I'll put my things next door. I'll call for you in a few minutes,' he said.

Was Hugh's bedroom anything like this? she wondered. Were there things from his childhood that would give her a clue about what made him tick?

Not that she should be thinking about any of that. She was simply doing him a favour and playing a part. None of this was *real*, she reminded herself.

To distract herself, she went and looked out of the window. The room overlooked the garden at the back of the house: a perfectly striped lawn, with borders all full of tulips, and a stone wall at the end of the lawn with what looked like espaliered trees full of blossom. It was a million miles away from her own suburban upbringing. How wonderful it must have been to have a garden like that to run around in and explore as a child.

Then there was a knock at the door. 'Bella?'

'Come in.'

Hugh remained in the doorway. 'Ready?'

She nodded. 'I was just looking at the view. It's gorgeous.'

'Yes, it's pretty good. I guess I didn't really appreciate it when I was younger.' He took a deep breath. 'Let's go and face the hordes.'

She walked over to join him. 'Though you might have to roll your eyes at me to remind me to be Miss Ditzy. I already made a couple of mistakes with your mum.'

'It'll be fine,' he said. 'I know you're going to do a great job. That's why I asked you.'

'So you didn't ask me just because you were desperate?'

His eyes crinkled at the corners. 'That, too. But mainly because I think you'll do this brilliantly.'

Funny how the compliment warmed her all the way through. Maybe that was because he was being sincere.

Then again, she hadn't spotted Kirk's lies, had she? For all she knew, Hugh could be lying, too.

She took a deep breath. '"Once more unto the breach, dear friends."'

He laughed. 'It won't be that bad.'

Once they got downstairs, Bella wasn't so sure. The dining room held the biggest table she'd ever seen in her life. And every place was already filled, except two.

Hugh introduced her swiftly to everyone before they sat down. She'd already met his mother, but now there was his father, his brothers and their partners and baby Sophia, various aunts and uncles, and his grandparents. And it was all just a little bit overwhelming—especially as Bella could see the shock on all their faces, even though it was quickly masked and everyone was very polite to her.

She knew that she was playing a part and Hugh's intention had been to bring someone home who was so out of place that his family would stop pressuring him to settle down, but even so she didn't enjoy their scrupulous politeness. It looked as if this was going to be a very long weekend.

A maid came in carrying a tray with silver teapots and what Bella guessed were silver jugs of hot water to refresh the tea. Porcelain jugs of milk and dishes with slices of lemon were already on the table, along with a selection of finger sandwiches, tiny pastries, slices of cake and what looked like still-warm scones. A butler followed the maid, carrying a magnum of champagne; once everyone's glass was filled, Hugh's father made a brief speech and proposed a toast to Nigel and his new fiancée, Victoria.

The food was amazing, and in other circumstances Bella knew she would've really enjoyed it. It was a shame that she had to play a part. Until she'd had a chance to work out who was who and the best way to play it, she decided to keep quiet.

But then the old lady sitting next to her—Hugh's great-aunt Lavinia—went very pale and looked as if she was about to faint.

'Are you all right?' Bella asked her, worried.

'I do feel a bit odd,' Lavinia admitted.

'Can I get you a glass of water?'

Lavinia looked grateful. 'Yes, please.'

Miss Ditzy might not know what to do, but Bella couldn't possibly keep playing that part when the old lady clearly wasn't very well and needed help. Hugh wouldn't mind her breaking out of role for this, would he? So she had a quiet word with the maid to get some water, persuaded Lavinia to eat a sandwich, and sat quietly with the old lady until the colour had come back into her face.

'I think I might go and have a little lie-down,' Lavinia said.

'I'll see you up to your room,' Bella said. 'As long as you can direct me, that is. I'm afraid I don't know my way round the house.'

Lavinia patted her hand. 'Thank you, dear. That's very good of you.'

'My pleasure.' Bella helped the old lady back to her room, and stayed with her for a little while to make sure she was quite all right.

'You're a lovely girl, very kind,' Lavinia said. 'I can see what Hugh sees in you.'

Which was totally the opposite of what Bella was supposed to be doing. And she knew that Hugh didn't see anything in her anyway, apart from her being his graphic designer who was probably too outspoken and had been crazy enough to agree to help him in his even crazier scheme. She'd have to hope that her outrageous clothes would distract everyone else from seeing who she really was.

But going back to face everyone in the dining room felt really daunting. She didn't have a clue what to say. To her relief, Hugh met her in the hallway. 'Thanks for looking after my great-aunt. Is Lavinia OK?'

'She's fine—just having a little rest,' Bella said, and gave the same reassurances to Hugh's mother when Libby asked her the same question.

Libby gave her a searching look, then a nod of what looked very much like approval.

Oh, help. She'd really have to work at being unsuitable now. Hugh's mother wasn't supposed to approve of her. She was meant to stick out like a sore thumb.

After the tea party, everyone disappeared to get changed for the cocktail party.

'Come and knock on my door when you're ready,' Hugh said when they reached her bedroom door.

'OK.' Bella wished again that she'd brought a normal black dress with her, rather than going along with Hugh's plans, but it was too late now.

When she'd changed, she knocked on Hugh's door.

'Come in,' he called.

When she pushed the door open, she could see that he was sitting on the end of the bed, checking something on his phone. He looked up and burst out laughing. 'Well. I really didn't expect that. You actually found that in a charity shop?'

'The material, yes—it was originally a pair of curtains. One of my friends from art school specialised in textiles, so she ran this up for me.' She narrowed her eyes at him. 'Why didn't you expect it?'

'I guess I really ought to give you advance warning,' he said. 'The curtains in the ballroom are, um, exactly the same material as your dress.'

'The same material?' She stared at him in shock. 'No way. You're *kidding*.'

He coughed. 'Afraid not.'

She covered her face with her hands. 'Oh, no. I thought I was being so clever, having a Maria moment. It never occurred to me your parents might have curtains like this. I should've run this past you before we came. And I haven't got a spare dress with me.' She blew out a breath. 'Oh, well. I'll just have to change into the leopard-skin thing again.'

He came over to her and rested his hand on her shoulder. Again, her skin tingled where he touched her. 'Relax. Stay as you are. It'll be fine,' he soothed.

She rolled her eyes at him. 'I can hardly go to a party wearing a dress made out of the same curtains that are in the room, can I?'

'Actually, you can,' he said. 'You're the one person I know who can pull this off.'

She really wasn't convinced. And it didn't help that Hugh was wearing a dinner jacket with grosgrain silk lapels that matched the fabric on the buttons, a white pleated-front shirt, and a properly tied black grosgrain silk bow tie. He looked sleek, elegant and perfect.

She blew out a breath. 'You look very nice. Very James Bond, though I think you might actually have the edge on Daniel Craig.'

'Thank you.' He inclined his head in acknowledgement of the compliment. 'You look very nice, too.'

'In a dress that matches your parents' curtains and clashes with my hair?' she asked, raising her eyebrows. 'Hardly.'

'Remember, you have chutzpah,' he said.

'Maybe I should stay here. You could say I drank too much champagne earlier and have a headache.'

He shook his head. 'Have the courage of your convictions, Bella.'

She scoffed. '*Your* convictions, you mean. If we'd done it my way, I wouldn't be here and you would've shown your family how great you are at your job.'

'Let's agree to disagree on that one, because I know you can do this,' he said. 'Ready?'

No. But she had no other choice. 'Sure,' she said. 'Let's go.'

CHAPTER FIVE

BELLA'S FACE WAS pale beneath her make-up, but she lifted her chin high and pulled her shoulders back.

For a moment, Hugh thought about calling this whole thing off—someone in the house was bound to have a spare dress that she could borrow for the evening—but they'd agreed that the idea was to present Bella as Miss Totally Unsuitable. To the point where his family would all breathe a collective sigh of relief when he announced next week that the relationship was over, and they'd stop nagging him about settling down.

Bella was the only woman he knew who could pull off an outfit like this one. And he knew he was asking a huge amount from her. When they were back in London, he'd do something nice for her to make up for what he was putting her through right now. Maybe he could send her on a spa weekend with her sister or something.

He suppressed the thought that he'd like to take her away and make a fuss of her himself. She'd made it clear that she was single and wanted to stay that way. The same was true for him. Bella Faraday might make his pulse beat that little bit faster: but she was his employee, and that made her completely off limits.

They went downstairs and he ushered her into the ballroom. As they walked through the doorway, he felt her hand tighten on his arm just a fraction. And the gasps of surprise as people saw her and took in what she was wearing were actually audible.

The ground obviously wasn't going to open up and swallow her, and turning back time wasn't physically possible either. Bella glanced at Hugh for a cue about how to react and what to do—after all, this was his family and he knew them way better than she did—but he seemed to have frozen.

Nothing fazes a Faraday girl. The mantra she shared with Grace echoed through her head. Wrong. This had definitely fazed her.

Then again, Hugh had asked her to play the part of his unsuitable girlfriend. Which was exactly how she felt right now—awkward and out of place, absolutely not fitting in. What would an unsuitable girl do when she was the centre of attention? The only thing Bella could think of was to draw even more attention to her gaffe and ham it up a little.

She walked over to the curtains and did a little curtsey. 'I promise I didn't make my dress from these,' she said, gesturing to the curtains. 'Because my name isn't Maria and I'm fairly sure you're the Moncrieffs and not the von Trapp family—right?'

There was still an uneasy silence.

Had she gone too far? Or did she need to go further still? 'Well, then,' Bella said, and began to sing 'Do Re Mi' very softly.

Hugh looked at Bella, totally stunned. He'd had no idea that she could sing—especially this beautifully. It made him think of Jessie, and how his ex had bewitched him with her voice.

But Jessie wasn't half the woman that Bella Faraday was. Jessie was an ambitious, lying cheat, whereas he knew that Bella was completely open and honest. Even though at the moment she was playing a part: that was solely because he'd asked her to do it.

And right now all the heat was on her—Hugh's unsuitable new girlfriend in her even more unsuitable dress. He could hear Bella's voice faltering and he knew he ought to rescue her. Especially because this whole fiasco was his fault. He needed to step in and take the heat off her. Now.

She'd even given him the perfect cue.

Yet that would mean performing in public. Something he hadn't done since Jessie had walked out on him. And singing a duet... The whole idea of it made him feel sick to his stomach, bringing back the misery and disappointment he'd felt when he'd learned the truth about how much of a fool he'd been, and the dismay when he'd realised the ramifications for Insurgo. He really didn't want to do this.

Yet how could he be a snake and leave Bella to face everyone's disapproval alone? This whole thing had been his idea, and she was doing him a favour. It wasn't fair that she should bear the brunt of it.

It left him no real choice.

Taking a deep breath, he walked over to Bella and took her hand. 'Von Trapp, you said? I believe that's my cue.' And then he began to sing 'Edelweiss'.

Bella smiled, and to his surprise she joined him in the song.

It had been a long, long time since Hugh had sung a duet with someone. Jessie. Who'd sung like an angel, promised him paradise, and left him in hell. This should've made him want to run for the hills as fast as possible. Instead, it felt as if something in the region of his heart had just cracked a tiny bit, enough to let in some unexpected warmth. His hand tightened just that tiny bit more round hers; and when she squeezed his fingers back the crack around his heart grew just that little bit wider.

When the song finished, everyone clapped and the tension in the ballroom had dissolved.

Then Nigel came over to him. 'Hugh, I need a favour.'

Considering that he'd just almost wrecked his brother's engagement party, Hugh felt guilty enough to agree to whatever it was. 'Sure. What do you need?'

'Excuse us, Bella,' Nigel said, and led Hugh off to a quiet corner. 'The band I hired for tonight just called to say that their van's broken down and they're running an hour late. Would you play for us until they get here?' He inclined his head towards the baby grand piano in the corner of the ballroom.

'You could've had the pick of my artists. And they would've been here on time,' Hugh said mildly.

'I know, but the singer of the band happens to be Vicky's friend. Vicky asked her to do it before I had a chance to suggest asking you to recommend someone.'

Hugh laughed. 'Nice save.'

'I know I'm asking a lot of you,' Nigel said softly. 'I know why you don't play in public any more.'

Because of Jessie's betrayal. It had sucked all the joy out of music for him. He didn't write songs any more. Today was the first time he'd sung in public since she'd left. Right now though, he was punch-drunk, not quite sure how he felt—happy and sad were all mixed up together, with him smack in the centre of the whirlpool.

'Yeah.' Hugh took a deep breath. This was a big ask. But, in the circumstances, there wasn't a nice way to say no. And Hugh did love his brother. This was his chance to help, to do something nice for his family. How could he turn that down? 'All right. I'll play until the band gets here. But I'm not singing any more, and neither is Bella, OK?'

'OK.' Nigel patted his shoulder. 'Thanks. I appreciate it.'

Hugh walked back over to Bella. 'Will you be OK if I play the piano for Nigel and Victoria until the band turns up?' he asked.

'Sure,' she said, giving him what looked like a brave smile. Clearly she didn't think she'd be OK at all.

'Of course she will. I'll look after her,' his mother said, coming over and catching the end of the conversation.

That was almost what Hugh was most afraid of.

But before he could say anything his mother had swept Bella away and Nigel was looking anxiously towards the piano. What could he do but give in and sit down at the baby grand? 'Let's get your party started, O brother mine,' he said and began to play.

'I think you need some champagne after that, Bella,' Libby said, and snaffled a glass from the nearest waiter.

'I'm so sorry, Mrs Moncrieff,' Bella said, accepting the glass. 'About the dress. And… And…' She shook her head, not knowing where to start. Just that she needed to apologise. She'd thought she was being so clever, making a dress out of a curtain. And she'd ended up being horrifically rude. This wasn't who she was. At all. And it made her squirm inside. She'd come here under false pretences and she'd behaved appallingly.

'It's Libby,' Hugh's mother reminded her gently. 'My dear, I can see exactly why Hugh fell for you.' Libby patted her arm. 'What you did just now—that was very brave.'

'Or very foolish in the first place,' Bella said softly. There was a huge lump in her throat. She really hadn't expected Hugh to come to her rescue like that. The last time a man had left her in a sticky situation, he'd left her to deal with it alone. Yet Hugh had been right there by her side, supporting her and sorting it out with her. 'I didn't know Hugh could sing like that—or that he could play the piano.' Considering that Hugh owned a record label and he'd told her how much he loved producing the songs and turning them from raw material to the finished product, she should've guessed that music was more than just a money-making venture to him. But Hugh wasn't listed on Insurgo's website as one of the label's artists, and nobody in the office had even hinted that he'd ever been any kind of performer. He hadn't even sung along with the music in the car on the way to Oxfordshire.

But she'd overheard Nigel saying something about knowing why Hugh didn't play in public any more. Something really awful must've happened. And there was no way she could possibly ask Hugh about it, not without opening up what might be some very painful scars. She'd have to tread very carefully.

'Hugh was very cagey when I asked him about how you'd met,' Libby said. 'Are you one of his artists?'

Bella winced. 'Not *quite* in the way you think. I'm not a singer and I don't play an instrument.'

Was it her imagination, or did Libby Moncrieff suddenly look relieved? And why? Did that have something to do with the reason why Hugh didn't play in public?

'So how did you meet?' Libby asked.

Bella could hardly be completely honest about that, either. Not unless she wanted to tell a story that made her sister look bad, and that wasn't fair. The best she could do was give the bare bones of the truth. Which would probably be the safest thing in any case, because then she wouldn't have to remember which fibs she'd told and end up in a muddle. 'I'm an artist—and by that I mean a graphic designer, not a recording artist—and Tarquin interviewed me for the job at Insurgo.'

'Ah.'

That earlier look of relief hadn't been her imagination, then, because Libby suddenly looked wary again.

Was Insurgo the problem? Hugh had said that his family worried about him because the music business was so risky. Maybe this was her chance to bat his corner for him and get his mother to see just how good he was at his job and how much the recording label meant to him.

'As I said, I'm not a singer,' Bella said, 'but I do like music, and Insurgo produces some of the very best music around. I used to be a freelance designer, but my best client went bust a few months ago, owing me rather a lot of money. My parents would've bailed me out if I'd told them, but I wanted to stand on my own two feet rather than rely on them—so that's why I applied to Insurgo when I saw the job advertised. Hugh had nothing to do with me getting the job. Tarquin interviewed me.' She spread her hands. 'I didn't even meet Hugh until after I'd accepted the job.'

To her relief, Libby looked a bit less wary again.

She took a sip of champagne. 'It's a good place to work. I've never been anywhere with a sense of team spirit like there is at Insurgo. Everyone looks out for each other. And the musicians all love coming in to the office because they feel we listen to them. Hugh doesn't treat them just as cash cows or as if they're stupid. He listens to what they want, and he gives them advice—and they listen to him because they know he wants to help them be the best they can be. They know he'll take their raw material and polish it—but he'll still keep their vision.'

Libby nodded, but said nothing.

'Insurgo wouldn't be the success it is without Hugh. He's its heart,' Bella said. 'And he really loves what he does. There aren't many people who can say that nowadays.'

'But the music business is so precarious,' Libby said.

'It is,' Bella agreed. 'But Hugh doesn't take stupid risks. He's really sharp and he makes exactly the right business decisions—though nobody in the office will ever ask him anything on a Monday morning.'

'Why not?'

'He's, um, not really a Monday morning person. Though I guess, as his mum, you already know that.' She smiled, and told Libby about the name-cards she'd made for everyone in the office.

Libby laughed. 'You didn't do that on a Monday morning, I hope.'

Bella laughed back, feeling properly at ease for the first time since she'd arrived. 'I wouldn't have dared. No, it was a Thursday. And he was still pretty grumpy.'

'So you can sketch people really quickly?'

'Not just people.' Bella fished in her bag and took out a pen and a small spiral-bound notebook. 'Give me a few seconds,' she said with a smile. She sketched swiftly. Then she handed the notebook with the line drawing to Libby. Sitting patiently next to a cake and wearing hopeful expressions as they stared at it were Lennie, Wilf and Sukie.

'Oh, that's wonderful,' Libby said. 'May I keep it?'

'Of course.' Bella detached the page and handed it to her.

'Thank you. So what exactly did you draw on Hugh's name-card?' Libby asked, sounding intrigued.

'You're his mother. I can hardly show you.'

Libby laughed. 'I used to have to get him out of bed on Monday mornings when he was a teen. I think I've seen him at his very grumpiest.'

'Well, if you put it that way,' Bella said, 'how can I resist?' She drew another sketch. And, before she realised it, she had a circle of people around her, all wanting to see her drawings and all asking for a sketch.

Oh, help. She was supposed to be playing Miss Ditzy and Unsuitable, not making friends with everyone the way she always did. Hugh was going to be furious. She'd just have to work out how to extract herself from this before the band turned up and he could leave the piano.

Hugh finally managed to get away from the piano when the band turned up, all flustered and apologetic. He went to rescue Bella from his mother, only to find her right in the middle of a crowd. Everyone around her was laughing and joking, and he noticed that she had a pen and paper in her hand.

She looked as if she belonged.

Oh, no. That wasn't supposed to happen. His bright idea was going completely pear-shaped. His family had obviously seen way beyond Bella's surface unsuitability. And Bella herself had clearly forgotten that she was playing the part of Miss Ditzy and Unsuitable.

Then again, hadn't he also told her just to be herself? Which was exactly what she was doing. Bella, the graphic artist, the woman who'd fitted in to their team at the office as if she'd been there since day one.

Right now, she lit up the room. Which scared him and drew him in equal measures. He wanted her—but he didn't want to risk his whole life imploding again, the way it had after Jessie. He needed to be sensible about this. And right now the sensible thing to do would be to get her out of there before she said anything that made his family guess at the truth.

And she was meant to be his girlfriend, so everyone would expect him to walk over and drape his arm round her shoulders. 'Sorry to desert you like that, darling.'

She looked up at him, her beautiful blue eyes wide. 'Hugh!'

'But I'm here now. Shall we dance?'

'I...' She looked flustered. Which was pretty much how he felt, too, so close to her that he could smell her perfume and feel the warmth of her body against his.

'May I finish my sketch first?' she asked.

'Sure.' He took a step back. Putting a bit of distance between them was probably a good idea, given that right now he wanted to pull her closer.

Hugh had seen what she could produce at the Insurgo office, but he'd never actually watched her working before. And he was amazed by how deft her hands were. He also noticed how she caught the tip of her tongue between her teeth when she was concentrating, and it made him want to kiss her.

Maybe dancing with her would be a bad idea after all. It would make her way, way too tempting.

But then she finished a sketch of Lennie with his father—lightning fast and seriously good—and handed it over to Oliver with a smile.

'Thank you, my dear. That's marvellous.' Oliver kissed her cheek. 'And maybe I could ask you to sketch Libby with Sukie for me, later?'

'Of course,' Bella said, smiling back. 'But I'll require payment in advance, you know. You'll have to dance with me first.'

He positively beamed at her. 'With absolute pleasure, my dear.'

Amazing. Even wearing a dress made out of a curtain which matched the ones in the ballroom and which clashed badly with her bright red hair—two things that Hugh was sure should've annoyed Oliver Moncrieff immensely—Bella had still managed to charm his father. Just, Hugh thought, by being herself. She couldn't help it. Bella was the kind of woman who brought out the best in people.

He led her off to the other side of the dance floor. 'I was going to apologise for throwing you to the wolves, but it looks to me as if you've managed to turn them all into little fluffy-wuffy lapdogs.'

She laughed. 'Hugh, don't be so mean. Your family's nice.'

He scowled. 'Maybe. When they're not nagging me.'

'Really, Hugh. They're *nice*.' She blew out a breath. 'And I should be apologising to you. I'm afraid I kind of forgot to be unsuitable. I was telling your mum about the name-cards I did in the office last week, and I ended up drawing the dogs for her, and…' She bit her lip, and Hugh had to suppress the urge to kiss the sting away. 'It snowballed a little bit. Sorry. I'll remember to be dim and scatty and unsuitable for the rest of the weekend, I promise.'

'Hmm,' Hugh said. He didn't think she'd be able to remember it for very long. Because he realised now that Bella wasn't a natural deceiver. What you saw was what you got. There were no hidden agendas. 'It's as much my fault as it is yours. I shouldn't have left you on your own.'

'But you couldn't have refused to help your brother.' She paused and gave him a curious look. 'I didn't know you could play the piano.'

'Lavinia taught me.'

'Lavinia, as in your great-aunt I sat next to this afternoon?'

He nodded. 'Before arthritis wrecked her hands, she was an amazing pianist.'

She frowned. 'So your family does understand about music, then.'

'Lavinia does,' he admitted. 'The rest don't. They still think I should give it up and join the family business.'

She looked thoughtful. 'So you play and you sing— I've heard that for myself. I'm guessing that you probably write your own stuff, too.'

He had. Once upon a time. Not any more.

She wasn't letting it go. She ignored his silence. 'And you own a record company. Do you ever record anything of your own?'

'No,' he said, knowing that he sounded abrupt and rude, but not being able to help himself.

But it didn't seem to put Bella off. 'Why not?' she asked. 'You're good. And I'm not just saying that because you're my boss. You, a piano and a love song— you'd have women swooning all round the globe. You'd make gazillions for the label.'

Hugh had written songs for Jessie, and he'd thought about recording them as duets with her. Then Jessie had dropped her bombshell that she was moving to another record label instead of signing the new contract with Insurgo, and by the way she'd met someone else…who just so happened to be the head of her new label.

And then Hugh had realised that maybe Jessie had never loved him at all. She'd just seen him as a stepping stone in her career, and it looked as if she was doing exactly the same with her new man. He'd been so shocked and hurt that he hadn't written anything since, and he couldn't remember the last time he'd touched the piano; the joy he'd once found in playing felt tainted with memories of her betrayal. Tonight was the first time he'd sung with anyone since he'd broken up with Jessie. The first time he'd played in public again.

And he didn't want to analyse that too closely. Or why it had felt so natural to sing with Bella, after the initial shock.

'I don't want to be a performer,' he said. 'I prefer being a producer. Seeing the rough diamond of the songs and how I can make them shine. You know, like Lacey's album—putting the cello in and a double bass made it just that bit more haunting and gave the sound some depth.'

'Fair enough.' She shrugged. 'I think I understand where you're coming from, because for me it's the other way round. I absolutely love designing, but I wouldn't want to own or run a gallery. The idea of having to organise a bunch of creative people…' She groaned. 'It'd be like herding cats. No, thanks.'

He smiled. 'It's very satisfying when it goes right.'

'Each to their own,' she said.

Hugh danced with her all evening, only stepping to

one side when his three brothers and his father all demanded a dance with Bella. And then he found himself dancing with his sisters-in-law and his mother, all of whom were singing Bella's praises loudly.

'She's perfect for you,' Victoria said. 'Even if her dress sense is a little, um, unusual.'

There was nothing he could say to that. If he protested, everyone would take it as a token protest; if he agreed, they'd have a date set for the wedding within the hour.

'I really should rescue her from Pa,' he said, and fled in Bella's direction.

'Is everything all right?' Bella asked when Hugh was dancing with her again.

'I think our plan might have crashed and burned a bit,' he said ruefully.

She winced. 'Sorry. That's my fault.'

'No. You were right. It was a daft idea in the first place.'

'I'm glad you can admit when you're wrong,' she said with a smile. 'That's a good thing.'

'Mmm.' He wasn't convinced.

She stroked his face. 'Hugh. Let's just forget it for now and enjoy the party.'

Her touch made every nerve-end sit up and pay attention. He had to stop himself from turning his head and pressing a kiss into her palm. Distance. He needed a tiny bit of distance between them, before he lost his head completely and gave in to his body's urging. He snagged a couple of glasses from one of the waiters and toasted her. 'I still can't believe you stood up there in front of those curtains, in that dress, and sang "Do Re Mi".'

'Says Captain von Trapp,' she retorted with a grin.

'Oh, please.' He rolled his eyes. 'Ma loves *The Sound of Music*.'

'So do I. It's one of the best films ever.' She hummed a snatch of 'My Favourite Things'.

'I hated that film,' Hugh said.

She blinked at him, clearly taken aback. 'Why?'

'The way the guy just ignored his kids made me so angry. And it wasn't so much a stick the guy had up his backside as a whole tree.'

'And you don't?' she teased.

What? Hugh stared at her in surprise. Was she saying that she thought he was stuffy? 'No, I don't,' he said, faintly put out.

'Prove it,' she challenged.

He narrowed his eyes at her. 'How?'

'Dance the samba with me.' She raised her eyebrows at him. 'After all, this is a party, and the samba is the best party dance I know.'

'Sorry.' He spread his hands. 'I would, but I'm afraid I don't know the steps.' It was a feeble excuse, but a valid one. If the samba meant dancing close to her and touching her... That would be way too risky. He needed to be sensible about this, not getting closer to her.

'It's easy. I'll teach you. Gracie and I go to a dance aerobics class where half the moves are based on samba.' She grinned. 'Just follow my lead.' Then she paused, batted her eyelashes at him, and drawled, 'Unless you can't take direction from a woman?'

He had the distinct impression that she was flirting with him. Even though he knew he ought to resist, he found himself flirting right back. 'I can take direction.' He stared at her mouth. 'When it's *appropriate*.'

Her skin heated, then, clashing spectacularly with her hair. 'Hugh!'

And her voice was all breathy. He was about to tease her when he realised that he couldn't speak, either, because right now his head was full of the idea of kissing her. And that breathiness in her voice was incredibly sexy. His mouth was actually tingling. All he had to do was lean forward and touch his lips to hers...

They ought to stop this.

Right now.

As if she was channelling his thoughts, she muttered, 'Back in a moment.'

But what she did next was to go and speak to the band. He recognised the song from the first couple of bars: 'Livin' la Vida Loca'.

So Bella wasn't going to let him off. To pay him back for making her blush, she taught him how to samba, making him repeat the basic steps and arm actions until his movements were fluid. He was surprised by how much he enjoyed the bouncy, shimmery nature of the steps.

Other people were watching them, but when Bella realised that she was having none of it. As the band continued to play songs with a similar beat, she went round and taught everyone else in the room how to do the basic steps. The women seemed to cotton on much quicker than the men—which didn't surprise him that much, because hadn't Bella said something about learning this kind of thing at an aerobics class?—but finally the whole room was dancing. Including relatives Hugh had never actually seen get up on the dance floor before.

How on earth had she managed that?

'You certainly know how to get a party going,' he said when she came back over to him.

She laughed and tossed her hair back. 'I *love* parties.'

He could tell. She was really lit up from the inside, and it was infectious. Being with her made him smile and forget just about everything else. How long had it been since he'd last felt this happy and carefree?

Then the band slowed it all down again. He held out one hand to her. 'May I have this dance, Ms Faraday?'

She gave him a shy smile and took his hand. 'Of course, Mr Moncrieff.'

He drew her into his arms and held her close, swaying with her. Weird how she fitted perfectly into his arms, all warm and soft and sweet. Maybe the romance of the engagement party had got to him, or maybe he'd drunk too much champagne, but he couldn't resist holding her just that little bit closer, dancing cheek to cheek with her. He could smell the soft floral scent she wore—gardenia, perhaps? It was enchanting: much like Bella herself.

And from dancing cheek to cheek it was the tiniest, tiniest move to kissing her. All he had to do was twist his head ever so slightly and brush the corner of her mouth with his lips.

Should he?

And what would she do if he did?

If she moved away, he'd stop, he promised himself.

Except she didn't move away. When he kissed the corner of her mouth, she twisted her head ever so slightly towards him, so her mouth brushed against his properly.

And Hugh was completely lost.

He tightened his arms round her and kissed her again, teasing her mouth with tiny, nibbling kisses until she let her lips part and he could deepen the kiss. It felt as if he were floating on air. Every sense was filled by her. And it had been a long, long time since he'd felt anything even approaching this.

He wasn't sure how long it was until he broke the kiss. But her mouth was reddened and her eyes were wide and bemused; he was pretty sure he looked in a similar state.

They needed to get out of here, before someone noticed or commented.

'Come with me?' he asked softly. 'Away from the crowd?'

She nodded, and he tangled his fingers with hers and led her quietly out of the ballroom and down the corridor to a room he knew would still be in darkness.

'Where are we?' Bella asked when Hugh led her into a darkened room.

'The orangery,' he said.

Once her eyes grew accustomed to the light, she realised that one whole wall was made of glass, and the moonlight shone through onto an ancient chequered red and cream flagstone floor. All along the walls were massive terracotta pots containing what she presumed were citrus trees; there were a couple of what looked like wrought-iron benches between the pots.

'Wait,' he said, and let go of her hand.

A few moments later, she heard a soft click, and then suddenly the room was glowing softly with dozens of tiny fairy lights twined round the stems of the trees.

'Hugh, this is amazing,' she said in delight. 'It's magical.'

'Isn't it just?' he said. 'We had a film crew here when I was in my teens, and the set designer said this was where people would sneak off for some privacy at a Regency house party, among the lemons and limes and oranges.

She reckoned they'd have had candles and it would've been beautiful.'

'Just like this.'

He nodded. 'Someone suggested fairy lights as a modern take on it without the fire risk. Since then, we've often sat out here after the sun sets, just watching the stars, with the fairy lights on. And a heater, in winter, because otherwise it's absolutely freezing.' He came back to hold her hand, and drew her over to one of the benches. 'This is probably my favourite place in the house. Even in the daytime, it's lovely.'

He'd promised her a guided tour of the house tomorrow, and she intended to hold him to that. But right now, when he sat down on one of the wrought iron benches and drew her onto his lap, she couldn't think straight. All she could do was to put her arms round his neck for balance. And from there it was one tiny step to kissing him again.

Time seemed to stop. It was just them, the moonlight and the fairy lights. Nobody came out to find them or ask Hugh to play the piano or Bella to sketch. They could've been light years away from anywhere.

But they could still hear the music.

'Dance with me?' he asked.

Even though part of her knew that this wasn't sensible—it was too intimate, just the two of them in the orangery among the fairy lights—how could she resist?

They swayed together in the room.

Any moment now, she thought, he'd say something to remind her that they were both playing a part.

And yet he didn't. He just danced with her. Held her close. Cherished her.

It was so long since she'd been held like that. It made her feel warm inside. Warm all over. And when Hugh rested his cheek against hers, even though she'd promised herself she'd be sensible, she found herself moving that little bit closer to him. Turning her head so her mouth made contact with the corner of his. His arms tightened round her and he moved his head too, so his lips brushed against hers. Once, twice: and then he was kissing her with abandon, and she was kissing him right back.

She was dizzy with desire when he broke the kiss.

'Hugh—I, we...' She couldn't think straight. There was something important she had to say, but for the life of her she couldn't remember what it was. She just wanted him to kiss her again.

She trailed her fingertips across his cheek, liking the very faint scratch of stubble. 'You're beautiful,' she said. 'Poster-boy beautiful.'

He turned his head and pressed a kiss into her palm. 'Less of the boy, thank you.'

Oh, yes. He was all man. 'I didn't mean it that way,' she said. 'Just that you're beautiful.'

'So are you.' He kissed her again. 'You make me ache.'

She dragged in a breath. 'Ditto.' An ache of wanting, of need. He was driving her crazy with his nearness.

'I know this isn't supposed to be happening, but right now,' he said softly, 'I don't want to go back and join the others. I want to carry you up the stairs to your bed.'

The big, wide four-poster.

'I want to make love with you, Bella.'

A shiver of pure desire ran down her spine.

She knew they shouldn't be doing this. It wasn't what they'd agreed. She was his pretend girlfriend, not his real one. He was her boss. It could have major repercussions and she could end up in another financial mess. They really ought to stop this right now and remember who and where they were. She opened her mouth, intending to say that they shouldn't.

Then again, this wasn't real. And she knew neither of them was looking for for ever. Kirk had wiped out her trust in relationships, and from the little Hugh had said about his ex she was pretty sure that he felt the same way. He wasn't looking for The One, any more than she was.

They were both adults.

There was no reason why they shouldn't act on the attraction between them, just for one night.

So instead, she said softly, 'Tonight's just tonight. A one-off.'

His eyes looked almost navy blue in the soft light. 'No strings.'

'No promises.' She didn't believe in promises any more. 'No for ever.'

'No promises and no for ever,' he echoed.

'Then do it,' she said softly.

He kissed her once. Hard. And then he scooped her up into his arms, pausing only to switch off the fairy lights, and carried her down the corridor and up a quiet flight of stairs to her bedroom.

CHAPTER SIX

THE NEXT MORNING, Bella woke to find a warm body curled round hers. For a moment, she couldn't place where she was and why on earth a naked male body would be in her bed at all, let alone wrapped round her.

Then she remembered.

Hugh.

She went hot as she thought about the previous night. The way he'd kissed her in the orangery among the fairy lights until she'd been dizzy. The way he'd actually carried her up to her bed. The way he'd undressed her, and then made love to her until she'd seen stars.

Right now, the way he was holding her made her feel special. Even though she wasn't really Hugh's girlfriend, and they weren't in any kind of relationship other than that of employee and boss—just for a moment, Bella could imagine what it would be like if this was the real deal instead of an elaborate fiction. She'd spent the last six months feeling stupid and useless and pathetic, after Kirk's betrayal. Last night, Hugh had made her feel good again. Not just the sex, either. He'd danced with her, laughed with her—*believed* in her.

Would last night have changed everything between them? They'd agreed that this was a one-off. No strings.

No promises. No for ever. But could they still work together after this? Or would she have to resign?

They'd have to talk—*really* talk—and maybe redraw the ground rules.

Nothing fazes a Faraday girl, she reminded herself.

Except the mantra felt hollow.

Right now, she really didn't know what to do. Did she stay where she was and wait for him to wake up? Or did she creep out of bed and get dressed—or would that make facing him even more awkward?

Hugh woke to find himself curled round a warm female body.

Bella.

He remembered the previous night in full Technicolor, and panic slid down his spine. Why had he been so stupid?

It was a physical thing, that was all, he told himself. It was obvious why it had happened. He hadn't satisfied any physical urges for a while. Maybe it'd been the same for her. They'd both drunk too much champagne, they'd danced together, they found each other attractive, and they'd just given in to the temptation.

He sighed inwardly. Just who was he trying to kid?

If he was honest with himself, he'd been attracted to Bella since the first moment he'd met her. Her bright blue eyes, her bubbly personality, the way she opened her mouth and just said what was in her head without thinking it through. Not to mention the way she'd been there for her sister; Bella Faraday had a good heart. He really liked that about her.

But he still shouldn't have let things go this far between them. They were going to have to talk, *really* talk, and redraw the ground rules. Because Bella was a great designer, perfect for Insurgo, and Tarquin would have his guts for garters if she left the company just because Hugh hadn't been able to keep his hands—or anything else, for that matter—to himself.

He lay there, trying to think what to say. Even though they'd both agreed that last night was a one-off, would she feel differently this morning? And, if she did, how was he going to handle it?

He knew that Bella wasn't like Jessie. But he just didn't trust his own judgement any more. He didn't want to take the risk of getting involved with anyone, so it was easier not to start something that was likely to end up in a mess.

Eventually he became aware that Bella's breathing was no longer deep and even, and her body was slightly tense. Clearly she was awake.

Was she, too, remembering what had happened?

Did she, too, think about turning round and kissing him hello, the way he wanted to kiss her right now?

Or was she full of regrets and awkwardness and embarrassment?

Right now, he didn't have a clue. But he knew he was going to have to do the right thing rather than ignoring the rest of the world and making love with her all over again. They had to talk.

'Bella?' he whispered.

'Uh-huh.' She sounded worried.

He resisted the urge to kiss her bare shoulder. No matter how much he wanted to touch her, taste her, he had to keep himself in check. Carefully, he withdrew his arms from round her. Odd how cold it made him feel. 'I think we need to talk.'

'Uh-huh,' she said again, and turned to face him. 'OK. I'll say it first. I know we agreed that last night was a one-off, but it really shouldn't have happened at all.'

Relief coursed through him. If she knew it, too, then it meant that things weren't going to be awkward between them. They could still work together. He wouldn't have to find another designer.

He tried to ignore the fact that another emotion under-pinned the relief. It was ridiculous to feel disappointed, especially as he didn't want to risk starting another relationship. He knew he was better off on his own, con-centrating on his business.

'Last night was last night,' he said,

'Exactly. You know the Vegas principle?'

'The Vegas principle?' he asked, not quite following her train of thought.

'You know—what happens in Vegas, stays in Vegas,' she explained.

'Ah. Yes.'

'I think we should apply that to last night,' she said carefully.

He agreed. Completely. 'So you're not going to resign because I couldn't keep my hands to myself?' he asked.

'And you're not going to sack me because I didn't stick to our plan?'

Clearly she didn't want to leave her job, either. Which was a very, very good thing. 'Apart from the fact that I don't have any grounds to sack you, you're good at your job. Tarquin would kill me if I made you leave.'

Was it his imagination, or was there a flash of disap-pointment in her eyes?

He wasn't going to analyse that too closely. Much bet-ter to let each other off the hook instead than to get tied up with all the complications. And he definitely shouldn't tell her that he didn't want her to leave because he liked having her around. That'd be way too much pressure on both of them.

'What happened last night—we don't talk about it ever again. And it's not going to be repeated,' she said.

'Agreed,' he said.

She took a deep breath. 'So we stick to the plan from here on, and I'm back to playing Miss Ditzy this morning.'

'Uh-huh.' Even though he knew she wasn't very good at it. Yesterday, although she'd tried, her true self had just shone through the play-acting. And his family had responded in kind: warmth generating warmth.

If only he'd met her years ago. When he was still able to trust. But there was no point in wishing for something he couldn't have.

'What's the agenda for today?' she asked. 'You promised me a guided tour of the house.'

And he'd make very sure that the orangery wasn't part of that. Because then he'd remember how it had been last night and he'd want to kiss her again. It would be very stupid to put himself back in the path of temptation. 'Of course,' he said, 'and everyone's going for a walk between breakfast and lunch.'

'I have a really unsuitable outfit for that,' she said. 'Totally impractical spike-heeled mules that I can totter about in.'

'They sound perfect.' He paused. 'I guess we ought to, um, get up and face everyone downstairs for breakfast. I'll, um, go next door and have a shower.' Even though part of him would much prefer staying here and having a shower with her.

'Uh-huh.'

Was she relieved or disappointed that he was going? He hadn't a clue. And he wasn't going to ask. 'I'll knock for you when I'm ready, shall I?'

This time she definitely looked relieved. He winced inwardly. Did she really think that he'd leave her to find her own way through the house, and then face his family on her own? Or maybe that was the way her ex had treated her. Again, he couldn't really ask. Not without maybe ripping open some scars, and he didn't want to hurt her.

'See you in a bit, then,' she said. And then she closed her eyes.

Was she feeling shy? Or was she trying to spare his blushes?

He climbed out of bed, pulled on his boxer shorts, grabbed the rest of his clothes—and then made the mistake of glancing back at the bed. She looked so cute, lying there. Warm and sweet. He almost dropped his clothes back on the floor and climbed back in beside her again. Especially as he remembered last night so clearly. Touching her. Tasting her. The look of sheer pleasure in her eyes just before she'd fallen apart. The soft little cry she'd made when she'd climaxed in his arms.

No, no and absolutely no.

Common sense won—just—and he managed to get back to his own room without bumping into anyone in the corridor.

Showering helped to restore a little more of his common sense, once he'd turned the temperature of the water right down. Once he'd dressed, he stripped the bed, threw everything into his case, and knocked on Bella's door.

'Come in,' she called.

She was just closing the lid of her suitcase, and she was wearing a strappy top and the shortest pair of denim cut-offs he'd ever seen. Her legs went on for ever. And his tongue felt as if it was glued to the roof of his mouth.

It grew even worse when she gave a little wiggle. Her bottom had the most perfect curve, and it made him want to touch her again.

'Is this ditzy enough?' she asked with a grin, seemingly oblivious to the desire coursing through him.

'Uh—yeah.' And now he sounded like a total troglodyte. He didn't want her to guess the effect she had on him, particularly as he knew she wasn't doing it deliberately. Bella wasn't a game-player. 'I need some coffee,' he gabbled wildly. 'You know I'm not a morning person.'

'Coffee sounds good. Would you mind, um, showing me where I can make some?'

'There's probably already a pot on the go downstairs.'

Though now they had to face his family at the breakfast table. Please don't let any of them start asking questions about where he and Bella had disappeared to last night, he begged silently.

When he ushered Bella into the kitchen, his brothers and their partners were all sitting there, along with Sophia in her high chair; his mother was bustling around and his father was deep in the Sunday newspapers. He narrowed his eyes at them all in warning that they were absolutely not to say a single word, and to his relief they actually went along with him, saying nothing more awkward to her than a cheerful, 'Good morning.'

Without another word, he pulled out a chair at the table for Bella, then sat down next to her.

'Would you like tea or coffee?' Libby asked, coming over to them.

'Coffee, please,' Bella said. 'Can I do anything to help?'

'No, sweetie, it's fine. Bacon sandwich? I'm just about to do another batch.'

'Yes, please.' Bella smiled. 'Bacon and sandwich have to be the two most perfect words for a Sunday morning.'

'And coffee,' Nigel added with a smile. 'Don't forget coffee. Especially where Hugh's concerned.'

'I reckon it'll be another twenty minutes before we get a civil word out of our Hugh,' Julian teased.

'And the rest! He only ever grunts before midday,' Alastair added. 'Even *with* coffee.'

'Now, now, children,' Libby said, mock-warning.

Bella was really enjoying the byplay between Hugh and his brothers. She missed chatting in the kitchen with her mum and her sister on Sunday morning, when her dad would be deep in the Sunday papers in the living room and they would talk about anything and everything—from films to books to seriously girly stuff that would make her dad squirm.

Then her smile faded. If any of her family knew what had happened last night... Well. Nobody would be surprised. If there was a way to mess things up, Bella would be the one to find it. But she and Hugh had agreed that they'd act as if last night hadn't happened.

She just hoped that he meant it.

The kitchen was amazing, a huge room with cream cupboards and tiled floors, with an Aga and an island workstation as well as the breakfast area with the massive table looking out onto the garden. There were comfortable-looking dog beds next to the Aga, but Bella had already worked out that the Labrador, the Westie and the spaniel were all sitting under the table, waiting patiently for treats to be sneaked down to them. 'Your kitchen's really lovely, Libby,' she said.

'Thank you,' Libby replied, putting a plate of bacon sandwiches onto the table. 'Has Hugh shown you the rest of the house yet?'

Only the orangery. And Bella had to fight to prevent the blush that threatened to betray her. 'Not yet,' she said.

'I promised I'd do that before we go out for our walk,' Hugh drawled.

'Make sure you do,' Libby said.

Bella noticed that little Sophia was fussing in her high chair; both Poppy and Julian looked exhausted, and she guessed that Sophia had slept badly during the night, meaning that so had her parents. 'Can I give her a cuddle?' Bella asked.

Poppy looked torn between wariness and gratitude.

'One of my friends does music classes for babies and toddlers,' Bella said. 'So I know a few things that might help distract her—then you might be able to have your breakfast in peace.'

'You haven't had your own breakfast yet,' Poppy said.

'I'll be fine.' Bella shrugged and smiled. 'So can I?'

Poppy smiled back at her. 'Thank you.'

Bella didn't quite dare look at Hugh as she scooped Sophia out of the high chair and then settled the baby on her lap. But Sophia clearly enjoyed being bounced to 'Humpty Dumpty' and 'Row, Row, Row Your Boat' and the other nursery songs Bella could remember, and she was gurgling with delight when Julian picked her up from Bella's lap again.

'Eat your bacon sandwich before it gets cold,' he said, patting her shoulder. 'And thank you for cheering up Miss Grumpy here.'

'Any time,' Bella said with a smile.

'Can I help with the washing up?' Bella asked when she'd finished her sandwich.

Libby shook her head. 'No, sweetie. Thank you for the offer, but it's fine.'

'The kitchen is Ma's domain,' Nigel explained.

'My mum's the same, except we all pitch in and help when we have family over for lunch, because it's really not fair to make someone peel all the veg on their own,' Bella said.

'Well, if you really want to, you can help me with the veg,' Libby conceded. 'But let Hugh show you round first.'

'Hint taken,' Hugh said and stood up. 'Come on, Bella.'

She took his hand and let him lead her out of the kitchen.

He dropped her hand again, the minute they were out of sight. 'Guided tour,' he said, and proceeded to whisk her through the house. The house was glorious, with mullioned windows upstairs and floor-to-ceiling windows downstairs.

'Hugh,' she said when he'd taken her swiftly through the library, not even letting her browse a single shelf in the acres of shelving.

'What?'

'What did I do wrong?' she asked.

'Nothing.' But his voice was clipped.

She sighed. 'Was it because I cuddled the baby? I *like* babies, Hugh. And I like your family.'

'You're meant to be unsuitable,' he reminded her.

'Even unsuitable girlfriends can like babies.'

'Hmm,' he said. 'Drawing room.' There were com-

fortable chairs and amazing artwork on the walls, and a
den with a state of the art television and music system.

'Dining room.'

She'd already seen this the previous day, and the ballroom—though it was much less intimidating now it was
empty. She was almost tempted to ask him to play something for her on the piano, something soft and gentle for
a Sunday morning, but there was an odd expression on
his face and she didn't quite dare.

So much for the Vegas principle. He was clearly finding it hard to ignore what had happened between them.

And that was probably why he didn't show her the
orangery in daylight. It would've been too much of a reminder of how reckless they'd been.

'Do you want your family to think we've had a fight?'
she asked when he'd finished the tour and was leading
her back to the kitchen.

'Fight? Oh.' The penny clearly dropped, and he took
her hand again.

Except it felt grudging.

Considering that *he'd* been the one to come up with
the idea of the unsuitable girlfriend in the first place,
Bella wanted to shake him by the scruff of his neck.
'You have to be the most difficult man in the universe,'
she muttered.

He didn't disagree with her. And she had the nasty
feeling that she was going to be looking for another job,
pretty soon. She just hoped that Tarquin would give her
a decent reference—she certainly wasn't going to ask
Hugh. And she wasn't telling Grace about any of this.
So much for standing on her own two feet and getting
her life in shape. She'd just messed up again. Big time.

In the kitchen, everyone was still drinking coffee.

Libby looked at her shoes. 'You need to borrow some wellingtons, Bella, or you'll risk ruining those lovely shoes.'

'I guess they're probably not that suitable for a walk in the garden,' she said, playing Miss Ditzy—though her heart really wasn't in this any more.

'Hugh will find you something in the boot room,' Oliver said.

She blinked. 'You have a room just for *boots*?' Hugh hadn't shown her that.

'It's for boots, coats and muddy dogs to dry off in,' Hugh explained.

The boot room turned out to be just off the kitchen. The room had a stone chequered floor that reminded Bella a bit of the orangery, teamed with white tongue and groove panelling on the cabinets. There were shelves of wellington boots, pegs for coats, and a couple of wicker picnic baskets on shelves; there were also a washing machine and tumble dryer, and she guessed that there would be an iron and ironing board in one of the cupboards.

Hugh checked her shoe size and came up with a pair of green wellington boots and an ancient waxed jacket that was too big for her. 'You'll need socks,' he said, and rummaged in one of the wicker baskets for an old but clean pair of what looked like rugby socks.

And at least borrowing a jacket meant she had pockets to shove her hands into and she wouldn't have the temptation of being hand-in-hand with Hugh—or the awkwardness if she tried to hold his hand and he rejected her, which she thought would be the most likely outcome.

Hugh's brothers and their partners all joined them on the walk, along with Sophia in her pushchair, and the dogs romped along happily beside them.

'So we're going for a walk in the nearby woods or something?' she asked.

Hugh nodded. 'They're part of the estate.'

Well, of course a huge manor house like this would come with an estate rather than just a garden. How stupid of her not to think of that before.

But her awkwardness turned to delight when they walked through the narrow paths in the woods and she could see bluebells everywhere. 'That's gorgeous!'

'It's still a bit early for them yet,' Hugh said, 'but they're like a blue haze when they're fully out.'

'A real bluebell carpet—how lovely,' she said. It made her itch to sit out here with a pad of cartridge paper and a box of watercolours. 'I love the colour of new leaves, that really bright lime-green that means spring's really here.'

'Yeah.'

Somehow, Hugh was holding her hand again, and it sent a shiver of pure desire through her.

He met her gaze. 'I'm not coming on to you,' he said in a low voice. 'Everyone will expect me to hold my girl-friend's hand.'

'Of course,' she said, but she had to swallow her disappointment. Which was ridiculous in any case. She didn't want a relationship and she didn't want to mess up her job. Hugh was off limits and this was simply a bit of play-acting for his family's benefit. They'd agreed. And the fact that he was holding her hand simply meant that the bluebells had just got rid of his Monday morning-itis, which was actually more like *every* morning-itis.

Back at the house, the others all disappeared to sort out various things, and Hugh's father called him to come and help with something. Feeling a bit like a spare part,

Bella went in search of Libby in the kitchen. 'I promised to help you with the vegetables.'

'You really don't have to,' Libby said. 'You're a guest.'

'Even so,' Bella said. 'Is that beef I smell roasting?'

'Yes.'

'I could make the Yorkshire puddings, if you like.' She laughed. 'I admit I'm a terrible cook, but I'm actually quite good at cupcakes, pancakes and Yorkshire puddings. I guess it's because they're light and fluffy, like me.'

Libby gave her look as if to say that she knew there was much more to Bella than that, or Hugh wouldn't be dating her. 'You're playing a part, this weekend, aren't you?'

Uh-oh. She hadn't expected Libby to call her on it. 'A part?' Bella asked, trying not to panic. 'What makes you say that?'

'Because the real you keeps shining through. The way you brought me my favourite chocolates, the way you looked after Lavinia yesterday afternoon, the way you drew those pictures for everyone, the way you haven't minded a muddy dog draped all over you, the way you sat and cuddled Sophia this morning during breakfast and sang nursery songs to her.' Libby ticked them off on her fingers. 'If you were the dreadful airhead that you and Hugh clearly want us all to think you are, I'm not so sure you would've done any of that.'

There was no way she could keep up the pretence any more. 'Busted, I guess. But please don't tell Hugh you know.'

'I won't,' Libby said softly. 'But what I don't understand is why you both feel that you have to play a part.'

'I did tell him Plan B would be better,' Bella said with a rueful smile.

Libby's frown deepened. 'What's Plan B?'

Bella held up both hands in a surrender gesture. 'Just ignore me. I'm rambling.'

'No, I think this is something I need to know,' Libby said.

Bella bit her lip. 'Please, please don't shoot the messenger, because you've all been so kind and I don't want to be rude and ungrateful. Even though I've already been rude and obnoxious.'

'Now you're really worrying me,' Libby said. 'What's plan B?'

'To tell you the truth about his job and make you see how he feels. Hugh isn't a stockbroker at heart,' Bella said, 'he's a music producer. He loves his job and he's really, really good at it. I really don't mean to be rude or to offend you, but he seems to believe that you all want him to toe the line—to sell Insurgo Records to the highest bidder and join the family firm instead. If he does that, you're going to break his heart and his spirit. He'd hate it so much and he'd spend all his time wishing he was somewhere else. And then he might grow to resent you all instead of loving you like he does now.'

Libby was silent for so long that Bella thought she'd gone too far.

'Mrs Moncrieff? Libby?' she asked anxiously.

Libby's eyes were glistening with tears. 'Those were very wise words,' she said softly. 'And they came from the heart.'

Hugh was halfway down the corridor to the kitchen when he heard his mother ask, 'So are you his real girlfriend pretending to be his fake girlfriend?'

What?

Oh, no. He knew his mother was perceptive. He needed to go in and head her off. Or had Bella already caved in and told her the truth?

To his horror, he heard Bella say, 'That all sounds so complicated. But I was telling you the truth when I said I'm the designer at Insurgo.'

Oh, hell. She *had* caved in. She'd blown their cover completely. And he was shocked by how hurt and disappointed he was. He'd been telling himself that Bella wasn't like Jessie—and yet she'd let him down, too. She'd promised to play a part and she'd gone back on her word. Betrayed his trust. Ratted him out to his mother, so his subterfuge was well and truly uncovered. So much for thinking that she was different. Obviously his judgement was still way off.

'That,' Libby said, 'figures.'

'What does?' Bella asked.

Hugh went cold. Please don't let his mother start talking about Jessie. He only realised he was holding his breath when Libby said, 'If he hasn't told you, I won't break his confidence.'

'That's not very fair, given that I've just done that,' Bella said.

She'd even admitted what she'd done. And it made him feel sick. How far had she gone?

He strode into the kitchen. 'Breaking my confidence?' he asked.

Bella went white. 'Hugh. I didn't know you were there.'

'Obviously.' He shook his head in disgust. 'Well, thanks a bunch. I guess that'll teach me to trust you. So do you blab Insurgo's business all over social media, too, the same way you've just blabbed my personal business to my mother?'

'Hugh, that's not fair,' Libby said. 'She was trying to help.'

'She was gossiping about me.' And that hurt.

'I wasn't gossiping at all,' Bella said. 'Right now, I want to tip this Yorkshire pudding batter all over your stupid head. But I'm not going to waste food and put your mum in an awkward position. Instead I'm going to walk outside in the garden, in this stupid outfit I found to fit your even more stupid idea. And *you*,' she said, walking over to him and stabbing her finger into his chest, 'are going to sit down with your mum and talk. Really talk.'

He was too taken aback to say anything. Not that he could've got a word in edgeways, because Bella was on a roll.

'You're going to tell her how you feel about your business and how it's not just your job, it's your passion, and for you it's like breathing. And you're going to tell her that you're great at business and you don't take unnecessary risks—that you save being a total idiot for the other bits of your life. You three,' she added to the dogs, 'you're coming with me and we're going to find some tennis balls, and I'm going to pretend they're Hugh's head and kick them as hard as I can.'

'Bella—' he began, knowing that he needed to apologise.

'No. Talk to your mum,' she said. 'Right now, I don't want to talk to you. I'm going out with the dogs.'

'Take whatever you need from the boot room, love,' Libby said. 'And I'll shout at him for you.'

Bella shook her head. 'I'd much rather you listened to him,' she said softly. 'Even though right at this moment I don't like him very much, I respect him when it comes to business—and I think you both need to listen to each other.' And she walked quietly out of the kitchen, followed by the dogs.

Hugh found himself talking—*really* talking—to his mother about the most important thing in his life. And she listened. Understood. Just as he could now see that the worrying and fussing were driven by love rather than a need to make him toe a family line that didn't actually exist.

Without Bella's intervention, this would never have happened, and he knew it.

When he'd finished, Libby said, 'You owe that girl—'

'—a huge apology,' he cut in. 'I know.'

She hugged him. 'You're my youngest son, Hugh, and I love you, but I don't like you very much today.'

'I don't like myself very much, either,' he admitted.

'She isn't Jessie,' Libby said softly.

'I know.' Jessie would never have offered to help prepare the vegetables. Yes, musicians had to look after their hands, because an accidental cut or burn would affect their ability to play an instrument—but Jessie wouldn't have offered to do something that didn't risk her hands, either. She wouldn't have played with Sophia. He knew that his family hadn't taken to her—they'd been polite but reserved. But everyone had instantly warmed to Bella, from his great-aunt to his brothers and even his father. 'I need to go and talk to her.'

'Be nice,' Libby said softly. 'She's got a good heart. She didn't break your trust. She found a better way to deal with things than any of us did.'

Hugh hugged his mother back. 'I know.' And he'd messed this up. Big time.

He went outside to find Bella. She looked as if she'd

been crying, and he felt a total heel. How could he have been so unkind to her?

'Bella. I'm sorry,' he said.

'Hmm.' She didn't look in the slightest bit mollified by his apology.

'You were right and I was wrong.'

She folded her arms. 'That's rather stating the obvious.'

'And I'm sorry I was obnoxious to you. I shouldn't have said any of that.'

'Also stating the obvious,' she said.

'I can't even blame it on Monday morning-itis.' He sighed. 'How do I make it up to you?'

'You've made it clear that you don't trust me. So, actually, I don't think you can,' she said.

He blew out a breath. 'I don't have a clue what to say or what to do. Only that I'm sorry for hurting you. And, without you, I don't think my family would ever have understood what Insurgo means to me. And I wouldn't have understood how they really feel, either. I appreciate that.'

She shrugged. 'Even so, I'm not your personal punch-bag. Hugh, I don't enjoy people lashing out at me. I was only playing Miss Ditzy because you asked me to. I'm not an actress. Your mum saw right through the whole thing. And I did tell you it was a stupid idea.'

'You were right,' he said again. 'I know you probably want to be a million miles away from here right now, so if you want me to drive you straight home, then I'll do it. But I think my family would like you to stay for lunch. They like you. And I mean they like the *real* Bella Faraday,' he clarified. 'The one who looks out for elderly aunts, cuddles babies, plays ball with the dogs, is an amazing artist and brings out the best in everyone. The woman who really is the life and soul of the party—because I've never seen my entire family get up on the dance floor before you came along.'

Her eyes sparkled with tears; he brushed away the single one that spilled over her lashes.

'They don't hate me for lying to them?' she whispered.

'No. They really, really like you.' And so did he. Though now wasn't the time to say so. After the way he'd hurt her, she wouldn't believe him—and he couldn't blame her.

'Come and have lunch,' he said.

'For your mum's sake. Not yours.'

'I know,' he said softly. 'And thank you.'

Although Bella didn't say much to him once they were back in the house, she sparkled all the way through Sunday lunch. She insisted on helping to clear things away and on cuddling Sophia again when his niece had another fit of the grumps. And when his family said goodbye to her, it was with a warm, heartfelt hug rather than the formal handshakes they'd always given Jessie.

'Come back soon,' Libby said. 'And I mean *really* soon. You have to see the bluebells when they're at their best.'

'I'd love to,' Bella said, hugging her back. 'Thank you so much for having me.'

His brothers and their partners all got hugs, too, along with the baby. And so did his father, who then shocked Hugh immensely by saying, 'Come and paint the bluebells for my study, and I'll cook you my famous chicken biryani.'

Since when had his father ever cooked? Let alone something as exotic as biryani?

Hugh was so stunned that he didn't say a word until they were halfway home. And then it was only because Bella was the one to start the conversation.

'I think we need to talk,' she said carefully.

'Talk?'

She took a deep breath. 'I'm sorry I messed up your plans. If you want me to resign and go quietly from Insurgo, I'll accept that and write you an official resignation letter as soon as we're back in London.'

'No, that's not fair.' And he didn't want her to leave.

'You asked me to play your unsuitable girlfriend, and I didn't do it right.'

'I also told you to be yourself,' he said. 'And you were. Though I don't get how you do it.'

'How I do what?' she asked, sounding confused.

'Fit in so effortlessly. When you joined Insurgo, within a couple of days it was as if you'd been one of the team right from the start. And my family. They took to you like they never did to—' He stopped abruptly.

'Never did to whom?' she asked softly.

'Never mind.'

'The girl who broke your heart? The one you worked with?'

He gave her a sidelong glance. 'Fishing, Bella?'

'No—but I can hardly ask you straight out about it, can I? You're not exactly approachable.'

'My past isn't any of your—' he began, then stopped, knowing that he was being completely unfair to her. 'Sorry. That was rude and unkind. Especially as you've just given up your whole weekend to do me a favour, and I've already treated you badly. I apologise unreservedly. And you have the right to stamp all over me in spike heels.'

'Spike heels?'

'Your "three strikes and you're out" rule. I've broken that several times.'

'That's bravado,' Bella said, sounding sad. 'I don't really stomp on people.' And he felt even guiltier when she added, 'Besides, you're right. Your past isn't any of my business.' She sighed. 'Did you hear everything I said to your mum?'

'Only from when she asked you if you were my real girlfriend pretending to be my pretend girlfriend.' He gave her another swift look. Guilt was written all over her face. 'Is there more I should know about?'

'I told her that you're Insurgo's heart—and joining the family firm would break your spirit and make you resent them instead of loving them and being exasperated by them as you do now.'

If Hugh hadn't been driving, he would've closed his eyes in horror. 'We never talk about that sort of stuff.'

'I think you might do, in future,' Bella said softly. 'But, as I said earlier, I understand if you want me to resign.'

'Right now,' Hugh said, 'I think the best thing would be if neither of us said another word until we get back to London.'

'OK,' Bella said, and lapsed into silence.

Which made Hugh feel even more mean and guilty. He knew she'd said everything with the best of intentions. But his head was in a whirl. Bella Faraday knocked him seriously off balance, and he didn't trust himself to say what he really meant. He wasn't even sure what he really felt, other than being completely mixed up, so it was better to say nothing.

It didn't help that he could still smell her perfume, and

that made him remember kissing her in the orangery last night. That kiss—and what had happened afterwards—was something he really couldn't dare to repeat. So it was better to put a little bit of metaphorical distance between them. Wasn't it?

Finally he pulled up in the road outside her flat. 'I'll see you to your door.'

'There's no need,' Bella said. 'Thank you for the lift. And I won't ask you in. Not because I'm being rude, but because I'm sure you're busy. And, tomorrow morning, when we're back in the office, this weekend never happened.'

'Agreed,' he said.

Even though he didn't see her to the door, Hugh waited until she'd closed her front door behind her before he drove away. That was the very least he could do. And as for the damage to their working relationship... He'd better hope that he could fix it. Because the only way he could keep Bella in his life was as a colleague—and he didn't want to lose her.

What a weekend, Bella thought as she closed the front door behind her.

She changed swiftly into a more comfortable—not to mention demure—pair of jeans and a normal T-shirt, and bustled about sorting out things in her flat. There was a message on her phone from Grace.

Give me a ring when you're back and let me know how it went xxx

Yeah, right. Bella rolled her eyes. She could hardly admit to her sister what she'd done: slept with her boss, gone completely off brief, interfered and told his mother the truth, and then had a huge row with Hugh. Even though he'd apologised, she still hated the fact that he thought he couldn't trust her. Maybe his ex had broken his ability to trust, the way Kirk had broken hers; but it still hurt that he could think of her in that way. Did he not know her at all?

So she left it until late in the evening to text a reply to Grace: Just got back. That was stretching a point, but it was only a tiny fib. Too late to call. That bit was true. All fine. That bit might not be true. But she hoped that Grace wouldn't push her for more details—and that things would be OK in the office tomorrow. That she and Hugh could pretend that nothing had ever happened. Because, otherwise, she'd be looking for another job.

And, if she left Insurgo, it wasn't just the job she'd miss.

CHAPTER SEVEN

ON MONDAY MORNING, Bella was slightly nervous as she walked in to the Insurgo offices. She bought a double-shot cappuccino from the café downstairs to give her courage. Would Hugh be the same with her as he usually was, or would he avoid her? Would he be more difficult than he usually was on Monday mornings?

But he wasn't in the office. He'd left Tarquin a message to say that he was in a meeting across town and probably wouldn't make it in to the office until very late that day, if at all. Bella wasn't sure if she was more relieved at not having to face him or disappointed at missing him; though she knew that she couldn't let anyone guess how she was feeling. Nobody knew she'd been in Oxfordshire with Hugh, and it had to stay that way. As far as everyone at the Insurgo offices was concerned, he was the boss and she was simply the graphic designer. Full stop.

By Wednesday, Hugh knew that he had to show his face in the office or Tarquin would start working things out for himself. But he wasn't sure if he could do what Bella had suggested and work on the Vegas principle.

On paper, it was easy. What had happened in Oxfordshire should stay in Oxfordshire.

The problem was, he could still remember what it felt like to wake up wrapped round her. And, worse still, he wanted to do it again.

But he couldn't see a way of making this work. He already knew that from his experience with Jessie. Even though Bella wasn't anything like Jessie, the equation was the same: business plus relationship equals disaster.

So either he dated her and she left the company—which wouldn't be good for Insurgo, because she was a great designer—or she stayed in her job and he'd have to keep a lid on his feelings. It made business sense for it to be the latter. Plus he was used to keeping a lid on his feelings.

But that had been before Bella Faraday exploded into his life. Before he'd taken her home as his 'unsuitable' girlfriend. Before she'd turned his world upside down.

Bella was aware of every time Hugh walked into the room, even when her back was to the door.

She looked up several times from her work when he was in the main office, talking to Tarquin, and caught his eye. He looked away again almost immediately. And, because Hugh was so good at being impassive, she didn't have a clue what he was thinking.

Was he thinking about what had happened between them? Did he feel the same pull, the same awareness, as she did? Or was he regretting every single moment?

She was half tempted to text him and suggest that they talked. But that would be needy and pathetic, and that wasn't who she was. She'd got through Kirk's betrayal, and this situation with Hugh wasn't anywhere near that on the scale of awfulness.

Things would all settle down, soon enough. She

would get to the stage where she could look at Hugh without remembering how it had felt when he'd touched her and kissed her. Where she could look at him without wanting him to kiss her again. It would just take a bit of time, that was all. Until then, she'd just have to keep a lid on her feelings. This wasn't appropriate, and she wasn't in a position where she dared do anything to jeopardise her job.

Hugh sat in front of his computer with his elbows resting on the desk and his chin propped in his hands. This was ridiculous. He never, ever let anything distract his focus from his work.

But he couldn't stop thinking about Bella.

Maybe he should call her. Text her. Tell her he'd like to change his mind about the Vegas principle and see her now they were back in London. Ask her out to dinner or to a show.

But then things would start to get complicated in the office, and he didn't want that. He knew that keeping his distance from her was the sensible thing to do.

All the same, he was antsy. He couldn't settle to anything. And he knew it was making him snappy with everyone.

On the Thursday, he was glad that one of his artists was in the studio in the basement, recording an album. It gave him an excuse to stay out of the office and focus on producing the music—the part of his job he loved most. That would keep his head too busy to let him think about Bella Faraday.

And he actually managed it...until lunchtime, when Tarquin brought Bella down to meet the band and talk about the cover art concept.

She'd changed her hair colour again, Hugh noticed. Today she was brunette. It was a huge change from the almost fire-engine-red she'd sported in Oxfordshire, but it suited her and it brought out the depths of her eyes. It made her look seriously pretty.

How he wanted to twirl the ends of her hair round his fingers. Feel how soft and silky it was. And then touch his mouth to hers...

What made it worse was that she was dressed in faded jeans which hugged her curves, and spike-heeled ankle boots. She'd teamed it with a black T-shirt with the Insurgo logo on the front, clearly going for the rock chick look. And she carried it off beautifully.

He wasn't surprised that she charmed the band as quickly as she'd charmed his family. Just by being herself: bright, vivacious Bella with her ready laugh, and the way she touched people's hands or arms or shoulders when she spoke. She was very tactile; and yet she didn't make you feel as if she'd invaded your personal space. It felt natural. Easy.

Hugh caught her eye. Was it his imagination, or was there the faintest blush in her cheeks as she looked at him? Probably his imagination, he decided, because she was totally professional and almost cool with him. Clearly she didn't have a problem with the Vegas principle.

They discussed the album concept and cover with the band, and Bella made a few sketches and notes. Hugh could barely take his eyes off her hands. He remembered how they'd felt against his skin, and it made him ache.

When would he stop wanting her?

Tarquin had also organised a buffet lunch for all of them, sent down by the café on the ground floor. Being together in a more social setting would be awkward, Hugh thought, but no way could he or Bella get out of this. He hadn't said a word to Tarquin about the situation and he was pretty sure that she hadn't said anything, either, or his business partner would've had quite a lot to say about it.

Well, they'd just have to roll with it and pretend that everything was normal. Even though it wasn't.

He noticed that Jet, the band's lead singer, was flirting with Bella during lunch. She wasn't encouraging him at all; she was professional and polite and made sure that she included the rest of the band in the conversation. Hugh couldn't fault her behaviour. But he really wanted to snarl at Jet and tell him to back off, because Bella wasn't available. Which would put her in an impossible situation, so he kept his tongue firmly under control.

But then he reached for the plate of sandwiches at the same time as Bella did. As his fingers brushed against hers, he felt the heat zing through him. And when his gaze caught hers, her pupils went just that little bit darker and wider. So was it the same for her, too? This crazy, raging need that sent him into a flat spin?

And just what were they going to do about this?

The more time Hugh spent with her, the more he wanted her—and this wasn't fair to either of them. But right at that moment he couldn't see a way of making things better. Not without complicating things or risking things getting a whole lot worse.

To his relief, after lunch Bella made an excuse to go back up to the office with Tarquin, which left him to concentrate on the music and the band and working on the arrangements.

Jet turned to him at the end of the next song. 'I was going to ask you—could you give me Bella's number?'

'To discuss the album cover?' Hugh asked, deliberately misunderstanding the other man. 'Just call the usual office number and someone will put you through to her.'

'No, I meant...'

'What?' Uh-oh. He really hoped that Jet hadn't picked up how short his tone was.

But the singer didn't seem fussed in the slightest. 'Dating her, man,' he said with a grin. 'I know you're dedicated to your work, Hugh, but surely even *you* have noticed how hot she is?'

Of course he'd noticed. More than noticed. 'She's my colleague,' he said crisply. 'I never mix business and relationships.'

Jet gave him a look as if to say, *more fool you.* 'So can you give me her number?'

'She might already be involved with someone.'

Jet held his gaze. 'And she might not.'

'I'll let her know you asked, and leave it up to her if she wants to call you,' Hugh said. And he seriously hoped she didn't. Even though he knew he was being a complete dog in the manger, given that he wasn't actually in a relationship with Bella. For all he knew, she might actually want to date Jet. But he'd be much happier if she didn't. 'Now, let's get back to work and go through the next song, shall we?'

Later that afternoon, when the band had left, Hugh walked back into the office. Bella was working at her desk, but he knew by the sudden tension in her shoulders that she knew he was there.

'Jet asked for your number,' he said abruptly.

Her head snapped up and she stared at him. 'Jet?'

'The lead singer of the band. You were talking to him at lunch.' And Jet had most definitely been flirting with her. Surely she'd been aware of that?

'Oh.'

'I told him to ring the office and someone would put him through, if he wants to discuss the album cover.'

'Uh-huh.'

He couldn't tell anything from her expression. Which left him with no choice; he'd have to raise the issue. 'Jet didn't want to discuss business.'

'Then what did he want?'

He gave her a speaking look. Wasn't it obvious? 'I told him that relationships and business don't mix.'

And now there was the tiniest, tiniest glint in her eyes. Amusement? Anger? Pity? He wasn't sure. There was no way he could ask without betraying himself, and until he knew what was going on in her head he didn't want her to know what he was feeling.

'Did you, now?' she drawled.

'I said I'd tell you he'd asked.'

'I might,' Bella said, 'already be committed to someone.'

'So you might,' he said. And he had to suppress the wish that it was him.

'I'll make sure he knows that,' she said.

So she wasn't going to date the guy? He was shocked by the way it made him feel as if a massive weight had been lifted from his shoulders. 'Thank you.' But he didn't want her to realise he was glad for selfish reasons. 'I like the office to run smoothly,' he added coolly.

'Noted, Mr Moncrieff.'

And then she did something that nearly finished

him off. She moistened her lower lip with the tip of her tongue, so her lips looked as shiny as if she'd just been kissed. *Just as she'd looked when he'd kissed her.*

'Right,' he said, and left for his own office. While he still could.

Back at his desk, he rested his elbows on the table and propped his face in his hands. When was he going to stop wanting this woman? When was his common sense going to come back? He knew it wouldn't work between them. It couldn't.

Yet he still wanted her.

By the end of the next week, Hugh was near to going insane. Throwing himself into work wasn't making any difference at all. And when he was at home he actually found himself sitting down with a guitar in his hand or at the piano, something he hadn't done in a long time. There were little snatches of songs buzzing round in his head—nothing he recognised, so he knew they were his own compositions. There were bits of melodies, bits of introductions, and bits of a middle eight. None of them fitted together and none of the melodies had proper words to go with them, but Hugh knew that he was starting to write songs again.

And that worried him even more.

It had taken him a year to get over the mess that Jessie's betrayal had caused. He didn't want to leave himself open to the risk of feeling that low ever, ever again—even though part of him was glad that the music he loved so much was bubbling up inside him again, and he knew it was all due to Bella.

But this was all too complicated.

He was just going to have to get over these growing

feelings for Bella and ignore them. And ignore the hints from his parents that the bluebells were starting to look really pretty and the dogs would love to go for a run with him. They might just as well have texted him in capitals to say WE WANT TO SEE BELLA.

Well, it wasn't happening.

What happened in Oxfordshire, stayed in Oxfordshire. They'd agreed it. Their relationship had been strictly business from that Sunday afternoon onwards.

So why couldn't Bella get Hugh out of her head? Why could she still feel the warmth of his body wrapped round her? Why, every time she closed her eyes, did she remember him kissing her among the fairy lights until they were both dizzy?

'Are you OK, Bella?' Tarquin asked.

'Fine.' She smiled at him. 'Just a bit of a headache.' A headache called Hugh Moncrieff. Not that she would ever admit that to anyone at Insurgo. Since they'd been back, Hugh's cool and professional behaviour towards her had made it clear that their relationship was strictly business. And she didn't want to cause tension in the office. Even so, she couldn't help asking, 'Tarq, have you known Hugh for very long?'

'We were at school together, so yes. Why?'

'I just wondered,' she said, 'why he has this thing about not mixing business and relationships.'

'Ah. That's not my story to tell, sweet-cheeks,' Tarquin said softly. 'Why? Are you...?'

Oh, no. He hadn't guessed how she felt about Hugh, had he? 'No, no, not at all,' she fibbed hastily. 'It's just something he said when Jet from the band asked for my number.'

'OK.'

But Tarquin looked curious, and Bella wished she hadn't said anything. 'Just being nosey,' she said sweetly. 'Obviously something's happened in the past that made things difficult for everyone in the office, so he doesn't want people to get involved with people they have to work with. I get it.'

'Something like that,' Tarquin said.

But he still looked oddly at her, and she knew she had to do something to distract him. 'I'm going to do a tea and coffee run. What do you want?' Even if that did mean going upstairs to the staff kitchen and being even closer to Hugh's office, it would hopefully distract Tarquin and he wouldn't start working things out or leaping to conclusions.

'I'd love a coffee, thank you, sweetie,' Tarquin said, and to her relief the sticky moment was over.

On Friday evening, Tarquin walked into Hugh's office and tapped the face of his watch with an exaggerated motion. 'Right, you. Time to turn the computer off.'

Hugh frowned. 'Not now, Tarq. I've got a couple of things to do.'

'They can wait. We're meeting Ro, or had you forgotten?'

Roland was their other best friend from school. And both Hugh and Tarquin had been worried about him for months; their regular fortnightly meeting was their way of keeping an eye on him, under the guise of rescuing Hugh from being a total workaholic. 'I'd forgotten what today was,' Hugh admitted. He glanced at the screen. 'OK. Let me save the file and shut the computer down, and we'll go.'

* * *

Roland walked into the bar at roughly the same time they did, and raised his hand to show he'd seen them.

But although Hugh had thought this was all about keeping an eye on Roland, he was in for a surprise when Tarquin turned to him after ordering two beers and a mineral water for Roland.

'All righty. You're being more of a nightmare than usual in the office, Hugh. I'm pretty sure it's got something to do with your brother's engagement party—and, as I haven't been able to get it out of you, Ro's going to do the thumbscrews.'

Roland spread his hands. 'That pretty much sums it up. So you can tell us now, or we can nag you until you tell us. Your choice, but I'd advise saving all the drag of us droning on at you and just telling us.'

Hugh raked a hand through his hair. 'Nothing's wrong.'

'Or,' Roland suggested, 'I could call your mother and tell her that Tarq and I are worried about you. She'll tell us what you're not saying.'

Which was what Hugh and Tarquin had done to Roland, the previous year, out of sheer desperation. It had worked, but they'd had an unspoken pact since then that calling any of their mothers was off limits.

'No. *Don't* call Ma. Please.' Hugh had been avoiding his mother's calls, too, returning her answering machine messages with a brief text to say he was up to his eyes at work and would call her soon. If his two best friends tag-teamed her and she told them the information he'd been keeping back, he wouldn't stand a chance. He put his hands up in a gesture of surrender. 'OK. I'll talk.' At least then maybe he could do some damage limitation.

Tarquin handed him a beer and gestured to one of the quieter tables in the corner.

They really weren't going to let him off this, were they? He suppressed a sigh and went to sit down.

'Tell us, sweet-cheeks,' Tarquin said. 'What happened at Nigel's party?'

Hugh blew out a breath. 'I thought I was being so clever. I took someone with me. A pretend girlfriend. Someone unsuitable. The idea was that they'd all be so horrified by her that they'd be glad when I told them it was all over—and then they'd back off.'

Tarquin and Roland exchanged a glance. 'But?' Tarquin asked.

Hugh grimaced. 'They saw through it. And they liked her. A lot.'

'Hmm. If you liked her enough to ask for her help, and she liked you enough to go along with it, and your family all liked her, then it sounds to me as if you're looking at this from completely the wrong direction,' Roland said. 'Why don't you just date the girl properly?'

'You know why,' Hugh said. 'After Jessie, there's no way I'm getting involved with anyone again. Nothing serious. I'm concentrating on the business. That's how I like my life.'

'Not all women are like Jessie,' Tarquin said. 'There's no reason why you can't try again with someone else.'

Hugh folded his arms. 'I *know* not all women are like Jessie. But I don't trust my own judgement any more. I was stupid enough to let her fool me, so what's to say I won't make the same mistake again?'

'Because you're too bright to do that,' Tarquin said. 'Think about it. You earned a first class degree.'

'Plus you own the hottest indie record label in the

country and the business is going from strength to strength,' Roland said.

It was now. Thanks to a lot of hard work—and Roland's investment. But Hugh knew just how much damage had been done to his business by letting his heart rule his head over Jessie.

'Tarq has a point,' Roland continued. 'It's been a while. Surely you're lonely?'

Yes. He was. And he wanted Bella. Hugh's temper flared. 'That's rich, coming from you.'

'That's a different kettle of fish altogether,' Roland said, his voice very quiet.

Hugh saw the emptiness in his best friend's eyes and flinched. 'Ro, I'm sorry—that was way, way below the belt. I apologise unreservedly. I shouldn't have said that.' Roland was single, but not from choice; his wife had died in a car crash eighteen months ago, and he was still mourning her. Some well-meaning friends had tried matchmaking over the last few months, but every attempt had failed spectacularly.

'Apology accepted.' But Roland's voice was completely neutral, and Hugh knew he'd overstepped the mark. Big time. Exactly the way he'd lashed out at Bella—and for exactly the same reason.

The only way he could think of to make amends was to tell the truth. Well, some of it. 'I *am* sorry, Ro. This whole thing makes me antsy, and I shouldn't have taken it out on you. I'm just as horrible at work, and...' He shrugged. 'I hate being like it. Everyone else hates it just as much. But I don't seem to be able to stop myself.'

Tarquin patted his arm. 'You're in Monday morning mode. We get it. Now spill.'

'I like her. A lot. And it scares me stupid,' he admitted. 'The way I feel about her is like nothing else I've ever known. Not even Jessie. I just can't get her out of my head.'

'Are you going to tell us anything about her?' Roland asked.

Hugh squirmed. How could he do this without giving away too much? 'She's bright, she's funny, and she makes me feel as if the world's full of sunshine.'

'Which sounds perfect. So why aren't you dating her officially?' Tarquin asked.

'It's complicated,' Hugh hedged.

'Complicated how?' Roland asked.

Hugh put his face in his hands. There was no way out of this, any more. He was going to have to bite the bullet. 'Because she works for Insurgo,' he muttered. '*Now* do you get why it's a problem?'

Tarquin groaned. 'No. Please. Not Bella. Tell me you didn't take Bella with you to Oxfordshire.'

'Who's Bella?' Roland asked, looking mystified. 'And why would it be so bad if Hugh was with her?'

'Bella's our new designer,' Tarquin explained. 'She's really good at her job, and she makes everyone in the office laugh for all the right reasons. She fitted in from the moment she walked in to Insurgo. She's adorable. If I was straight, I'd be tempted to ask her to marry me. Which gives you an idea of just how great she is.' He looked at Hugh, unsmiling. 'All righty. Bottom line. How does she feel about you?'

'I don't know.' Hugh looked away.

Tarquin groaned. 'I've got a bad feeling about this. I thought she'd been a bit wary of you in the office, this last week or so. And you've been grumpier than usual. I assumed it was because of your family—but it's not, is it?'

'Bella Faraday and I are not an item,' Hugh said calmly. 'Don't worry, Tarq. It'll be absolutely fine. Things will settle down. We talked about it.'

'Did you tell her about Jessie?' Roland asked.

'No. The subject didn't come up.' Which was a big fat lie. The subject *had* come up, but his family hadn't told her quite enough for her to work it out for herself, and Hugh had refused flatly to discuss it. He'd even been rude to Bella when she'd asked. Unkind. Unfair.

Tarquin rolled his eyes. 'Great. So now I'm going to have to scour London for a new designer—one as good as she is and who'll fit in as quickly as she has. Which is practically impossible. You *idiot*. I could shake you until your teeth rattle.'

'It's fine,' Hugh repeated. 'She's staying. We understand each other.'

'You mean you've both said all the right words,' Roland said. 'And neither of you have said what you're really thinking.'

'Neither of us wants any complications,' Hugh insisted.

'But you complicated it anyway?' Tarquin asked dryly.

'Yes,' Hugh admitted. He told them about her dress and the curtains in the ballroom, making them both laugh. 'And I sang with her.'

His best friends both went still. 'She sings?' Roland asked, his voice very soft.

'Not professionally,' Hugh said. 'Tarq already told you that she's a graphic artist. She really loves what she does. She doesn't want to be a pop star.'

'Ro, this isn't a re-run of the Jessie situation,' Tarquin said. 'Bella's nothing like Jessie at all. If someone came and offered her ten times her salary to work for them instead of for Hugh, she'd tell them to get lost. She's loyal, she's sweet and she's utterly lovely.' He looked at Hugh. 'And you know it, too. Actually, now I think about it, she's absolutely perfect for you and she might even make you into a nicer man. Except you're such an idiot that you won't give her a chance.'

Hugh folded his arms. 'You know how I feel about the situation, and you know I'm right. Mixing business and your love life is a recipe for disaster.'

'No. Getting mixed up with Jessie was a recipe for disaster,' Roland corrected. 'How many people meet their partners at work and there's a happy ending?' He paused. 'I met Lynette at work. And, if it hadn't been for the car accident, we'd still be together now.'

Hugh patted his shoulder awkwardly. 'What happened to her was beyond awful, Ro.'

'Yeah. But,' he said, surprising Hugh, 'I've decided it's time to make the effort. Lyn wouldn't have wanted me to spend the rest of my life on my own, missing her and being lonely. She would've wanted me to live life to the full.'

'So you're going to date again? Have you actually met someone?' Tarquin asked.

'No. But I'm going to try,' Roland said. 'Jessie, on the other hand, would want you to be on your own and miserable, Hugh. Which is because she's totally self-absorbed and wants the universe to revolve round her. Are you really going to let her make the rest of your life as lonely and empty as it's been for the past year, when you've met someone you actually like and you have a chance of grabbing happiness with both hands?'

'You,' Hugh said, 'are trying to pull a guilt trip on me.'

'No,' Tarquin said. 'He's telling you that it's OK to feel let down by Jessie, but it's not OK to wallow in it. Talk to Bella. Find out how she feels about you. Then, if she feels the same way you do, just sweep her off her feet.'

Could he?

Should he?

Would it all go wrong anyway?

'Maybe,' Hugh said. 'Now, can we please change the conversation and lighten this evening up a bit?'

'Flowers for the best sister in the world,' Bella said, dumping a large bunch of flowers into Grace's arms. 'And pudding.' She swung the carrier bag from one finger, and added with a grin, 'I bought it rather than made it, so it'll be edible.'

Grace simply laughed. 'Oh, Bel. You're going to have to learn to cook, one day, you know.'

'No, I won't. I have an excellent plan. I'm going to win a million on the lottery and have a housekeeper,' Bella retorted.

'In your dreams,' Grace teased back. 'Come and sit down. The kettle's on.'

'Just what I wanted to hear. So how's the flat-hunting going?' Bella asked.

Grace wrinkled her nose. 'I'm still looking. But when I have to leave here at the end of the week, Charlene's letting me use her spare room because her flatmate's spending a month in Australia. And that'll hopefully give me enough breathing space to find somewhere.'

'You can stay at mine, any time,' Bella said. 'I know it'll be a squeeze, but I'll never see you out on the streets, Gracie.'

Grace hugged her. 'I know. And the same goes for you.'

Bella enjoyed dinner—until Grace made them both a cappuccino and said, 'So when are you going to tell me?'

'Tell you what?' Bella asked, feigning innocence and trying frantically to work out how she could distract her sister.

'About what really happened in Oxfordshire? You've been way too quiet about it.'

Bella laced her fingers together. 'There's nothing to tell.'

Grace coughed. 'Try the truth.'

'I messed it up,' Bella confessed.

'So does that mean you're looking for another job?'

'Yes and no,' Bella hedged.

'You're not making a lot of sense.'

'I know.' Bella sighed. 'I don't know where to start.'

'Try the beginning?' Grace suggested gently.

'OK. I managed the afternoon tea bit OK, and I looked after his great-aunt when she wasn't feeling well.'

Grace frowned. 'That doesn't sound like messing up, to me.'

'It's not what an unsuitable girlfriend would do,' Bella pointed out.

'I guess—but it's what a decent person would do, and I know you, Bel. You couldn't have just left her to be unwell. So then what?'

'My dress for the cocktail party.' Bella blew out a breath. 'It turned out that the curtains in the ballroom were the same material as my dress.'

Grace put her hands up in a 'stop' gesture. 'Wait. Let me get my head round this. They have a *ballroom* in their house?'

Bella nodded. 'They live in an Elizabethan manor house—it's been used as a location for a few period dramas, Hugh said. Oh, Gracie, the house is utterly gorgeous, and his family's so lovely. Libby—his mum—

she's so like our mum. And his oldest brother and sister-in-law have the cutest baby, and they have three dogs.'

'I think I'm beginning to see what you meant about messing up,' Grace said. 'They didn't think you were unsuitable at all, did they?'

'Um—no.' Bella squirmed. 'I guess they kind of liked me.'

'Of course they liked you. Everyone who meets you likes you,' Grace said.

'Except Mrs Concrete Hair,' Bella said, referring to Grace's almost mother-in-law.

Grace laughed. 'I don't think she likes anyone. So his family are nice and you get on. Was that a problem for Hugh?'

'Possibly,' Bella said. 'We haven't exactly spoken much since we've been back.'

'It's difficult between you at work?'

'We pretty much ignore each other—unless we're in a meeting together, which isn't that often,' Bella said. 'And I'm just hoping that nobody in the office has noticed that it's a bit strained between us.'

'Maybe they haven't,' Grace said. 'So—back to your dress. What happened?'

'I brazened it out,' Bella said. 'I said I hadn't cut it from their curtains because they weren't the von Trapps—and then I sang "Do Re Mi".'

Grace laughed. 'That's *so* you, and I bet everyone joined in.'

'No. It was a bit awkward. And then Hugh sang "Edelweiss".' She bit her lip. 'That's something else odd, Gracie. The band his brother booked for the party was late, so Hugh played the piano until they turned up. He's really talented. And he has a gorgeous voice. I can't understand why he doesn't release records as well as produce them—and his brother said something about knowing why Hugh doesn't sing or play in public. His mother kind of let something slip, too. And Tarquin in the office, this week... I was subtle when I asked.'

Grace laughed. 'Bel, you don't do subtle.'

'Subtle for *me*, then.' She frowned. 'I might be putting two and two together and making ten, but I think Hugh fell for someone he worked with and it went pear-shaped.'

'Have you asked him about it?'

'Sort of—and he said it was none of my business. Which is quite right,' Bella added hastily, seeing Grace's eyes narrow in annoyance. 'It was rude of me to ask. And I wasn't subtle when I asked him. Anyway, we danced together. And he sneaked me off to the orangery—Gracie, it was the most romantic place ever, just the two of us and the darkness outside and fairy lights wrapped round the base of the orange trees, and he k—' She stopped, realising that maybe she shouldn't have admitted that much.

But Grace had clearly realised anyway. 'He kissed you?' she asked softly.

There was no point in trying to deny it. Especially as Grace was sensible enough to help her work out how to deal with it, and her sister could only do that if Bella told her the truth. She nodded. 'And it was like seeing stars—it's never been like that for me before.'

'Me, neither,' Grace said, sounding wistful. Then she frowned. '*Just* kissing?'

Bella winced. 'No. But we took precautions. And the next morning we agreed it'd be like the Vegas principle—what happened there, stayed there.'

'Uh-huh,' Grace said. 'So what's the situation now?'

'I don't really know,' Bella admitted. 'I like him, Gracie. I mean *really* like him. Which is crazy. We've only known each other for a few weeks. And yet in some ways I feel I've known him for ever. He's a good man. Look at the way he rescued us. And I know from talking to some of the artists that he's gone way beyond the call of duty for them. He's one of the good guys. He'd never do anything like what Kirk did.'

'Not if he wanted to keep all his bits intact, he wouldn't,' Grace said crisply.

Bella gave her sister a wan smile. 'I don't know what to do, Gracie. After Kirk, I don't really believe in love any more. And I don't want to mess up my job by falling for my boss, knowing that he doesn't believe in mixing work and relationships. One of the bands came in to record an album and the lead singer wanted to ask me out, and Hugh told him straight out that work and relationships don't mix.'

'Because he wants you for himself?'

That was the big question. Bella dragged in a breath. 'I don't actually know,' she said miserably. 'I don't know what to do, Gracie. I mean, I know I'm scatty and disorganised outside work and it's usually fine, but right now I feel as if I'm in the middle of a whirlwind, and it's really not very comfortable. I don't like feeling this way.'

'I think, love, you're going to have to take a risk and talk to him,' Grace said. 'If he likes you and you like him, then it's simple.'

'But what if he doesn't like me?'

'Bel, you're sweet and you're warm and you're funny and you're beautiful. What's not to like?'

'You're my sister. You're supposed to think that.' Bella folded her arms. 'And I don't know what he thinks of me.'

'For what it's worth,' Grace said, 'you've already said he's not like Kirk. And from what you said he's not like Howard, either—he was right there by your side when you sang "Do Re Mi". So it sounds to me as if he likes you.'

'And his family's definitely not like Mrs Concrete Hair and Mr Toad,' Bella added, referring to Howard's parents.

'Well, then. Talk to him. What's the worst that could happen?'

'That he turns me down and then it's too awkward to work with him,' Bella said.

'But isn't it already awkward working with him?' Grace asked.

'A bit,' Bella admitted. 'So I've been half thinking that I might need to find another job anyway.'

'And if you don't say anything, what's the worst that could happen?' Grace asked.

Bella knew that her sister wouldn't let her get away with being feeble. 'I'll always regret not talking to him and seeing if we could make a go of it. And maybe he'll meet someone else, and he'll never know how I felt about him because I was too much of a coward to try.'

'And you're not a coward, Bel. You're brave and you're honest and you're lovely,' Grace said. 'Talk to him.'

'I'll try,' Bella promised.

But would Hugh talk to her? Or would he keep himself shut off?

CHAPTER EIGHT

'ARE YOU SURE you don't want to leave this until the morning, sweet-cheeks?' Tarquin asked, the following Tuesday evening. 'It's late and you've already put in a lot of hours.'

'I'm sure,' Bella said firmly. 'It won't take me very long to get this finished and I really hate leaving things.'

'OK. Just let Hugh know when you leave, so he can lock up,' Tarquin said. 'I'll let him know you're working late so he doesn't accidentally lock you in or anything.'

A frisson went through her. So she and Hugh would be alone in the building?

Well, not completely alone—she knew that there would be people downstairs in the café—but there would be just the two of them in the office.

Maybe she could be brave and talk to him tonight...

'See you tomorrow, Tarq,' she said brightly. 'Have a nice evening.'

'You, too—and don't work too late, do you hear?'

She smiled and blew him a kiss; smiling back, Tarquin left her to it. Bella managed to concentrate on what she was doing and finished the piece of art she'd been working on all day. Once she'd turned off her computer and checked all the other switches in the main office, she paused by the staircase. Time to face Hugh.

Would she have the nerve to talk to him about the unfinished business between them?

She took a deep breath, headed upstairs and rapped on Hugh's closed door.

'Yes?' he called.

She opened the door and leaned against the door jamb. 'Tarquin said to tell you when I was leaving so you could lock up.'

'OK. Thanks.' He barely glanced at her, concentrating on a file on his desk.

He looked tired, she thought, as if a gazillion things were on his mind and stopping him sleeping. She knew the feeling. He clearly wasn't going to bring up the subject, because he was too stubborn. Which meant that she'd have to be the one who initiated the conversation. She walked over and sat on the edge of his desk. Hugh looked up at her again and glowered. 'What?'

She wasn't fooled by the brusqueness. 'You were in earlier than everyone else, and you're here later than everyone else. It's been like that ever since we got back from Oxfordshire. Carry on like this and you're going to risk burn-out.'

'Thank you for your concern, but my mother doesn't need anyone to help her nag me.'

His tone was snippy enough to make her back off. Except she'd seen that tiny glint of vulnerability in his eyes before he'd looked away. So maybe Grace was right and he was feeling as antsy as she was, and for the same reasons. She knew she was taking a huge risk here and it could all go horribly wrong, but on the other hand if she didn't try then she knew she'd always regret it. She leaned over and stroked the hair back from his forehead. 'Hey,' she said softly.

He looked at her again, and his pupils were huge. So he *did* react to her then.

'You've done enough for today,' she said. 'Come and have dinner with me.'

He was silent for so long that she thought he was going to refuse. She was about to back away and tell him to ignore anything she said because she was sleep-deprived and that meant her mouth wasn't in sync with her brain, when he asked softly, 'Are you asking me out on a date, Bella Faraday?'

His voice was deep. Slightly raspy. Just as he'd sounded when he'd made love with her and whispered her name. And it sent a thrill right the way through her.

'I'm asking you back to my place,' she said. 'There's not going to be anything super-fantastic on the menu, just a stir-fry, because I'm really *not* a very good cook. But it does mean that you won't have to make anything for yourself when you finally leave here and go home.'

He looked at her, wide-eyed with surprise. 'You're mothering me?'

She gave him a rueful smile. 'As you said, your mother doesn't need any help.'

He grimaced. 'Sorry. That was rude and unfair of me.'

'And a defence mechanism. You're snippy when you want people to back off.'

He raised an eyebrow. 'So you're a psychologist as well as an artist, now?'

'Nope. Just someone who also uses a defence mechanism. Except mine's sunshine rather than grumpiness.'

He smiled, then, and rested his hand against her cheek. 'Bella. Go home.'

His touch made heat zing throughout her body. And

maybe short-circuited her brain, because she said, 'Not without you.'

'Bella—I've already told you, I don't do relationships.'

'Neither do I.' She dragged in a breath. 'But you and I, we've been circling each other in the office ever since we went to Oxfordshire. And I think we need to...'

He was staring at her mouth. 'Need to what?'

She twisted her head to one side and pressed a kiss into his palm. 'Talk.'

His pupils dilated even more, making his eyes seem completely black. 'Uh-huh.'

'Maybe among other things,' she admitted. Because talking wasn't all she had in mind. Particularly when he was this close to her.

He moistened his lower lip with the tip of his tongue. 'Do you really think it's a good idea for you and me to be alone in a room that might have a bed nearby?'

She smiled. 'Who needs a bed?'

He groaned. 'Bella, you're killing me.'

'Maybe,' she said, 'we need to get this out of our systems. Unfinished business and all that.'

'I don't do for ever,' he warned.

'Neither do I.' And this time she leaned forward and touched her mouth to his. Really, really lightly. Every nerve-end in her lips tingled.

Was he going to kiss her back? Pull her into his arms and really kiss her? Anticipation danced through her. Any second now. Any second...

Hugh dragged in a breath. 'Bella. Right now, my self-control is hanging by the thinnest thread. We can't do this. Go home.'

It was enough of a confession to give her the courage to ignore his protests. She curled her thumb and fingers into her palm and widened the gap between her first and middle finger, as if her hand were a pair of scissors, then smiled at him and 'snipped'. 'Come home with me,' she said softly.

She could see the struggle in his face. Hugh the honourable man, who wanted to do the right thing and keep his employee at a respectable distance, versus Hugh the lover, who remembered how in tune their bodies had been and wanted to do it all over again.

Then he pulled her into his arms and she knew that the lover had won.

When she surfaced from the kiss, she whispered, 'Ready?'

'Not in a million years.' He kissed her again. 'We need to lock up.'

His head and heart were still warring, she guessed.

She waited for him to lock up, then took his hand.

'My car's outside,' he said.

She nodded, and followed him out to the tiny car park behind the offices. He actually opened the passenger door for her; she loved his old-fashioned good manners.

Then he drove her home and parked outside the road by her flat.

'Do I need a parking permit or anything?' he asked.

Yes, but she didn't want him to have time to think about this and change his mind. 'There won't be any traffic wardens around at this time of night,' she said.

He kissed her. 'I wouldn't bet on that, but OK. You're worth a parking ticket.'

She grimaced. 'Now you've made me feel guilty.'

'Good.' He gave her a slow, sensual smile. 'You can make it up to me.'

He held her hand all the way between the car and her

front door. Once they were inside, he slid his hands into her hair and kissed her until she was dizzy. 'I can't get you out of my head,' he said, holding her close.

'Me, too,' she admitted. She slid her hand under the hem of his T-shirt and splayed her hands against his abdomen. 'Every time I close my eyes, I see you. And I want you, Hugh. It's driving me crazy.'

'Me, too,' he admitted. 'Let's do something about it.'

She took his hand and led him to her room. Slowly, she took off his T-shirt; then she took a step backwards, looked at him and sucked in a breath. 'I want to paint you.'

'Oh, yes?'

'Like Michelangelo's David.'

He grinned. 'I'm hardly a fourteen-foot-tall statue.'

'Scaled down,' she said, grinning back. 'But you're still wearing too much.'

'So are you,' he pointed out.

She spread her hands. 'Do something about it, then.'

He kissed her, then stripped off her T-shirt; and then it was her turn to get rid of his jeans. He followed suit, stroking every inch of skin he uncovered as he removed the soft denim, then making her whimper when he kissed the soft undersides of her breasts and drew a path downwards.

Bella wasn't sure who finished stripping whom, but finally they were naked and in her bed and he was inside her. And the world felt very right indeed.

As they lay curled up together afterwards, her stomach rumbled. 'Sorry,' she said, feeling the heat flare into her cheeks.

He laughed and kissed her. 'It's not just you. Sorry. I was hungrier for you than I was for food.'

'Me, too,' she admitted. 'It's been driving me crazy this last couple of weeks, seeing you in the office and knowing I was supposed to keep my hands off you.'

'That's why I've been skulking in my office instead of coming downstairs with the rest of the team,' he said, and kissed her again. 'Bella, we need to talk. We need to work out how we're going to deal with this.'

'The Vegas principle again?' she asked.

'Maybe,' he said.

'Let's eat, first,' she suggested. 'It might get some brain cells working properly.'

'Good idea.' He climbed out of bed and started to get dressed.

Bella was tempted to tell him not to bother putting his T-shirt back on, but a wave of shyness stopped her; she, too, scrambled out of bed and pulled on her clothes.

'Take a seat,' she said in the main room of her flat, gesturing to the little bistro table in her kitchen area.

'Now I think I know why your desk is so untidy,' he teased.

'Because there's more room on it than there is in my flat?' she asked wryly.

'It's, um, bijou,' he said.

'I like it.'

He stroked her face. 'It's a nice flat.'

'But the whole thing's hardly bigger than the boot room in the house where you grew up.'

'Isn't there a saying that lovely things come in small packages?' he asked. He kissed her lightly. 'Starting with you.'

'Hmm. Sit down and I'll feed you,' she said.

Except when she was making the stir fry, she managed to burn the chicken slightly, and then the noodles caught on the bottom of the wok as well, and the vegetables had somehow gone watery. The whole thing looked disgusting and smelled disgusting—and she dreaded to think what it would taste like. Even a sachet of sweet chilli sauce wouldn't be able to disguise the burned or watery bits.

No way could she serve him this.

'I'm so sorry,' she said, and bit her lip. 'This has all gone a bit wrong. I wish I was more like Gracie—she's a great cook and I've never got the hang of anything more than cupcakes, pancakes and Yorkshire puddings,' she finished miserably.

Hugh came over to her, gave her a hug and kissed her frown away. 'It's no big deal. Actually, I'm an OK cook. Ma taught us all before we left for uni. Do you mind me taking over your kitchen?'

'But I was supposed to cook for you, because you're tired. I can't make you cook for me.'

He kissed the tip of her nose. 'The thought was there, and it's appreciated. But right now you're stressed, and cooking relaxes me anyway. Let me do this for you.'

'OK. And thank you. But I need to get rid of this mess first.' She gestured to the wok.

'Sure.'

She scraped the ruined stir fry into the bin and put the burned pan to soak in the sink. 'Would you like a glass of wine?' she asked.

He shook his head. 'Thanks for the offer, but I'm driving.'

Obviously he wasn't planning to stay the night, then. Well, she shouldn't have expected it. He'd made it very clear that he didn't do relationships. Neither did she, really; so this was just unfinished business to get it out of their systems. 'You'd still be under the limit with one glass,' she pointed out.

'My best friend's wife was killed by a drunk driver, eighteen months ago,' he said softly. 'Since then, none of our group of friends touches a drop of alcohol if we're driving.'

Her eyes widened. 'Oh, poor Tarquin! But I thought he was…' Her voice faded. 'Um. Well.'

'Not Tarquin,' he said. 'His partner—who is indeed male—is just fine. I was talking about Roland. He went to school with Tarq and me. He's a silent partner in Insurgo.' He gave her a sidelong look. 'Though I guess it's a bit greedy, having two best friends.'

Just lucky, Bella thought. She'd been perfectly happy with one—until it had all gone wrong. 'There's nothing wrong with having two best friends,' she said. 'So can I get you a coffee instead?'

'Thanks. That'd be good.'

'I'm afraid it's instant,' she warned. Because Kirk had taken their posh coffee machine as well, and replacing it had been a wee bit out of her budget.

'Instant's fine,' he reassured her.

She made coffee for them both while he rummaged in her cupboards and her fridge. Within ten minutes he'd made the best pasta carbonara she'd ever eaten in her life.

'Is there anything you're not good at?' she asked.

He laughed. 'My ego says thank you.'

'Seriously. You're good at business, you're good at music, you can dance, you're good in b—' She stopped, feeling her face heat. 'Well.'

'Have you gone shy on me, Bella?' His eyes glittered with amusement, but she knew he was laughing with her rather than at her.

'I'm going to shut up and eat my dinner. Which really I should've made for you, except there's no way I could produce anything as excellent as this.'

They ate in silence that wasn't quite companionable but wasn't quite awkward either, then shared a tub of posh ice cream from her freezer.

'I guess,' he said when they'd sorted out the washing up, 'we need to deal with the elephant in the room.'

'You and me.'

'Yeah.' He blew out a breath. 'Bella, I don't do relationships—nothing more than casual, anyway. And I never, ever mix work and relationships.'

'Something obviously happened to make you feel that way,' she said. She'd picked up that much from his family and Tarquin. But would he trust her enough to tell her?

There was a long, long pause. Then he nodded. 'It was a couple of years ago. Insurgo had just hit the big time, and this woman came to the offices to ask if I'd sign her. I said no, because right at that moment my list was full, and she asked me for two minutes to change my mind. And then she sang for me.' He looked away. 'She sang "The First Time Ever I Saw Your Face". She was good. Seriously good. I fell in love with her voice.'

'I love that song,' Bella said. 'There was a version a while back that I really liked—who sang it?' She thought about it. 'Oh, I remember now. Jessie Harrison.'

'That would be her,' Hugh said softly.

'Jessie Harrison? Seriously?' She stared at him. 'But she isn't one of your artists.' Jessie wasn't on the list that Tarquin had given her. Bella would've recognised her name.

'Not any more, she isn't.'

Bella had a nasty feeling where this was going. 'You were dating her?'

'Yes. It happened one night when we were in the studio. She'd been working on a song and couldn't get it right, and she wanted my help.' He paused. 'I played piano for her and did the harmonies, and suggested a few changes to the music—and then somehow I ended up taking her home. A couple of months later, she moved in with me.'

Now Bella was beginning to understand what his brother had been getting at. Obviously the reason why Hugh didn't play the piano or sing in public was because it reminded him of being with Jessie. Working with her, loving her, having his heart broken by her.

Yet he'd sung 'Edelweiss' with Bella, to take the heat off her when their plan to make her his unsuitable girlfriend had gone wrong. And she realised now that it must have brought back memories and hurt him.

'I'm sorry,' she said softly.

'I loved her, and I thought she loved me,' Hugh said, 'but it turned out I was her stepping stone to a bigger label and a bigger career. Six months after she moved in with me, I did something very stupid. Because I was in love with her, I assumed she was just being scatty and hadn't got round to signing her new contract. I'd already put a lot of work into her new album, and I'd put a lot of money into promotional stuff.'

'And it didn't happen?' Bella asked softly.

'It didn't happen,' he confirmed. 'She told me she was leaving Insurgo for another label.'

'What about all the work you'd done—all the things you'd paid out for?'

'It was her word against mine. She hadn't signed anything and I'd gone ahead on an assumption I should never have made. There was nothing I could do except absorb the losses.' He dragged in a breath. 'But it was a really bad business decision that put the label at risk for a while, until Ro decided to invest. I hate that I let everyone down because I let my heart rule my head.'

'I know that feeling,' Bella said. 'It's not much fun.'

'Jessie didn't just leave Insurgo. She left me, too.' He shrugged. 'I found out she'd been having an affair with the head of her new label. That's how, she, um, got him to sign her.'

'That's a really vile way to treat someone.' Bella could understand now why Hugh didn't want to mix work and relationships. He'd been badly burned. But she wasn't Jessie and she would never behave like Jessie had. Surely Hugh could see that?

'I've kind of lost my faith in relationships since then,' he said.

She could appreciate that, too. 'Yeah. It's hard to get your trust back when someone lets you down.'

'That sounds personal.'

She nodded. 'You told me the truth about your past, so I guess I should tell you about mine. Even though it makes me feel so stupid.' She sighed. 'I'd been living with Kirk for six months, though we'd been dating for a year before that. He'd gone all secretive on me for a few weeks. I thought he was going to ask me to marry him, and he was planning this amazing proposal—which was why he was acting oddly, because he wanted it to be a surprise—and I was so happy. I was going to say yes.'

She blew out a breath. 'Except it turned out he'd been seeing my best friend. Instead of proposing to me, he went off with her.'

Hugh winced. 'Your boyfriend and your best friend? That's a double betrayal. Nasty.'

She might as well tell him the worst. Just so he knew how naïve and stupid she'd been. 'He cleared out our bank account as well. Which is why it hit me so badly when my client went bust a couple of months back.' She grimaced. 'Thankfully Grace is an accountant. When I went freelance, she told me that I should always put my tax money to one side in an account I never touched as soon as a client's payment cleared, and to keep a cushion of three months' salary in my bank account. So, although Kirk wiped out my cushion, at least I can still pay my tax bill without worrying where to find the money.'

'But how did he manage to take all the money out of your account?' he asked.

'Online banking—he just transferred all the money to a different account. When you have a joint current account, it seems it doesn't matter how much you each put in to the account; you can both take out however much you like because the bank treats it as jointly owned money,' she explained. 'The bank said if it'd been a savings account, that would've been different and I could've taken him to court for theft. But it was a current account, so I couldn't because he had as much right to the money as I did.' She sighed. 'And how stupid does that make me?'

'Not stupid. Naïve, perhaps,' Hugh said. 'But you loved him and you had no reason not to trust him. Were there any signs that he was going to take all your money?'

'No. He'd been seeing a lot of my best friend, but I thought it was all to do with the secret proposal and that she was helping him plan it. It was the same as you and Jessie, really. You loved her and you had no reason not to trust her, either.' She looked levelly at him. 'You and I—we both made the same kind of mistake, and we both paid for it.'

'Very true.'

'So where does that leave us now?' she asked.

He blew out a breath. 'I'm attracted to you, Bella. Seriously attracted.'

And it was mutual, she thought.

'You're the first person I've really wanted to date since Jessie.'

'And you're the first person I've wanted to date since Kirk.' The first person she'd slept with since Kirk. 'But?' she asked. Because it echoed as loudly in her head as if he'd actually said the word.

'But,' he said softly, 'I learned from my mistakes. I'm never going to mix business and relationships again.'

She narrowed her eyes at him. 'Are you saying, if we start dating then I have to find another job?'

He paused for a long, long time. And then he said, 'Yes.'

She frowned. 'That's totally unreasonable, Hugh. I'm not Jessie, just as you're not Kirk.'

'I know.'

'We can keep it strictly business in the office and see each other outside. There's no reason why we can't separate our relationship from work. We're both grown-ups.'

'You came up to my office tonight and kissed me,' he pointed out.

She blinked. 'So you're saying that this is all my fault?'

He raked a hand through his hair. 'No. Just that it's not negotiable. If we see each other, we can't work together.'

'So I have to choose between seeing you and keeping my job.' She frowned. 'Can you not see how unreasonable that is?'

'Yes,' he said. 'But it doesn't stop me feeling it. I can't keep working with you and seeing you.'

'I admire the fact you have strong principles,' Bella said, 'but actually, right now I think you're being really stubborn and inflexible. You're not taking into account that life doesn't stay the same all the time. Things *change*, Hugh.'

'Not this.'

She stared at him. 'Think about this, then: whatever I decide to do, I lose something. According to your rules, I have to give something up—either you or my job.'

'We can't work together,' he said again.

And he didn't have to give anything up. Admittedly, Insurgo was his company and his last relationship had put it all at risk, so she could understand why he was so antsy about getting involved with someone he worked with. But she was going to be the one making all the sacrifices—which wasn't fair. 'I need time to think about this,' Bella said. 'And I think you, do, too.'

'Yes.' He looked at her, unsmiling. 'So I guess I'll see you tomorrow. Or not.'

Depending on whether she chose him or his job. Or neither, though he hadn't seemed to consider that as an option. Which made her even antsier.

'I guess,' she said.

Unless she could find an argument to convince him

that there was another way. One that didn't involve either of them making a sacrifice. But would he be able to compromise? Or had he been hurt too badly to let himself try again?

CHAPTER NINE

BELLA SAT MISERABLY on the sofa with her knees drawn up and her arms wrapped around her legs for half an hour after Hugh left. Then she pulled herself together and went to splash her face with water.

She needed to think about this—and, better still, to think aloud and work out what to do. Right now there was only one person she knew who'd let her talk and help her see her way through this. She picked up the phone and called her sister. 'Gracie? It's Bella.'

'Are you OK, sweetie?' Grace asked.

'Sure,' Bella fibbed.

'You don't sound it. What's happened?'

Bella sighed. 'I talked to Hugh.'

'I'm coming straight over,' Grace said. 'Hold on. I'll be with you in twenty minutes.'

'You don't have to—' Bella began, but the phone line was already dead.

Twenty minutes later, Grace used her spare key to Bella's flat, walked in and gave her a hug.

'You didn't have to come over,' Bella said.

'I most certainly did,' Grace corrected her. 'You're my little sister, and there's no way I'm letting you cry yourself to sleep.' She hugged Bella. 'Right. Cake and hot chocolate.'

'I don't have any cake,' Bella said miserably.

'I do,' Grace said, and took a wrapped cake from her bag. 'Emergency ginger cake.' While the milk for the hot chocolate was heating in the microwave, Grace cut them both a slice of cake, then finished making the hot drinks and sat down with Bella on the sofa. 'Right. Tell me everything.'

Bella did so, ending with, 'So it seems I have a choice. Either I lose him or I lose my job.'

'Maybe,' Grace said carefully, 'you might be better off without both of them.'

'How do you mean?'

'If you choose the job, it's going to be hard to work with him.'

Bella sighed. 'He's being totally unreasonable about this.'

'Which is why I'm worried,' Grace said. 'Supposing you choose him and you find another job—and then he lets you down?'

'I'm not exactly planning to live with him and open a joint bank account with him,' Bella said dryly.

'OK. You've already told me he's not like Kirk. And, although I wasn't in a fit state to remember much when I met him, you've said he has a good heart and I trust your judgement. So I guess, when it comes down to it, the real question is what do *you* want?' Grace asked.

'I want Hugh,' Bella said. 'But, because he's being stubborn about it, that means losing my job—which I can't afford to do.'

'I've got savings,' Grace said immediately. 'I can cover

your bills. So you don't have to worry about money. Not now and not ever.'

'That's so lovely of you, and I appreciate it,' Bella said, 'but I'm going to say no. Not because I'm an ungrateful, spoiled brat, but because I want to stand on my own two feet. I want to be able to hold my head high, instead of having to rely on you or Mum and Dad to bail me out all the time.' She sighed. 'I want Hugh, but I can't be with someone who's not prepared to even consider meeting me halfway. Having principles is a good thing—something that Kirk didn't have—but Hugh's at the opposite extreme of the spectrum. And if he can't learn to compromise, then we don't stand a chance.' She looked plaintively at her sister. 'Why can't life be simple?'

Grace squeezed her hands. 'I wish I could wave a magic wand for you, Bel.'

'You already have. You came straight over when I called, you brought me cake and you listened.' Bella swallowed hard. 'The only person who can sort this out is me.'

'Together with Hugh.' Grace bit her lip. 'I feel guilty, because I'm the one who told you to talk to him in the first place.'

'No. You were right. We needed to talk.' Bella lifted her chin. 'And now I have to think about it. Long and hard. And then...' She sighed. 'Then I need to make a decision.'

'Sleep on it,' Grace advised. 'And if you want to talk to me about it, even if it's stupid o'clock in the morning and you've just woken up, then just pick up the ph—. No, actually, scratch that,' she corrected. 'You don't need to call me, because I'll be right here. I'll stay with you tonight.'

Bella hugged her. 'I love you. But you really don't

have to stay.' Her bed was only big enough for one and her sofa wasn't big enough to sleep on, which meant that one of them would have an uncomfortable night on the floor. And she knew that Grace would be the one to insist on taking the floor.

'I can sleep on the fl—' Grace began, unconsciously echoing her younger sister's thoughts.

'No, you can't. And, although I can lend you pyjamas and toiletries, my clothes would be totally unsuitable for a day at your office. Not to mention the fact that you're four inches taller than I am, so nothing I own would fit you properly anyway,' Bella pointed out.

'True,' Grace said. 'In that case, go and have a shower and get into your pyjamas. We're going to snuggle up on your sofa under a throw and watch a rerun of *Friends* for a bit.'

Exactly what Bella had done with Grace on the very first day she'd met Hugh—the day when Hugh had rescued them from the Fifty Shades of Beige party. And she was pretty sure her sister remembered that, too. Tears pricked her eyelids. 'Oh, Gracie.'

'It'll work out,' Grace said gently. 'You're strong and you're brave, and you'll make the right decision when you've slept on it.'

Snuggling up with her sister on the sofa—with the help of their favourite comedy, more cake and more hot chocolate—made Bella feel marginally less miserable. But she knew that Grace needed to be up early tomorrow for work and it wasn't fair to keep her up late. Especially as she could see her sister's eyelids drooping.

'Go home, sweetie,' she said. 'You've got work tomorrow.'

Grace shook her head. 'I don't want to leave you.'

'I'll be fine,' Bella reassured her. 'Really. I'm already a lot better than I was.'

'I'll go,' Grace said, 'but only on condition you promise to ring me if you need me. Any time. And I mean *any* time.'

Bella knew she meant it. 'I will, and thanks.'

'And I meant it about covering your bills. Even if you insist on it being a temporary loan,' Grace said. 'If you decide to leave Insurgo, I can help you out until you find another job. It doesn't mean you're stupid or pathetic or needy—it's what sisters do. You had my back when I called off my wedding to Howard. And I've got yours now.'

Bella had to blink back the tears. 'I love you,' she said.

'I love you, too.'

'Text me when you get home.'

Grace laughed. 'You sound as if you're turning into me.'

Good, Bella thought. Maybe Grace's capable, calm togetherness would rub off on her and help her make the right decision.

She didn't sleep much that night. Every time she looked at the clock, the minute hand barely seemed to have moved. The next morning, she felt groggy and her head ached. She washed her hair, drank two big glasses of water and took some paracetamol.

Time to make her decision. Hugh or her job? Whatever she did, she'd lose.

She thought about it for a long time, and eventually came to the conclusion that this was the only way forward. She typed a text to Hugh on her phone, but didn't send it; she needed to bite the bullet, first.

She rang the Insurgo office, hoping that Hugh wouldn't

be the one to answer. She actually crossed her fingers as the call connected and she heard the ringing tone, and then to her relief Tarquin answered.

'Hi, Tarq, it's Bella.'

'You sound terrible,' he said immediately. 'Are you calling in sick?'

'I, um—no, actually.' She sighed. 'I'm, um, afraid I'm resigning. For personal reasons. With immediate effect. Anything of mine in the office, just give to the local charity shop if nobody else wants it.'

'What?' He sounded utterly shocked. 'Bella, sweetie, are you all right? What's happened? Is there anything I can do, anyone I can ring for you?'

His concern and kindness nearly undid her. But she lifted her chin. She needed to do the right thing and stand on her own two feet. 'No, I'm fine.' As fine as you could be with a broken heart. 'I'm sorry to let you down. To let everyone down.'

'Sweetie—I don't know what to say, but I'm worried about you.'

'I'll be fine. Really. And I've loved working at Insurgo. I'm sorry to let you all down.' She'd call the café later, wield her credit card and get them to deliver cake to the team on her behalf to say goodbye. 'I need to go now, Tarq.' Before she let herself down by bursting into tears. 'All the best.'

Once she'd hung up, she pressed the button on her phone to send the text to Hugh.

And then she switched off her phone.

Hugh's phone buzzed as he was walking up the stairs to his office. He checked the screen.

Bella.

His heart skipped a beat. So she'd made her decision?
He flicked into the message.

Am leaving Insurgo

She'd chosen him. Thank God. He closed his eyes
with relief, realising just how much he'd wanted her to
make that choice.

His phone beeped again, and he looked at the screen.
Another message from Bella.

Am leaving Insurgo but I can't be with someone who
gives me impossible ultimatums. I wish it could've been
different. Sorry.

What the hell? But she'd just said...

He looked at the previous message. At the bottom, in
a different script, it said: This message has only been
partially downloaded.

Yeah. And how.

He really hadn't expected this. He'd given her the
choice of a working relationship or a proper relationship. He'd never dreamed that she'd pick a different option: neither.

He was still trying to get his head round it when his
best friend stormed in to his office and slammed the
door behind him.

'What the hell did you do?' Tarquin asked. 'Bella's
resigned and, after the conversation we had with Ro, I
know it's your fault. What did you do?'

'Something very stupid. Don't worry. I'll find you another designer,' Hugh said wearily.

'Not like Bella, you won't. And nobody can believe

she's just left like that. Just what did you do?' Tarquin asked again.

Hugh shook his head. 'You know how I feel about things. I can't mix work and relationships.'

'So you're seeing her?'

That had been the plan. But he'd got that wrong. 'No.'

'Then what the…?' Tarquin shook his head. 'I don't understand what's going on.'

Hugh handed over his phone. 'Here. Read it for yourself.'

Tarquin read the text, then stared at Hugh with narrowed eyes. 'What was the ultimatum?'

'Work and relationships don't mix,' Hugh said.

'You mean you actually asked her to choose between you and Insurgo?'

Hugh winced. 'Put like that, it sounds bad.'

'Sounds bad? It *is* bad, Hugh. Really bad,' Tarquin said. 'I can't believe you did that.'

Hugh was rather beginning to wish that he hadn't, either.

'You,' Tarquin said, 'are my best friend as well as my business partner. Which is why I can tell you that you're also the most stupid, stubborn, *unreasonable* man I've ever met, and right now I don't want to work with you. I don't want to see your face in the office this week. I don't want to speak to you—and, quite frankly, you're lucky the rest of us aren't all walking out on you as well. As of now, you're taking a week's leave.'

Hugh coughed. 'I'm the senior partner.'

'True. But I'm in charge of personnel,' Tarquin reminded him, 'which means that in this case *you* do what *I* say.'

Hugh had never seen his best friend so angry. And he

knew he only had himself to blame. 'I can't take a week off. We've got people in the studio.'

'Most of them are outside bookings. There's only one Insurgo artist due in, and I'll rearrange that for at least a week's time—when your head might be in a fit state to deal with it. I'm not letting you do any more damage this week,' Tarquin said firmly.

'Ouch,' Hugh said, but he knew that he deserved it—and that Tarquin was telling the truth. 'OK. Call me if you need anything.'

'From you? I'll tell you what I need,' Tarquin said. 'I need you to go and have a long, hard think. Look at yourself, look at your life, and think about what you really want. And when you come to your senses and realise that Bella Faraday is the best thing to happen to you—as in the best thing *ever*—you'd better find a fantastic way to apologise to her. And you'd better hope that she's a better person than you are and will actually forgive you. In her shoes, I'm not so sure I would.'

'Noted,' Hugh said dryly.

'Don't you try your Mr Grumpy-in-the-mornings act on me,' Tarquin said, scowling at him. 'Now go home and sort your life out.'

Sorting his life out was easier said than done.

By the time he got back to his house, Hugh was half surprised not to have had a barrage of calls from his family to ask him what he thought he was doing. He was grateful that Tarquin clearly hadn't told his mother or his brothers; though he knew Tarquin had told Roland because his other best friend simply sent him a text saying, You are *such* a moron.

Nothing felt right. Everything felt two-dimensional.

And he knew exactly why: it was because Bella had walked out of his life.

He picked up the phone and called her. A recorded message informed him that her mobile phone was switched off, so please try later or send a text. He tried her landline next, but it went through to voicemail. Which didn't exactly leave him much of an option. Awkwardly, he said, 'Bella, it's Hugh. I'm sorry. I've been a complete idiot. Can we talk? Please call me.'

But she didn't return his call.

He tried both lines again later, several times, with the same result: her mobile was switched off and her landline was switched through to voicemail. Was she avoiding him? Or was she just busy?

Going to her flat in person didn't help, either. Although he rang the bell, there was no answer. He knew Bella wouldn't refuse to answer the door, so clearly she was out. He had no idea where she was and no idea how else to contact her; she was close to her sister, but an internet search to find a phone number for Grace Faraday in London when he couldn't narrow it down to any particular part of the city left him frustrated and grumpy.

It looked as if he'd just have to wait for Bella to contact him. Even though waiting wasn't something that sat well with him.

He paced round the house for a bit, flicked through various television channels without finding anything remotely interesting, and couldn't even lose himself in music. Though he found himself wide awake at three a.m. with music filling his head. He lay there for a bit, trying to ignore it, but the urge was too strong.

In the end, he pulled on a pair of jeans and padded downstairs to his piano. Luckily the houses in his road were well insulated, and he'd installed soundproofing in his music room when he moved in, or the neighbours wouldn't be too happy with him playing the piano at stupid o'clock. He grabbed a manuscript book and a pencil, scribbled down the words in his head, and then started to work out the tune to go with them. By the time it was light again, he'd finished the song.

And he knew exactly what he was going to do.

He showered and changed, though he didn't bother shaving; he just wanted the rest of his life to hurry up and start now. He drove to Bella's and rang the doorbell. There was no answer, but the curtains were still closed—so surely she was there? He rang again and waited, but there was still no answer. Panicking slightly, he leaned on the doorbell.

She opened the door abruptly, rubbing her eyes. 'All right, all right, give a girl time to wake up... Oh,' she said, taking in who was standing on her doorstep.

'I'm sorry. I'm an idiot, please forgive me and—' He broke off, not quite ready to say the three little words yet. 'Come for breakfast.'

'Breakfast?' She blinked, looking confused.

'Breakfast,' he confirmed. 'At my place, and I'm cooking.'

'Hugh, it's the crack of dawn,' she protested.

'It's half past seven,' he pointed out.

'Same thing.'

'No, it isn't. I saw the sun rise this morning, and I'm pretty sure it was about five o'clock.'

She frowned. 'But you're not a morning person. What on earth were you doing up at five o'clock?'

'Finishing.'

'Finishing what?'

'Come for breakfast and I'll show you.'

'Hugh…'

'You don't have to dress up,' he said. 'Just grab some clothes. Please.'

She paused for so long that he thought she was going to say no. But then she gave a weary nod. 'Come in and make yourself a coffee while I have a shower.'

'Thank you.' Though he didn't bother with coffee. He simply paced around her tiny flat, music running through his head. He felt more alive than he'd been in months. Than he'd ever been, if he was honest with himself. And once he'd opened his heart to Bella, told her how he really felt about her, he just hoped she'd give him a second chance.

At last, Bella emerged from the bathroom wearing jeans and a T-shirt. Clearly she'd taken the time to shower, as her hair was damp and not styled, but she hadn't bothered with make-up—and she'd never looked more beautiful to him.

'Ready for this?' he asked softly.

She nodded, and he drove her back to his house. Once he'd made coffee and they'd gone through a stack of pancakes with maple syrup, he said, 'We need to talk.'

'I thought we did all our talking the other night, back at my flat,' she said.

'No, we didn't, because I wasn't thinking straight,' he said. 'I was wrapped in panic because I was so scared of repeating my past mistakes—even though I know you're not Jessie and you'd never behave like her in a million years.' He dragged in a breath. 'I wrote a song for you.'

She looked surprised. 'You wrote a song for me?'

'That's why I was up in the middle of the night. I had music in my head—music you inspired—and…oh, look, why am I blathering on about it? I need you to hear something. That's why I brought you here.'

He led her into his music room and she curled up on his easy chair. Then he sat down on the piano stool and played the song to her.

It was the most beautiful song Bella had ever heard and she knew it came straight from the heart. Hugh's voice kept catching with emotion as he sang, 'You're the missing piece of my heart.'

When the last chord had died away, he turned round to face her. 'I love you, Bella. Yes, I have issues, and I'm probably not going to be the easiest person to share your life with, but I love you and that's not ever going to change. I think I fell in love with you when I saw you bouncing out of Insurgo and into my taxi, that Friday night. I love everything about you—your warmth and your vitality and your brightness. You make my world feel a better place. And I meant everything I sang to you, because you really are the missing piece of my heart,' he said simply.

She simply stared at him. 'I can't believe you wrote this song for me.'

'You took down all the barriers I'd put round myself and set the music free again.' He smiled at her. 'I'm a nicer person when I'm writing music. And you make me a better man.' To Bella's shock, he moved off the piano stool and dropped to one knee in front of her. 'I was totally wrong about not being able to mix business and a relationship. With you by my side, I can do anything; and without you everything just feels wrong. Will you marry me, Bella Faraday?'

She stared at him, not quite sure she was really hearing this. 'But the other night you wanted me to choose between you and my job.'

'Because I was scared. Because I was stupid. But a few hours on my own to think about it and what I could be losing means I've worked through that,' he said. 'I admit, you might still need to tell me I'm stubborn and unreasonable at various points in the future, but I promise I'll listen to you and I'll take it on board—and, more importantly, I'll talk things over with you instead of brooding. So will you give me a second chance? Will you come back to Insurgo?'

'You really think you can work with me?'

'I work a lot better with you than without you. And you're a great designer. Everyone misses you. And they're all pretty mad at me for being an idiot and driving you away,' he admitted.

'So do I still have to choose between you and my job?' she checked.

He shook his head. 'And you took the option I never even considered—not because I'm arrogant but because being without you in any way is so unthinkable. I was wrong, and I'm sorry. Please come back to Insurgo. And—even more importantly—please will you marry me?'

Words she'd expected to hear six months ago from someone else—from a man she'd thought she'd known but she'd been so wrong. So foolish.

And now Hugh—a man she'd known for only a few weeks—was saying those words to her. Offering her for ever. Sweeping her off her feet.

She knew he'd still be grumpy in the mornings. And obstinate. There would be days when he'd drive her crazy.

But, the very first time she'd met him, he'd been there

for her. He'd given her help when she'd needed it, without any strings. And he'd believed in her, been there right by her side when the pretend girlfriend plan had gone wrong.

With Kirk, she'd had dreams. Castles built on sand.

With Hugh, she had reality. Something solid.

'We haven't known each other very long,' he said, as if picking up on her worries, 'but I think you know when you've met the right one. It feels different with you. Like nothing else I've ever known.'

'Me, too,' she whispered.

'And I think that's why I asked you to come home to Oxfordshire with me,' he said. 'Because, even then, I knew you were the right one. The woman who'd just be herself and my family would love her as much as I did— even though I was in major denial at the time.'

'And you let me wear a dress made out of the same curtains your parents had.'

'That's when I knew.' He coughed. 'May I point out that I'm still on one knee, waiting for an answer?'

She leaned over and stroked his face. 'You're not Kirk. You're not going to run off with my best friend and the contents of my bank account. Though you did run off with my heart. Which I guess is why I agreed to go to Oxfordshire with you instead of sending you off with a flea in your ear.' She smiled. 'The answer's yes.'

'To coming back to Insurgo? Or to marrying me?'

'Both,' she said, 'because I love the job—and I love you.'

'I love you, too. So much.' Hugh kissed her, then stood up, scooped her out of the chair, sat down in her place and settled her on his lap. 'One thing. You might have noticed that I'm not very good at waiting.'

'Meaning?' she asked.

'Meaning that I don't want this to be a long engage-ment.'

'Gracie was engaged to Howard for four years,' she said.

'Way, way, way too long,' he said. 'This is going to be a very short engagement. As short as we can possi-bly make it.'

'So you're telling me I don't get an engagement party like Nigel and Victoria's—a tea party with your older rel-atives, a dress made out of curtains and a sneaky dance in the orangery?' she asked.

'How about a wedding in a tiny parish church in Ox-fordshire, a party afterwards in my parents' ballroom, and as many sneaky dances as you like in the orangery and a walk in the bluebell woods with the full carpet out?' he countered.

She blinked. 'But the bluebells are out now.'

'And they'll still be out for the next three weeks,' he said softly. 'I reckon we can organise a wedding in three weeks—don't you?'

She grinned. 'I see what you mean about not being good at waiting. Yes, we probably can organise a wed-ding in three weeks, but we're going to need help.'

'I have a feeling that the Moncrieffs and the Faradays are all going to be very happy if we ask them to help us sort things out,' he said. 'Plus Tarquin and Roland.'

'Hmm. It sounds to me as if we're going to have two best men,' she said.

'Is that OK?' He looked worried.

She kissed him. 'It's very OK. I haven't met Roland yet, but if he's anything like Tarq we'll get on famously. Though, Hugh, if we're working to a deadline of three weeks, we're going to have to start asking people now.'

He grabbed his phone. 'OK. We'll start with a synchronised text to our parents, siblings and best fr—' He stopped. 'Um. Sorry.'

'Don't apologise. You haven't brought back any bad stuff. I do still have a best friend,' Bella said softly, 'but she's usually known to the world as my sister.'

'And I hope also as our chief bridesmaid.' He paused. 'How many bridesmaids can we have? Can we ask my sisters-in-law? Because, um, they all told me you were perfect for me at Nigel and Victoria's engagement.'

'Oh, bless.' Bella smiled. 'Of course. And we need Sophia—she'll be perfect as the flower girl.'

'You are utterly wonderful. And I intend to tell you that every single day. As well as telling you how much I love you.' He typed in a message on his phone.

Bringing Bella to see the bluebells this weekend. Need everyone there for family meeting to plan our wedding.

'How about this?' he asked, and handed the phone to her.

She read it swiftly. 'Perfect. OK.' She handed his phone back and grabbed hers from her pocket. '"Going to see the bluebells at Hugh's parents' in Oxfordshire at weekend. Need you to come with us as is also family meeting to plan our wedding,"' she said as she typed.

'Perfect,' he said.

They both put all the phone numbers in to the right place and smiled at each other. 'Ready?' he asked.

She nodded. 'Go.'

Simultaneously, they pressed Send.

'What do you think—maybe ten seconds before we get a response?' Hugh asked.

'About that,' Bella agreed.

They counted.

On cue, both their phones started ringing and beeping with texts from the people who were obviously trying to call and discovering that the line was engaged.

'And let the wedding planning craziness begin,' Bella said with a grin.

EPILOGUE

Three weeks later

WHEN THEIR PARENTS had gone down to the hotel reception to wait for the other bridesmaids to arrive, Grace turned to Bella. 'Are you absolutely sure about this? Because if you've got even the *slightest* doubt, you walk away now and we'll all support you.'

'I'm absolutely sure,' Bella confirmed. 'Hugh's everything I want.'

'Then I wish you both a lifetime of happiness together,' Grace said softly. 'And you look amazing.'

'So do you. And I can't believe we've organised everything in less than three weeks.'

Grace laughed. 'With Team Faraday and Team Moncrieff joining together—of course we've managed to organise everything in the shortest space of time possible between us!'

'You're all pretty awesome,' Bella agreed.

'And your new in-laws are fantastic,' Grace said. Neither of them said it but both were thinking, the Moncrieffs were so unlike the Suttons, and how nearly Grace had been trapped in a lifetime of misery.

'Thankfully you're not a Bridezilla, so it was relatively easy to sort everything out,' Grace said.

'It's not the dress or the food or even the venue that's the most important bit of a wedding,' Bella said. 'It's the vows and the people there.'

'Totally,' Grace agreed. 'Though I have to admit I'm glad it's the perfect day for an early summer wedding—much better to have bright sunshine than trying to dodge the showers.'

Bella hugged her. 'Sorry. I'm being selfish. This must be so hard for you, considering that right now you should've been just back from your honeymoon.'

'Actually, no,' Grace corrected. 'You're not selfish at all, and today's confirmed for me that I did the right thing. When you and Hugh are together, you both glow—and that's not how it was for Howard and me. I think we both owed it to each other to let ourselves find the person who'd make us light up and who we could light up in return.'

'But you just blinked away tears,' Bella pointed out.

'Those are tears of happiness,' Grace said softly, 'because I'm so glad for you. You've got the kind of love you deserve.'

There was a knock on the hotel room door and their parents came in, followed by Hugh's sisters-in-law and little Sophia, all dressed up in their wedding finery.

'Look at you all—you're gorgeous,' Bella said in delight.

'Bel-Bel,' Sophia cooed, and Bella scooped her up for a kiss.

'My little Sophia.' She grinned. 'We're so going to do "Row, Row, Row Your Boat" later.'

'Bo!' Sophia said happily.

'Careful,' Poppy said, 'or she'll have us all singing that down the aisle.'

'What an excellent idea.' Bella laughed. 'So are we all ready to get this show on the road?'

'We certainly are,' Harriet said. 'Even though we still can't quite believe how fast this is all happening.'

'Sorry. I did kind of steal your and Nigel's thunder, Victoria,' Bella said.

'No, you didn't. It's good to see Hugh happy,' Victoria said. 'And it could be worse. You could've made us all wear bridesmaid dresses made out of curtains.'

In response, Poppy started singing 'Do Re Mi', and everyone joined in, ending in gales of laughter.

Finally it was time to go downstairs, where the bridal cars were waiting to take everyone to the tiny country church where Hugh and Bella were getting married—the church where Hugh's parents had been married and Hugh himself had been christened.

'I'm not even going to ask you if you're sure about this,' Bella's father said when they were in the car. 'Apart from the fact that I know Gracie's already asked you, I can see it in your eyes. Hugh's the right one for you.'

'Absolutely yes,' Bella said.

'Will you please stop checking your watch, sweet-cheeks?' Tarquin asked in exasperation. 'She'll be here. She might be a couple of minutes late, because it's traditional, but she'll be here.'

'She loves you to bits,' Roland added.

'I know. I'm just antsy.' Hugh dragged in a breath. Standing here by the altar, waiting, was much more nerve-racking than he'd anticipated. He'd been there before as Roland's best man, but being the groom gave you a totally different perspective. The ancient Cotswold stone church was full to bursting, there were flowers everywhere he looked, and the sun was shining through the stained glass in the windows, spilling pools of colour over the congregation. Everything was perfect.

Or it would be, when Bella was here.

And then a memory surfaced that made him even more antsy. 'Did I ever tell you, her sister cancelled her wedding three weeks before the big day?'

'And you've had three weeks to organise yours,' Tarquin said. 'But, from what Bella told me, Grace would've been donning a ball and chain instead of a wedding ring, and she did absolutely the right thing in calling it off.'

'Even so, cancelling it just three weeks before the actual day—surely she must've known earlier that she didn't want to get married?' Roland said with a frown. 'She sounds a bit princessy to me. Obviously she's nothing like her sister.'

'Grace is all right, actually—but she is pretty much the opposite of Bella,' Tarquin agreed.

'You would've met her and found out for yourself if you hadn't been off on a conference when the rest of us were doing wedding organising stuff,' Hugh pointed out mildly.

Roland rolled his eyes. 'If you will insist on getting married with practically no notice, Moncrieff...'

'We wanted the rest of our lives to start as soon as possible,' Hugh said softly. 'There was no reason to wait.'

'Hang on. You're not...?' Tarquin asked.

'Expecting a baby?' Hugh finished. 'No. We just didn't want to wait. Because we're sure this is the right thing for us.'

'I remember that feeling,' Roland said softly.

Hugh patted his shoulder. 'I know. And I'm sorry.'

'Don't be sorry. It was the best day of my life. Just as this will be yours,' Roland said.

Suddenly, the organ music changed from Bach to the processional music from *The Sound of Music*.

'So very Bella to choose this one to walk down the aisle to,' Tarquin said with a grin. Then he looked over his shoulder. 'Oh, my. Ro. Look.'

Roland looked. 'Hugh, you definitely need two best men, one either side—because otherwise your knees are going to go weak and you'll fall flat on your face when you turn round and see her. She looks incredible.'

Fortified by their warnings, Hugh looked round to see Bella walking down the aisle towards him on her father's arm. She looked absolutely amazing. Being Bella, she'd made a few alterations to the traditional wedding gown. Her dress was in cream silk and chiffon, with a strapless sweetheart neckline and a ballerina-type skirt which came to just above her ankles and showcased her strappy high heels—which were exactly the same dark red as the bouquet of sunflowers she was holding, the bridesmaids' dresses and the waistcoats and cravats of the men in the wedding party. He knew that Grace had talked her out of dyeing her hair the same colour as the sunflowers, but today she'd gone back to being platinum blonde. Just like the first day he'd seen her.

And she looked like an angel.

'I love you,' Hugh mouthed at her as she joined him at the altar, and was rewarded with a smile that felt as if it lit up the whole church.

They both pledged to love, honour and cherish each other, in front of a whole church full of family and friends. And then came the bit he'd been waiting for. The moment when he could kiss his beautiful bride.

Signing the register and walking back down the aisle as man and wife passed in a blur, and then they were walking on the path outside the church with dried white delphinium petals raining down on them. Hugh's face was aching, but he didn't care because he couldn't stop smiling. Even posing for endless photographs, both at the church and back at his parents' home under the wisteria, didn't try his patience: Roland had been absolutely right, he thought, because this was really the happiest day of his life.

'Libby, Oliver, this is so perfect—thank you so much,' Bella said, hugging them both inside the marquee on the lawn in the back garden.

'It was a team effort between the Moncrieffs and the Faradays,' Oliver said. 'The men put up the marquee and the women did the flowers and the table arrangements.'

'And what gorgeous flowers,' Bella said happily. There were alternating arrangements of red and yellow sunflowers in the centre of the table.

'Come and see the cake,' Hugh said. 'Victoria says the top tier is red velvet, the middle one's vanilla and the bottom one's chocolate.'

In keeping with the rest of the theme, red sunflowers made from fondant icing spilled down the side of the cake in a cascade. 'Just brilliant,' Bella said. 'We're so lucky, Hugh. We have the best joint family in the entire world.'

'We do indeed,' Hugh said.

The meal was perfect, too, and Roland and Tarquin did the perfect double act for the best man's speech, teasing Bella about her ever-changing hair colour and Hugh about having to learn to be less grumpy in the morning now he was married. Oliver welcomed Bella to the Moncrieff family. 'Though I still have to stop myself calling her Maria,' he teased at the end, 'and I'm going to have to check the curtains for cut-outs before she and Hugh leave tonight.'

Bella laughed and raised a glass to him. 'I promise—no scissors, so your curtains are safe. For today, at least!'

Ed welcomed Hugh to the Faraday family. And Hugh's own speech was simple but heartfelt. 'I do enough talking in my day job, so I just want to say that Bella's made me the happiest man alive and I intend to make her the happiest woman alive, I'm glad you're all here to celebrate with us, and I hope everyone else has as happy a day as we're having.'

After the speeches were over and the cake had been cut, the party moved to the ballroom for the dancing. Oliver and Libby had decorated the room with fairy lights, so it looked completely romantic and utterly gorgeous.

Hugh took Bella's hand. 'You know we don't always do things the traditional way,' he said, 'and the first dance is no exception—because we're not actually going to dance to the first song. We also know most of you are pretty sure we're going to use "Edelweiss" or something else from *The Sound of Music* as "our song", because of the first time a lot of you met Bella in this very room. But instead,' he said, 'it's this.' He sat down at the baby grand piano, pulling Bella onto his lap, and began to play the song he'd written for her—'The Missing Piece of My Heart'.

She joined him when he sang the chorus.

And there wasn't a dry eye in the house when they'd finished.

'That's our song,' Hugh said softly. 'The one Bella

inspired. Because she really is the missing piece of my heart. Now, please, I want you all to dance and drink champagne and enjoy yourselves—because today's all about celebrating.'

'Today and the rest of our lives,' Bella said softly.

'The rest of our lives,' Hugh echoed.

* * * * *

HIS BOARDROOM MISTRESS

EMMA DARCY

Many thanks to Phil Asker and his wonderful team for providing me with so many amazing experiences on The Captain's Choice Tour of South-East Asia—all in such a safe and friendly atmosphere. Great memories!

CHAPTER ONE

'THE kind of man you want, Liz, is the marrying kind.'

The quiet authority of her mother's voice cut through the buzz of suggestions being tossed around by her three sisters, all of whom had succeeded in marrying the men of their choice. This achievement made them feel qualified to hand out advice which Liz should take, now that she had been forced to confess her failure to get a commitment from the man who'd been her choice.

Brendan had told her he felt their relationship was stifling him. He needed space. So much space he was now in Nepal, half a world away from Sydney, planning to find himself or lose himself in the Himalayas, meditate in a Buddhist monastery, anything but make a life with a too managing woman.

It was shaming, humiliating to have to admit his defection to her family, but there was no excuse for not attending her father's sixtieth birthday luncheon today and no avoiding having to explain Brendan's absence.

The five of them—her mother, her sisters and herself—were in the kitchen, cleaning up after the long barbecue lunch which had been cooked by the male members of the family, now relaxing out on the patio of her parents' home, minding the children playing in the backyard.

Liz knew she had to face up to her situation and try to move on from it, but right now she felt engulfed by a sense of emptiness—three years of togetherness all drained away—and her mother's statement hit a very raw place.

'How can you know if they're the marrying kind or not?' she tossed back derisively.

Mistake!

Naturally, her wonderfully successful siblings had the answers and leapt in to hit Liz over the head with them.

'First, you look for a man with a good steady job,' her oldest sister, Jayne, declared, pausing in her task of storing leftovers in the refrigerator to deliver her opinion. 'You want someone to support you when the kids come along.'

Jayne was thirty-four, the mother of two daughters, and married to an accountant who'd never deviated from forging a successful career in accountancy.

'Someone with a functional family background,' Sue contributed with a wise look. 'They value what they've had and want it for themselves.'

Sue was thirty-two, married to a solicitor from a big family, now the besotted father of twin sons, loving his wife all the more for having produced them.

Liz silently and bitterly conceded two black marks against Brendan who'd never held a steady job—preferring to pick up casual work in the tourist industry—and had no personal experience of a functional family background since he'd been brought up by a series of foster parents.

There was no longer any point in arguing that she earned enough money to support them both. A small family, as well, if Brendan would have been content to be a house husband, as quite a few men were these days. The traditional way was not necessarily the *only* way, but Jayne and Sue weren't about to appreciate any other view but theirs, especially with the current inescapable proof that Liz's way hadn't worked.

'What about your boss?'

The speculative remark from her younger sister, Diana, jolted Liz out of maundering over her failures. 'What about him?' she retorted tersely, reminded that Diana, at only twenty-eight, was rather smug at having scooped the marriage pool by snagging her own boss, the owner of a chain of fashion boutiques for which she was still a buyer since they had no immediate plans to start a family.

'Everyone knows Cole Pierson is rolling in money, probably a billionaire by now. Isn't his divorce due to go through? He's been separated from his wife for ages and she's been gallivanting around, always in the social pages, linked to one guy or another. I'd certainly count Cole Pierson available and very eligible,' Diana declared, looking at Liz as though she'd been lax at not figuring that out for herself.

'Get real! That doesn't mean *available* to me,' Liz threw back at her, knowing full well she didn't have the female equipment to attract a man of his top-line attributes.

'Of course it does,' Diana persisted. 'He's only

thirty-six to your thirty, Liz, and right on the spot for you to snaffle. You could get him if you tried. After all, being his P.A. is halfway there. He depends on you...'

'Cole Pierson is not the least bit interested in me as a woman,' Liz snapped, recoiling absolutely from the idea of man-hunting where no love or desire was likely to be kindled.

Besides, she'd long ago killed any thought of her boss *that way* and she didn't want to do anything that might unsettle what had become a comfortable and satisfying business relationship. At least she could depend on *its* continuing into the foreseeable future.

'Why would he be interested?' Diana countered, apparently deciding she'd done her share of the cleaning up, propping herself on a stool at the island bench and examining her fingernails for any chipped varnish. 'You've been stuck with Brendan all the time you've been working for Cole Pierson, not giving out any availability signals,' she ran on.

'He is quite a hunk in the tall, dark and handsome mould,' Jayne chimed in, her interest sparked by the possibility of Liz linking up with the financial wizard who managed the money of several of her accountant husband's very wealthy clients. As she brought emptied salad bowls to the sink where their mother was washing up and Liz drying, she made a more direct remark. 'You must feel attracted to him, Liz.'

'No, I don't,' she swiftly denied, though she certainly had been initially, when he'd still been human and happily married. He'd been very distractingly attractive *then,* but being the remarkable man he was and having a beautiful wife in the background, Liz had listed him in the no hope category.

Besides, she'd just found Brendan—a far more realistic and reachable choice for her—so she'd quelled any wayward feelings towards her boss.

'How couldn't you be?' Sue queried critically, frowning over what she assumed was totally unnatural. 'The few times I've dropped in on you at your office and he's appeared...the guy is not only a stunner but very charming. Fantastic blue eyes.'

Cold blue eyes, Liz corrected.

Cold and detached.

Ever since he'd lost his baby son eighteen months ago—a tragic cot death—Cole had retreated inside himself. The separation from his wife six months later had not come as a surprise to Liz. The marriage had to be in trouble. Her boss had moved beyond *connecting* to anyone.

He switched on a superficial charm for clients and visitors but there was no real warmth in it. He had a brilliant brain that never lost track of the money markets, that leapt on any profitable deal for his clients' investments, that paid meticulous attention to every critical detail of his business. But it was also a brain that blocked any intrusion to whatever he thought and felt on a personal level. Around him was an impenetrable wall, silently but strongly emitting the message—*keep out*.

'There's just no spark between us,' she told Sue, wanting to dampen this futile line of conversation. 'Cole is totally focused on business.'

Which made *him* appreciate her management skills,

she thought with black irony. He certainly didn't feel *stifled* by her being efficient at keeping track of everything. He expected it of her and it always gave her a kick when she surprised him by covering even more than he expected. He was a hard taskmaster.

'You need to shake him out of that one-track mind-set,' Diana advised, persisting with her get-the-boss idea.

'You can't change what drives a person's life,' Liz flashed back at her, realising she'd been foolish to think she could change any of Brendan's ingrained attitudes.

Diana ignored this truism. 'I bet he takes you for granted,' she rattled on, eyeing Liz assessingly. 'Treats you as part of the office furniture because you don't do anything to stand out from it. Look at you! When was the last time you spent money on yourself?'

Liz gritted her teeth at the criticism. It was all very well for Diana, who had a rich husband to pay for everything she wanted. *She* didn't need to siphon off most of her income to make the payments on a city apartment. Liz had figured the only way she'd ever have a home to call her own was to buy it herself. Besides which, real estate was a good solid investment.

'I keep up a classic wardrobe for work,' she argued, not bothering to add she had no use for fancy clothes anyway. She and Brendan had never gone anywhere fancy, preferring a much more casual lifestyle, using whatever spare money they had to travel where they

could. Jeans, T-shirts and jackets took them to most
places.

'Dullsville,' Diana said witheringly. 'All black
suits and sensible shoes. In fact, you've let yourself
get positively drab. What you need is a complete
makeover.'

Having finished putting everything away, her two
older sisters joined Diana on stools around the island
bench and jumped on this bandwagon. 'I've never
thought long hair suits you,' Jayne remarked critically. 'It swamps your small face. And when you
wear it pulled back like that, it does nothing for you
at all. Makes your facial bones appear sharper. No
softening effect. You really should get it cut and
styled, Liz.'

'And coloured,' Sue said, nodding agreement. 'If
you must wear black suits, mouse brown hair doesn't
exactly give you a lift.'

'There's no *must* about it,' Diana declared, glaring
a knowing challenge as she added, 'I bet you simply
took the cheap route of having a minimal work wardrobe. Am I right or not, Liz?'

She couldn't deny it. Not making regular visits to
a hairdresser saved her time and money and it was
easy enough to slick back her long hair into a tidy
clip at the back of her neck for work. Besides,
Brendan had said he liked long hair. And the all-
purpose suits she wore meant she didn't have to think
about putting something smarter together—a sensible
investment that actually cost less than a more varied
range of clothes.

'What does it matter?' she countered with a vexed

sigh at being put under the microscope like this. 'I get by on it,' she added defiantly. 'Nobody criticises me at work.'

'The invisible handmaiden,' Diana scoffed. 'That's what you've let yourself become, and you could be a knockout if you made the effort.'

'Oh, come off it!' she protested, losing patience with the argument. 'I've always been the plain one in this family. And the shortest.'

She glared at tall, willowy Jayne with her gorgeous mane of dark wavy hair framing a perfectly oval face and a long graceful neck. Her eldest sister had thickly fringed chocolate brown eyes, a classical straight nose, a wide sensuous mouth, and a model-like figure that made everything she wore look right.

Her gaze moved mockingly to Sue who was almost as tall but more lushly feminine, round curves everywhere topped by a pretty face, sparkling amber eyes and soft, honey-coloured curls that rippled down to her shoulders.

Lastly she looked derisively at Diana, a beautiful blue-eyed blonde who turned heads everywhere she went, her long hair straight and smooth like a curtain of silk, her lovely face always perfectly made up, her tall slim figure invariably enhanced by fabulous designer clothes. Easy for her to catch the eye of *her* boss. He'd have to be blind not to appreciate what an asset she was to him.

Next to her sisters Liz felt small, and not just because she was only average height and had what could be called a petite figure. She felt small in every sense. Her hair was a mousy colour and far too thick to manage easily. It did swamp her. Not only that, her eyes were a murky hazel, no clear colour at all, there was a slight bump in her nose, and her cheek-bones and chinline *were* sharply angular. In fact, her only saving grace was good straight teeth.

At least, people said she had a nice smile. But she didn't feel like smiling right now. She felt utterly miserable. 'It's ridiculous to pretend I could be a knock-out,' she stated bitingly. 'The only thing I've got going for me is a smart brain that keeps me in a good job, and it's been my experience that most men don't like too much smart in their women when it comes to personal relationships.'

'A smart man does, Liz,' her mother said quietly.

'And Cole Pierson is incredibly smart,' Diana quickly tagged on. 'He'd definitely value you on that score.'

'Would you please leave my boss out of this?' Liz almost stamped her foot in frustration at her younger sister's one-track mind. Any intimate connection with Cole was an impossible dream, for dozens of reasons.

'Regardless of your boss, Liz,' Jayne said in a serious vein. 'I truly think a makeover is a good idea. You're not plain. You've just never made the most of yourself. With some jazzy clothes and a new hairdo...'

'A lovely rich shade of red would do wonders for your hair,' Sue came in decisively. 'If you had it cut and layered to shape in just below your ears, it could look fantastic. Your skin is pale enough for red to look great with it and such a positive contrast would bring out the green in your eyes.'

'They're not green!' Liz cried in exasperation. 'They're...'

'More green than amber,' Sue judged. 'Red would definitely do the trick. Let me make an appointment with my hairdresser for you and I'll come along to advise.'

'And I can take you shopping. Outfit you in some smashing clothes,' Diana eagerly tagged on.

'At a discount price,' Jayne leapt in. 'Right, Diana? Not making it too frightfully expensive?'

'Right!'

'Hair first, clothes second,' Sue ordered.

'A visit to a beautician, too. Get the make-up right to match the new hair.'

'And accentuate the green in her eyes.'

'Don't forget shoes. Liz has got to get out of those matronly shoes.'

'Absolutely. Shapely legs should be shown off.'

'Not to mention a finely turned ankle.'

They all laughed, happy at the thought of getting their hands on their little sister and waving some magic wand that would turn her into one of them. Except it couldn't really happen, and as her sisters continued to rave on with their makeover plan, bouncing off each other, meaning well...she knew they *meant well*...Liz found herself on the verge of tears.

'Stop! Please stop!' she burst out, slamming her hands onto the island bench to gain their undivided attention. 'I'm me, okay? Not a doll for you to dress up. I'm okay as me. And I'll live my life my own way.'

The shaking vehemence in her voice shocked them

into silence. They stared at her, hurt showing on their faces at the blanket rejection of their ideas. They didn't understand where she was coming from, had never understood what it was like to be *her,* the odd one out amongst them. The tears pricked her eyes, threatening to start spilling.

'I'd like some time alone with Liz.'

Her mother's quiet demand floated over Liz's shoulder. She was still at the sink, wiping it back to its usual pristine state. Without a word of protest, her other three daughters got to their feet and trooped out to the patio. Liz turned to her mother, who slowly set the dishcloth aside, waiting for the absolute privacy she'd asked for, not turning until the others were gone.

Having screwed herself up for more talking, Liz was totally undone when her mother looked at her with sad, sympathetic understanding. Impossible to blink back the tears. Then her mother's arms were around her in a comforting hug and her head was being gently pressed onto a shoulder that had always been there for her to lean on in times of strife and grief.

'Let it out, Liz,' her mother softly advised. 'You've held in too much for too long.'

Control collapsed. She wept, releasing the bank of bad feelings that had been building up ever since Brendan had rejected all she'd offered him, preferring to be somewhere else.

'He wasn't right for you,' her mother murmured when the storm of tears eased. 'I know you tried to make him right for you, but he was never going to be, Liz. He's footloose and rootless and you like to be grounded.'

'But I did enjoy the travelling with him, Mum,' she protested.

'I'm sure you did, but it was also a way of going off independently, not competing with your sisters. You may not think of it like that, but being different for the sake of being different is not the answer. By attaching yourself to Brendan, you virtually shut them out of your life. They want back in, Liz. They want to help you. They're your sisters and they love you.'

She lifted her head, looking her mother in the eye. 'But I'm not like them.'

'No, you have your own unique individuality.' Her mouth curved into a tender, loving smile. 'My one brilliant daughter.'

Liz grimaced. 'Not so brilliant. Though I am good at my job.'

Her mother nodded. 'That's not the problem, is it? You're not feeling good about yourself as a woman. I don't think you have for a long time, Liz. It's easy to sweep away your sisters' makeover plan as some kind of false facade, but you could treat it as fun. A new look. A new style. It might very well give you a lift. Don't see it as competing with them. See it as something new for you.'

'You're urging me to be their guinea pig?'

This drew a chiding shake of the head. 'They're proud of your career in high finance, Liz. They admire your success there. How about conceding that they have expertise in fields you've ignored?'

She winced at the pointed reminder that in the feminine stakes, her sisters certainly shone and undoubt-edly had an eye for things she hadn't bothered with. 'I guess they do know what they're talking about.'

'And then some,' her mother said dryly.

Liz sighed, giving in more because she was bereft of any plans for herself than in any belief that her life could be instantly brightened, along with her hair. 'Well, I don't suppose it will hurt.'

'You could be very pleasantly surprised. Jayne is right. You're not plain, Liz. You're just different.' Her mother patted her cheek encouragingly. 'Now go and make peace with them. Letting them have their way could be a very positive experience for all of you.'

'Okay. But if Diana thinks a new me will make any difference to Cole Pierson, she's dreaming.'

Her boss occupied a different planet.

A chilly one.

Even fiery red hair wasn't about to melt the ice in that man's veins. Or make him suddenly see her as a desirable woman. Why would he anyway, when he'd had Tara Summerville—a top-line international model—as his wife? Even Diana wasn't in that class.

A totally impossible dream.

CHAPTER TWO

HIS mother was upset.

Cole didn't like his mother being upset. It had taken her quite a while to get over his father's death and establish a life on her own. For the past few years she'd been happy, planning overseas trips and going on them with her bridge partner, Joyce Hancock, a retired school principal who was a natural organiser, a person he could trust to look after his mother on their travels. As misfortune would have it, Joyce had fallen and broken her hip so the tour they'd booked to South-East Asia had to be cancelled.

He'd spent the whole weekend trying to distract his mother with his company, cheer her up, but she'd remained down in the dumps, heaving miserable sighs, looking forlorn. Now, driving her back to her Palm Beach home after visiting Joyce in Mona Vale Hospital, Cole saw she was fighting tears. He reached across and squeezed her hand, trying to give sympathetic comfort.

'Don't worry about Joyce. Hip replacement is not a dangerous procedure,' he assured her. 'She'll be up and about soon enough.'

'She's annoyed with me for not going ahead with the trip by myself. But I don't want to go on my own.'

Unthinkable to Cole's mind. His mother would undoubtedly get flustered over the tour schedule, leave things in the hotel rooms, be at the wrong place at the wrong time. She'd become quite fluffy-headed in her widowhood, not having to account to anyone anymore, just floating along while Cole took care of any problems that were troublesome. He saw to the maintenance of her far too large but beloved home and looked after her finances. It was easier than trying to train her into being more responsible for herself.

'It's your choice, Mum. Joyce probably feels guilty about disappointing you,' he soothed.

She shook her head dejectedly. 'I'm disappointing her. She's right about *The Captain's Choice Tour Company*. Their people do look after everything for you. They even take a doctor along in case anyone gets sick or injured. Joyce wants me to go so I can tell her all about it. She says I'll meet people I can talk to. Make new friends...'

'That's easy for her to say,' Cole said dryly, knowing Joyce was the kind of person who'd bulldose her way into any company and feel right at home with it. His mother was made of more fragile stuff.

Her hands twisted fretfully. 'Maybe I should go. Nothing's been cancelled yet. I was going to do it tomorrow.'

Clearly she was torn and would feel miserable either way. 'You need a companion, Mum,' Cole stated categorically. 'You'll feel lost on your own.'

'But there's no one in our social circle who's free to take up Joyce's booking.'

He frowned at this evidence of her actively trying to find someone congenial to travel with. 'You really want to go?'

'I've been looking forward to it for so long. Though without Joyce…' Her voice wavered uncertainly.

Cole made a decision. It meant a sacrifice on his part. Liz Hart had been on vacation for the past two weeks and her fill-in had tested his tolerance level to the limit. He hated doing without his efficient personal assistant. Nevertheless, when it came to entrusting the management of his mother to someone else, he couldn't think of anyone better. No hitches with Liz Hart.

'I'll arrange for my P.A. to take up Joyce's booking and accompany you on the tour,' he said, satisfied that he'd come up with the perfect solution, both for his mother's pleasure and his peace of mind.

It jolted her out of her gloom. 'You can't do that, Cole.'

'Yes, I can,' he asserted. 'I'll put it to Liz first thing in the morning. I'm sure she'll agree.'

'I don't even know the girl!' his mother cried in shocked protest.

'You can come into the city tomorrow and I'll set up a lunch meeting. If you approve of her…fine. If you don't, I'm afraid the trip will be off.'

The lure of the tour clearly held a lot of weight. After a few moments, his mother gave in to curiosity. 'What's she like…this personal assistant of yours?'

'She's the kind of person who can handle anything I throw at her,' he replied, smiling confidently.

'Well, she'd have to be, wouldn't she, to keep up with you, Cole,' came the dryly knowing comment. 'I meant…what is she like as a person?'

He frowned, not quite sure how to answer. 'She fits in,' was the most appropriate description he could come up with.

This earned an exasperated roll of the eyes. 'What does she look like?'

'Always neat and tidy. Professional.'

'How old is she?'

'Not sure. Late twenties, I guess. Maybe early thirties.'

'What colour are her eyes?'

He didn't know, couldn't recall ever noticing. 'What does eye colour have to do with anything?'

His mother sighed. 'You just don't look, do you? Not interested. You've closed off all involvement with anyone. You've got to get past this, Cole. You're still a young man.'

He gritted his teeth, hating any reference to all he'd put behind him. 'Her eyes are bright.' he answered tersely. 'They shine with intelligence. That's more important to me than colour.'

The blank look her temporary fill-in had given him too many times over the past fortnight had filled him with frustration. He'd have to second somcone else to take Liz Hart's place while she was off with his mother.

'Is she attractive...pretty...big...slight...tall... short...?'

Cole sighed over his mother's persistence on irrelevant detail. 'She's ordinary average,' he said impatiently. 'And always obliging, which is the main point here. Liz will ensure you have a trouble-free tour, Mum. No worries.'

His mother sighed. 'Do try to tell me more about her, Cole.'

She should be satisfied with what he'd already told her but he stretched his mind to find some pertinent point. 'She likes travel. Spends most of her time off travelling somewhere or other. I expect she'll jump at the chance of accompanying you to South-East Asia.'

'Then it won't be a completely burdensome chore for her, escorting me around?'

'Of course not. I wouldn't load you with a sourpuss. I'm sure you'll find Liz Hart a delight to be with.'

'Do you?'

'Do I what?'

'Find her a delight to be with.'

'Well, I'll certainly miss her,' he said with feeling.

'Ah!'

He glanced sharply at his mother. Her 'Ah!' had carried a surprising depth of satisfaction, making him wonder what she was thinking.

She smiled at him. 'Thank you, Cole. You're quite wonderful at fixing things for me. I'll look forward to meeting your Liz tomorrow.'

'Good!'

Problem solved.

His mother wasn't upset anymore.

Monday morning…

Cole heard Liz Hart arrive in the office which adjoined his—promptly at eight-thirty as she did every workday. Totally reliable, he thought with satisfaction.

He had not qualms whatsoever about entrusting his mother's well-being and pleasure in this upcoming South-East Asia tour to his punctual and efficient personal assistant.

It didn't occur to him that the request he was about to make was tantamount to inviting Liz Hart into his personal and private life. To his mind it was simply a matter of moving people into position to achieve what had to be achieved. He could manage another two weeks more or less by himself, asking the absolute minimum of another temporary P.A., while his mother enjoyed a stress-free trip. Once the fortnight was over, everything would shift back to normal.

He rose from his desk and strode to the connecting door, intent on handing the tour folder to Liz so she could get straight to work on doing what had to be done to become Joyce Hancock's replacement. In his business, time was money and his time was too valuable to waste on extraneous matters. Liz would undoubtedly see to everything required of her—passport, visas, whatever.

He opened the door to find some stranger hanging her bag and coat on Liz's hatstand, taking up personal space that didn't belong to her. Cole frowned at the unexpected vision of a startling redhead, dressed in a clingy green sweater and a figure-hugging navy skirt with a split up the back—quite a distracting split, leading his gaze down a pair of finely shaped legs encased in sheer navy stockings, to pointedly female high-heeled shoes.

Who was this woman? And what did she think she was doing, taking up Liz's office? He hadn't been informed that his P.A. had called in, delaying her scheduled return to work. Unexplained change was not acceptable, especially when it entailed having someone foisted on him without his prior approval.

His gaze had travelled back up the curve of thigh and hip to the indentation of a very small waist before the unwelcome intruder turned around. Then he found himself fixated on very nicely rounded breasts, emphatically outlined by the soft, sexy sweater, with more attention being drawn to them by a V-neckline ending in a looped tie that hung down the valley of her cleavage.

'Good morning, Cole.'

The brisk, cool greeting stunned him with its familiarity. His gaze jerked up to an unfamiliar mouth, painted as brightly red as the thick cropped hair that flared out in waves and curls on either side of her face. The eyes hit a chord with him—very bright eyes—but even they looked different, bigger than they normally were and more sparkly. This wasn't the Liz Hart he was used to. Only her voice was instantly recognisable.

'What the devil have you done to yourself?' The words shot out, driven by a sense of aggrievement at the shock she'd given him.

A firmly chiseled chin which he'd previously thought of as strong, steady and determined, now tilted up in provocative challenge. 'I beg your pardon?'

He was distracted by the gold gypsy hoops dangling from her earlobes. 'This is not you, dammit!' he grated, his normal equilibrium thrown completely out of kilter by these changes in the person who worked most closely with him, a person he counted on not to rock his boats in any sense whatsoever.

Her eyes flashed a glittery warning. 'Are you objecting to my appearance?'

Red alert signals went off in his brain…sexual discrimination…harrassment…Liz was calling him on something dangerous here and he'd better watch his step. However disturbingly different she looked today, he knew she had a core of steel and would stand up for herself against anything she considered unreasonable or unjust.

'No,' he said decisively, taking firm control over the runaway reactions to an image he didn't associate with her. 'Your appearance is fine. It's good to have you back, Liz.'

'Thank you.' Her chin levelled off again, fighting mode discarded. She smiled. 'It's good to be back.'

This should have put them on the correct footing but Cole couldn't help staring at her face, which somehow lit up quite strikingly with the smile. Maybe it was the short fluffy red hair that made her smile look even whiter and her eyes brighter. Or the bright red lipstick. Whatever it was, she sure didn't look average ordinary anymore.

He wanted to ask…why the change? What had happened to her? But that was personal stuff he knew he shouldn't get into. He liked the parameters of their business relationship the way they were. Right now they felt threatened, without inviting further infringements on them.

He had to stop staring. Her cheeks were glowing pink, highlighting bones that now seemed to have an exotic, angular tilt. They must have always been like that. It made him feel stupid not to have noticed before. Had she been deliberately playing herself down during business hours, hiding her surprisingly feminine figure in unisex suits, keeping her hair plain and quiet, wearing only insignificant make-up?

'Is that something for me to deal with?' she asked, gesturing to the folder he was holding.

Conscious that his awkward silence had driven her to take some initiative, he didn't stop to reconsider the proposition he'd prepared. 'Yes,' he said, gratefully seizing on the business in hand. 'I need you to go to South-East Asia with my mother,' he blurted out.

She stared at him, shocked disbelief in her eyes.

Good to serve it right back to her, Cole thought, stepping forward and slapping the folder down on her desk, a buzz of adrenalin shooting through him at regaining control of the situation.

'It's all in here. The Captain's Choice Tour. Borneo, Burma, Nepal, Laos, Vietnam, Cambodia— all in fifteen days by chartered Qantas jet, leaving on Saturday week. You'll require extra passport photos for visas and innoculation shots for typhoid, hepatitis, and other diseases. You'll see the medical check list. I take it you have a usable passport?'

'Yes,' she answered weakly.

'Good! No problem then.'

She seemed frozen on the spot, still staring at him, not moving to open the folder. He tapped it to draw her attention to it.

'All the tickets are in here. Everything's been paid

for. You'll find them issued in the name of Joyce
Hancock and first thing to do is notify the tour company that you'll be travelling in her place.'

'Joyce Hancock,' she repeated dazedly.

'My mother's usual travelling companion. Broke
her hip. Can't go. None of her other friends can take
the trip at such short notice,' he explained.

Liz Hart shook her head, the red hair rippling with
the movement like a live thing that wasn't under any
control. Very distracting. Cole frowned, realising she
was indicating a negative response. Which was un-
acceptable. He was about to argue the position when
she drew in a deep breath and spoke.

'Your mother...Mrs. Pierson...she doesn't even
know me.'

'*I* know you. I've told her she'll be safe with you.'

'But...' She gestured uncertainly.

'Primarily my mother needs a manager on this trip.
I have absolute faith in your management skills, not
to mention your acute sense of diplomacy, tact, understanding, and generally sharp intelligence. Plus
you're an experienced traveller.' He raised a challenging eyebrow. 'Correct?'

Another deep breath, causing a definite swell in the
mounds under the clingy sweater which was a striking
jewel green, somewhere between jade and emerald, a
rich kind of medieval colour. The fanciful thought
jolted Cole. He had to get his mind off her changed
appearance.

'Thank you. It's nice to have my...attributes...
appreciated,' she said in a somewhat ironic tone that
sounded unsure of his end purpose. 'However, I do
think I should meet with your mother...'

'Lunch today. Book a table for the three of us at Level 21. Twelve-thirty. My mother will join us there. She is looking forward to meeting you.'

'Is Mrs. Pierson…unwell?'

'Not at all. A bit woolly-headed about directions in strange places and not apt at dealing with time changes and demanding schedules, but perfectly sane and sound. She'll lean on you to get things right for her. That's your brief. Okay?'

'She's…happy…about this arrangement?'

'Impossible for her to go otherwise and she wants to go.'

'I see. You want me to be her minder.'

'Yes. I have every confidence in your ability to provide the support she needs to fully enjoy this trip.'

'What if she doesn't like me?'

'What's *not* to like?' he threw back at her more snappishly than he'd meant to, irritatingly aware that his mother would think this new version of Liz Hart was just lovely. And she would undoubtedly mock his judgment at having called his P.A. ordinary average.

No answer from Liz. Of course, it would be against her steely grain to verbally put herself down. Which increased the mystery of why she had *played* herself down physically these past three years. Had it been a feminist thing, a negation of her sexuality because she wanted her intellect valued?

Why had she suddenly decided to flaunt femininity now?

Dammit! He didn't have time to waste on such vagaries.

He tapped the folder again. 'I can leave this with you? No problems about dealing with it?' His eyes locked onto hers with the sharp demand of getting what he expected.

'No problems I can see,' she returned with flinty pride.

Her eyes were green.

With gold speckles around the rim.

'Fine! Let me know if you run into any.'

He stalked off into his own office, annoyed at how he was suddenly noticing every detail about a woman who'd been little more than a mind complementing his up until this morning. It was upsetting his comfort zone.

Why did she have to change?

It didn't feel right.

Just as well she was going off with his mother for two weeks. It would give him time to adjust to the idea of having his P.A. looking like a fiery sexpot. Meanwhile, he had work to do and he was not about to be distracted from it. Bad enough that he had to take time off for the lunch with his mother, which was bound to be another irritation because of Liz Hart's dramatic transformation.

Bad start to the morning.

Bad, bad, bad.

At least the food at Level 21 was good.

Though he'd probably choke on it, watching his mother being dazzled by her new travelling companion. No way was *she* going to be upset by a *colourful* Liz Hart, which was some consolation, but since he was decidedly upset himself, Cole wasn't sure that balanced the scales.

CHAPTER THREE

LIZ took a deep, deep breath, let it out slowly, then forced her feet to walk steadily to her desk, no teetering in the high-heels, shoulders back, correct carriage, just as Diana had drilled her. It was good to sit down. She was still quaking inside from the reaction her new image had drawn from Cole Pierson.

Diana had confidently predicted it would knock his socks off but Liz had believed he would probably look at her blankly for a few seconds, dismiss the whole thing as frivolous female foibles, then get straight down to business. Never, in a million years, would she have anticipated being *attacked* on it. Nor looked at so...so *intensely*.

It had been awful, turning around from the hatstand and finding those piercing blue eyes riveted on her breasts. Her heart had started galloping. Even worse, she'd felt her nipples hardening into prominent nubs, possibly becoming visible underneath the snug fit of the cashmere sweater.

She'd clipped out a quick greeting to get his focus off her body, only to have him stare at her mouth as though alien words had come out of it. Even when he had finally lifted his gaze to hers, she'd been totally rattled by the force of his concentration on how she looked. Which, she readily conceded, was vastly different to what he was used to, but certainly not

31

warranting the outburst that came. Nor the criticism it implied.

Her own fierce response to it echoed through her mind now—*I will not let him make me feel wrong. Not on any grounds.*

There was no workplace law to say a woman couldn't change the colour of her hair, couldn't change the style of her clothes, couldn't touch up her make-up. It wasn't as if she'd turned up with hair tortured into red or blue or purple spikes or dreadlocks. Red was a natural hair colour and the short layered style was what she'd call conservative modern, not the least bit outlandish. Her clothes were perfectly respectable and her make-up appropriate—certainly not overdone—to match the new colouring.

In fact, no impartial judge would say her appearance did not fit the position she held. All her sisters had declared she was now perfectly put together and Liz herself had ended up approving the result of their combined efforts. Her mother was right. It did make her feel good to look brighter and more stylish. She'd even started smiling at herself in the mirror.

And she wasn't about to let Cole Pierson wipe *that* smile off her face, just because he'd feel more comfortable if she merged into the office furniture again so he could regard her as another one of his computers. Though he had attributed her with management skills, diplomacy, tact, understanding, and sharp intelligence, which did put her a few points above a computer. And amazingly, he trusted her enough to put his mother into her keeping!

Having burned off her resentment at her boss's totally intemperate remarks on what was none of his business, Liz focused on the folder he'd put on her desk. Surprises had come thick and fast this morning. Apart from Cole's taking far too much *physical* notice of her, she had been summarily appointed guardian to a woman she'd never met, and handed a free trip to South-East Asia, no doubt travelling first-class all the way on The Captain's Choice Tour.

Right in the middle of this, Cole had listed Nepal amongst the various destinations.

Brendan was in Nepal.

Not that there was any likelihood of meeting up with him, and she didn't really want to...did she? What was finished was finished. But there was a somewhat black irony in her going there, too. Especially in not doing everything on the cheap, as Brendan would have to.

You can do better than Brendan Wheeler, her mother had said with a conviction that had made Liz feel she had settled for less than she should in considering a life partner.

Maybe her mother was right.

In any event, this trip promised many better things than bunking down in backpacker hostels.

On the front of The Captain's Choice folder was printed 'The leader in luxury travel to remote and exotic destinations.' Excitement was instantly ignited. She opened the folder and read all about the itinerary, delighted anticipation zooming at the places she would be visiting, and all in a deluxe fashion.

The accommodation was fantastic—The Hyatt Regency Hotel in Kathmandu, The Opera Hilton in

Hanoi, a 'Raffles' hotel in Phnom Penh. No expense spared anywhere...a chartered flight over Mount Everest, and a chartered helicopter to Halong Bay in Vietnam, another chartered flight to the ancient architectural wonder of Angkor Wat in Cambodia, even a specially chartered steam train to show them some of the countryside in Burma.

She could definitely take a lot of this kind of travel. No juggling finances, no concern over how to get where, no worry about making connections, no trying to find a decent meal...it was all laid out and paid for.

Even if Cole's mother was a grumpy battleaxe, Liz figured it couldn't be too hard to win her over by being determinedly cheerful. After all, Mrs. Pierson had to want this trip very much to agree to her son's plan, so mutual enjoyment should be reached without too much trouble.

Tact, diplomacy, understanding...Liz grinned to herself as she reached for the telephone, ready now to get moving on sealing her place for this wonderful new adventure. Her changed appearance had probably knocked Cole's socks off this morning, though in a more negative way than Diana had plotted, but he had still paid her a huge compliment by giving her this extra job with his mother. Better than a bonus.

It made her feel good.

Really good.

She zinged through the morning, booking the table at Level 21—no problem to fit Cole Pierson's party in at short notice since he regularly used the restaurant for business lunches—then lining up everything necessary for her to take Joyce Hancock's place on the tour.

Cole did not reappear. He did not call her, either. He remained secluded in his own office, no doubt tending meticulously to his own business. At twelve-fifteen, Liz went to the Ladies' Room to freshen up, smiled at herself in the mirror, determined that nothing her boss said or did would unsettle her again, then proceeded to beard the lion in his den, hoping he wouldn't bite this time.

She gave a warning knock on the door, entered his office, waited for him to look up from the paperwork on his desk, ignored the frown, and matter-of-factly stated, 'It's time to leave if we're to meet your mother at twelve-thirty.'

Since Cole's financial services company occupied a floor of the Chifley Tower, one of the most prestigious buildings in the city centre, all they had to do was catch an elevator up to Level 21, which, of course, was also one of Sydney's most prestigious restaurants. This arrangement naturally suited Cole's convenience, as well as establishing in his clients' minds that big money was made here and this location amply displayed that fact.

Cold blue eyes bored into hers for several nerve-jangling moments. He certainly knew how to put a chill in a room. Liz wondered if she should have put her suitcoat on, but they weren't going outside where there was a wintery bite in the air. This was just her boss, being his usual self, and it was good that he had returned to being his usual self.

Though as he rolled his big executive chair back

from his work station and rose to his full impressive height, Liz did objectively note that Sue was not wrong in calling him tall, dark and handsome, what with his thick black hair, black eyebrows, darkly toned skin, a strong male face, squarish jaw, firm mouth, straight nose, neat ears. And those piercing eyes gave him a commanding authority that accentuated his *presence*.

The Armani suits he invariably wore added to his presence, too. Cole Pierson had dominant class written all over him. Sometimes, it really piqued Liz. It didn't seem fair that anyone should have so much going for him. But then she told herself he wasn't totally human.

Although the robotic facade *had* cracked this morning.

Scary stuff.

Better not to think about it.

Move on, move on, move on, she recited, holding her breath as Cole moved towards her, mouth grim, eyes raking over her again, clearly not yet having come to terms with her brighter presence.

'Did you call up to see if my mother had arrived?' he rapped out.

'No. I considered it a courtesy that we be there on time.'

'My mother is not the greatest time-keeper in the world.' He paused beside Liz near the door. 'Which is why she needs you,' he rammed home with quite unnecessary force.

'All the more reason to show her I'm reliable on that point,' she retorted, and could have sworn he breathed steam through his nostrils as he abruptly waved her to precede him out of both of their offices.

It made Liz extremely conscious of walking with straight-backed dignity. It was ridiculous, given his icy eyes, that she felt the bare nape of her neck burning. He had to be watching her, which was highly disconcerting because usually his whole attention was claimed by whatever was working through his mind. She didn't want his kind of intense focus trained on her. It was like being under a microscope, making her insides squirmish.

She breathed a sigh of relief when they finally entered the elevator and stood side by side in the compartment as it zoomed up to Level 21. Cole held his hands loosely linked in front of them and watched the numbers flashing over the door. It looked like a relaxed pose, but he emanated a tension that erased Liz's initial relief.

Maybe he was human, after all.

Was it *her* causing this rift in his iron-like composure, or the prospect of this meeting with his mother?

This thought reminded Liz that *she* should be thinking about his mother, preparing herself to answer any questions put to her in a positive and reassuring manner. Of course, her response depended largely on the kind of person Cole's mother was. Liz hoped she wasn't frosty. Cole had said fluffy, but that might only mean her mind wasn't as razor-sharp as his.

Liz was fast sharpening her own mind as they were met at the entrance to the restaurant by the maitre d' and informed that Mrs. Pierson had arrived and was enjoying a drink in the bar lounge.

'Must be anxious,' Cole muttered as they were led to where a woman sat on a grey leather sofa, her attention drawn to the fantastic view over the city of Sydney, dramatically displayed by the wall of windows.

Her hair was pure white, waving softly around a slightly chubby face which was relatively unlined and still showing how pretty she must have been in her youth. About seventy, Liz judged, taking heart at the gentle, ladylike look of the woman. Definitely not a battleaxe. Not frosty, either. She wore a pink Chanel style suit with an ivory silk blouse, pearl brooch, pearl studs in her ears, and many rings on her fingers.

'Mum!'

Her son's curt tone whipped her head around, her whole body jerking slightly at being startled. Bright blue eyes looked up at him, then made an instant curious leap to Liz. Her mouth dropped open in sheer surprise.

'Mum!' Cole said again, the curt tone edged with vexation now.

Her mouth shut into a line of total exasperation and she gave him a look that seemed to accuse him of being absolutely impossible and in urgent need of having his head examined.

Liz thought she heard Cole grind his teeth. However, he managed to unclench them long enough to say, 'This is my P.A., Liz Hart...my mother, Nancy Pierson.'

Nancy rose to her feet, her blue eyes glittering with

a frustration that spilled into speech as she held out her hand to Liz. 'My dear, how *do* you put up with him?'

Tact and diplomacy were right on the line here!

'Cole is the best boss I've ever had,' Liz declared with loyal fervour. 'I very much enjoy working with him.'

'Work!' Nancy repeated in a tone of disgust. 'Tunnel vision...that's what he's got. Sees nothing but work.'

'Mum!' Thunder rolled through Cole's warning protest.

Liz leapt in to avert the storm. 'Cole did cover your trip to South-East Asia this morning, Mrs. Pierson.' She beamed her best smile and poured warmth into her voice as she added, 'Which I think is wonderful.'

It did the trick, drawing Nancy out of her grumps and earning a smile back. She squeezed Liz's hand in a rush of pleasure. 'Oh, I think so, too. Far too wonderful to miss.'

Liz squeezed back. 'I'm simply over the moon that Cole thought of me as a companion for you. Such marvellous places to see...'

'Well...' She gave her son an arch look that still had a chastening gleam. 'Occasionally he gets some things right.'

'A drink,' Cole bit out. 'Liz, something for you? Mum, a refill?'

'Just water, thank you,' Liz quickly answered.

'Champagne,' Nancy commanded, and suddenly there was a wickedly mocking twinkle in her eyes.

'I'm beginning to feel quite bubbly again, now that I've met your Liz, Cole.'

His Liz? Exactly what terms had Cole used to describe her to his mother? Nothing with a possessive sense, surely.

'I'm glad you're happy,' he said on an acid note and headed for the bar.

Nancy squeezed Liz's hand again before letting go and gesturing to the lounge. 'Come and sit down with me and let us get better acquainted.'

'What would you like to know about me?' Liz openly invited as she sank onto the soft leather sofa.

'Not about work,' came the decisive dismissal. 'Tell me about your family.'

'Well, my parents live at Neutral bay...'

'Nice suburb.'

'Dad's a doctor. Mum was a nurse but...'

'She gave it up when the family came along.'

'Yes. Four daughters. I'm the third.'

'My goodness! That must have been a very female household.'

Liz laughed. 'Yes. Dad always grumbled about being outvoted. But he now has three sons-in-law to stand shoulder to shoulder with him.'

'So your three sisters are married. How lovely! Nice husbands?'

Under Nancy's eager encouragement, Liz went on to describe her sisters' lives and had just finished a general rundown on them when Cole returned, setting the drinks down on the low table in front of them and dropping onto the opposite sofa. Into the lull following their 'thankyous,' Nancy dropped the one question Liz didn't want to answer.

'So what about your social life, Liz? Or are you like Cole...' a derisive glance at her son. '...not having one.'

It instantly conjured up the hole left by Brendan's defection. She delayed a reply, picking up the glass of water, fiercely wishing the question hadn't been asked, especially put as it had been, linking her to her boss who was listening.

Unexpectedly he came to her rescue. 'You're getting too personal, Mum,' he said brusquely. 'Leave it alone.'

Nancy aimed a sigh at him. 'Has it occurred to you, Cole, that such a bright, striking young woman could have a boyfriend who might not take kindly to her leaving him behind while she travels with me?'

He beetled an accusing frown at Liz as though this was all her fault, then sliced an impatient look at his mother. 'What objection could a boyfriend have? It's only for two weeks and you can hardly be seen as a rival.'

'It's short notice. The trip takes up three weekends. They might have prior engagements,' came the ready arguments. 'Did you even ask this morning, or did you simply go into command mode, expecting Liz to carry through your plan, regardless?'

A long breath hissed through his teeth.

Liz felt driven to break in. 'Mrs. Pierson...'

'Call me Nancy, dear.'

'Nancy...' She tried an appeasing smile to cover the angst of her current single state. '...I don't have a boyfriend at the moment. I'm completely free to take up the amazingly generous opportunity Cole handed me this morning. I would have told him so if I wasn't.'

Tact, diplomacy…never mind that the hole was humiliatingly bared.

'Satisfied?' Cole shot at his mother.

She smiled back at him. 'Completely.' It was a surprisingly smug pronouncement, as though she had won the point.

Liz was lost in whatever byplay was going on between mother and son, but she was beginning to feel very much like the meat in the sandwich. Anxious to get the conversation focused back on the trip, she offered more relevant information about herself.

'I haven't been to Kuching but I have travelled to Malaysia before.'

Thankfully, Nancy seized on that prior experience and Liz managed to keep feeding their mutual interest in travel over lunch, skilfully smoothing over the earlier tension in their small party. Cole ate his food, contributing little to the table talk, though he did flash Liz a look of wry appreciation now and then, well aware she was working hard at winning over his mother.

Not that it was really hard. Nancy seemed disposed to like her, the blue eyes twinkling pleasure and approval in practically everything Liz said. Oddly enough, Liz was more conscious of her boss watching and listening, and whenever their eyes met, the understanding that flashed between them gave her heart a little jolt.

This had never happened before and she tried to analyse why now? Because his mother made this more personal than business? Because he was looking at her from a different angle, seeing the woman behind the P.A.? Because she was doing the same thing, seeing him as Nancy's son instead of the boss?

It was confusing and unsettling.

She didn't want to feel...*touched*...by this man, or close to him in any emotional sense. No doubt he'd freeze her out again the moment this meeting with his mother was over.

'Now, are you free this Saturday, my dear?' Nancy inquired once coffee was served.

'Yes?' Liz half queried, wondering what else was required of her.

'Good! You must come over to my home at Palm Beach and check my packing. Joyce always does that for me. It eliminates doubling up on things, taking too much. Do you have a car? It's difficult to get to by public transport. If you don't have a car...'

Liz quickly cut in. 'Truly, it won't be a problem. I'll manage.'

She'd never owned a car. No need when public transport was not only faster into the city, but much, much cheaper than running a car. Palm Beach was, however, a fair distance out, right at the end of the northern peninsula, but she'd get there somehow.

'I was going to say Cole could bring you.' She smiled at her son. 'You could, dear, couldn't you? Don't forget you're meeting with the tradesman who's going to quote for the new paving around the pool on Saturday.' She frowned. 'I think he said eleven o'clock. Or was it one o'clock?'

Cole sighed. 'I'll be there, Mum. And I'll collect and deliver Liz to you,' he said in a tone of sorely tried patience.

Oh, great! Liz thought, preferring the cost of a taxi to being a forced burden loaded onto her boss's shoulders. But clearly she wasn't going to get any say in this so she might as well grin and bear it. Though she doubted Cole would find a grin appropriate. He was indulging his mother but the indulgence was wearing very, very thin.

'You'd better come early. Before eleven,' Nancy instructed, then smiled at Liz. 'We'll have a nice lunch together. I've so enjoyed this one. And, of course, we have to be sure we've got all the right clothes for our trip.'

Liz had been thinking cargo pants and T-shirts for daywear and a few more stylish though still casual outfits for dinner at night, but she held her tongue, not knowing what Nancy expected of her. She would see on Saturday.

A great pity Cole had to be there.

He was probably thinking the same thing about her.

In fact, Liz wondered if Nancy Pierson was deliberately putting the two of them together to somehow score more points off her son. She might be fluffy-headed about time, but Liz suspected she was as sharp as a tack when it came to people. And she was looking smug again.

'Everything settled to your satisfaction, Mum?' Cole dryly inquired.

'Yes.' She smiled sweetly at him. 'Thank you, dear. I'm sure I'll have a lovely time with your Liz. So good of you to give her to me. I imagine you'll be quite lost without her.'

'No one is indispensable.'

A chill ran down Liz's spine. She threw an alarmed look at Cole, frightened that she'd somehow put her job on the line by courting his mother. The last thing she wanted at this uncertain point in her life was to lose the position that gave her the means to move on.

Cole caught the look and frowned at the flash of vulnerability. 'Though I must admit it's very difficult to find anyone who can remotely fill Liz's shoes as my P.A.,' he stated, glowering at her as though she should know that. 'In fact, I may very well take some time off work while she's away to save myself the aggravation.'

Both Liz and Nancy stared at him in stunned disbelief.

Cole taking time off work was unheard of. He ate, drank, and slept work.

Surprises were definitely coming thick and fast today!

The best one, Liz decided with a surge of tingling pleasure, was the accumulating evidence that Cole Pierson really valued her. That made her feel better than good. It made her feel...*extra special.*

CHAPTER FOUR

COLE had expected Liz Hart to manage his mother brilliantly. That had never been in doubt. However, while the meeting had achieved his purpose—his mother happily accepting his P.A. as her companion for the trip—there were other outcomes that continued to niggle at his mind, making the rest of Monday afternoon a dead loss as far as any productive work was concerned.

Firstly, his mother considered him a blind idiot.

That was Liz's fault.

Secondly, his mother had neatly trapped him into some ridiculous matchmaking scheme, forcibly coupling him with Liz on Saturday.

While he couldn't entirely lay the blame for that at his P.A.'s door, if she hadn't completely changed how she looked, his mother wouldn't have been inspired to plot this extraneous togetherness.

Thirdly, what had happened to the boyfriend? While Cole had never met the man in Liz Hart's life and not given him a thought this morning, he had been under the impression there was a long-running relationship. The name, Brendan, came to mind. Certainly on the few occasions Liz had spoken of personal travel plans, she'd used the plural pronoun. 'We...'

Had she lied to put a swift end to the fuss his

mother had made? Surely insisting her boyfriend wouldn't object could have achieved the same end.

Cole wanted that point cleared up.

Maybe the departure of the boyfriend had triggered the distracting metamorphosis from brown moth to bright butterfly.

Lastly, why would Liz feel insecure about her job? She had every reason to feel confident about holding her position. He'd never criticised her work. She had to know how competent she was. It was absurd of her to look afraid when he'd said no one was indispensable.

The whole situation with her today had been exasperating and continued to exasperate even after she left to go home. Cole resolved to shut it all out of his mind tomorrow. And for the rest of the working week. Perhaps on the drive to his mother's house on Saturday he'd get these questions answered, clear up what was going on in Liz's head. Then he'd feel comfortable around her again.

On Tuesday morning she turned up in a slinky leopard print outfit that totally wrecked his comfort zone, giving him the sense of a jungle cat prowling around him with quiet, purposeful manoeuvres. She also wore sexy bronze sandals with straps that crisscrossed up over her ankles, making him notice how fine-boned they were.

Wednesday she gave the tight navy skirt with the slit up the back a second wearing, but this time topped with a snug cropped jacket in vibrant violet, an unbelievably stunning combination with the red hair. Cole found his gaze drawn to it far too many times.

Thursday came the leopard print skirt with a black sweater, and the gold hoop earrings that dangled so distractingly. *Striking,* his mother had said, and it was a disturbingly apt description. Cole was struck by thoughts he hadn't entertained for a long time. If Liz Hart was free of any attachment...but mixing business with pleasure was always a mistake. Stupid to even be tempted.

Friday fueled the temptation. She wore a bronze button-through dress which wasn't completely buttoned through, showing provocative flashes of leg. A wide belt accentuated her tiny waist, the stand-up collar framed her vivid hair and face, and the strappy bronze sandals got to him again. The overall effect was very sexy. In fact, the more he thought about Liz Hart, the more he thought she comprised a very desirable package.

But best to leave well enough alone.

He wasn't ready for a serious relationship and an office affair would inevitably undermine the smooth teamwork they'd established at work. Besides which, he reflected with considerable irony, Liz had not given any sign of seeing *him* in a sexual light. No ripple of disturbance in her usual efficiency.

She did seem to be smiling at him more often but he couldn't be sure that wasn't simply a case of the smile being more noticeable, along with her mouth, her eyes, and everything else about her. Nevertheless, the smile was getting to be insidious. More times than not he found himself smiling back, feeling a lingering pleasure in the little passage of warmth between them.

No harm in being friendly, he told himself, as long

as it didn't diminish his authority. After all, Liz had worked in relative harmony with him for three years. Though getting too friendly wouldn't do, either. A line had to be drawn. Business was business. A certain distance had to be kept.

That distance was clearly on Liz's mind when she entered his office at the end of their working week, and with an air of nervous tension, broached the subject—'About tomorrow…going to your mother's home at Palm Beach…'

'Ah, yes! Where and when to pick you up.'

Her hands picked fretfully at each other. 'You really don't have to.'

'Easier if I do.' Cole leaned back in his chair to show that he was relaxed about it.

'I've worked out the most efficient route by public transport. It's not a problem,' she assured him.

'It will be a problem for me if I arrive without you,' he drawled pointedly.

'Oh!' She grimaced, recalling the acrimony between mother and son. Her eyes flashed an anxious plea. 'I don't want to put you out, Cole.'

'It's my mother putting me out, not you. I don't mind obliging her tomorrow, Liz.' He reached for a notepad. 'Give me your address.'

More hand-picking. 'I could meet you somewhere on the way…'

'Your address,' he repeated, impatient with quibbling.

'It will be less hassle if…'

'Do you have a problem with giving me your address, Liz?' he cut in.

She winced. 'I live at Bondi Junction. It would mean your backtracking to pick me up...'

'Ten minutes at most from where I live at Benelong Point.'

'Then ten minutes back again before heading off in the right direction,' she reminded him.

'I think I can spare you twenty minutes.'

She sighed. 'I'd feel better about accepting a lift from you if we could meet on the way. I can catch a train to...'

'Are you worried that your boyfriend might object if I pick you up from your home?' The thought had slid into his mind and spilled into words before Cole realised it was openly probing her private life and casting himself in the role of a rival.

She stared at him, shocked at the implications of the question.

Cole was somewhat shocked at the indiscretion himself, but some belligerent instinct inside him refused to back down from it. The urge to know the truth of her situation had been building all week. He stared back, waiting for her answer, mentally commanding it.

A tide of heat flowed up her neck and burned across her cheekbones, making their slant more prominent and her eyes intensely bright. Cole was conscious of a fine tension running between them, a silent challenge emanating from her, striking an edge of excitement in him...the excitement of contest he always felt with a clash of wills, spurring on his need to win.

'I told you on Monday I don't have a boyfriend,' she bit out.

'No. You told my mother that, neatly ending her blast at me.'

'It's the truth.'

'Since when? The last I heard, just before you left on vacation, you had plans to travel with...is it Brendan?'

Her mouth compressed into a thin line of resistance.

'Who's been floating around in your background for as long as you've been working with me,' Cole pushed relentlessly. 'Probably before that, as well.'

'He's gone. I'm by myself now,' she said in defiant pride.

'Send him packing, did you?'

'He packed himself off,' she flashed back derisively.

'You're telling me he left you?'

'He didn't like my style of management.'

'Man's a fool.'

Her mouth tilted into a wry little smile. 'Thank you.'

No smile in her eyes, Cole noted. They looked bleak. She'd been hurt by the rejection of what she was, possibly hurt enough to worry about how rightly or wrongly she managed her job, hence the concern about losing it, too.

Satisfied that he now understood her position, Cole restated his. 'I shall pick you up at your home. Your address?'

She gave it without further argument, though her tone had a flat, beaten quality he didn't like. 'I was only trying to save you trouble,' she muttered, excusing her attempt to manage him.

'I appreciate the value you place on my time, Liz.' He finished writing down her address and looked up, wanting to make her feel valued. 'You're obliging my mother. The least I can do is save *you* some of your leisure time. Does ten o'clock suit?'

'Yes. Thank you.' Her cheeks were still burning but her hands had forgotten their agitation.

He smiled to ease the last of her tension. 'You're welcome. Just don't feel you have to indulge all my mother's whims tomorrow. Do only what's reasonable to you. Okay?'

She nodded.

He glanced at his watch. 'Time for you to leave to get those injections for the trip.' He smiled again. 'Off you go. I'll see you in the morning.'

'Thank you,' she repeated, looking confused by his good humour.

Cole questioned it himself once she left. He decided it had nothing to do with the fact she was free of any attachment. That was irrelevant to him. No, it was purely the satisfaction of having the mysteries surrounding her this week resolved. Even the change of image made sense. Given that Brendan was stupidly critical, no doubt she'd been suppressing her true colours for the sake of falling in with what he wanted.

Liz was well rid of that guy.

He'd obviously been dragging her down.

Cole ruefully reflected that was what his ex-wife had accused him of doing, though he'd come to recognise it had been easier to blame him than take any responsibility herself for the breakdown of their marriage. At the time he hadn't cared. All that had been good in their relationship had died...with their baby son.

For several moments the grief and guilt he'd locked away swelled out of the sealed compartment in his mind. He pushed them back. Futile feelings, achieving nothing. The past was past. It couldn't be changed. And there was work to be done.

He brought his concentration to bear on the figures listed on his computer monitor screen. He liked their logical patterns, always a reason for everything. Figures didn't lie or deceive or distort things. There were statiticians who used them to do precisely that, but figures by themselves had a pure truth. Cole was comfortable with figures.

He told himself he'd now be comfortable again with Liz Hart. It was all a matter of fitting everything into place—a straightforward pattern built on truth and logic. It wouldn't matter what she wore or how she looked tomorrow, he wouldn't find it distracting. It was all perfectly understandable.

As for the sexual attraction...a brief aberration.

No doubt it would wear off very quickly.

His desk telephone rang, evoking a frown of annoyance. No Liz to intercept and monitor his calls. He didn't talk to clients off the cuff, but it could be an in-house matter being referred to him. Hard to ignore the buzzing. He snatched up the receiver.

'Pierson.'

'Cole…finally,' came the distinctive voice of his almost ex-wife.

'Tara…' It was the barest of acknowledgments. He had nothing to say to her. An aggressive tension seized his entire body, an instinctive reaction to anything she might say to him.

'I tried to get hold of you all last weekend. You weren't at the penthouse…'

'I was with my mother at Palm Beach,' he cut in, resenting the tone that suggested he should still be at Tara's beck and call. She'd been *enjoying* the company of several other men since their separation, clearing him of any lingering sense of obligation to answer any of her needs.

'Your mother…' A hint of mockery in her voice.

It had been one bone of contention in their marriage that Cole spent too much time looking after his mother instead of devoting his entire attention to what Tara wanted, which was continual social activity in the limelight. Not even her pregnancy and the birth of their baby son had slowed her merry-go-round of engagements. If they hadn't been out at a party, leaving David in the care of his nanny…

'Get to the point, Tara,' he demanded, mentally blocking the well-worn and totally futile *if only* track in his mind.

She heaved a sigh at his bluntness, then in a sweetly cajoling tone, said, 'You do remember that our divorce becomes final next week…'

'The date is in my diary.'

'I thought we should get together and…'

'I believe our respective solicitors have covered

every piece of that ground,' he broke in tersely, angry at the thought that Tara was thinking of demanding even more than he had conceded to her in the divorce settlement.

'Darling, you've been more than generous, but…do we really want this?'

The hair on the back of his neck bristled. 'What do you mean?' he snapped.

She took a deep breath. 'You know I've been out and about with a few men since our separation, but the truth is…none of them match up to you, Cole. And I know you haven't formed a relationship with anyone else. I keep thinking if David hadn't died…'

His jaw clenched.

'It just affected everything between us. We both felt so bad…' Another deep breath. 'But time helps us get over these things. We had such a good life going for us, Cole. I was thinking we should give it another shot, at least try it for a while…'

'No!' The word exploded from him, driven by a huge force of negative feelings that were impossible to contain.

'Cole…we could try for another child,' she rolled on, ignoring his response, dropping her voice to a soft throaty purr that promised more than a child. 'Let's get together tomorrow and talk about it. We could have lunch at…'

'Forget it!' he bit out, hating what could only be a self-serving offer. Tara had never *really* wanted a child, hadn't cared enough about David to spend loving time with him. The nanny had done everything

Cole hadn't done himself for his son—the nanny who'd been more distraught than Tara when…

'I'll be lunching with Mum tomorrow,' he stated coldly, emphasising the fact he was not about to change any plans at this point. 'I won't be doing anything to stop the divorce going through. We reached the end of our relationship a long time ago, Tara, and I have no inclination whatsoever to revive it.'

'Surely a little reunion wouldn't hurt. If we could just talk…'

'I said forget it. I mean precisely that.'

He put the receiver down, switched off his computer, got up and strode out of the office, the urge for some intense, mind-numbing activity driving him to head for the private gymnasium where he worked out a couple of times a week.

He didn't want sex with his almost ex-wife.

It was sex that had drawn him into marrying Tara Summerville in the first place. Sex on legs. That was Tara. It had blinded him to everything else about her until well after the wedding. And there he'd been, trapped by a passionate obsession which had gradually waned under one disillusionment after another.

He might have held the marriage together for David's sake, but he certainly didn't want back in. No way. Never. If he ever married again it would be to someone like…he smiled ironically as Liz Hart popped into his mind.

Liz, who was valiantly trying to rise above being dumped by her long-term lover, revamping herself so effectively she'd stirred up feelings that Cole now recognised as totally inappropriate to both time and circumstance.

No doubt Liz was currently very vulnerable to being desired. It was probably the best antidote for the poison of rejection. But he was the wrong man in the wrong place to take advantage of the situation. She needed to count on him as her boss, not suddenly be presented with a side of him that had nothing to do with work.

Still the thought persisted that Liz Hart could be the perfect antidote to the long poisonous hangover from Tara.

Crazy idea.

Better work that out of his mind, too.

CHAPTER FIVE

FORTUNATELY, Liz wasn't kept waiting long at the medical centre. The doctor checked off the innoculations on the yellow card which went straight into the passport folder, along with the reissued tickets and all the other paperwork now acquired for the trip to South-East Asia. *Done,* Liz thought, and wished she was flying off tomorrow instead of having to accompany Cole Pierson to his mother's home.

It was quite scary how conscious she'd become of him as a man. All this time she'd kept him slotted under the heading of her boss—an undeniably male boss but the male part had only been a gender thing, not a sexual thing. This past week she'd found herself looking at him differently, reacting to him differently, even letting her mind dwell on how very attractive he was, especially when he smiled.

As she pushed through the evening peak hour commuter horde and boarded the train for Bondi Junction, she decided it had to be her sisters' fault, prompting her into reassessing Cole through their eyes. Though it was still a huge reach to consider him a possible marriage prospect. First would have to come…no, don't think about steps towards intimacy.

If her mind started wandering along those lines while she was riding with him in his car tomorrow, it could lead her into some dubious response or glance that Cole might interpret as trouble where he didn't want trouble. As it was, he was probably putting two and two together and coming up with a readily predictable answer—boyfriend gone plus new image equals man-hunting.

She would die if he thought for one moment she was hunting him. Because she wasn't. No way would she put her job at risk, which would certainly be the case if anything personal between them didn't work out. Bad enough that this trip with his mother had bared private matters that were changing the parameters of how they dealt with each other.

It didn't feel *safe* anymore.

It felt even less safe to have Cole Pierson coming to her home tomorrow, picking her up and bringing her back. Liz brooded over how he'd torpedoed her alternative plan, making the whole thing terribly personal by questioning her about Brendan and commenting on the aborted relationship.

She must have alighted from the train at Bondi Junction and walked to her apartment on automatic pilot, because nothing impinged on her occupied mind until she heard her telephone ringing in the kitchen.

It was Diana on the line. 'How did it go today?' Eager to hear some exciting result that would make all her efforts worthwhile.

'My arm is sore from the injections,' Liz replied, instinctively shying from revealing anything else.

'Oh, come on, Liz. That bronze dress was the pièce de résistance. It had to get a rise from him.'

'Well, he did notice it…' making her feel very self-conscious a number of times '…but he didn't *say* anything.'

Diana laughed. 'It's working. It's definitely working.'

'It might be angry notice, you know,' Liz argued. 'I told you how he reacted on Monday.'

'Pure shock. Which was what he needed to start seeing you in a different light. And don't worry about anger. Anger's good. Shows you've got to him.'

'But I'm not sure I want to get to him, Diana. It's been a very…uneasy…week.'

'No pain, no gain.'

Liz rolled her eyes at this flippant dictum. 'Look!' she cried in exasperation. 'It was different for you. A fashion buyer operates largely on her own, not under her boss's nose on a daily basis. There was room for you to pursue the attraction without causing any threat to your work situation.'

'You're getting yourself into a totally unnecessary twist, Liz. Cole Pierson is the kind of man who'll do the running. All you have to do is look great, say *yes,* and let things happen.'

'But what if…'

'Give that managing mind of yours a rest for once,' Diana broke in with a huff of impatience. 'Spontaneity is the key. Go with the flow and see where it takes you.'

To not being able to pay the mortgage if I lose my job, Liz thought. Yet there was something insidiously tempting about Diana's advice. She'd been *managing* everything for so long—*stifling* Brendan—and where had it got her?

On the discard shelf.

And Diana was right about Cole. He'd rolled right over the arrangements she'd tried to manage for tomorrow. If there was any running to be done, he'd certainly do it his way. Of course the choice to say yes or no was hers, but where either answer might lead was still very tricky.

'Maybe nothing will happen,' she said in her confusion over whether she wanted it to or not.

'He's taking you to a meeting with his mother tomorrow, isn't he?'

Liz wished she hadn't blabbed quite so much to Diana on Monday night. 'It's just about the trip,' she muttered.

'Wear the camel pants-suit with the funky tan hip belt and leave the top two buttons of the safari jacket undone,' came the marching orders.

'That's too obvious.' The three buttons left undone on her skirt today had played havoc with her nerves every time Cole had glanced down.

'No, it's not. It simply telegraphs the fact you're not buttoned up anymore. And use that *Red* perfume by Giorgio. It smells great on you.'

'I'm not good at this, Diana.'

'Just do as I say. Got to go now. Ward's arrived home. Good luck tomorrow and don't forget to smile a lot.'

Liz released a long, heavy sigh as she put the receiver down. This linking her up with Cole Pierson was turning into a personal crusade for her younger sister. Liz had tried to dampen it down, to no avail. She had the helter-skelter feeling that wheels had been set in motion on Monday and she had no control over where they were going.

At least she'd had little time to feel depressed over her single state. This weekend could have looked bleak and empty without Brendan. Instead of fretting over how to act with Cole, she should be grateful that the Piersons—mother and son—had filled up tomorrow for her.

Besides, she had Diana's instructions to follow and she carried them out to the letter the next morning, telling herself the outfit would undoubtedly please Nancy Pierson's sense of rightness. Classy casual. Perfect for a visit to a Palm Beach residence, which was definitely in millionaire territory. After all, she did want to assure Cole's mother she was a suitable companion for her in every way.

Her doorbell rang at five minutes to ten. Cole had either given himself more time than he needed to get here, or was keen to get going. Liz grabbed her handbag on the way to the door, intent on presenting herself as ready to leave immediately. She wasn't expecting to have her breathing momentarily paralysed at sight of him, but then she'd never seen him dressed in anything other than an impeccably tailored suit.

Blatant macho virility hit her right in the face. He wore a black polo sweater, black leather jacket, black leather gloves, black jeans, his thick black hair was slightly mussed, adding an air of wild vitality, and his eyes were an electric blue, shooting a bolt of shock straight through Liz's heart.

'Hi!' he said, actually grinning at her. 'You might

need a scarf for your hair. It's a glorious morning so I've put the hood of my car down.'

Scarf…the tiger print scarf for this outfit, she could hear Diana saying. 'Won't be a moment,' she managed to get out and wheeled away, heading for her bedroom to the beat of a suddenly drumming heart, leaving him standing outside her apartment, not even thinking to invite him in. Her mind was stuck on the word, scarf, probably because it served to block out everything else.

Despite the speedy collection of this accessory, Cole had stepped into her living room and was glancing around when she emerged from the bedroom. 'Good space. Nice high ceilings,' he commented appreciatively.

'Built in the nineteen thirties,' she explained on her way to the door, feeling his intrusion too keenly to let him linger in her home.

'Do you own or rent?' he asked curiously.

'It's partly mine. I'm paying off the bank.'

'Fine investment,' he approved.

'I think so. Though primarily I wanted a place of my own.'

'Most women acquire a home through marriage,' he said with a slightly cynical edge.

Or through divorce, Liz thought, wondering how much his almost ex-wife had taken him for and whether that experience had contributed to his detachment from the human race.

'Well, I wasn't counting on that happening,' she said dryly, holding the door and waving him out—a pointed gesture which was ignored.

'You like your independence?' he asked, cocking a quizzical eyebrow at her.

She shrugged. 'Not particularly. I've just found it's better to only count on what I know I can count on.'

'Hard lesson to learn,' he remarked sympathetically.

Had he learnt it, too?

Liz held her tongue. He was finally moving out, waiting for her to lock the door behind them. She didn't know what to think of the probing nature of his conversation. Or was it just casual chat? Maybe she was too used to Cole's habit of never saying anything without purpose.

Still, the sense of being targeted on a personal level persisted and it was some relief that he didn't speak at all as they descended the flight of stairs to street level. Perversely the silence made her more physically aware of him as he walked beside her. She was glad when they emerged into the open air.

It was, indeed, a glorious morning. There was something marvellous about winter sunshine—the warmth and brightness it delivered, the crisp blue of a cloudless sky banishing all thought of cold grey. It lifted one's spirits with its promise of a great day.

'Lucky we don't have to be shut up in the office,' Liz said impulsively, the words accompanied by a smile she couldn't repress.

'An unexpected pleasure,' Cole replied, his smile raising tingles of warmth the sun hadn't yet bestowed.

Liz was piqued into remarking, 'I thought work was the be-all and end-all for you.'

His laser-like eyes actually twinkled at her. 'My life does extend a little further than that.'

Her heart started fluttering. Was he *flirting?* 'Well, obviously, you do care about your mother.'

'Mmmh…a few other things rate my attention, too.'

His slanted look at her caused a skip in her pulse beat and provoked Liz into open confrontation. 'Like what?'

He laughed. He actually laughed. Liz was shocked into staring at him, never having seen or heard Cole Pierson laugh before. It was earth-shaking stuff. He suddenly appeared much younger, happily carefree, and terribly, terribly attractive. The blue eyes danced at her with wicked amusement, causing her to flush in confusion.

'What's so funny?' she demanded.

'Me…you…and here we are.' Still grinning, he gestured to the kerb, redirecting her gaze to the car parked beside it.

Hood down, he'd said, alerting her to the fact that he had to be driving some kind of convertible. If anything, Liz would have assumed a BMW roadster or a Mercedes sports, maybe even a Rolls-Royce Corniche—very expensive, of course, but in a classy conventional style, like his Armani suits.

It was simply impossible to relate the car she was seeing to the boss she knew. She stared at the low-slung, glamorous, silver speed machine in shocked disbelief, her feet rooted on the sidewalk as Cole moved forward and opened the passenger door for her.

'You drive…a Maserati?' Her voice emerged like a half-strangled squawk.

'Uh-huh. The Spyder Cambio Corsa,' he elaborated, naming the model for her.

'A Maserati,' she repeated, looking her astonishment at him.

'Something wrong with it?'

She shook her head, belatedly connecting his current sexy clothes to the sexy car and blurting out, 'This is such a change of image…'

'Welcome to the club,' he said sardonically.

'I beg your pardon?'

She was totally lost with this Cole Pierson, as though he'd changed all the dimensions of his previous persona, emerging as a completely different force to be reckoned with. To top off her sense of everything shifting dangerously between them, he gave her a sizzling head-to-toe appraisal that had her entire skin surface prickling with heat.

'You can hardly deny you've subjected me to a change of image this week, Liz,' he drawled, 'And that was at work, not at play.'

Was he admitting the same kind of disturbance she was feeling now? Whatever…the old boat was being severely rocked on many levels.

'So this is you…at play,' she said in a weak attempt to set things right again.

'One part of me.' There was a challenging glint in his eyes as he waved an invitation to the slinky low black leather passenger seat. 'Shall we go?'

Diana's voice echoed through her head… *Go with the flow.*

Liz forced her feet forward and dropped herself onto the seat as gracefully as she could, swinging her legs in afterwards. 'Thanks,' she murmured as the door was closed for her, then trying for a light note, she smiled and added, 'Nothing like a new experience.'

'You've never ridden in a high-performance car?' he queried as he swung around to the driver's side.

'First time,' she admitted.

'Seems like we're clocking up a few first times between us.'

How many more, Liz thought wildly, acutely aware of him settling in the seat next to her, strong thigh muscles stretching the fabric of his jeans.

'Seat belt,' he reminded her as he fastened his own.

'Right!'

He watched her pull it across her body and click it into place. It made Liz extremely conscious of the belt bisecting her breasts, emphasising their curves.

'Scarf.' Another reminder.

She flushed, quickly spreading the long filmy tiger-print fabric over her hair, winding it around her neck and tying the floating ends at the back.

'Sunglasses.'

It was like a countdown to take-off.

Luckily she always carried sunglasses in her handbag. Having whipped them out and slipped them on, she dared a look at him through the tinted lenses.

He gave her a devil-may-care grin as he slid his own onto his nose. 'You want to watch those jungle prints, Liz. Makes me wonder if you're yearning for a ride on the wild side.'

Without waiting for a reply—which was just as well because she was too flummoxed to think of one—he switched on the engine, put the car into gear, and they were off, the sun in their faces, a wind whipping past, and all sorts of wild things zipping through Liz's mind.

CHAPTER SIX

LIZ couldn't help feeling it was fantastic, riding around in a Maserati. The powerful acceleration of the car meant they could zip into spaces in the traffic that would have closed for less manoeuvrable vehicles. Pedestrians stared enviously at it when they were stopped at traffic lights. They looked at her and Cole, too, probably speculating about who they were, mentally matching them up to the luxurious lifestyle that had to go with such a dream car. After one such stop, Liz was so amused by this she burst out laughing.

'What's tickling your sense of humour?' Cole inquired.

'I feel like the Queen of Sheba and a fraud at the same time,' she answered, grinning at the madness of her being seen as belonging to a Maserati, which couldn't be further than the truth.

'Explain.'

The typical economical command put her on familiar ground again with Cole. 'It's the car,' she answered happily. 'Because I'm your passenger, people are seeing me as someone who has to be special.'

'And you think that's funny?'

'Well, it is, isn't it? I mean you are who you are...but I'm just your employee.'

'Oh, I don't know.' His mouth quirked as he

glanced at her. 'You do have a touch of the Queen of Sheba about you today.'

This comment wasn't boss-like at all. Liz tried to laugh it off but wasn't sure the laughter sounded natural. She was glad he was wearing sunglasses, dimming the expression in the piercing blue eyes. As it was, the soft drawl of his voice had curled around her stomach, making it flutter.

'And why shouldn't they think you're special?' he continued with a longer glance at her. 'I do.'

Liz took a deep breath, desperate to regather her scattered wits. 'That's not the point, Cole. I mean...this car...your wealth...I'm sure you take it all for granted, but it's not me.'

'Do you categorise anyone born to wealth as *special?*' he demanded critically.

'Well...they're at least privileged.'

'Privileged, yes. Which, more times than not, means spoiled, not special.' He shook his head. 'I bought a Maserati because I like high performance. You've remained my P.A. because you give me high performance, too. In my view, you match this car more than any other woman who has ridden in that passenger seat.'

More than the fabulous Tara Summerville?

Liz couldn't believe it.

Unless Cole had acquired the Maserati *after* the separation with his wife.

On second thoughts, he'd been talking performance, not appearance, which reduced the compliment to a work-related thing, puncturing Liz's bubble of pleasure.

'You know, being compared favourably to how well an engine runs doesn't exactly make a woman feel special, Cole,' she dryly informed him.

He laughed. 'So how do I answer you? Hmm...' His brow furrowed in concentration. 'I think you were being a fraud to yourself all the time you were with Brendan, but now you're free of him, the real you has emerged in a blaze of glory and everyone is seeing the shine and recognising how special you are, so you're not a fraud today.' He grinned at her. 'How's that?'

She had to laugh. It was over the top stuff but it did make her feel good, as though she really had shed the miserable cloak of feeling less—deserving less— than her beautiful sisters. 'It wasn't so much Brendan's influence,' she felt obliged to confess. 'I guess I've had a problem with self-esteem for a long time.'

'What on earth for?' he demanded, obviously seeing no cause for it.

She shook her head, not wanting to get into analysing her life. 'Let me relish *blaze of glory*. I can smile over that for the rest of the trip.' Suiting action to words, she gave him her best smile.

He shook his head, still puzzled. 'Would it help for you to know I hold you in the highest esteem?'

'Thank you. It's very kind of you to say so.'

'I can hear a *but* in there.'

Her smile turned rueful. 'I guess what you're giving me is respect for what I can carry out for you. And I'm glad to have your respect. Please don't think I'm not. But I've never felt...incompetent...in that area, Cole. Though I have wondered if being too damned smart is more a curse than a blessing.'

'It's a gift. And it's stupid not to use it. You won't be happy within yourself if you try denying it. You know perfectly well it pleases you to get things right, Liz.'

'Mmmh…but I'm not happy living in a world of my own. I want…' She stopped, realising just how personal this conversation had become, and how embarrassing it might be in retrospect, especially on Monday when she had to face Cole at work again.

'Go on,' he pressed.

She tried shrugging it off. 'Oh, all the usual things a woman wants.'

'Fair enough.'

To Liz's immense relief, he let it go at that. She'd been running off at the mouth, drawn into speaking from her heart instead of her head, all because Cole had somehow invaded her private life and was involving himself in it.

Her gaze drifted to the leather gloved hands on the steering wheel. Power controlling power. A convulsive little shiver of excitement warned her she should get her mind right off tempting fantasies. But it was very difficult with Cole looking as he did, driving this car, and dabbling in highly personal conversation.

She did her best to focus on the passing scenery, a relatively easy task once they hit the road along the northern beaches, passing through Dee Why, Collaroy, Narrabeen, then further on, Bilgola, Avalon, Whale Beach. Apart from the attraction of sand and sea, there were some fabulous homes along the way, making the most of million dollar views. Liz had never actually visited this part of Sydney, knew it only by repute, so it was quite fascinating to see it firsthand.

Finally they came to Palm Beach, right at the end of the peninsula, where large mansions overlooked the ocean on one side and Pittwater the other. Cole turned the Maserati into a semicircular driveway for what looked like a palatial Mediterranean villa with many colonnaded verandahs. It was painted a creamy pink and positively glowed in the sunshine. A fountain of dolphins was centred on the front lawn and a hedge of glorious pink and cream Hawaiian hibiscus lined the driveway.

'Wow!' Liz breathed.

'It is far too large for my mother, requires mountainous maintenance, but she won't leave it,' Cole said in a tone of weary resignation.

'Neither would I,' Liz replied feelingly, turned chiding eyes to Nancy's son. 'She must love it. Leaving would be a terrible wrench.'

Cole sighed. 'She's alone. She's getting old. And she's a long way out from the city.'

Liz understood his point. 'You worry about her.'

He brought the Maserati to a halt, switched off the engine. 'She is my mother,' he stated in the sudden quiet.

And he loved her, thereby passing the functional family background test, unlike Brendan. Liz clamped down on the wayward thought and pushed her mind back onto track.

'I *will* look after her on this trip, Cole.'

He smiled. 'I know I can count on you. And while your ex-boyfriend may not have appreciated your responsible streak, I do. And I don't count on many people for anything.'

Over the past year she had considered him totally self-sufficient. Coldly self-sufficient. It gave Liz a rush of warm pleasure to hear him express some dependence on her, even if it was only peripheral.

No man is an island, she thought.

No woman is, either.

Liz was very conscious of needs that remained unanswered. They'd just been highlighted by Cole's comparing himself to Brendan.

Deliberately highlighted?

For what purpose?

He took off his sunglasses and tucked them into the top pocket of his leather jacket. Liz was prompted into taking hers off, too. She was about to meet his mother again and she didn't need any defensive barrier with Nancy Pierson.

'Want to remove your scarf before we go inside?'

She'd forgotten the scarf, forgotten her hair. Cole sat watching as she quickly unwound the protective cover and tucked it under the collar of her jacket, letting the ends fall loose down the front. Having whipped out a brush from her handbag, she fluffed up her flattened hair and trusted that she hadn't eaten off her lipstick because painting her mouth under Cole's gaze was not on. As it was, she was super conscious of him observing her actions and their effect.

'Okay?' she asked, turning to show herself for his approval.

His eyes weren't their usual ice blue. They seemed to simmer over her face and hair, evoking a flush as he drawled, 'All things bright and beautiful.'

Then he was out of the car and at the passenger door before Liz found the presence of mind to release her seat belt. As she freed herself and swung her feet to the ground, he offered his hand for the long haul upright. It was an automatic response to take it, yet his grip shot an electric charge up her arm and when she rose to her full height, they were standing so close and he seemed so big, she stared at the centre of his throat rather than risk looking up and sparking any realisation of her acute physical awareness of him.

She could even smell the leather, and a hint of male cologne. His broad shoulders dwarfed hers, stirring a sense of sexual vulnerability that quite stunned her because she'd never felt overwhelmed by the close presence of any other man. And this was her boss, who should have been familiar, not striking these weird chords that threatened to change everything between them.

'I didn't realise you were so small,' he murmured in a bemused tone.

Her head jerked up as a sense of belittlement shot through her. The gold sparks in her green eyes blazed at him. 'I hate being *small*.'

His brows drew together in mock concern. 'Correction. Dainty and delicate.'

'Oh, great! Now I sound breakable.'

'Woman of steel?'

His eyes were twinkling.

She took a deep breath and summoned up a wry smile. 'Sorry. You hit a sore point. Unlike you, I was behind the door when God gave out height.'

He openly grinned. 'But you weren't behind the door when God gave out quick wit. Which you'll undoubtedly have to use to keep my mother in line.'

With that comment he led off towards the front door of the pink mansion and Liz fell into step beside him, still fiercely wishing she was as tall as her sisters, which would make her a much better physical match for him. Somehow that 'small' comment felt as though she'd been marked down in the attraction stakes.

On the other hand, she was probably suffering from an overactive imagination to think Cole was attracted at all, and she'd do well to concentrate her mind on exercising the quick wit he credited her with, because the real purpose of this trip was about to get under way.

The front door was opened just as they were stepping up onto the ground floor verandah. 'At last!' Nancy Pierson cried in a tone of pained relief.

Cole checked his watch. 'It's only just eleven, Mum.'

'I know, dear, but I've been counting the minutes since Tara arrived. You could have warned me...'

'Tara?' Cole's face instantly tightened. 'What the devil is she doing here?'

Nancy looked confused. 'She said...'

'You shouldn't have let her in.'

The confusion deepened, hands fluttering a helpless appeal. 'She *is* still your wife.'

'A technicality. One that will end next week.'

This evoked a huff of exasperation from his mother. 'Tara gave me the impression it was arranged for her to meet you here.'

'There's no such arrangement. You've been manipulated, Mum.'

'Well, I'm glad you recognise Tara's skill at doing that, Cole,' came the swift and telling retort. Clearly Nancy held no warm feelings for the woman her son had married. 'I set out morning tea in the conservatory. She's there waiting for you, making herself at home as though she had every right to.'

'Makes for one hell of a scene,' Cole ground out.

'Well, it's not my place to shut her out of your life. It's you who has to make that good. If you have a mind to.'

'Tara's made you doubt it?'

Another huff of exasperation. 'How am I supposed to know what you feel, Cole? You never talk about it. For all I know, you've been pining over that woman...'

'No way!'

'Then you'd better go and convince her of that because she's acting as though she only has to crook her little finger at you and...'

'An act is what it is, Mum.' He flashed a steely glance at Liz. 'As you've just heard, we have some unexpected company for morning tea.'

'I'll take Liz upstairs with me,' Nancy rushed out,

shooting an anguished look at her. 'I'm sorry, dear. This isn't what I planned.'

'Which is precisely why you won't scurry off with Liz,' Cole broke in tersely. 'I will not have her treated like some backroom nonentity because my almost ex-wife decides to barge in on us.'

Nancy looked shocked. 'I didn't mean...'

'It's an issue of discretion, Cole,' Liz quickly supplied. 'I don't mind giving you privacy.'

'Which plays right into Tara's scheme. We're not changing *anything* for her.' Angry pride shifted into icy command. 'Mum, you will lead back to the conservatory. Liz, you will accompany my mother as you normally would. We are going to have the morning tea which has been prepared for *us*.'

He gestured her forward, unshakable determination etched on his face. Liz glanced hesitantly at his mother whom she was supposed to be pleasing today. The anguish was gone from Nancy's expression. In fact, there seemed to be a look of smug delight in her eyes as she, too, waved Liz into the house.

'Please forgive me for not greeting you properly, dear,' she said with an apologetic smile. 'These problems in communication do throw one out.'

'Perfectly understandable,' Liz assured her. Then taking her cue from Cole's command to act normally, she smiled and said, 'I love the look of your home, Nancy. It's very welcoming.'

'How nice of you to say so!' Nancy beamed her pleasure as she hooked her arm around Liz's and drew her into a very spacious foyer, its tiled floor laid out in a fascinating mosaic pattern depicting coral and seashells. 'I picked everything myself for this house. Even these tiles on the floor.'

'They're beautiful,' Liz said in sincere admiration, trying not to be too conscious of Cole closing the door behind them, locking them into a scene that was bound to be fraught with tension and considerable unpleasantness, since Tara Summerville had obviously come expecting to gain something and Cole was intent on denying her.

Nancy continued to point out features of the house as she showed Liz through it, feeding off the interest expressed and enjoying telling little stories about various acquisitions, quite happy not to hurry back to her uninvited guest. Liz suspected Nancy was taking satisfaction in keeping Tara waiting.

Cole didn't push his mother to hurry, either, seemingly content to move at her pace, yet Liz sensed his seething impatience with the situation that had been inflicted on all of them by the woman he'd married.

He must have loved her once, Liz reasoned.

Had the love died, or had husband and wife been pulled apart by grief over the loss of their child?

She had never speculated over her boss's marriage—none of her business—but the exchange between mother and son at the door had ignited a curiosity Liz couldn't deny now. She wanted to see how Cole and Tara Summerville reacted to each other, wanted to know the cause of the ruction between them, wanted to feel Cole was now truly free of his wife...*which may not be the case.*

Surely a private meeting would have served his purpose for ending it more effectively.

Was his angry pride hiding a vulnerability to his wife's power to manipulate his feelings?

Was he using Liz and his mother as a shield, not trusting himself in a one-on-one situation?

As they approached the conservatory, Nancy's prattling began to sound nervous and the tension emanating from Cole seemed to thicken the air, causing Liz to hold her breath. She sensed something bad was about to happen.

Very bad.

And she found herself suddenly wishing she wasn't in the middle of it.

CHAPTER SEVEN

LIZ caught a quick impression of abundant ferns, exotic plants, many pots of gorgeous cyclamens in bloom, all forming a glorious backdrop to settings of cane furniture cushioned in tropical prints. However, even as she entered the conservatory her gaze was drawn to the woman seated at the far end of a long rectangular table.

'Cole, darling...' she drawled, perfect red lips pursing to blow a kiss at him as she rose from her chair, giving them all the full benefit of what the media still termed 'the body' whenever referring to Tara Summerville.

She wore a black leather jacket that moulded every curve underneath it, with enough buttons undone to promise a spillage of lush feminine flesh if one more button was popped. This was teamed with a tight little miniskirt, also in black leather, and with a front split that pointed up the apex of possibly the most photographed legs in history—long, long legs that led down to sexy little ankle high boots. A belt in black and white cowhide was slung jauntily around her hips and a black and white handkerchief scarf was tied at the base of her very long throat.

Her thick mane of tawny hair tumbled down to her shoulder-blades in highly touchable disarray and her artfully made-up amber eyes gleamed a provocative challenge at the man she was intent on targeting. Not so much as a glance at Liz. Nor at Nancy Pierson. This was full power tunnel vision at Cole and Liz suspected the whole beam of it was sizzling with sexual invitation.

'I'm glad you're on your feet, Tara,' Cole said in icy disdain of this approach. 'Just pick up your bag and keep on walking, right out of this house.'

'Very uncivil of you, darling, especially when *your mother* invited me in,' she returned with a cat-like smile, halting by a side chair and gripping the back of it, making a stand against being evicted.

'You lied to her,' came the blunt rebuttal.

'Only to get past your pride, Cole. Now that I'm here for you, why not admit that pride is…' She rolled her hips and moved her mouth into a sensual pout. '…a very cold bedfellow.'

'Waste of time and effort, Tara. Might as well move on. I have,' he stated emphatically.

'Then why haven't I heard a whisper of it?' she mocked, still exuding confidence in her ability to get to him.

'I no longer care to mix in your social circle.'

'You're *news,* Cole. There would have been tattle somewhere if you'd…*moved on.*'

'I prefer to guard my privacy these days.'

He was stonewalling, Liz thought. If there'd been any woman in his life since Tara, some evidence of the relationship would have shown up, at least to her as his personal assistant—telephone calls, bookings to be made, various arrangements. Was it pride, resisting the offer Tara was blatantly making? Or did he truly not want her anymore?

'Don't tell me you've taken to slumming it,' Tara tossed at him derisively.

'Not every woman has your need for the limelight,' Cole returned, icy disdain back in his voice. 'And since I'll never be a party to it again, I strongly recommend you go and find yourself a fellow game player to shine with. You're not about to win anything here.'

Her eyes narrowed, not caring to look defeat in the face. For the first time, her gaze slid to Liz. A quick up and down appraisal left her feeling she'd been raked to the bone. The fact that Nancy was still hugging her arm didn't go unnoticed, either. Without any warning, Tara flashed a bolt of venom at Cole's mother.

'You never did like me, did you, Nancy?'

Liz felt the older woman stiffen under the direct attack, but she was not lacking in firepower herself. 'It's difficult to like such a totally self-centred person as yourself, Tara,' she said with crisp dignity.

A savagely mocking smile was aimed right back at her. 'No doubt you've been producing sweet little protégées for Cole ever since I left.' Her glittering gaze moved to Liz. 'So who and what is this one?'

'*I* brought Liz with me,' Cole stated tersely. 'Her presence here has nothing to do with you and your exit is long overdue.'

'*Your* choice, Cole?' One finely arched eyebrow rose in amused query. 'In place of *me?*'

The comparison was meant to humiliate, but on

seeing his wife in the flesh again, Liz had already conceded she'd never be able to compete in the looks department. She just didn't have the female equipment Tara Summerville had. Not even close to it. But since it could be argued there was something positive to be said for an admirable character and an appealing personality—neither of which was overly evident in Cole's wife—the nasty barb didn't hit too deeply. What actually hurt more was Cole's response to it.

'Oh, for God's sake! Liz has been my personal assistant for the past three years. You used to waltz past her on your way to my office in times gone by, though typically, you probably didn't bother noticing her.'

It was a curt dismissal of the *his choice* tag, implying there was no chance of her ever being anything more than his personal assistant. It shouldn't have felt like a stab to her heart, but it did.

'The little brown mouse!' Tara cried incredulously, then tossed her head back as laughter trilled from her throat.

Liz's stomach knotted. She knew intuitively that Tara Summerville hadn't finished with her. The nerve-jangling laughter was bound to have a nasty point to it. The amber eyes glinted maliciously at her as the remarks rolled.

'How handy, being Cole's P.A.! Saw your chance and took it, jazzing yourself up, making yourself *available,* and here you are, getting your hooks into Mummy, as well, playing Miss All-Round-Perfect.'

The rush of blood to Liz's head was so severe she didn't hear what Cole said, only the angry bark of his voice. She saw the response to it though, Tara swinging back to pick up her bag, slinging the strap of it over her shoulder, strutting towards Cole, pausing to deliver one last broadside.

'You've been *had,* Cole. No doubt she's hitting all the right chords for you...but I bet she can't match me in bed. Think about it, darling. It's not too late to change your mind.'

Both of them left the conservatory, Tara leading off like a victor who'd done maximum damage, Cole squeezing Liz's shoulder first in a silent gesture of appreciation for her forebearance, then following Tara out to enforce her departure and possibly have the last word before she left.

Liz was so sick with embarrassment, she didn't know what to do or say. The worst of it was, Tara had literally been echoing Diana's calculated plan to *get the boss.* While that had not been part of Liz's motivation for going along with her sisters' makeover plan, Tara's accusations had her squirming with guilt over the feelings that had emerged this past week, the growing desire for Cole to find her attractive.

Fortunately, Nancy moved straight into hostess mode, drawing Liz over to the table and filling the awkward silence with a torrent of words. 'Tara always did make an ugly scene when she wasn't getting her own way. You mustn't take anything she said to heart, dear. Pure spite. You just sit yourself down and relax and I'll make us a fresh pot of tea. Help yourself to a pastry or a scone with strawberry jam and cream. That's Cole's favourite. I always make him Devonshire tea.'

Liz sat. Her gaze skated distractedly over a selection of small Danish pastries with fillings of glazed fruit—apricot, apple, peach—the plate of scones beside dishes of cream and strawberry jam. Nothing prompted an appetite. She thought she would choke on food.

Nancy moved to what was obviously a drinks bar, easily accessible to the swimming pool beyond the conservatory. She busied herself behind it, apparently unaffected by the suggestion that Liz and Cole were having an affair, though she must be suspecting it now, adding in the fact that Cole had arranged for his P.A. to accompany her on a pleasure trip. It was, after all, an extraordinary thing to do, given there was no closer connection between them than boss and employee.

Liz couldn't bear Nancy thinking she was Cole's mistress on the side. It made her seem underhand, sleazy, hiding the intimacy from his mother, pretending everything was straight and aboveboard.

'I'm not having a secret affair with Cole. I've never slept with him...or...or anything like that,' she blurted out, compelled to clear any murkiness from their relationship.

Nancy looked up from her tea-making, startled by the emphatic claim. Her blue eyes were very direct, projecting absolute certainty as she replied, 'I have no doubt whatsoever about that, dear. I questioned Cole about you before we met on Monday. His answers revealed...' She heaved a deep sigh. '...he only thought of you as very capable.'

The flush in Liz's cheeks still burned. Although she'd known Cole had not been aware of her as a woman, certainly not before this past week, that truth was not quite so absolute now. He *was* seeing her differently, and even though it might not *mean* what Diana wanted it to mean, Liz couldn't let Tara's interpretation of her changed appearance go unanswered.

'I'm not out to *get* him, either.'

Nancy heaved another deep sigh, then gave her a sad little smile. 'I almost wish you were, dear, but I don't think it's in your nature.'

It startled Liz out of her wretched angst. 'You wish...?'

'I probably shouldn't say this...' Nancy's grimace revealed her own inner angst. '...but I'm very afraid Cole is still stuck on Tara. What she said is all too true. And I'm sure you must know it, as well. There hasn't been any other woman in his life since she left him. It's like he's sealed himself off from every normal social connection.'

Liz nodded. She was well acquainted with *the untouchable ice man.*

Nancy rattled on, voicing her main concern. 'But if Tara is now determined on getting her hooks into him again...' A shake of the head. 'I can only hope Cole has the good sense to go through with the divorce and have done with her.'

Liz kept her mouth shut. It wasn't appropriate for her to comment on Cole's personal life when it had nothing to do with her. The stress of Tara's visit had wrung this confidence from Nancy, just as it had driven Liz to defend herself. Where the truth lay about Cole's feelings for his wife, she had no idea.

Though now that Nancy had spelled out her viewpoint, it did seem he had to be carrying a lot of emotional baggage from his marriage—baggage he'd systematically buried under intensive work.

Was the physical confrontation with his wife stirring it all up? He hadn't come back from seeing her out of the house. Maybe they were still talking, arguing as couples do when neither of them really wanted to let go. Any foothold—even a bitter one— was better than none. And Cole was unhampered by witnesses now. What if Tara had thrown her arms around him, physically pressing for a resumption of intimacy? Was it possible for him to be totally immune to what 'the body' was offering?

A sick depression rolled through Liz. Cole had only noticed her this past week because *the little brown mouse* didn't fit that label anymore. Which was probably still an annoyance to him. Or a curiosity, given his questioning about Brendan. Nothing to do with a sudden attraction which she'd probably fabricated out of her own secret wanting it to be so.

A foolish fantasy.

Why on earth would a man like him—a handsome billionaire—be attracted to her when he could snap his fingers and have the Tara Summervilles of this world? She must have been mad to let Diana influence her thinking. Or desperate to feel something excitingly positive after being dumped by Brendan.

'Oh! There's Cole with the tradesman!' Nancy cried in relief.

The remark halted Liz's miserable reverie and directed her gaze out to the pool area where Nancy was looking. Cole was, indeed, with another man, pointing out a section of paving and leading him towards it.

'He must have arrived while Cole was seeing Tara out. They've come down the side path,' Nancy prattled on, her spirits perking up at this evidence that her son's delayed return did not mean he was being vamped by his almost ex-wife. 'The appointment was at eleven o'clock, after all. So fortuitous.'

It didn't guarantee that Cole had maintained his rejection of any reunion, but it certainly minimised the opportunity for persuasion on his wife's part. Liz found herself hoping that Tara had not *won* anything from him, and not just because of being interrupted by the arrival of the tradesman. Nancy didn't like the woman and Liz certainly had no reason to. But no doubt the power of sex could turn some men blind to everything else.

'Now we can enjoy our morning tea,' Nancy declared, carrying an elegant china teapot to the table and setting it down with an air of happy satisfaction. Clearly danger had been averted in her mind. She settled on the chair opposite to Liz's and eyed her with bright curiosity.

'Pardon me for asking, dear, but was it just this week that you...uh...jazzed yourself up?'

'During my vacation,' Liz answered, not minding the question from Nancy, knowing she could find out from Cole anyway. 'My sisters ganged up on me, saying I'd let myself become drab, and hauled me off to do their Cinderella trick.'

'Well, whatever they did, you do look lovely.'

'Thank you.'

'Tea?'

'Yes, please.'

Nancy poured. 'So you came back to work on Monday with a new image,' she said, smiling encouragement.

'Yes.'

'Did Cole notice any difference?'

Liz grimaced. 'He didn't like it.'

'Didn't like how you looked?'

'Didn't like me looking different, I think.' Liz shrugged. 'No doubt he'll get used to it.'

'Milk and sugar?'

Liz shook her head. 'Just as it is, thank you.'

'Do have a scone, dear.'

Liz took one out of politeness, though she did feel calmer now and thought there'd be no problem with swallowing. It was a relief to have Nancy understanding her situation. It would have been extremely uncomfortable accompanying Cole's mother on the trip, with her still thinking all sorts of horribly false things.

Having cut the scone in half, Liz was conscientiously spooning strawberry jam and cream onto her plate when her ragged nerves received another jolt.

'Oh, good! Cole is coming in for his tea,' Nancy announced, causing Liz to jerk around in her chair to see her boss skirting the pool and heading for the conservatory, having left the tradesman to measure the paving area and calculate the cost of the work to be done.

Totally mortified by the tide of heat that rushed up her neck again, Liz focused hard on transferring the jam and cream to the halved scone. If she shoved the food into her mouth and appeared to be eating, she reasoned that Cole might only speak to his mother. It might be a cowardly tactic but she didn't feel up to coping with his penetrating gaze and probing questions. She didn't even want to look at him. He might have lipstick smudged on his mouth.

Which was none of her business!

Why she felt so violent about that she didn't know and didn't want to know. She just wanted to be left out of anything to do with Tara Summerville.

She heard a glass door slide open behind her and it felt as though a whoosh of electric energy suddenly permeated the air. Her hands started trembling. It stopped her from lifting the scone to her mouth. She glared at her plate, hating being affected like this. It wasn't fair. She'd done nothing wrong.

'Liz…'

She gritted her teeth.

He had no right to put her on the spot, commanding her attention when they weren't even at work. She was here in her spare time, as a favour to his mother, not as *his* personal assistant.

'Are you okay?' he asked, amazingly in a tone of concern.

Pride whipped her head around to face him. There was no trace of red lipstick on his mouth. His expression was one of taut determination, the piercing blue eyes intensely concentrated, aimed at searching her mind for any trouble.

Her chin tilted in direct challenge as she stated, 'I have no reason not to be okay.'

He gave a slow nod. 'I didn't anticipate a collateral hit from Tara. I regret you were subjected to it.'

'A hit only works if there's damage done. I've assured your mother there's no truth in what was assumed about me…and you.' *And don't you dare think otherwise,* she fiercely telegraphed to him.

His gaze flicked sharply to Nancy. 'You didn't believe that rank bitchiness, did you, Mum?'

'No, dear. And I told Liz so.'

'Right! No harm done then,' he said, apparently satisfied. 'Got to get back to check that this guy knows what's he's quoting on.'

'What about your tea?' Nancy asked.

'I'll have it later.'

He stepped outside, closed the door, and to all intents and purposes, the nasty incident with Tara Summerville was also closed. Liz certainly wasn't about to bring the subject up again. She realised her hands were clenched in her lap and consciously relaxed them. The scone was waiting to be eaten. She'd eat it if it killed her. It proved she was okay.

'Well, isn't that nice?' Nancy remarked, beaming pleasure at her as Liz lifted one half of the scone from her plate.

She looked blankly at Cole's mother, completely lost on whatever had struck her as *nice*.

'He cares about you, dear.' This said with a benevolent smile that thoroughly approved of the supposed caring.

Liz felt too frazzled to argue the point.

She only hoped that Cole had completely dismissed the idea—planted by Tara—that his personal assistant was focused far more on climbing into bed with him than doing the work she was employed to do.

CHAPTER EIGHT

MAKE another baby...

Cole seethed over Tara's last toss at him and all the memories it aroused. He ended up accepting the quotation for the paving work around the pool without even questioning it. He didn't care if the guy was overcharging. As long as the job was done by a reputable tradesman, the cost was irrelevant. All the money in the world could not buy back the life of the baby son he'd lost. Though it could obviously buy back a wife who was prepared to pay lip-service to being a mother again.

A mother...

What a black joke that was!

And the gross insensitivity of Tara's even thinking he'd consider her proposition was typical of her total lack of empathy to how he felt. God! He wouldn't want her in the same house as any child of his, let alone being the biological mother to it, having the power to affect its upbringing in so many negative ways.

David had only ever been a show-off baby to her—trotting him out in designer clothes when it suited her, ignoring him when he needed her. *Their son* hadn't even left a hole in her life when he died, and she'd resented the huge hole he'd left in Cole's—impatient with his grief, ranting about how cold he was to her,

93

seeking more cheerful company because he was such *a drag.*

Did Tara imagine he could forget all that just because they'd started out having great sex and she still had 'the body' to excite him again if she put her mind to it?

He hadn't even felt a tingle in his groin when she'd tried her come-on this morning.

Not a tingle.

Though he had felt a blaze of fury when she'd painted Liz in her own manipulative colours, casting her as a calculating seductress, mocking her efforts to look more attractive. Which she certainly did, though Cole had no doubt the change had been motivated by a need to lift herself out of the doldrums caused by Brendan's defection. Nothing to do with him.

If Liz withered back into a little brown mouse now...because of Tara's bitchiness...Cole seethed over that, too, as he made his way back to the conservatory after seeing the tradesman off. Liz had insisted she was okay, but she hadn't wanted to look at him when he'd asked. When she had turned to answer, her eyes had been all glittery, her cheeks red hot. She'd denied any damage done but Cole suspected her newly grown confidence in herself as a woman had been badly undermined. He wanted to fix that but how...?

Liz and his mother were gone from the conservatory by the time he returned to it, Just as well, since he had no ready antidote for Tara's poison. At least he could trust his mother to be kind to Liz, involve her in the business of packing for their trip. Probably overkind, trying to make up for the nasty taste left behind by her uninvited guest.

He'd made one hell of a mistake marrying that woman. Five more days and the divorce would become final. Thursday. It couldn't come fast enough for Cole.

He made himself a fresh pot of tea, wolfed down a couple of scones, found the morning newspaper and concentrated on shutting Tara out of his mind. She didn't deserve space in it and he wouldn't give it to her.

Having read everything he deemed worth reading, he was attacking the cryptic crossword when his mother returned to the conservatory, wheeling a traymobile loaded with lunch things. Liz trailed behind her, looking anywhere but at him.

'Well, we've worked everything out for the trip,' his mother declared with satisfaction. 'Do clear the table of that newspaper, Cole. And if you'd open a good bottle of red—Cabernet Sauvignon?'

'What are we eating?' he asked, hoping some mundane conversation would make Liz feel more relaxed in his company.

'Lasagne and salad and crispy bread, followed by caramelised pears. And we must hurry because Liz needs to do some shopping and it's after one o'clock already.'

'How much shopping?' he asked as he moved to the bar. 'Mum, have you been pressing Liz to buy a whole lot of stuff to fit what *you* think is needed?'

'Only a few things,' she answered airily. 'Liz didn't understand about the colonial night at The

Strand Hotel in Rangoon where the ladies are invited to wear white, and…'

'Surely it's not obligatory.'

'That's not the point, dear. It's the spirit of the thing.'

He frowned, wondering how much expense his mother was notching up for her companion—costs he simply hadn't envisaged. 'I didn't mean for Liz to be out of pocket over this trip.'

His mother gave him one of those limpidly innocent smiles that spelled trouble. 'Then you could take her shopping so she'll feel right…everywhere we go together.'

'No!' Liz looked horrified by the suggestion, stopping in her setting of cutlery on the table to make a firm stand on the issue. 'You're giving me the trip free, Cole,' she reminded him with vigour. 'And Nancy, I'll get plenty of use out of what I buy anyway. It's no problem.'

The line was drawn and her eyes fiercely defied either of them to cross it.

Cole felt the line all through lunch.

He was her boss.

She was here on assignment.

She would oblige his mother in every way in regard to the trip, but the block on any personal rapport with the man who employed her was rigidly adhered to. She barely looked at him and avoided acknowledging his presence as much as she could without being openly rude. It was very clear to him that what Tara had said about her—and him—was preying on Liz's mind.

It was even worse in the car travelling back into the city. She sat almost scrunched up in the passenger seat, making herself as small as possible, her hands tightly interlinked in her lap. No joy in riding in the Maserati this time, though Cole sensed she was willing the car to go as fast as it could, wanting the trip over and done with so she could get away from him.

It made him angry.

He hated Tara's power to do this to her.

Just because Liz wasn't built like Tara didn't make her less attractive in her own individual way. He liked the new hairstyle on her. It was perky. Drew more attention to her face, too, which had a bright vitality that was very appealing. Very watchable. Particularly her eyes. A lot of power in those sparkly green eyes. As for her figure, certainly on the petite side, but definitely feminine. Sexy, too, in the clothes she'd been wearing. Not in your face sexy. More subtle. Though strong enough to get to him this past week.

Cole was tempted to say so, but he wasn't sure she'd want to hear such things from him, coming on top of Tara's coupling them as she had. It might make Liz shrink even more inside herself, thinking he *was* about to make a move on her. It was damned difficult, given their work situation and her current fragile state.

'I'd appreciate it if you'll drop me off along Military Road at the Mosman shopping centre,' she said abruptly.

He glanced at his watch. Almost three o'clock. Most shops closed at five o'clock on Saturday, except in tourist areas, and Mosman was more a classy suburb. 'I'll park and wait for you. Take you home when you're through shopping.'

'No, please.' Almost a panicky note in her voice. 'I don't want to hold you up.'

'*You'll* be held up, getting public transport home. Apart from which, you wouldn't be shopping but for my mother making you feel you have to,' he argued. 'I'll sit over coffee somewhere and wait for you.'

'I truly don't want you to do that, Cole.' Very tense. 'It will make me feel I have to hurry.'

'Take all the time you want,' he tossed back at her, assuming a totally relaxed air. 'I have nothing in particular to go home to.'

And he didn't like the sense of her running away from him.

A compelling urge to smash the line she had drawn prompted him into adding, 'Actually, I think I'll tag along with you. Give an opinion on what looks good.'

That shocked her out of her defensive shell. Her head jerked towards him. The sunglasses hid the expression in her eyes but if it was horror, he didn't care.

'I will not let you buy anything for me,' she threw at him, a feisty pride rising out of the assault on her grimly held sense of propriety. 'You are not responsible for…for…'

'My mother's love of dressing up for an occasion?' he finished for her, grinning at the steam he'd stoked. 'I couldn't agree more. The responsibility is all yours for indulging her. And you probably don't need me along. Have to admit the clothes you've been wearing this past week demonstrate you have a great eye for what looks good on you.'

Got in that little boost to her confidence, Cole thought, and continued on his roll with a sense of triumphant satisfaction. 'But most women like a man's opinion and since I'm here on the spot, why not? More interesting for me than sitting over coffee by myself.'

'Cole, I'm your P.A., not your…your…'

Lover? Mistress? Wife?

Clearly she couldn't bring herself to voice such provocative positions. Cole relieved her agitation by putting their relationship back on terms she was comfortable with.

'As your boss, who instigated this whole situation, it's clearly within my authority to see that you don't spend too much on pleasing my mother.'

'I'm not stupid!' she cried in exasperation. 'I said I'd only buy what I'll make use of again.'

'Then you can't have any objection to my feeling right about this. Besides, I'll be handy. I'll carry your shopping bags.'

She shook her head in a helpless fashion and slumped back into silence. Cole sensed that resistance was still simmering but he was now determined on this course of action and he was not about to budge from it. Tara was not going to win over Liz Hart. One way or another, he was going to make Liz feel great about herself.

As she should.

She was great at everything she did for him.

Probably make a great mother, too.

Cole grimaced over this last thought.

Time he got Tara out of his head, once and for all. She'd left one hell of a lot of scar tissue but that was no reason for him not to move on. In fact, he'd told her he had, which had spurred the attack on Liz.

Well, at least he was moving on neutralising that—one step in the right direction.

CHAPTER NINE

LIZ's heart was galloping. Why, why, why was Cole being so perverse, insisting on going shopping with her, foiling her bid to escape the awkwardness she now felt with him? Didn't he realise how personal it was, giving his opinion on what clothes she chose, carrying her shopping bags, acting as though they were *a couple?*

She took several deep breaths in an attempt to calm herself down. Her mind frantically re-examined everything he'd said, searching for clues that might help her understand his motivation. It came as some relief to realise he couldn't think she'd been making a play for him this past week. His comment on the clothes she'd worn to work had been a compliment on her taste, no hint of suspicion that they could have been especially aimed to attract *his* notice.

He'd said he had nothing in particular to go home to and tagging along with her would be more interesting than drinking coffee alone. But weren't men bored by clothes shopping? Brendan had always been impatient with any time spent on it. *That'll do,* had been his usual comment, never a considered opinion on how good anything looked on her.

Maybe with having a famous model as his wife, Cole had learnt some of the tricks of the trade, but thinking of Tara made Liz even more self-conscious about parading clothes in front of him. She couldn't compete. She didn't want to compete. She just wanted to be left alone to lick her wounds in private.

But Cole was already parking the car, pressing the mechanism that installed the hood, getting ready to leave the Maserati in the street while he accompanied her. She knew there'd be no stopping him. Once Cole Pierson made up his mind to do something, no force on earth would deter him from pursuing his goal. But what was his goal here?

Was it just filling in time with her?

She could minimise the shopping as much as seemed reasonable to him.

Reasonable might be the key. He'd said he wanted to *feel right* about what she bought. Which linked this whole thing back to indulging his mother. Nothing really personal at all.

The frenzy in her mind abated. She could cope with this. She had to. Cole was now out of the car and striding around it to the passenger door. Liz hastily released her safety belt and grabbed her handbag from the floor. The door was opened and once again he offered his hand to help her out. Ignoring it was impossible. Liz took it and was instantly swamped by a wave of dynamic energy that fuzzed the coping sector in her mind.

Thankfully he didn't hold on to her hand, releasing it to wave up and down the street, good-naturedly asking, 'Which way do you want to go?'

Liz paused a moment to orient herself. They were in the middle of the shopping centre. Mosman had quite a number of classy boutiques, but her current budget wasn't up to paying their prices, not after the big splurge she'd just had on clothes. She hadn't wanted to ask Diana for help with these extras for the trip. Her sister would inevitably pepper her with questions about her boss, and Liz didn't want to hear them, let alone answer them. There was, however, one inexpensive shop here that might provide all she needed.

'Across the road and to our left,' she directed.

Cole automatically took her arm to steer her safely through the cruising traffic to the opposite sidewalk. She knew it was a courtesy but it felt like a physical claim on her. She was becoming far, far too conscious of her boss as a man. It wasn't even a relief when he resumed simply walking side by side.

'Do you have a particular place in mind?' he asked, glancing at display windows they passed.

'Yes. It's just along here.' She kept her gaze forward, refusing to be tempted by what she couldn't afford. It was the middle of winter but the new spring fashions were already on show everywhere.

'Hold it!' Cole grabbed her arm to halt her progress and pointed to a mannequin dressed in a gorgeous green pantsuit. 'That would be fantastic on you, Liz.'

'Not what I'm looking for,' she swiftly stated, knowing the classy outfit would cost mega-dollars.

He frowned at her as she tugged herself loose and kept walking. 'What are you looking for?'

'A couple of evening tops to go with black slacks and something in white,' she rattled out.

'Black,' he repeated in a tone of disapproval.

'You're going into the tropics, you know. Hot and humid. You should be wearing something light.'

'Black goes anywhere,' she argued.

'I like green on you,' he argued back.

'What you like isn't really relevant, Cole. You won't be there,' she reminded him, glad to make the point that she wasn't out to please *him*.

'My mother would like what I like,' he declared authoritatively. 'I think we should go back and...'

'No. I'm going to look in here,' she insisted, heading into the shop she had targeted.

It was somewhat overcrowded with racks of clothes, but promising a large range of choice which was bound to yield something suitable. However, Liz had barely reached the first rack when Cole grabbed her hand and hauled her outside.

'A second-hand shop?' he hissed, his black brows beetling down at her.

'Quite a lot of second-hand designer wear,' she tersely informed him. 'Classy clothes that have only been worn a few times, if that. They're great bargains and perfectly good.'

'I will not have you wearing some other woman's cast-offs,' he said so vehemently Liz was stunned into silence, not understanding why he found it offensive. His hand lifted and cupped her cheek, his thumb tilting her chin up so the piercing blue eyes bored into hers with commanding intensity. 'I will not have you thinking you only rate seconds. You're a class act, Liz Hart. Top of the top. And you are going to be dressed accordingly.'

He dropped his hand, hooked her arm around his

and marched her back down the street before Liz could find her voice. Her cheek was still burning from his touch and her heartbeat was thundering in her ears. It was difficult to think coherently with his body brushing hers, his long stride forcing her to pick up pace to keep level with him. Nevertheless, something had to be said.

'Cole, I've…I've spent most of my spare money on…on…'

'I'll do the buying,' he cut in decisively. 'Consider it a bonus for being the best P.A. I've ever had.'

Bonus…best P.A….top of the top…the heady words buzzed around her brain. The compliments were so extraordinary, exhilarating. And suddenly she recalled what his mother had said—*He cares about you.*

Her feet were almost dancing as he swept her into the boutique she had bypassed before. 'We'll try that green,' he told the saleswoman, pointing to the pant-suit on the display mannequin.

There was such a strong flow of power emanating from Cole, the woman virtually jumped to obey. Liz was ushered into a dressing-room and handed the garments in her size in double-quick time.

'I want to see that on,' Cole continued in commanding vein. 'And while Liz is changing, you can show me anything else you have that might do her justice.'

Wearing second-hand clothes had never bothered her, but Cole's determination to *do her justice* was too intoxicating to resist. She fell in love with the apple green pantsuit and his raking look of male ap-

preciation and resounding, 'Yes,' set her heart fluttering with wild excitement. He really did see her as
special…and attractive.

Next came a lime green cotton knit top, sleeveless
but with a deep cowl neckline that could be positioned many clever ways. It was teamed with white
pants printed with lime green pears, strawberries and
mangos—the kind of fun item she'd never indulged
in. But it did look brilliant on her and she was
tempted into striking a jaunty pose when showing the
outfit to Cole. He grinned at her, giving a thumbs up
sign, and she grinned back, enjoying the madness of
the moment. Both green tops would dress up her
black slacks, she decided, trying to be a bit sensible.

'That's it for here,' he declared. 'We'll try somewhere else for the white.'

Somewhere else turned out to be a Carla Zampatti
boutique, all stocked up with the new spring range
from one of the top designers in Australia. With the
help of the saleswoman Cole selected a white broderie
anglaise skirt with a ruffle hem and a matching peasant blouse. The correct accessories included a dark
auburn raffia hip belt featuring a large red, brown and
camel stone clip fastening, long Indian earrings dangling with beads and feathers in the same colours,
high wedge heeled sandals in white, with straps that
crisscrossed halfway up Liz's calves.

The whole effect was absolutely stunning.

Liz couldn't believe how good she looked.

Fine feathers certainly did make fine birds, she
thought giddily, waltzing out of the dressing-room on
cloud nine. Cole's gaze fastened on her ankles and

slowly travelled up, lingering on her bare shoulder where the saleswoman had pulled down the peasant neckline for *the right effect*. A sensual little smile was directed at the exotic earrings and when he finally met her eyes, she saw the simmer of sexual interest in his—unmistakable—and felt her toes curling in response.

'This strappy bandeau top in camel jersey also goes with that skirt,' the saleswoman informed, showing the garment.

'Yes,' Cole said eagerly. 'Let's see it on.'

It fit very snugly, moulding her small firm breasts, which didn't go unnoticed by Cole whose interest in dressing her as *he* liked seemed to gather more momentum. 'I like that filmy leopard print top, too,' he said, pointing to a rack of clothes.

'The silk georgette with the hanky hemmed sleeve?' It was held up for his approval.

'Mmmh...very sexy.'

'It teams well with the bronze satin pants, and the bronze tassel belt,' the saleswoman encouraged, seizing advantage of the obvious fact that Cole was in a buying mood.

Liz felt driven to protest. 'I don't need any more. Truly.'

'Just this one extra lot then,' came the blithe reply. He grinned at her. 'I know you've got bronze shoes. Saw you wearing them last week. And the jungle motif is definitely your style.'

He would not be deterred. Liz couldn't help feeling both elated and guilty as they left the boutique, both of them now laden with shopping bags.

'Happy?' he asked, triumph sparkling in his eyes.

'Yes. But I shouldn't have let you do that.'

He arched a cocky eyebrow at her. 'The choice was all mine.'

She heaved a sigh in the hope of relieving the wild drumming in her chest. 'You've been very generous. Thank you.'

He laughed. 'It was fun, Liz. Maybe that's what both of us need right now. Some fun.'

His eyes flirted with hers.

It was happening. It really was happening. Just as Diana had predicted. But could a classy appearance achieve so much difference in how one was viewed? It didn't seem right. Surely attraction shouldn't depend entirely on surface image. Yet Cole had *married* Tara Summerville, which pointed to his being heavily swayed by how a woman looked.

But he knows me, the person, too, Liz quickly argued to herself. We've worked together for three years. *Best P.A. I've ever had.* And he did like her. Trust and respect were also mixed in with the liking. So this suddenly strong feeling of attraction was acceptable, wasn't it? Not just a fleeting thing of the moment?

They reached the Maserati and Cole unlocked the boot to stow away the host of shopping bags. 'What we should do now…' he said as they unloaded themselves. '…is drop this stuff off at your apartment, then go out to dinner to celebrate.'

'Celebrate what? Your outrageous extravagance?'

'Worth every cent.' He shut the lid of the boot with an air of satisfaction, then smiled at her. 'Pleasure can't always be so easily bought, Liz, and here we are, both of us riding a high.'

She couldn't deny it, but she knew her high was fired by feelings that hadn't been stirred for a very long time, feelings that had nothing to do with new clothes. Not even fabulous clothes. 'So we're celebrating pleasure?'

'Why not?' He took her arm to steer her to the passenger side, opening the door for her as he added, 'Let's put the blight of our ex-partners aside for one night and focus on having fun.'

One night…

The limitation was sobering. So was the reference to ex-partners. As Liz stepped into the car and settled on the passenger seat, she forced herself to take stock of what these remarks could mean. She herself had completely forgotten the blight left by Brendan in the excitement of feeling the sizzle of mutual attraction with Cole. However, she did have three weeks' distance since last being with Brendan. Cole had been very freshly reminded of his relationship with Tara this morning.

Earlier, before the shopping spree, he'd said he had nothing to go home to. Tara had clearly left a huge hole in his life. Had he just been buying a filler for that hole? As well as some sweet private revenge on the woman who'd taken him for much more than Liz would ever cost him?

She glanced sharply at him as he took the driver's seat beside her. One night of fun could mess with their business relationship. Had Cole thought of that or was he in the mood not to care?

He switched on the engine and threw her a smile that quickened her pulse-beat again. 'How about Doyle's at Rose Bay? Feel like feasting on oysters and lobster?'

Oh, why not? she thought recklessly. There was nothing for her to go home to, either. 'Sounds good. But it's Saturday night. Will we get a table?' The famous seafood restaurant on Sydney Harbour was very popular.

'No problem,' he confidently assured her. 'I'll call and book from your apartment.'

No doubt he wouldn't care what it cost for the restaurant to *find* an extra table for two. Cole was on a roll, intent on sweeping her along with him, and Liz decided not to worry about it. Fun was the order of the night and there was nothing wrong with taking pleasure in each other's company.

Diana's advice slid into her mind.

Go with the flow.

For too much of her life Liz had been managing situations, balancing pros and cons, thinking through all the possible factors, choosing what seemed the most beneficial course. She wanted to be free of all that...if only for one night...to simply *go with the flow* and let Cole take care of whatever happened between them.

After all, he was the boss.

The man in command.

CHAPTER TEN

COLE had never thought of his P.A. as delightful, but she was. Maybe it was the influence of the champagne, loosening inhibitions, bringing out bubbles in her personality. It was the first time she'd ever drunk alcohol in his presence. First time they'd ever been away from their work situation, dining together as a social twosome. She was enjoying the fine dinner at Doyle's and he was thoroughly enjoying her company.

Aware that she liked travelling, he'd prompted her into relating what trips she'd like to take in future— the old silk route from Beijing to Moscow, the northwest passage to Alaska, the Inca trail in South America—places he'd never thought of going himself. He'd hit all the high spots—New York, London, Paris, Milan, Hong Kong—but they hadn't been adventures in the sense Liz was talking about—reliving history and relating culture to geography.

Watching her face light up with enthusiasm, her eyes sparkle in anticipation of all there was yet to see and know, Cole mentally kicked himself for allowing his world to become so narrow, so concentrated on the challenge of accumulating more and more money. He should take more time out, make a few journeys into other areas. Though he'd probably need Liz to guide him into seeing what she saw.

Future plans…he had none. Not really. Just keep on doing what he'd been doing. He looked at Liz, taking pleasure in her vitality, in her quest for new experiences, and a question popped into his mind—a question he asked without any forethought of what its impact might be on her.

'Does marriage and having a family fit anywhere in your future, Liz?'

A shadow instantly descended, wiping the sparkle from her eyes, robbing her face of all expression. Her lashes lowered to half mast, as though marking the death of her hopes in that area, and Cole mentally kicked himself for bringing up what must be a raw subject for her with Brendan having walked away from their long-term relationship.

Her shoulders squared. An ironic little smile tilted one corner of her mouth. Her eyes flashed bleakly at him. 'I guess I'm a failure at being desirable wife material. I haven't met anyone who wants to marry me,' she said in a tone of flat defeat.

Cole barely bit down on the urge to tell her she was intensely desirable in every way. Words were useless if they didn't match her experience. But they were true nonetheless. It had been growing on him all day…how different she was to Tara, how much he liked her, how sexy she looked in the right clothes.

His gaze fastened on her mouth. He wanted to kiss away the hurt that had just been spoken, make her smile with joy again, as she had this afternoon, twirling around in that very fetching white skirt. She'd felt all woman then, failing in nothing, and certainly stirring a few pressing male fantasies in Cole.

'What about you?' she asked. 'Would you come at marriage again?'

It jolted him into a harsh little laugh. 'Not in a hurry.'

'Bad experience?'

'Bad judgment on my part.' He shrugged, not wanting to talk about it. 'Though I would like to be a father again,' he added, admitting that joy and sorrow from his marriage.

She nodded, her eyes flashing heartfelt sympathy. 'I would hate to lose a child of mine.'

It had barely caused a ripple in Tara's life, which made her proposition today all the more obscene. He had no doubt Liz would manage motherhood better, probably dote on a child of her own. He recalled her speaking of a number of sisters to his mother and asked about her family, moving the conversation on.

She was an aunt to two nieces and nephews, had a big extended family, lots of affection in her voice. Good people, Cole thought, and wondered how much he'd missed by being an only child. His father hadn't wanted more, even one being an intrusion on the orderly life he'd liked. Though he had been proud of Cole's achievements.

His mother would have liked a daughter. Someone like Liz with whom she could really share things. Not like Tara.

Liz Hart...

Why hadn't he thought of her like this before?

Blind to what was under his nose.

Tara getting in the way, skewing his view, killing

any desire to even look at a woman, let alone involve himself with one.

Besides which, Liz had been attached—might still be emotionally attached—to the guy who'd used her for years, then dumped her. Though clearly she'd been trying to rise out of those ashes, firing herself up to make something else of her life. Still, she'd definitely been burned, thinking of herself as a failure in the female stakes.

It wasn't right.

And on top of that, Tara putting her down this morning.

So wrong.

The rank injustice that had been done to Liz lingered in Cole's mind, even as he drove her home from Doyle's. She was quiet, the bubbles of the night having fizzed out. Facing the prospect of a lonely apartment, he thought, and memories that would bring misery. He didn't like this thought. He didn't like it one bit.

It was just a one off night, Liz told herself, trying to drum it into her foolish head. And she'd probably talked far too much about herself, her tongue let loose by the free flow of beautiful French champagne, delicious food, and Cole showing so much personal interest in her.

But it hadn't been a two way street. Very little had come back to her about him, and on the question of marriage, Cole's instant and derisive reply—*Not in a hurry*—had burst Liz's fantasy bubble. In fact, reflecting on his manner to her over dinner, Liz decided he undoubtedly dealt with clients in the same fashion, drawing them out, listening intently, lots of eye contact, projecting interest. *Charm,* Jayne had called it.

It didn't *mean* anything.

He'd spelled it out beforehand—one night of fun. And now he was driving her home. Nothing more was going to happen. She just wished her nerves would stop leaping around and she'd be able to make the parting smooth and graceful, showing she didn't expect any more from him.

But in her heart she wanted more.

And trying to argue it away wasn't working. The wanting had been building all day. It was now a heaviness in her chest that was impossible to dislodge. A tight heaviness that was loaded down with sadness, as well. Crying for the moon, she thought. Which had shone on her for a little while this evening but would inevitably keep moving and leave her in the dark again.

Cole parked the car outside her apartment, switched off the headlights. Liz felt enveloped in darkness—a lonely darkness, bereft of the vital power of his presence as he left her to stride around to the passenger side. *Get used to it, girl,* she told herself savagely. *He's not for you.*

The door opened and she stepped out, not taking the offered hand this time, forcing herself upright on her own two legs because if she took that hand it would heat hers, sending the tingling message of a warm togetherness that wasn't true. Cole was her boss. He would do her the courtesy of accompanying her to her door and then he would leave her. Back to business on Monday.

She put her head down and walked, acutely conscious of the sound of their footsteps—the quick clacking of her heels, the slower thump of his. They seemed to echo through the emptiness of her personal life, mocking dreams that had never been fulfilled, recalling her mother's words—*The kind of man you want, Liz, is the marrying kind.*

Why couldn't she meet someone who was?

Want someone who was.

Someone who was at least…reachable!

Tears blurred her eyes as they started up the stairs to her apartment. She shouldn't have drunk those glasses of champagne, giving her a false high, making the down worse. It was paramount now that she pull herself together, get out her door key, formulate a polite goodbye to her boss who had done her many kindnesses today. Kind…generous…making her feel special…

A huge lump rose in her throat. She blinked, swallowed, blinked, swallowed, managed somehow to get the key in the lock, turned it, pushed the door open enough for a fast getaway, retrieved the key, dropped it in her bag, dragged a deep breath into her aching chest, and turned to the man beside her.

'Thank you for everything, Cole,' she recited stiltedly and tried to arrange her mouth into a smile as she lifted her gaze, knowing she had to briefly meet his eyes and desperately hoping no evidence of any excess moisture was left for him to see. 'Goodnight,' she added as brightly as she could. 'It was fun.'

Cole's whole body clenched, resisting the dismissal. He stared at her shiny eyes. Wet eyes. Green pools, reflecting deep misery. The smile she'd forced was quivering, falling apart, no fun left to keep it in a natural curve.

He should let her go.

They were on very private ground now.

If he crossed it, there'd be no going back.

She was his employee...

Yet he stepped forward, his body responding to a primal tug that flouted the reasonable workings of his mind. Raising a hand, he gently stroked the tremulous corner of her mouth, wanting to soothe, to comfort, to make her feel safe with him. A slight gasp whispered from her lips. Her eyes swam with a terrible vulnerability, fearful questions begging to be answered.

It laid a responsibility on him, instantly striking a host of male instincts that rose in a strangely exultant wave, urging him to fight, to hold, to take, to protect—the age-old role of man before current day society had watered it down into something much less.

A sense of dominant power surged through his veins. She would submit to it. He would draw a positive response from her. He sensed it waiting behind the fear and confusion, waiting to be ignited, to flare into hot fusion with the desire pounding through him.

He slid his hand over her cheek, felt the leap of warmth under her skin, the firm yet fragile line of her jaw, the delicate curl of her small ear. Even as his thumb tilted her chin, his fingers were reaching to the nape of her neck, ready to caress, to persuade, to possess.

He lowered his head...slowly, savouring the moment of impact before it came. She had time to break away. His hold on her was light. She stood still, as though her entire being was poised for this first intimate contact with him, caught up in a breathless anticipation that couldn't be turned aside.

His lips touched hers, settling over their softness, drawing on them with light sips, feeling their hesitant response, teasing them into a more open kiss, wanting an exchange of sensation, reining in the urge to plunder and devour. She was willing to experiment, her tongue tentatively touching his as though she wasn't sure this was right. It fired a fierce desire in Cole to convince her it was. He turned the kiss into a slow, sensual dance, intent on melting every inhibition. She followed his lead, seduced into playing his game, savouring it herself, beginning to like it, want it, initiating as well as responding.

Excitement kicked through Cole. This was so different to Tara's all-too-knowing sexual aggression. He had to win this woman, drive the memory of her lost partner out of her mind and supplant it with what *he* could make her feel. The challenge spurred him into sweeping her into his embrace.

Her spine stiffened, whether in shock or resistance he didn't know. Shock was probably good. Resistance was bad. Before he could blast it with a passionate onslaught of kisses, her palms pressed hard against his chest and her head pulled back from his—a warning against force that he struggled to check, sensing her need for choice here, even while gathering himself to sway it his way.

He felt the agitated heave of her breasts as she sucked in a quick breath. Her lids fluttered, lashes half veiling the eloquent confusion in her eyes. Satisfaction welled in him, despite the frustration of being halted. It wasn't rejection on her mind. She didn't understand what was going on in his.

'Why are you doing this?' The words spilled out, anxious, frightened of consequences that he should know as well as she.

The lack of any calculation in her question, the sheer exquisite innocence of it evoked a streak of tenderness that Cole would have sworn had died with his son. His own chest heaved with the sudden surge of emotion. He dropped a soft kiss on her forehead.

'Because it feels right,' he murmured, feeling the sense of a new beginning so strongly, his heart started racing at the possibility it was really true. He could move past Tara. Even past David. Perhaps it was only hope but he wasn't about to step away from this opportunity of taking a future track which might bring him all he'd craved in his darkest nights.

'But I'm not really a…a date, am I?' she argued, trying to get a handle on what he meant by kissing her.

'No. You're much more.'

She shook her head, not comprehending. 'Cole, please…' Anguished uncertainty in her eyes. '…we have to work together.'

'We do work together. That's precisely the point. We work very well together.' He stroked the worry line between her brows. 'I'm just taking it to another level.'

'Another level?' she repeated dazedly.

He smiled into her eyes, wanting to dispel the cloudiness, to make her see what he saw. 'This feels right to me, Liz. Don't let it feel wrong to you because it's not,' he insisted, recklessly intent on carrying her with him. On a wild burst of adrenalin he added, 'I'm damned sure I can give you more than Brendan ever could or would.'

'Bren...dan.'

The name seemed to confuse her further. Cole silently cursed himself for bringing it up. He didn't want to compete. He wanted to conquer—wipe the guy out, take the woman, make her his. He didn't care how primitive that course was. It burned in his gut and he acted on it, sweeping Liz with him into her apartment, closing the door, staking his claim on her territory.

Before she could even think of protesting, he threw off his leather jacket, needing no armour against the cold in here, nor any barrier to the enticing heat of her body, and he captured her within the lock of his arms, intent on her surrender to his will. She felt small against him, and all the more intensely feminine because of it, but he knew she had a backbone of steel that could defy the might of his physique. Triumph zinged through his brain as her spine softened, arched into him, and her hands slid up over his shoulders, around his neck, and she lifted herself on tiptoe, face tilted to his, ready to be kissed again.

The darkness of the room seemed to sharpen his

senses. He could smell her perfume, enticingly erotic. His fingers wove through the silky curls of her hair, revelling in the tactile pleasure of it. His body hardened to the yielding softness of hers. He was conscious of their breaths mingling as his mouth touched hers, touched and clung with a voracious need that demanded her compliance.

She kissed him back with a passionate defiance that challenged any sense of dominance over her. No submission. It was as though a fire had erupted in her and Cole caught the flame. It flared through him, firing his desire for her to furnace heat. The power of it raced out of control, taking them both, drawing them in, sucking them towards the intense thrill of merging so completely there could be no turning back.

He removed her jacket.

She lifted his sweater, fearless now in matching him step for step.

Discarding clothes...like walls coming down, crashing to the floor, opening up the way...the ravenous excitement of flesh meeting flesh, sliding, caressing, hot and hungry for more and more intimacy.

Kissing...like nothing he knew, sliding deep, a sensual mating of tongues, a fierce response generated in every cell of his body, the sense of immense strength, power humming.

He scooped her off her feet, cradled her against his chest, carried her, intuitively picking the route to the room where she had gone to get her scarf this morning. Her head rested on his shoulder, her face pressed to his neck, the whole feel of her soft and warm and womanly, giving, wanting what he wanted.

She made him feel as a man should feel.

Essentially male.

And all that entailed.

CHAPTER ELEVEN

LIZ was glad of the darkness. It wasn't oppressive now. It was her friend and ally, heightening the vibrant reality of Cole making love to her while it hid the same reality in comforting shadows. It allowed her to stifle the fear of facing the sheer nakedness of what they were doing and revel in the incredible pleasure of it. She could even believe she was as desirable as Cole made her feel. In the darkness.

He laid her on the bed—a bed she had shared only with Brendan—and she felt a sharp inner recoil at the memory, not wanting it. Why had Cole referred to him? Brendan was gone. Long gone from her bed. And he'd made mincemeat of her heart—the heart that was now pounding with wild excitement as Cole loomed over her, so big and strong and dynamically male, as different as any man could be to Brendan.

Purpose…action…energy focused on carrying through decisions…and unbelievably that focus was now on her…a totally irresistible force that kept swamping the reservations that should be in her brain, but he'd blown them away as though they didn't count. And maybe they didn't at this level, wherever this level was taking them.

She could barely think. Couldn't reason anymore. His arms slid out from under her and the solid mass of him straightened up, substance not fantasy, Cole taking charge, wanting her with him like this. She saw his arm reach for the bedside lamp and reacted with violent rejection of the action he had in mind.

'No!'

The arm was momentarily checked. 'No what?' he demanded.

'No light. I don't want light.'

'Why not?'

'You'll see...'

'I want to see you.'

'It won't be right,' she argued desperately. Her mind was screaming, *I'm not built like Tara. My breasts are small. My legs aren't long. I don't have voluptuous curves.*

'I promise you it will be,' he said, his voice furred with a deep sensuality that did promise, yet she couldn't believe he wouldn't compare her body to that of the woman he'd married and find her wanting.

'I don't have red hair down there,' she cried frantically, clutching at anything to stop him from turning on the light. 'You'll see it and think of me as a little brown mouse again.'

'I never thought of you like that,' he growled. 'Never!'

It got him onto the bed, lying beside her, the lamp forgotten, his hand sliding down over her stomach, fingers thrusting into the tight curls below it. 'I always saw you as bright, Liz Hart. Bright eyes. Bright intelligence. And behind it a fire which occasionally leapt out at me. There's not an ounce of mouse in you.'

This emphatic string of statements was very reassuring as to her status in his eyes, but Liz was highly distracted from it by the further glide of his fingers, delving lower, probing soft sensitive folds, exciting nerve ends that melted into slick heat.

'I thought this past week…she's showing her true colours. Reflecting the real Liz instead of covering her up,' he went on, still wreaking exquisite havoc with his hand, caressing, tracing, teasing. 'You don't need a cloak of darkness. You can't hide from me anymore. I know the fire inside you. I can feel it…'

A finger slid inside the entrance to her body and tantalisingly circled the sensitive inner wall, raising convulsive quivers of anticipation for the ultimate act of intimacy. He leaned over, his face hovering above hers. She saw the flash of a smile.

'…and taste it.'

He kissed her, long and deeply, and the tantalising fingertip plunged inward, stroking in the same rhythmic action as his tongue, a dual invasion that drove her wild with passionate need, a need that swelled inside her, arching her body in an instinctive lift towards his, wanting, yearning. He didn't instantly respond so she reached for him with her hands, turned towards him, threw a leg over his, and her heart leapt at the hard muscular strength it met. Huge thighs. She'd forgotten how big he was, had a moment's trepidation…how would it be when he took her?

I promise you it will be right…

It had to be.

She didn't want to stop.

Not now.

Not when she was awash with a tumultuous

need to have him...if only this once. It was madness...dangerous madness...risking what should have been kept safe. But it was his choice. *She* was his choice. And feeling him wanting her—Cole Pierson wanting her—it was like being elevated above any other woman he could have had, above Tara, making her feel...marvellous!

He broke the kiss and moved, but not as she expected, craved. His mouth fastened over the pulse at the base of her throat, radiating a heat that suffused her entire skin. She heard herself panting, barely able to breathe. Her arms had locked around his neck, but his head slipped below their circle, his lips tracing the upper swell of one breast, shifting to its tip...

Her stomach contracted as the feeling of inadequacy attacked her again. Her breasts weren't lush. He'd be disappointed in them. Oh, why, why couldn't he just...

Sensation exploded through her as he drew the tense peak into the hot wetness of his mouth and sucked on it. Swept it with his tongue. Another rhythmic assault that moved in tandem with the caressing hand between her thighs, driving her to the edge of shattering. Her fingers scrabbled blindly in his hair, pressing, tugging, protesting, inciting.

He moved to her other breast, increasing her ache for him, and her flesh seemed to swell around his mouth, throbbing with a tight fullness that totally erased any concern about levels of femininity. He made her feel she was all the woman he wanted and he wouldn't be denied any part of her.

Again he shifted and her body jerked as his tongue

swirled around her navel, a hot sweep of kisses trailing lower, lower. Her hands grabbed ineffectually at the bunched muscles of his shoulders as fear and desire warred through her mind.

No hesitation in his. Ruthless purpose. Lips pressed to her curls, fingers parting the way, his tongue touching, licking. The intensity of feeling rocked her, drenched her with desire, rendered her utterly helpless to stop anything even if she'd wanted to. And she didn't. She was on fire and he was tasting her because he wanted to.

He wedged his shoulders between her thighs, lifted her legs, clamped his hands on her hips and held her fast as he replaced the caress of his hand with the incredibly intimate caress of his mouth, his lips encircling her, his tongue probing with such artful sensual skill, she couldn't breathe at all as the intensity of feeling grew, ripping through her. She tried to ride the tide of it, her hands gripping the bedcover, holding on, holding on, but a rush of heat broke through her inner walls, overwhelming her with a wave of excruciating delight. A cry broke from her throat as she lost all sense of self, falling into a deep well of pleasure that engulfed her in sweet, molten heat.

Then Cole was surging over her. She could see him, feel him, but her muscles were so limp, she was unable to react. Her mind was filled with awe that he had taken her this far before satisfying himself. Yet she sensed he was not unsatisfied with what he had done, but pleased, even triumphant, as though he'd found his feasting very much to his liking.

I promise you it will be right...

Impossible to deny it, feeling as she did.

Having set himself to enter her, he pressed forward, pushing into her slowly, letting her adjust to the thick fullness of him, a completely different sensation and one that re-electrified all her senses. He eased back, lifting her hips, stuffing a pillow under her.

'Put your legs around me,' he murmured.

Somehow she managed to do it, locking her ankles so that they wouldn't slip apart. This time his thrust was firm, pushing deep, deeper, filling her to a breath-taking depth, then bracing himself on his arms as he bent his head to join his mouth to hers, and the kiss was different, too, like an absolute affirmation of him being inside her, having him there, an intensely felt sensation of possessing and being possessed, exulting in it, absorbed by it.

'Now rock with me,' he instructed, flashing a smile as he lifted his head.

Joy rippled through her. He was happy with where they were. She was, too. It re-energised her body, making it easy now to move as he did, matching the repetitive undulation, even touching him, stroking him, encouraging him, running her hands over the warm skin of his back, inciting the rise of heat with each delicious rhythmic plunge.

It was a wild, primitive dance that she gloried in, flesh sliding against—into—flesh, fusing, yet still gliding with a strong, relentless purpose, friction building to ecstatic peaks, wave after wave of in-tense sensation rolling through her...so much to feel...flaring, swirling, pooling deep inside her, touching her heart, stirring indefinable emotions...too much to pin down…far beyond all her previous experience.

Rapture as he groaned and spilled himself inside her. She sighed his name as his hard body collapsed on her, spent, and she wrapped her arms around him, holding him close, loving him, owning him if only for these few precious moments in time. He'd given himself to her, all that he was, and she silently revelled in the gift, unable to see ahead to what came next, not caring, listening to his heart thundering, elated that he had reached a pinnacle of pleasure with her.

He raised himself to kiss her again, her name whispering from his lips as they covered hers, soft, lingering sips that demanded nothing, merely sealing a tender togetherness that tasted of true and total contentment. Then his arms burrowed under her and he rolled onto his back, carrying her with him so that she lay with her head under his chin, her body sprawled over his.

Done, she thought, and wondered where it would lead. But with no sense of anxiety. She felt too amazingly replete to worry about tomorrow. Only luxuriating in this blissful sense of peace mattered. As long as it lasted. It awed her that she had lived so many years without realising how fantastic intimacy could be with a man. With the right man. Cole…Cole Pierson. Was it asking too much to want him thinking the same about her?

Probably it was.

This could be just a timing thing with him—a backlash against Tara's assumption that she could rope him in again, making the alleged intimacy between him and his personal assistant real because it had been planted in his mind, and it was an act of defiance against any desire he might have left for his almost ex-wife.

People did do reckless things on the rebound.

Was he thinking of Tara now…mentally thumbing his nose at her?

Liz felt herself growing cold at these thoughts and fiercely set them aside. Cole was with her. He'd chosen her. She moved her hand, suddenly wanting to stoke his desire again, feel it burning through her, obliterating everything else with the intense sense of possession.

A long sensual caress from his armpit, down his rib-cage, over the hollows underneath his hipbones, his firm flesh quivering to her touch, pleasured by it. She levered herself to a lower position so she could close her mouth over his nipple, kissing it, lashing it with her tongue. His chest heaved, dragging in a sharp breath, reacting swiftly to the sexual energy that had roared around them and was sparking again, gathering momentum.

She reached further, her hand closing around him, fondling, stroking. He groaned, his whole body tensing as her thumb brushed delicately over the sensitive head of his shaft. Elated at his response, she seized him more firmly, felt the surge of rampant strength grow hard, harder…

Hands gripped her waist, lifting her. 'Straddle me,' came the gravelled command. 'Put me inside you.'

It was an even more incredible sensation, lowering

herself onto him, engineering the penetration herself, feeling her inner muscles convulse and adjust to the pressing fullness of him, loving the sense of taking him, owning him. His hands moved to her hips, helping her sink further as he raised his thighs behind her, forming a cradle for her bottom, a cradle he rocked to breathtaking effect.

'Lean forward.'

She wanted to anyway, wanted to kiss him as he'd kissed her when he was deep inside her. She placed her hands on his shoulders and merged her mouth with his, plunging into a cavern of wild passion, drawn into a whirlpool of need that he answered with ravishing speed, his hands on her everywhere, stroking, shaping, kneading, strong fingers clutching, gentle fingers loving, sensitising every inch of her flesh to his touch.

She lifted herself back and he rubbed his palms over her nipples, rotating the hardened buds, exciting them almost beyond bearing, then latching onto them one by one with his mouth, his hands back on her hips, moving her from side to side, up and down, stirring a frenzy of sensation that rocketed through her, shattering every last vestige of control.

Even as she started to collapse on him he caught her face, drew it down to his, and devoured her mouth again, a sweet devastating plunder that she could only surrender to, helplessly yet willingly because the intoxication of his desire for more and more of her was too strong an exhilaration to deny.

Then amazingly, he was surging upright, swinging his legs off the bed, holding her pinned to him across his lap, hugging her tightly, her breasts crushed so intimately against his chest, the beat of his heart seemed to pound through them, echoing the throb of her own. And he remained inside her, a glorious sensual fullness, as his fingers wound through her hair and his lips grazed over her ear.

'I have never felt anything as good as this,' he murmured, his voice furred with a wonderment that squeezed her heart and sent elation soaring through her bloodstream. He tilted her head back, rained kisses over her face, her forehead, her eyelids, her cheeks, his lips hovering over hers as he added with compelling urgency, 'Tell me it's so for you. Tell me.'

'Yes.' The word spilled out automatically, impossible not to concede the truth, and he captured it in his mouth and carried it into hers, exploding the force of it with a fierce enthralling passion, holding her caged in his arms, swaying to reinforce the sense of his other insertion, pressing the heated walls of the passage he filled, making her feel him with commanding intensity.

'So, good, it has to be right,' he said rawly as he broke the kiss and cupped her chin, his eyes burning into hers. 'So don't you doubt it tomorrow. Or on Monday. Or anytime in the future.'

Emphatic words, punching into her dazed mind. She wasn't sure what he was saying. Her brain formed its own message. 'Right…for one night,' she sighed, knowing she would never forget the feelings he'd aroused in her, was still arousing. She didn't care if it was only one experience. It was the experience of a lifetime.

'No.' His hands raked through her hair, pressing for concentration. 'This isn't an end. It's a beginning. You and me, Liz. Moving forward, moving together. Feel it. Know it. Come with me.'

He moved his thighs, driving an acute awareness of their sexual connection. He was still strongly erect, probing her inmost self, demanding she yield to him, and what else could she do? She wanted this deeper bonding, wanted it to last far beyond now.

'Liz…' An urgent demand poured through her name.

She lifted her limp, heavy arms and locked them around his neck…for better or worse, she thought, her mind aswim, drowning in the need for Cole to keep wanting her, making her feel loved as a woman.

'Yes.' It was the only word humming through her mind. Yes to anything, everything with him.

'Yes-s-s…' he echoed, but with a ring of triumphant satisfaction, powerfully realised.

One hand skated down the curve of her spine, curled under the soft globes of her bottom, clasping her to him as he rose to his feet and turned to lower her onto the bed again, her head and shoulders resting on the coverlet as he dragged pillows under her hips, then knelt between the spread of her legs, leaning over her, hands intertwining with hers, a wild grin of joy on his face.

'We'll both come,' he promised wickedly, then began to thrust in a fast driving beat, rocking deeply into her, and she felt her body receive him with an exultant welcome, opening to him over and over again. And he claimed all she gave, imprinting himself so completely on her consciousness, her entire body was focused on the erotic friction he built and built…only pausing, becoming still when he felt the powerful ripples of her release, savouring them before he picked up the rhythm again, all restraint whipping away as he pursued his own climax, broken breaths, moans of mounting tension, climbing, climbing, bursting into a long, intense rapture, waves of heat spilling, swirling, fusing them, lifting them into a space where they floated together in ecstatic harmony.

And Liz no longer questioned anything.

A sense of perfect contentment reigned.

Sliding slowly and languorously into a feast of sensuality that lasted long into the night…the night that he said was a beginning, not an end.

CHAPTER TWELVE

COLE was gone when Liz awoke. She vaguely remembered him kissing her, murmuring he had to keep an appointment. He'd been fully clothed, ready to leave. She was almost sure she'd mumbled, 'Okay,' before dropping back into a heavy sleep.

It came as a shock that her bedside radio now showed 11:47, almost midday. There was only one afternoon of the weekend left and she had washing to do, food shopping. She bolted out of bed and headed straight into the bathroom, cold wintry air hitting her nakedness, making her shiver.

A hot shower dispelled the chill and soaping her body brought back all the memories of last night's intimacies with Cole...delicious, indelible memories. If she wasn't in love with the man, she was certainly in lust with him. He was an incredible lover. And he'd made her feel sexier than she'd ever felt in her life. Sexy, beautiful, special...

Her mind flitted to how it had been with Brendan. Why had she accepted *so little* from him? Compared to Cole...but she hadn't known any better at the time. In fact, Brendan had been mean about a lot of things—a taker, not a giver. Whereas Cole...the beautiful clothes yesterday, the sumptuous dinner last night, the loving...she felt wonderfully spoilt, as though all her Christmases had come at once.

She desperately hoped it *was* right to have plunged into this intimate relationship with him. Her job was very definitely at risk if it turned wrong. Oddly enough, work security didn't weigh so heavily on her mind now. Losing him would be far more devastating. Which was the problem with being raised to giddy heights. The fall…

But she wasn't going to think about that.

Nor was she going to worry about Cole being her boss. As Diana had predicted, *he* had done the running, and Liz was now determined on *going with the flow,* wherever it took her. There really was no other choice, except dropping entirely out of his life. And why would she do that when he made her feel…so good?

The somewhat sobering recollection slid into her mind—he was in no hurry to marry again.

So what? she quickly argued. Did she have any prospects leaping out at her? Not a one. Besides, there was no guarantee of permanence with any relationship. It went that way or it didn't. Though everything within her craved for this new relationship with Cole to last, to become truly solid, to have it fulfil…all her impossible dreams.

As she stepped out of the shower, dried herself and dressed, a wry little smile lingered on her lips. Perhaps hope *was* eternal. In any event, it was a happy boost to her spirits. So was emptying yesterday's shopping bags, remembering the zing of parading the clothes in front of Cole as she hung them up in her wardrobe, knowing now that he did see her as a desirable woman—a woman he wanted.

She rushed through the afternoon, doing all the necessary chores, planning what she'd pack for the trip with Cole's mother, making sure everything was clean, ready to wear. She wondered what Nancy would think of her son becoming attached to his personal assistant. Better me than Tara, Liz cheerfully decided. Nancy hadn't liked Tara at all.

She was still riding a high when her telephone rang just past seven o'clock. She hesitated over answering it, thinking it might be Diana with another stream of advice. She didn't want to share what had happened with Cole. Not yet. It suddenly felt too precious, too fragile. And she didn't know how it might be tomorrow.

On the other hand, it might be her mother who wasn't pushing anything, only for her daughter to be happy about herself, and Liz was happy about herself right now, so she snatched up the receiver and spoke with a smile. 'Hi! Liz here.'

'Cole here,' came the lilted reply, warm pleasure threading his voice.

'Oh!' A dumb response but he'd taken her by surprise.

'Oh good, I trust?'

The light teasing note brought the smile back. 'Yes. Definitely good.'

He laughed. 'I've been thinking of you all day. Highly distracting.'

'Should I say I'm sorry?' It was fun to flirt with him, though it amazed her that she could.

'No. The distraction was very pleasurable.' He drawled the last words, sending pinpricks of excite-

ment all over her skin. 'I'm currently having to re-
strain myself from dashing to your door, telling myself I do need some sleep in order to function well
tomorrow.'

'You have a string of meetings in the morning,'
she said primly, playing the perfect P.A. while inwardly delighted that his restraint was being tested. It
spoke volumes about the strength of attraction he felt.
Towards *her*.

'Mmmh...I was wondering how to alleviate the
problem of people getting in the way of us.'

Us...such an exhilarating word. 'We do have work
to get through, Cole,' she reminded him, though if he
didn't care, she wasn't about to care, either.

'True. But you could wear that bronze dress with
the buttons down the front. Very provocative those
buttons. One could say...promising.'

Liz felt her thighs pressing together, recapturing the
sensations of last night when he'd...

'And wear stockings,' he continued. 'Not those
coverall pantihose. Stockings that end mid-thigh, under the skirt with the buttons. And no one will know
but you and me, Liz. I like that idea. I like it very
much.'

His voice had dropped to a seductive purr, and her
entire body was reacting to it, an exquisite squirming
that actually curled her toes.

'If you'll do that I think I'm sure to perform at a
high peak tomorrow,' he went on, conjuring up
breathtaking images that dizzied her brain. 'Won't
feel deprived at all during those meetings. There's
nothing quite like waiting on a promise.'

A shiver ran down her spine. Did he mean…after the meetings…at the office? He wanted sex with her there?

'Liz?'

'Yes?' It was like punching air out her lungs.

'Have I shocked you?'

'Yes…no,' she gabbled. 'I mean…I wasn't sure what you'd want of me tomorrow.'

'You. I want you. In every way there is,' he answered with a strength of purpose that thudded straight into Liz's heart, making her feeling intensely vulnerable about how he would deal with her in the end if she trod this path with him. Was it only sex on his mind? How much did she count as a person?

She couldn't find anything to say, her mind riddled by doubts and fears, yet physically, sexually, she was aware of an overwhelming yearning to follow his lead, to be the woman he wanted in every way.

'Remember how right it felt?' he dropped into her silence.

'Yes,' she answered huskily, her voice barely rising over a huge emotional lump in her throat.

'It will be tomorrow, too. That's my promise, Liz.' Warm reassurance.

'I'll come as you say,' she decided recklessly.

'Good! I'll sleep on that. Sweet dreams.'

The connection clicked off.

Goal achieved, she thought, then shook her head dazedly over the power Cole Pierson could and did exert. Being the focus of it was like nothing she had ever known before. In the past, she had always done the running, not very effectually where men were concerned. No truly satisfying success at all. In actual fact, a string of failures, probably because she'd tried to manage things to turn out right instead of them just being right.

She had no control with Cole.

He'd seized it.

Was still wielding it.

And maybe that was how it should be.

So let it be.

Cole sat at his desk in his office, his computer switched on, the screen flashing figures he should be checking, but he was too much on tenterhooks, waiting for Liz to arrive. He couldn't remember ever being this tense about seeing a woman again. Would he win or lose on last night's gamble?

He wasn't sure of her.

The sex on Saturday night had been fantastic. No doubting her response to everything they'd done together—a more than willing partner in pleasure, once he'd moved her past the initial inhibitions—storming barriers before she could raise them. Barriers that had undoubtedly been built during the Brendan era—damage done by a selfish lover who didn't have the sense to appreciate the woman he had.

Cole knew he could definitely reach her on the sexual level. It was what he was counting on to bind her to him. He'd moved too fast to take a slower route now, and be damned if he was going to let her slip away from him. He'd sensed her second thoughts during the telephone call. Perhaps the better move would have been to stay with her all yesterday. But her apartment was her ground and she would have had the right to ask him to go.

Best to keep the initiative.

She'd come to work this morning—his ground. And after their conversation over the phone, she would have gone to bed last night thinking of him, tempted by the promise of more pleasure, remembering what they'd already shared, wanting more...

Cole dragged in a deep breath, trying to dampen the wild surge of desire rising at the thought of what she would wear today. Compliance or defiance? At least the signal would be clear, the moment she walked into his office. Yes...no. He fiercely willed it to be yes. And why not? She had the fire in her to pursue pleasure. He'd lit the flame. She wouldn't let it go out...would she?

A knock on his door.

'Come in!' he called, his voice too terse, on edge.

She stepped into his office, wearing the bronze dress with the buttons down the front.

His heart thundered as a lightning burst of triumph flashed through his mind.

'Good morning,' she said brightly.

He saw courage in the red flags on her cheeks, in the high tilt of her head, the squared shoulders, the smile that wavered slightly at its corners. Courage defying fear and uncertainty. It touched him to a surprising depth.

'I think it's a great morning,' he rolled out, his smile ablaze with admiration and approval.

She visibly relaxed, walking forward, holding out

a Manila folder. 'I brought in the file for your first meeting.'

Straight into business.

Not quite yet, Cole thought. 'I seem to remember that the last time I saw you in that dress, there were several buttons towards the hem undone.'

It was a challenging reminder and she halted, looking down at her skirt in hot confusion.

'Three,' he said. 'I recall counting three undone.'

Her gaze lifted, eyes astonished. 'You counted them?'

He grinned. 'I'm good at counting.'

A little laugh gurgled from her throat. 'So you are.'

'And here you are all buttoned up today, which doesn't look right at all. I much preferred it the other way. I think you should oblige me and undo at least one button before we get down to serious business.'

'One button,' she repeated, her eyes sparkling at the mischievous nonsense.

Fun was the key here. There was never enough fun in anyone's life. She'd had fun trying clothes on during the buying spree on Saturday. What could be more relaxing and seductive than having fun with some knowingly provocative undressing?

'Okay. One button for now,' he agreed. 'Though I think it would relieve the pressure of these meetings if an extra button got undone after each session.'

'That makes four buttons.'

'I knew you were good at counting, too.'

She gave him an arch look, joining in the game he was playing. 'You might find that distracting.'

'No. I'll think of it as my reward for outstanding concentration.'

She placed the folder on the desk. Then with an air of whimsical indulgence, she flicked open the bottom button, straightened up, took a deep breath and boldly asked, 'Happy now?'

'We progress. Let's say I'm…briefly…satisfied.' He ran his gaze up the row of buttons from hem to neckline, then smiled, meeting her eyes with deliberately wicked intent.

She flushed, realising he had no intention of stopping anywhere. *And may she burn with anticipation all morning,* Cole thought as he drew the folder over to his side of the desk and opened it, ostensibly ready to familiarise himself with the financial details of the client who would soon be arriving.

He'd thrown his net, caught Liz with it, and he'd draw her closer and closer to him as the morning wore on. The whole encounter had sharpened his mind brilliantly. He felt right on top of the game.

An hour later, the first client had been dealt with. Without saying a word, Cole stared at Liz's skirt. Without a word from her, she undid a button, then handed him the next file.

Exhilarated by the silent complicity, Cole ploughed through the next meeting, sparking on all cylinders.

Another button hit the dust.

He could see above her knee now when she walked, the skirt peeping open far enough to tease him with flashes of leg. Was she wearing stockings as he'd requested?

Excitement buzzed through his brain. Restraint was

like a refined torture. He forced it over the desire simmering through him and satisfied the third client with a fast and comprehensive exposition on the state of the money markets. Even as he ushered the man out of his office, his gaze targeted the next button, wanting it opened, commanding it done…now…this instant.

He saw her hands move to do it as he walked his client through Liz's office. Anticipation roared through him. It was an act of will to keep accompanying the man to the elevator, farewelling him into the compartment before turning back to the woman who had to be wanting an acceleration of action as much as he did.

He'd planned the sexual tease. He'd meant it to go on all day, but here he was, too caught up with the need it had evoked in him to wait for tonight. To hell with work. It was lunch time anyway. Though his appetite for Liz Hart wiped out any thought of food. The energy driving him now did not require more fuel.

He strode into her office, locked the door against any possible interruption. She stood at one of the filing cabinets, putting the last folder away. The click of the lock caused her to throw a startled glance over her shoulder. Their eyes met, the sizzling intent in his causing hers to widen.

'It's all right,' he said, soothing any shock. 'We're alone. Private. And I want you very urgently, Liz Hart.'

She didn't move, seemingly entranced by the force of need emanating from him. Then he was behind her, his arms caging her, pulling her back against him, finding some solace for his fierce erection in pressing it against the soft cleft of her sexy bottom.

He heard, felt her gasp, kissed the delicate nape of her neck, needing to give vent to the storm of desire engulfing him. He was so hungry for her. His hands covered her stomach, pushing in, making her feel how much he wanted her. Then he remembered the buttons, stockings, bare thighs, and his desire for her took another turn. He dropped his hands, fingers moving swiftly, opening the skirt.

And yes, yes...it was how he'd envisaged, stockings ending, naked flesh above them, quivering to his touch, the crotch of her panties hot, moist, telling evidence of her excitement, boosting his.

He whirled her over to her desk, sat her on it, took her chair, spread her legs, lifting them over his shoulders as he bent to taste the soft, bare, tremulous inner walls of her thighs, kissing, licking, smelling her need for him, exulting in it, knowing she was his to take as he wanted.

Liz could hardly believe what was happening. He was spreading the silk of her panties tight, kissing her through the thin screen, finding the throbbing centre between her folds, sucking on it. Pleasure rushed from the heat of his mouth, sweeping through her like a tidal wave. She had to lie back on the desk to cope with it, though there was no coping, more a melting surrender to the flow of sensation.

And she had once thought him an ice man!

He let her legs slide from his shoulders as he rose,

seemingly intent on following her, bending over her, his eyes dark, ringed with burning blue—no ice!— and she felt the silk being drawn aside as the hot hard length of him pushed to possess the space waiting for him, aching for him.

The intense focus of his eyes captured hers, held it as he drove the penetration home. 'This is how it is…in the light,' he said raggedly. 'You don't need the dark, Liz. It's better this way, seeing, knowing…'

He withdrew enough to plunge again, and it *was* thrilling to see the tension on his face, the concentrated flare of desire in his eyes, to watch him moving in the driving rhythm that pleasured them both in ever increasing pulse beats of intense excitement. The final release was incredibly mutual, and instinctively she wrapped her arms around his head and drew his mouth to hers, kissing him with the sweet knowledge that his desire for her was very real, not some accident of fate because she was simply on hand at a time of need.

This was proven to her over and over again as the days—and nights—rolled on towards the date of departure for the trip to South-East Asia. For the most part, restraint ruled in the office, but then they would go to her apartment, his apartment, make wild needy love, proceed to a nearby restaurant for dinner, enjoy fine food and wine while they whetted their appetite for more lovemaking.

It was exhilarating, addictive, a whirlwind of uninhibited passion, and Liz was so completely caught up in it, she heartily wished she wasn't going off travelling with his mother…until Cole made an announcement over dinner on Thursday night that gave her pause for thought.

'My divorce was settled this afternoon. I'm finally a free man again.'

It was the relief in his voice that unsettled her, as though his freedom had remained threatened until the law had brought his marriage to Tara Summerville to an end. It instantly brought to mind the confrontation between them last Saturday, with Tara firing all her guns to win a reconciliation, and Cole savagely denying her any chance of it.

Since then—apart from Sunday when he had been occupied elsewhere—he had virtually immersed himself in a white-hot affair with the very woman Tara had accused of a sexual connection to Cole. Had it become so concentrated in order to keep Tara completely shut out? No space for her, not in his mind, not in his life, ensuring the final line was drawn on a marriage he'd written off as a case of bad judgment.

One could settle things in one's head that didn't necessarily get translated into physical and emotional responses. In a kind of reverse situation, Liz knew she'd reasoned out a million things about Brendan, trying to keep positive about their relationship, even when her body and heart were reacting negatively. The old saying, mind over matter, didn't really work. It only covered over stuff that kept bubbling underneath.

Liz couldn't help wondering if Cole had chosen her as the best possible distraction to take him through to the finishing line with Tara. Yet the sexual chemistry they shared had to be real. He couldn't perform as he did unless he felt it. And he'd noticed how many buttons had been undone on the bronze dress last week, before that meeting with Tara. Which surely meant Liz could trust the attraction between them.

It was just that Cole had such a formidable mind. Once he decided something, he went at it full bore until the goal was achieved. And Liz didn't know what his goal was with her, except to satisfy a very strong sexual urge—made right because she wanted the same satisfaction. Although secretly she wanted more from him. Much more.

But nothing was said about any future with her. Too soon, Liz told herself. After dinner, Cole drove her home. This was their last night together for more than two weeks while she toured through South-East Asia with his mother. She had Friday off to pack and generally get ready for the trip so she wouldn't be seeing him at work tomorrow. It had been arranged for her to meet Nancy Pierson at the airport Holiday Inn at six o'clock for a tour group dinner and they would fly off early Saturday morning.

Cole stayed late, seemingly reluctant to part from her even when he finally chose to leave. 'I wish you weren't going on this trip,' he said with a rueful smile, then kissed her long and hard, passionately reminding her of all the intimacy they'd shared. 'I'll miss you,' he murmured against her lips.

In every sense, Liz hoped, silently deciding the trip was a timely break, giving them both the distance to reflect on what they'd done, where they were going with it and why.

She felt she'd been caught up in a fever-pitch compulsion that completely blotted out everything else beyond Cole Pierson. Distance might give her enough perspective to see if it truly was good... or the result of influences that had pulled them somewhere they shouldn't be.

Which wouldn't be good at all.

CHAPTER THIRTEEN

BY MIDAFTERNOON Friday, Cole found himself totally irritated by the temporary assistant taking Liz's place. He wasn't asking much of her. Why did she have to look so damned intimidated all the time? He hoped his mother appreciated the sacrifice he was making, giving her Liz as a companion for this trip.

Which reminded him to call his mother before the limousine arrived to transport her to the airport Holiday Inn, make sure she wasn't in a tizz about having everything ready to go. He picked up the telephone and dialled the number for the Palm Beach house.

'Yes?' his mother answered breathlessly.

'Just calm down, Mum. The limousine can wait until you're sure you haven't left anything behind.'

'Oh, Cole! I was just going around the house to check everything was locked.'

'I'll drive out tomorrow and double-check the security alarm so don't worry about it. Okay?'

A big sigh. 'Thank you, dear. There's always so much to think about before I leave. I did call your Liz and she assured me she's all organised.'

His Liz. A pity she wasn't his right now. In more ways than one. 'She would be,' he said dryly.

'Such a nice girl!' came the voice of warm approval. 'I rather hope we do run into her boyfriend at

Kathmandu. I can't imagine he's not having second thoughts about leaving her.'

'What?' The word squawked out of the shock that momentarily paralysed Cole's brain.

'You must know about him,' his mother said reasonably. 'Brendan Wheeler. He and Liz have been together for the past three years.'

'Yes, I know about him,' Cole snapped. 'But not that he was in Kathmandu. When did Liz tell you this?'

'Last Saturday when we were working out what clothes to take. It seemed wrong that she didn't have a boyfriend, so I asked her…'

'Right!' *Before he'd made his move. She couldn't want the guy back now…could she?* 'Brendan dumped her, Mum, so don't be getting any romantic ideas about their getting together again,' he said tersely.

'But it might have been only a case of him getting cold feet over commitment, Cole. If he comes face to face with Liz over there…'

'I am not paying for my personal assistant to run off with a guy in Kathmandu!' Cole thundered into the receiver. 'If you assist this in any way whatsoever…'

'Oh, dear! I didn't think of that. Well, I don't think she would actually run off, Cole. As you said, Liz is very responsible. I'm sure she'd insist on Brendan following her back home to prove good faith.'

'Better that the situation be avoided altogether,' he grated through a clenched jaw.

'You can't block Fate, dear,' his mother said blithely.

Fate was a fickle fool, Cole thought viciously, recalling how quickly Liz had agreed to the trip. He'd listed off Nepal as one of the destinations when he put the proposition to her. She must have instantly thought…Kathmandu…Brendan. And she'd played his mother brilliantly at lunch that day, clinching the deal.

No reluctance at the possibility of meeting him over there.

She'd even told his mother where the guy was.

'Mum, you keep your nose right out of this,' Cole commanded. 'No aiding and abetting. I'm telling you straight. Brendan was no good for Liz.'

'No good?' came the critical reply. 'Then why did she stay with him so long? She didn't have a child to consider…like you did with Tara. And Liz didn't do the leaving,' his mother reminded him with pertinent emphasis.

He wanted to shout, *Liz is with me, now,* but knew it would be tantamount to ringing wedding bells in his mother's ears and Cole was not prepared to deal with that.

'He repressed her. He put her down. He made her feel like a failure,' he punched out. 'I know this, Mum, so just let it be. Liz is better off without him. Okay?'

A long pause, then…'You really do care about her, don't you?'

Care? Of course, he cared. And he certainly didn't want to lose her to an idiot who hadn't cared enough to keep her. However, what he needed here was to seal his mother's sympathy to the cause of holding Liz away from Brendan.

'She's had a rough time, Mum,' he said in a gentler tone. 'I want you to ensure she enjoys this trip. No pain.'

'I'll do my best,' came the warm and ready promise.

Mother hen to the rescue of wounded bird.

Cole breathed more easily.

'Right! Well, I hope you have a wonderful time together.'

'Thank you. I'm sure we will. Oh, there's the limousine now. Must go, dear. Goodbye! Thanks for all your help.'

Gone!

He put the receiver down and stared at the telephone for several seconds, strongly tempted to call Liz, but what more could he say? He'd told her last night he would miss her, shown her how very desirable she was to him. There could be no possible doubt in her mind that he wanted her back, wanted her with him.

Surely to God she wouldn't throw what they'd shared aside and take Brendan back!

She couldn't be that much of a fool!

Or did he have it all wrong?

Cole rose from his chair and paced around the office, unsettled by the sudden realisation that much of what he'd told his mother comprised assumptions on his part. Maybe Liz had felt secure enough in her relationship with Brendan not to bother about feminine frippery, saving money towards a marriage and having a family…which had slipped away from her because… *He didn't like my style of management.*

That was all she had actually told him about the relationship.

He'd interpreted the rest.

What if he was wrong?

He'd steamrolled Liz into a hot and heavy affair, to which she'd been a willing party, but he didn't really know what was going on in her mind. Was it rebound stuff for her? An overwhelming need to *feel* desired?

What if she did meet Brendan in Kathmandu and they clicked again, as they must have done in the beginning? Would she count the sex with her boss as meaning anything in any long-term sense? Had he made it *mean* anything to her?

All he'd said was it felt right.

And it did.

She'd agreed.

But was it enough to hold her to him?

Cole didn't know.

But there was nothing more he could do or say now to shift the scales his way.

Besides, Kathmandu was a big city. The tour schedule was jam-packed. The likelihood of her running into Brendan was very low. She had a full-time job to do—looking after his mother—and he'd just ensured, as best he could, that his mother wouldn't let Liz skip out on her responsibility.

Cole took a deep breath and returned to his desk.

Liz would come back.

He was wasting time, worrying over things he had no control over, but that very lack of absolute control where Liz Hart was concerned made him...uneasy.

CHAPTER FOURTEEN

LIZ quickly found she had no difficulty in travelling with Nancy Pierson. All the older woman needed was a bit of prompting on where they had to be at what time, and when their luggage was to be put outside their hotel room to be collected by the Captain's Choice staff, all of whom were brilliantly and cheerfully efficient. Nancy accepted the prompting goodnaturedly, grateful that Liz took the responsibility of ensuring they did everything right.

It was quite marvellous flying off on a chartered Qantas jet with almost two hundred other tourists, everyone excited about the adventure ahead of them. The party atmosphere on the plane was infectious, helped along by the champagne which flowed from the moment they were seated.

'Oh, I'm so glad you were able to come with me,' Nancy enthused, her eyes twinkling with the anticipation of much pleasure as she started on a second glass of champagne.

'So am I. This is great. But you want to go easy on the champers, Nancy. Don't drink it too quickly,' Liz warned, concerned about her getting tipsy.

Nancy laughed. 'I'm not a lush, dear. Just celebrating.' She leaned over confidentially. 'Cole's divorce was settled on Thursday. He's completely free of that woman now.'

'Well, I guess that's a good thing,' Liz said non-committally, unsure how she should respond.

'He'd make a wonderful husband to the right woman, you know,' Nancy went on, eyeing her with a spark of hopeful eagerness.

Liz could feel a tide of heat creeping up her neck and quickly brushed the subject aside. 'A failed marriage often puts people off the idea of marrying again.'

'But Cole absolutely adored his son. It was such a terrible tragedy losing David, and it's taken a long time for him to get over it, but I'm sure he'll want to have more children and he's not getting any younger,' Nancy argued.

'Men can have children any time they like,' Liz dryly pointed out. 'It's only women who have a biological clock ticking.'

'He doesn't want to get too old and set in his ways.' A sad sigh. 'His father—my husband—was like that, unfortunately. Didn't want more than one child. But I'm sure Cole is different. He loved being a father.'

'Then perhaps he'll be one again someday.'

This drew a sharp look. 'Do you want children, Liz?'

The flush swept into her cheeks. 'Someday.'

Another sigh. 'Someday I'd love to have a grand-child in my life again. Your mother must be delighted with hers.'

'Yes, she is. Particularly the twins, being boys, after having only daughters herself.'

Luckily, this turn of the conversation diverted

Nancy from pushing Cole as an eligible husband—a highly sensitive issue—and Liz was able to relax again. She didn't want to speculate on her new relationship with Nancy's son. It had happened so fast. She was banking on time away to bring some sort of perspective to it…on both sides.

When they arrived in Kuching, it was great to immerse herself in a completely different part of the world. Their hotel overlooked the Sarawak River with its fascinating traffic of fishing boats and sampans—smells and sights of the East. Kuching actually meant the city of cats and it even had a cat museum featuring an amazing collection of historical memorabilia on the feline species.

On their second morning, a bus took them to the Semengoh Orangutan Reserve where they were able to observe the animals closest to humans on the primate ladder, extinct now except here in Borneo. The orangutans' agility, swinging through the trees, was amazing but it was their eyes that Liz would always remember—so like people's eyes in their expression.

They also visited a long house where over a thousand men, women and children lived together in the old traditional way, with each family having their own quarters but sharing a large verandah as a communal area. No isolation here, as there was in modern apartment buildings, Liz thought. Ready company seemed to make for happy harmony, and sharing was obviously a way of life, clearly giving a sense of security and contentment in continuity.

It made her wonder how much had been lost in striving for singular achievement in western society.

She didn't want to live alone for the rest of her life, yet going back to her parents' home didn't seem right, either. She was thirty years old, had a mortgage on an apartment she was living in, but no one to share it with on any permanent basis. Her neighbours in the apartment block were like ships passing in the night. Where was she going with her life?

Would Cole ever think of marrying her?

Having a family with her?

Or was all this sexual intensity nothing more than a floodgate opening after a long period of celibacy?

It hurt to think about it. She knew the attraction had always been there on her side—suppressed because it had to be. Her boss was off limits for a variety of good reasons. Besides which, he'd shown no interest in her as a woman until…what exactly had triggered his interest? The new image? The fact that Brendan was no longer an item in her life, making her unattached and available? Simple proximity when he felt tempted by Tara's blatantly offered sexuality?

To Liz's mind, it wasn't something solid, something she could trust in any long-term sense. As much as she would like to explore a serious relationship with Cole, she wasn't sure it was going to develop that way, which made her feel very vulnerable about the eventual outcome.

She could end up in a far worse situation than when Brendan had decided enough was enough. Holding on to her job would be unthinkable, unbearable. Did Cole realise that? Had he even paused to think about it? What did *right* mean to him?

She wasn't at all sure that Diana's advice about

going with the flow was good—not if it led to a waterfall that would dash her to pieces. But there was no need to make any decision about it yet. Indeed, she didn't know enough to make a sensible decision.

The next day the tour group had a wonderful boat trip on the river to Bako National Park where they walked through a rainforest and swam in the South China Sea from a beautiful little beach. It felt like a million miles away from the more sophisticated life in Australia—primitive, sensual on a very basic level, simple but very real pleasures. Time slipped by without any worries.

They left Kuching and flew to Rangoon in Burma—or rather Yangon in Myanmar as it was now known. This had been one of the richest countries of South-East Asia and its past glories were abundantly evident. The Shwedagon Pagoda with its giant dome covered with sixty tonnes of gold and the top of the stupa encrusted with thousands of diamonds, rubies and sapphires, was absolutely awesome.

And the comfort of a past era was amply displayed in the old steam train chartered to take the tourists into the nearby countryside, through the green rice fields and the small villages where nothing had changed for centuries. Pot plants decorated the carriages, legroom was spacious, seats were far more comfortable than in modern trains, and provided with drink holders and ashtrays. The windows, of course, could be opened and it was fun waving to the people they passed, all of whom waved back.

'I feel like the queen of England,' Nancy commented laughingly. 'Such fun!'

Indeed, much of England lingered here, especially in the architecture of the city. The City Hall, Supreme and High Court Buildings, GPO, Colonial Offices—all of them would have looked at home in London, yet the city centre revolved around the Sule Pagoda which was stunningly from a very different culture, as were the temples.

On their last night in Rangoon a 'grand colonial evening' had been arranged for them at The Strand Hotel which had been built by an English entrepreneur and opened in 1901. It had once been considered 'the finest hostelry east of Suez, patronised by royalty, nobility and distinguished personages'—according to the 1911 edition of Murray's Handbook for Travelers in India, Burma and Ceylon.

The men were given a pith helmet to put them in the correct British India period, the women an eastern umbrella made of wood and paper printed with flowers. Everyone was asked to wear white as far as possible and as Liz dressed for the evening in the broderie anglaise peasant blouse and frilled skirt that Cole had bought for her, memories of their shopping spree came flooding back.

You're a class act, Liz Hart. Top of the top. And you are going to be dressed accordingly.

Cole hadn't been talking sex then.

If she really was the *top of the top* to him...but maybe that just referred to her efficiency as his P.A.

As much as she wanted to believe he could fall in love with her—was in love with her—Liz felt he only wanted sex, no emotional ties. And she'd been tempted into tasting the realisation of a fantasy which probably should have remained a fantasy. Except she couldn't regret the experience of having actually known what it was like to be his woman, if only for a little while.

'I just love that outfit on you!' Nancy remarked, eyeing her admiringly as they set off from their hotel room.

Liz bit her lips to stop the words, 'Your son's choice.' She forced a smile. 'Well I must say you look spectacular in yours, Nancy.'

She did. Her glittery white tunic was beaded with pearls at the neckline and hem, falling gracefully over a narrow skirt which was very elegant. In fact, Nancy had been right about the dressing on this tour. Casual clothes ruled during the day, but there was very classy dressing at the evening dinners which were invariably a special event.

The compliment was received with obvious pleasure. 'Thank you, dear. We must make the most of this last night here. It's off to Kathmandu tomorrow.'

Liz didn't reply. Kathmandu conjured up thoughts of Brendan. Was he happy with *the space* he'd put between them? If by some weird coincidence they should meet, would he think she had pursued him? What would his reaction be?

Didn't matter, Liz decided with a touch of bitterness. She'd wasted three years on him and wasn't going to waste another minute even thinking about their past relationship. But was she doing any better for herself with Cole? Would she look back in a few months' time and wonder at her own madness for getting so intimately involved with him?

A bus transported them to the Strand Hotel, the men laughing in their helmet hats—a pukka reminder of the British Raj—the women twirling their umbrellas with very feminine pizazz, embracing the sense of slipping back into a past era. They walked into a spacious, very old-world reception lobby, two storeys high with marvellous ceiling fans and chandeliers, wonderful arrangements of flowers, someone playing eastern music on a xylophone. Many waiters circulated with trays of cocktails and hors d'oeuvres, the refreshments adding to the convivial mood.

Overlooking the lobby was an upstairs balcony, a richly polished wood balustrade running around the four sides. Nancy was taking it all in, revelling in the ambience of the superbly kept period hotel. Liz heard her gasp, and automatically looked to where she was looking, her whole body jolting in shock as she saw what Nancy saw.

'Good heavens! There's Cole!'

He was on the balcony scanning the crowd below. Even as his mother spoke, his gaze zeroed in on them. His mouth twitched into a smile. He raised his hand in a brief salute then turned away, heading for the staircase which would bring him down to where they were.

Every nerve in Liz's body was suddenly wired with hyper-tension. Her mind pulsed with wild speculation over why Cole was here? He hadn't once suggested he might catch up with them on this trip. Had he felt compelled to check on her for some reason? Didn't he trust her with his mother?

'Well, well, well,' Nancy drawled, her voice rich

with satisfaction. 'Cole has actually taken time off work to be with us. Isn't that wonderful!'

It jerked Liz out of her turbulent thoughts. 'Did you…invite him to join us?' she choked out, her throat almost too tight to force words out.

Nancy shook her head in a bemused fashion. 'I didn't even think of it.' A lively interest sparkled in her eyes. 'Though I do find it very encouraging that he's done so just before we leave for Kathmandu.'

'Encouraging?' Liz echoed, not comprehending Nancy's point.

'Oh yes, dear. It's a very good sign,' she said with a complacent smile.

Of what?

Liz didn't have time to ask. Cole was already downstairs and heading towards them. He cut such an imposing figure and emanated such powerful purpose, people automatically moved aside to give him a clear path through the milling crowd, heads turning to stare after him, women eyeing him up and down. He looked absolutely stunning dressed in a white linen suit, made classy casual by the black T-shirt he'd teamed it with. A man in a million, Liz thought, her heart pounding erratically at his fast approach.

He grinned, his hands lifting into a gesture that encompassed them both as he reached them. 'Definitely the two best looking women here!' he declared.

His mother laughed. 'What a surprise to see you!'

'A happy one, I hope.' His gaze slid to Liz, the piercing blue eyes suddenly like laser beams burning into hers. The grin softened to a quirky smile. 'One day in the office with your replacement was enough to spur me into taking a vacation. You are…quite irreplaceable, Liz.'

In the office or in his bed? Did this mean he'd decided he couldn't do without her? Excitement fevered her brain. 'Have you arranged to join the tour?'

'Only for this evening. I'm actually booked into this hotel for a couple of days. I thought I'd have this one night with you…'

One night…in this hotel…

'…share what appears to be a very special occasion and escort you both to dinner.' He turned back to his mother. 'Are you enjoying yourself, Mum?'

'Immensely, dear. What are your plans for the rest of your vacation?'

'I thought I'd take a look at Mandalay while I'm in this country. It's always had a fascinating ring to it…Mandalay…'

'You're not coming to Kathmandu?'

'No.' He flicked a quick probing look at Liz. Trying to assess her reaction to this decision? Was she okay with only one night here? 'But I am flying on to Vietnam,' he added. 'I might meet up with you there.'

'We're very busy in Vietnam,' his mother warned.

He laughed. 'Perhaps I'll catch up with you for another dinner together. Hear all your news.'

Another night.

Liz's heart squeezed tight.

Was Cole expecting to whisk her away from his mother for a while…fit in a hot bit of sex?

If so, she wouldn't be a party to it, Liz fiercely decided, her backbone stiffening. She would not have his mother thinking there was some hanky-panky go-ing on between her son and his personal assistant, just as his ex-wife had suggested. Nancy might even leap to a rosy conclusion that was not currently on the cards—marriage and grandchildren!—and her happy allusions to it would be horribly embarrassing.

Best that she didn't so much as guess at any inti-mate connection. There were another eleven days of the trip to get through and every hour of it in Nancy's company. As it was, she was happily raving on to Cole about what they'd seen so far, accepting his presence here at face value. *Let it stay that way,* Liz grimly willed.

'What about you, Liz? Having fun?' he inquired charmingly.

'Yes, thank you.'

'No problems?' His eyes scoured hers, trying to penetrate the guard she'd just raised.

'None,' she answered sharply.

He frowned slightly. 'I haven't come to check up on you, if that's what you're wondering.'

She managed an ironic smile. 'That would com-prise bad judgment and a waste of time and money, Cole.'

He returned her smile. 'As always, your logic is spot on.'

'Thank you. I hope you enjoy your vacation.'

The distance she was putting between them was so obvious in her impersonal replies, he couldn't possi-bly mistake it. His eyes glittered at her, as though she'd thrown out a challenge he was bent on taking up with every bit of ammunition at his disposal. Liz burned with aggressive determination. Not in front of your mother, she wanted to scream at him.

'Time to move on to the ballroom,' Nancy announced, observing the people around moving forward, being ushered towards the next stage of the evening—dinner, entertainment and dancing in the Strand Hotel ballroom.

'Ladies…'

With mock colonial gallantry, Cole held out both of his arms for them to hook on to, ready to parade them in to dinner. His mother happily complied. Realising it would be rude to try avoiding the close contact, Liz followed suit, fixing a smile on her face and focusing on the people moving ahead of them, doing her level best to ignore the heat emanating from him and jangling every nerve in her body.

As they walked along, Nancy hailed various new acquaintances amongst the tour group, introducing her son, distracting Cole from any concentration on Liz, for which she was intensely grateful. It left her free to glance around the ballroom which was very elegant, panelled walls painted in different shades of pinky beige, huge chandeliers hanging from very high ceilings, a highly polished wooden floor, tables set for ten with white starched tablecloths and all the chairs had skirted white slip covers, adding to the air of pristine luxury.

Nancy insisted they sit at a table on the edge of the circle left free for dancing, saying she wanted to be close to whatever entertainment had been arranged for them. Cole obliged her by steering them to seats which had a direct view of the stage. Other people quickly joined them, making up the table of ten.

Liz was glad of the numbers. Although Cole had seated himself between her and Nancy, at least she had people to talk to on her other side, a good excuse to break any private tete-a-tete he might have in mind.

Even so, he shattered her hastily thought out defences by leaning close and murmuring, 'I look forward to dancing with you tonight.'

Dancing!

Being held in his arms, pressed into whatever contact he manoeuvred, moved right out of his mother's hearing for whatever he wanted to say to her…

Panic churned through Liz's stomach.

How was she going to handle this?

How?

CHAPTER FIFTEEN

Liz barely heard the choir of street children who had been rescued by the World Vision organization. They sang a number of songs. Another troup of children performed a dance. People made speeches she didn't hear at all. Food was placed in front of her and she ate automatically, not really tasting any of it. The man sitting beside her dominated her mind and played havoc with every nerve in her body.

A band of musicians took over the stage. They played a style of old time jazz that was perfect for ballroom dancing. A few couples rose from their tables, happily intent on moving to the music. Any moment now…

She could politely decline Cole's invitation to dance with him. He couldn't force her to accept. But given the level of intimacy there had been between them, he had every right to expect her compliance. A rejection would create an awkwardness that Nancy would inevitably rush into, urging Liz to *enjoy herself.*

She could say her feet were killing her.

Except she hadn't once complained about sore feet on this tour and Nancy might make a fuss about that, too.

Cole set his serviette on the table, pushed back his chair and rose to his feet. The band was playing

'Moon River', a jazz waltz which could only be executed well with very close body contact. Liz's stomach lurched as Cole turned to her, offering his hand.

'Dance, Liz?'

She stared at the hand, riven by a warring tumult of needs.

'Go on, dear,' Nancy urged. 'I'm perfectly happy watching the two of you waltz around.'

There really was no choice. Cole's other hand was already on the back of her chair ready to move it out of her way. Liz stood on jelly-like legs, fiercely resolving not to spend the night with him, no matter how deep the desire he stirred. It was an issue of... of...

She forgot what the issue was as his fingers closed around hers in a firm possessive clasp. An electric charge ran up her arm and short-circuited her brain. It seemed no time at all before his arm had scooped her against the powerful length of his body and his thighs were pushing hers into the seductive glide of the slow waltz.

He lowered his head and murmured in her ear. 'Why aren't I welcome, Liz?'

Her lobe tingled with the warmth of his breath. It was difficult to gather her scattered wits under the physical onslaught of his strong sexuality. The very direct question felt like an attack too, forcing her to explain her guarded behaviour with him.

'I'm with your mother,' she shot out, hoping he would see the need for some sense of discretion.

'So?' he queried, totally unruffled by any embarrassment she might feel about being pressed into some obvious closeness with him.

'It's not right to…' She struggled with the sensitivity of the situation, finally blurting out, '…to give her ideas…about us.'

'What's not right about it?' he countered. 'We're both free to pursue what we want.' His hand slid down the curve of her spine, splaying across the pit of her back, pressing firmly as his legs tangled with hers in an intricate set of steps and turns. 'I want you,' he said, again breathing into her ear. 'I thought you wanted me.'

She jerked her head back, her gaze wildly defying the simmering desire in his eyes. 'That's been private between us.'

'True. But I have no problem with making our private relationship public. And I can't imagine my mother would have any objection to it, either. She likes you.'

Resentment at his lack of understanding flared. 'That's not the point.'

He raised an eyebrow, mocking her contentious attitude. 'What is the point?'

Liz sucked in a quick breath and laid out what he apparently preferred to ignore. 'Nancy will want to think it's serious. She's already expressed her hope to me that you'll marry again and…and provide her with grandchildren.'

'And you don't see marriage on the cards for us?'

It sounded like a challenge to her. As though she had made a decision without telling him. And his eyes were now burning into hers with the determined purpose of finding out precisely what was on her mind.

Liz was flooded with confusion. 'You said…you said you had no intention of marrying again in a hurry.'

'Marry in haste, repent at leisure,' he quoted sardonically. 'Not a mistake I care to repeat. But I can assure you it won't take me three years to make up my mind.'

'Three…years?'

'That's what you spent on Brendan, Liz.'

She shook her head, amazed that he was linking himself in any way to her experience with Brendan. It was all so completely different. Why even compare a blitzkrieg affair to a long siege for commitment? In any event, it reminded her of a failure she preferred to forget. Surely Cole should realise that.

The music stopped.

The dancing stopped.

Cole still held her close, not making any move to disengage or take her back to the table. She dropped her hand from his shoulder, preparing to push out of his embrace. All the other couples were leaving the dance floor.

'Why didn't you tell me Brendan was in Nepal?'

'What?' Startled, her gaze flew up to meet his and was caught in the blaze of fierce purpose glittering at her.

'You heard me,' he stated grimly.

Her mind was whirling over knowledge he couldn't have…unless… 'Did Brendan try to contact me at the office?'

'Is that what you want to hear? Did you contact him with the news you were coming?'

'No...I...' She didn't understand what this was all about.

'Have you left a message for him to meet you in Kathmandu?' Cole bored in.

'It's over!' she cried, trying to cut through to the heart of the situation.

'Not for me, it isn't!' came the harsh retort.

She glanced wildly around the emptied dance floor. 'You're making a spectacle of us, standing here.'

'Then let's take the show on the road. You want private? We'll have private.'

Before Liz could begin to protest, he had her waist firmly grasped and was leading her straight to Nancy who was keenly watching them.

'I don't want private,' Liz muttered fiercely.

'I'm not going to let you take up ignoring me again, nor pretending there's been nothing deeply personal between us. Public or private, Liz. You choose.'

Aggression was pouring from him. He'd blow discretion sky-high if she insisted on staying at the table with the tour group. Liz frantically sought a way out of the dilemma Cole was forcing. Nancy was smiling at them, pleased to see them linked together. Liz inwardly recoiled from the interpretation she would put on their *togetherness* if Cole made it clear he was involved with his P.A. on more than a professional level.

Best to seize the initiative before he said something. Liz managed a rueful smile as they closed on his mother and quickly spoke up. 'Nancy, Cole and I have some business to sort out. Will you excuse us for a few minutes?'

'Might take quite a while,' Cole instantly inserted. 'Are you okay to get back to your hotel with the tour group, Mum?'

'Of course, dear.' She beamed triumphantly. 'I even have my room key with me. Liz always checks me on that.'

Trapped by her own efficiency.

'I'm sure we won't be so long, Cole,' she said, trying to minimise this *private* meeting.

'Best to cover all eventualities,' he smoothly returned. 'Given we run late sorting out this business, Mum, I'll escort Liz to your hotel and see her safely to your room, so no need to stay up and worry about her.'

Heat whooshed up Liz's neck and scorched her cheeks. Cole had to be planning more than just talk…

'Fine, dear,' came the ready acceptance to her son's plan. Nancy smiled benevolently at Liz. 'And don't you worry about disturbing me. It's been such a very busy day I'm sure I'll sleep like a log.'

Another excuse wiped out.

Cole picked up Liz's small evening bag from the table, taking possession of her money and her room key. 'Thanks, Mum,' he said by way of taking leave, then forcefully shepherded Liz towards the exit from the ballroom.

'Give me my bag,' she seethed through clenched teeth, determined not to have control taken completely out of her hands. If driven to it, she could arrange a taxi for herself.

'Going to do a runner on me, Liz?' he mocked.

'I don't like being boxed into a corner.'

'Right!' He passed it to her. 'So now you're a lady of independent means. Before you trot off in high dudgeon at my interference with your plans, I would appreciate your telling me what use I've been to you, apart from giving you a free ticket to Kathmandu.'

'What *use?*' She halted, stunned by what felt like totally unfair accusations. 'I didn't ask you for a free ticket!'

'This is not a private place.' To prove his point, he waved at the groups of smokers who had gathered out in the foyer to the ballroom. 'Since you don't want to cause gossip that might reach my mother's ears…'

He scooped her along with him, down the steps and through the passage to the hotel lobby, moving so fast Liz had barely caught her breath when he pressed the wall button beside an elevator.

'I am not going to your room,' she declared, furious at his arrogant presumption that she would just fall in with what he wanted.

His eyes seared hers in a savage assault. 'You had no problem with doing so last week.'

Liz's heart galloped at the sheer ferocity of feeling emanating from him. 'That…that was different.'

'How was it different? I'm making this as private as you had it then. Or was I just a stepping stone to boost your confidence enough to win with Brendan tomorrow?'

Brendan again!

The elevator doors opened while Liz was still shell-shocked by Cole's incredible reading of her actions.

He bundled her into the compartment and they were on their way up before her mind could even begin to encompass what he was implying. She stared at him in dazed disbelief. 'You think I went to bed with you to boost my confidence?'

'A frequent rebound effect,' he shot at her.

She was so incensed by the realisation he actually did think she had *used* him, the reverse side of that coin flooded into her mind. 'What about you, Cole?' she shot back at him. 'Quite a coincidence that on the very day Tara suggested I was obliging you in bed, you decided to make that true.'

He looked appalled. 'Tara had nothing to do with what I felt that night. Absolutely nothing!'

'So why do you imagine Brendan had anything to do with what I felt?'

'You didn't want the light on.'

'I didn't want you comparing me to your hot-shot wife. Finding me much less sexy.'

'You think I'd even look at a Tara clone after what I've been through with her?' he thundered.

Liz was stung into retorting, 'I don't know. She was the woman you married.'

'And divorced. As soon as it could be decently achieved after the death of our child.' A hard pride settled on his face. 'Tara is a user. She doesn't give a damn for anyone but herself. And believe me, that becomes sickeningly *unsexy* after you've lived with it for a while.' His eyes flashed venomously at her as he added, 'And I don't take kindly to being used by a woman I thought better of.'

'I didn't use you,' Liz cried vehemently.

'No? Then why the freeze-off tonight?'

'I told you. Your mother...'

'Not good enough!' he snapped, just as the elevator doors opened. He hustled her out into a corridor, jammed a key in a door, and pulled her into a private suite that ensured they'd be absolutely alone together.

Liz didn't fight the flow of action. The realisation had finally struck that this was not about having sex with her tonight. It was about sorting out their relationship and what it meant to them. And Cole was in a towering rage because he believed she meant to meet Brendan tomorrow, with the possible purpose of reigniting interest in a future together.

He released his hold on her as he closed the door behind them, apparently satisfied he had shut off all avenues of escape. 'Now...now I'll have the truth from you,' he said, exuding a ruthless relentlessness that perversely sent a thrill through Liz.

He cared.

He really cared.

Hugging this sweet knowledge to herself she walked on into the massive suite, past the opened door to a huge bathroom, past two queen size beds, through an archway to an elegant sitting room. She turned to face him in front of the large curtained window at the far end. He'd followed her to the archway where he stood with an air of fierce patience—a big, powerful man who was barely reining in violent feelings.

'I didn't tell you Brendan was in Nepal because it was irrelevant to us, Cole,' she stated quietly.

'Hardly irrelevant,' he gravelled back at her. 'Because of him you stopped hiding your light under a bushel and showed me a Liz Hart I'd never seen before.'

She shook her head. 'That was my sisters' idea. To brighten me up so that other men might see me as attractive. My mother insisted it would make me feel better about myself. Brendan was gone, Cole. I never thought for one moment of trying to get him back. It was over.'

'But then…having made me see you differently, which led to my proving how very desirable you were…you had a ticket to Nepal in your hand—the chance to show Brendan what he was missing.'

'We're going to Kathmandu. I have no idea where in Nepal Brendan is or if, indeed, he's still there. I don't care. If by some freakish chance I should run into him, it won't make any difference. I don't ever want him in my life again.'

He frowned. 'Is that how you feel about me, too? I've served your purpose of…feeling better about yourself?'

She lifted her chin in a kind of defiant challenge, telling herself she had nothing to lose now. 'You want the truth, Cole?'

'Yes.' Piercing blue eyes demanded it of her.

'I've always been attracted to you. But you were married. And I was no Tara Summerville anyway so it was absurd of me to even dream of ever having you. I guess you could say Brendan was a pragmatic choice for me and I tried quite desperately to make it work. Maybe that was what drove him away in the end…me trying too hard to make something that was never quite right into something I could live with.'

Another frown. 'You never indicated an attraction…'

'That would have been futile. And I liked working with you.'

He grimaced and muttered, 'My oasis in a desert.'

'Pardon?'

He managed an ironic smile. 'You helped make my life livable during its darkest days, just by being there, Liz.'

Her smile was wry. 'The handmaiden.'

'Oh, I wouldn't put you in that category. A handmaiden wouldn't talk back, put me in my place. More a helpmate.'

Liz took a deep breath and spilled out the critical question for her. 'Was I helping you to shut Tara out of your mind in those days—and nights—before your divorce was settled?'

He shook his head, clearly vexed by such a concept. 'She was gone. A lot longer gone than Brendan was for you, Liz. Part of me was angry because he'd made you feel a failure, made you feel less than you are. And Tara had put you down, as well. I wanted to lift you up…

'You took…*pity*…on me?' Everything within her recoiled from that idea.

'Good God, no!' He looked totally exasperated, frustrated by her interpretation, scowling as he gathered his thoughts to dispel it. 'I was angry that you felt so low, especially since you were worth so much more than the people who did that to you. I tried to tell you…show you….' He lifted his hands in an oddly helpless gesture. 'In the end, I couldn't stop myself from making love to you even though I knew I shouldn't risk our business relationship.'

'Making love…' She struggled to swallow the huge lump that had risen in her throat. 'It did feel like that, but then it seemed you only had sex on your mind. All the sex you could get.'

'With you, Liz. Only with you.' His eyes softened, warmed, simmered over her. 'You truly were like an oasis in the desert and when I finally got there, I wanted to revel in everything you gave me. It felt so good.'

So good… She couldn't deny it, didn't want to shade that truth by other things, but she needed to have all her doubts cleared away.

'To me, too,' she admitted. 'But I thought…maybe I was just handy and you were using me to…'

'No. Simply because you're you, Liz.'

'Tonight…when I saw you here…I decided I didn't want to be used like that. Not even by you, Cole.' She held tightly on to all her courage as she added, 'Though I want you more than any man I've known.'

His face broke into a smile that mixed relief with intense pleasure. 'Believe me. The feeling is entirely mutual.'

She let out the breath that had been caught in her lungs and an answering smile burst across her face. 'Really?'

'What do you think I've been fighting for?' He swiftly crossed the short distance between them and wrapped her in a tight hug, his eyes burning into hers with very serious intent. 'No pulling away from me now. We're going to see how well this relationship can work for us. Give it time. Okay?'

Not an impossible dream.

It was almost too much to believe. Her heart swelled with glorious hope. Her mind danced with future possibilities. She was being held very possessively by the man she wanted more than any other in the world. He'd left his work and flown to South-East Asia to fight anything that might part them, and now he was saying...

'Answer me, Liz.'

Commanding...

She loved this man...everything about him. Her arms flew up around his neck. 'Yes, Cole. Yes.' Joy in her voice, desire churning through her body. Mutual, she thought exultantly.

He kissed her, making *mutual* absolutely awesome.

They made love...wonderful, passionate, blissful love...long into the night. No inhibitions. Cole didn't have to sweep them away. Liz felt none. She believed she was the woman he wanted in every sense. He made her feel it. There was nothing she couldn't do with him, nothing she couldn't say to him. And she no longer worried about what his mother might think. Nancy would be happy for them.

It was almost dawn when Cole arranged for a car to transport them to the tour hotel. They'd both decided his mother might panic if Liz wasn't in their room when she woke up. Liz felt too exhilarated to sleep at all. She told herself she would have the opportunity later this morning, on the flight to Kathmandu.

Which reminded her…

'How did you know Brendan was in Nepal, Cole?'

'My mother told me, just before leaving on the trip.'

'Your mother?' Liz frowned over this unexpected source until she recollected having answered Nancy's questions on her ex-boyfriend. 'But why would she do that?'

Cole smiled. 'Maybe she guessed I cared about you and the suggestion that I might lose you was a prompt to action if I wanted to keep you.'

Liz sighed with happy contentment. 'Well, I'm glad you came.'

Cole squeezed her hand. 'So am I.'

She glanced down at their interlocked hands, suddenly recalling the horribly tense scene just after Tara had left the Palm Beach house and Cole had come to the conservatory to eliminate any distress she'd caused.

'Well, isn't that nice?' his mother had remarked. 'He cares about you, dear.'

Liz could now smile over the memory.

Maybe mothers knew best.

Cole did care about her.

And Liz certainly felt very, very good about herself.

CHAPTER SIXTEEN

Six months later...

LIZ and her sisters were in the kitchen, cleaning up after the Sunday lunch barbecue—an informal family celebration of her engagement to Cole who was happily chatting to her father and brothers-in-law out on the patio. Her mother and Nancy Pierson had their heads together in the lounge room, conferring about the wedding which Cole had insisted be held as soon as it could be arranged.

'That man of yours truly is charming. And mouth-wateringly attractive,' Sue declared, rolling her eyes teasingly at Liz. 'You have to admit it now.'

She laughed. 'He's improved a lot since we've been together.'

'Oh, you!' Sue flicked a tea-towel at her. 'You never give anything away. Still all buttoned up within yourself.'

'No, she's not!' Diana instantly disagreed. 'She's positively blossomed since we made her over. Best idea I ever had. And look what's come out of it.' She grabbed Liz's left hand out of the sink of washing up water and suds. 'Got to see your gorgeous ring again!'

It was a magnificent ruby, surrounded by diamonds. Liz smiled at the red gleams as Diana turned it to the light.

'That's the fire in you,' Cole had said when he'd slid it on her finger. 'Every time I think of you I feel warm.' Then a wicked grin. 'If not hot.'

'This is a very serious ring,' Diana decided. 'Definitely a *to have and to hold from this day forth* ring. High-powered stuff. I hope you realise what you're getting into with this guy, Liz.'

'I have known Cole for quite some time,' she answered dryly.

It evoked a gurgle of gleeful amusement. 'Nothing like marrying the boss.'

'What impresses me…' Jayne chimed in. '…is how good he is with the children. He's like a magnet to them. They're all over him and he obviously doesn't mind a bit.'

'He doesn't. Cole loved being a father.'

Jayne heaved a rueful sigh. 'So sad about the son he lost. Is he mad keen to have a family with you, Liz?'

'Definitely keen.'

'Liz…' her mother called from the doorway. 'Would you go and fetch Cole inside to us. Nancy and I need to talk to both of you.'

'Okay, Mum.'

Liz dried her hands on Jayne's tea-towel and headed for the patio. Behind her, her three sisters broke into a raucous chorus of, 'Here comes the bride…'

Liz was laughing at their high-spirited good humour as she stepped outside. It was so good to feel at one with them instead of shut out of their charmed circle, looking in. Not that they had ever shut her out.

Liz realised now she'd done that to herself, not feeling she could ever compete with them.

It was only with Cole that she'd come to understand that love had nothing to do with competition. Love simply accepted who you were. You didn't have to be like someone else…just who you were.

And she saw his love for her in his eyes as she walked towards him. It warmed her all through, made her feel special and brilliantly alive. She smiled, loving him right back.

'Our mothers want us in the lounge room with them. I think you've thrown them a bit, insisting on a quick wedding.'

'No way are we going to put it off,' he warned, and promptly excused himself from the company of the other men. He reached her in a couple of strides and wrapped an arm around her shoulders. 'We're standing firm on this, Liz. I want us married. I'm not waiting a day longer than I have to.'

'They won't be happy if they can't organise a proper wedding. And just remember, I only intend to be a bride once.'

He slanted a look at her that crackled with powerful purpose. 'I promise you, you'll have a proper wedding.'

Cole really was unstoppable when he had a goal in his sights.

Once they were in the lounge room, their mothers regaled them with the plans they'd made. A Saturday would be best for the wedding. Impossible to book a decent reception place at such short notice. Nancy had offered her home at Palm Beach, a marquee to be put up over the grounds surrounding the pool. Catering could be arranged.

'But, Liz,' her mother addressed her seriously. 'We really should have six weeks for the invitations to go out. People need that much time to...'

'No,' Cole broke in decisively. 'A month is it. If some invited guests can't make it, I'm sorry but we're not waiting on them.'

'What is the hurry, dear?' Nancy cried in exasperation.

His piercing blue eyes speared the question at Liz.

She nodded, feeling sure enough now to share their secret.

'Liz wouldn't agree to marry me until she was three months pregnant and feeling secure that everything was okay and she'd carry our baby full term.'

'Pregnant?' Her mother gaped at Liz.

'A baby!' Nancy clapped her hands in delight.

'If I'd had my way, we would have been married before she got pregnant,' Cole informed them. 'But Liz got this fixation about having a child...'

'*Our* child,' Liz gently corrected him.

He gave her a look that melted her bones. '*Our* child,' he repeated in a thrilling tone of possessive pride and joy.

'A grandchild,' Nancy said on a sigh of pleasure.

'And Liz doesn't want to look lumpy in her wedding dress,' Cole went on.

'Of course not!' Nancy happily agreed.

'Liz...' Having recovered from her initial shock, her mother rose from her armchair, shaking her head at her daughter as she came over to enfold her in a motherly hug. '…always bent on doing it your way. Congratulations, darling.'

'I'm so happy, Mum,' Liz assured her.

'As you should be.'

'And I'm so happy for both of you,' Nancy declared, leaving her chair to do some hugging herself. 'Liz is the right woman for you, Cole. I knew it the moment I met her.'

'Amazing how anyone can be blessed with such certainty at a moment's notice,' Cole drawled, his eyes twinkling at Liz.

'Mother's intuition,' she archly informed him. 'Maybe I'll get some of that myself in six months' time.'

'Mmmh…removing logical argument from our relationship?'

'More like shortcutting it.'

'This might be stretching my love for you.'

'You swore it would stretch on forever.'

He turned to his mother. 'You see, Mum? She's too smart for me.'

'Go on with you, Cole,' Nancy laughingly chided. 'You love it.'

He grinned. 'Yes, I do. And since we now have the wedding back on track, I'm going to whisk Liz off to show her how very much I love everything about her.'

And he did.

Six months later, Liz and Cole were the besotted parents of a baby daughter, Jessica Anne, whose tiny fingers curled around one of her father's and instantly enslaved him for life.

ACQUIRED BY HER GREEK BOSS

CHANTELLE SHAW

For Pippa Roscoe,
Thank you for being a wonderful editor,
for giving great advice, for the laughs we've shared
and your understanding (and occasional tear-mopping)
when I've struggled with a book!
Best wishes always,
Chantelle

CHAPTER ONE

'CAN I HELP YOU?' Alekos Gionakis said curtly, when he strode into his office on Monday morning and found an unknown woman making coffee with his espresso machine.

In the past month he'd had four temporary PAs, all of whom had proved inadequate to the task of organising his hectic schedule. But this morning his super-efficient personal assistant was due back at work after her holiday and Alekos was looking forward to his life running smoothly again. The idea that Sara might have delayed her return for some reason, and he would have to manage for even one more day with yet another temp, cast a dark cloud over his mood.

His rapier glance skimmed over the woman's hair that fell in loose waves around her shoulders and seemed to encompass every shade of brown from caramel to latte. Her delightfully curvaceous figure was packaged in a dusky pink blouse and a cream pencil skirt that was a good two inches shorter than knee length.

Moving his gaze lower, Alekos felt a jolt of masculine appreciation at her shapely legs, which were enhanced by her high-heeled shoes with cut-out sections at the front that revealed her bare toes. He noticed her toenails were varnished a flirty shade of hot pink that was more suited to a beach than to Gionakis Enterprises' prestigious offices in Piccadilly.

'Good morning, Alekos.'

He frowned at the sound of the familiar voice. Low-toned and melodious, for some reason it made him think of a cool, clear mountain stream.

'Sara?' Her *voice* was recognisable, but everything about his PA's appearance was definitely not. His brain was not playing tricks on him, Alekos realised when she turned her head. Even though she was standing several feet away from him, he was struck by the intense green of her eyes. They were her only remarkable features—or at least that had been true when Sara's style of workwear for the past two years had been a navy blue skirt and jacket, which she'd teamed with a plain white shirt, buttoned primly all the way up to her throat in the summer, or a black roll-neck sweater in colder weather.

Smart, practical and frankly unnoticeable was how Alekos would have described his PA's appearance before she had inconveniently decided to take a month's holiday in Spain. When he'd objected, she had reminded him that she hadn't used any of her annual leave since she'd started working for him, apart from one day to attend her mother's funeral. Sara had looked even more washed out than she usually did. Alekos was not renowned for his sensitivity, but he'd acknowledged that caring for her terminally ill mother must have been a strain and he'd reluctantly agreed to her taking an extended holiday.

He had vaguely imagined her on a scenic coach tour of Spain to visit places of historical and architectural interest. He knew she liked history. No doubt the majority of the other people on the tour would be pensioners and she would strike up a friendship with a spinster, or perhaps a widow who was travelling alone and who would be grateful for Sara's innately kind nature.

Alekos's rather cosy picture of his PA's holiday plans had been disrupted when she'd told him that she was going away on a YFS trip—which stood for Young, Free and Single. As their name suggested, the tour operator specialised in holidays for people in the twenty-something age bracket who wanted to spend every night clubbing, or partying on a beach. The media often reported scenes of drunken debauchery by Brits in Benidorm. When he had pointed out that a better name for the holiday company would be AFS—Available For Sex—Sara had laughed and, to Alekos's astonishment, told him she was looking forward to letting her hair down in Spain.

His eyes were drawn back to her hair. He visualised her as she had looked every weekday for the past two years. She had always worn her nondescript brown hair scraped back from her face and piled on top of her head in a no-nonsense bun that defied gravity with the aid of an arsenal of metal hairpins.

'You're wearing your hair in a new style,' he said abruptly. 'I was trying to work out why you look different.'

'Mmm, I had it cut while I was away. It was so long, almost waist length, and I was fed up of having to tie it up all the time.' She ran her fingers through the silky layers of her new hairstyle. In the sunshine streaming through the window, her hair seemed to shimmer like gold in places and Alekos felt an unexpected tightening sensation in his groin.

'And I finally ditched my glasses for contact lenses. Although I must admit they're taking a while to get used to.' Sara sounded rueful. 'My new contacts make my eyes water sometimes.'

Alekos was relieved that she wasn't fluttering her eyelashes at him seductively, but she was blinking presumably because her contact lenses felt strange. Without the thick-rimmed glasses he was used to seeing her wearing, her cheekbones were more noticeable and her face was prettier than his memory served him.

He wondered if she'd had some sort of surgical procedure to her lips. Surely he would have remembered the fullness of her lips—and, *Theos,* that faint pout of her lower lip that tempted him to test its softness with his own mouth. He forced his mind away from such a ridiculous idea and reminded himself that this was Miss Mouse, the name that one of his legion of leggy blonde mistresses had unkindly christened Sara.

The nickname had suited her plain looks but not her dry wit that frequently amused Alekos, or her sharp mind and even sharper tongue that he had come to respect, because Sara Lovejoy was the only woman he had ever met who wasn't afraid to state her opinion—even if it was different to his.

'I'll put your coffee on your desk, shall I?' Without waiting for him to reply, Sara walked across the room and placed a cup of coffee on the desk in front of Alekos's chair. He could not help himself from focusing on the sensual undulation of her hips as she walked, and when she leaned across the desk her skirt pulled tighter across the curves of her buttocks.

Alekos cleared his throat audibly and tightened his fingers on the handle of his briefcase as he moved it in front of him to hide the evidence that he was aroused. What the blazes was the matter with him? For the first time in a month he had woken in a good mood this morning, knowing that Sara would be back and between them they would clear the backlog of work that had built up while she'd been away.

But work was the last thing on his mind when she turned to face him and he noticed how her pink silk shirt lovingly moulded the firm swell of her breasts. The top two buttons on her blouse were undone, not enough to reveal any cleavage but more than enough to quicken his pulse as he visualised himself removing her shirt and her lace-edged bra that he could see outlined beneath the silky material of her top.

He forced his gaze away from her breasts down to her surprisingly slim waist and cleared his throat again. 'You…er…appear to have lost some weight.'

'A few pounds, as a matter of fact. I expect it was down to all the exercise I did while I was on holiday.'

What sort of exercise had she done on a young, free and single's holiday? Alekos was not usually prone to flights of imagination but his mind was bombarded with pictures of his new-look PA discarding her inhibitions and enjoying energetic nights with a Spanish Lothario.

'Ah, yes, your holiday. I hope you enjoyed yourself?'

'I certainly did.'

Her grin made him think of a satisfied cat that had drunk a bowlful of cream. 'I'm glad to hear it,' he said tersely. 'But you are not on holiday now, so I'm wondering why you've come to work wearing clothes that are more suitable for the beach than the office.'

When Alekos spoke in that coldly disapproving tone, people tended to immediately take notice and respond with the respect he commanded. But Sara simply shrugged and smoothed her hand over her skirt.

'Oh, I wore a lot less than this on the beach. It's perfectly acceptable for women to go topless on the beaches in the French Riviera.'

Had Sara gone topless? He tried to banish the vision of his prim PA displaying her bare breasts in public. 'I thought you went to Spain for your holiday?'

'I changed my plans at the last minute.'

While Alekos was registering the fact that his ultra-organised PA had apparently changed her holiday destination on a whim, Sara strolled towards him. Why had he never noticed until now that her green eyes sparkled like emeralds when she smiled? He was irritated with himself for thinking such poetic nonsense but he could not stop staring at her.

Along with her new hairstyle and clothes, she was wearing a different perfume: a seductive scent which combined spiky citrus with deeper, exotically floral notes that stirred his senses—and stirred a lot more besides, he acknowledged derisively when he felt himself harden.

'So, where do you want me?' she murmured.

'What?' He stiffened as a picture leapt into his mind of Sara sprawled on the leather sofa with her skirt rucked up around her waist and her legs spread wide, waiting for him to position himself between her thighs.

Cursing beneath his breath, Alekos fought to control his rampant libido and realised that his PA was giving him an odd look. 'Shall I sort out the pile of paperwork on my desk that I presume the temp left for me to deal with, or do you want me to stay in here and take notes from you?' she repeated patiently.

She put her hands on her hips, drawing his attention to the narrowness of her waist that served to emphasise the rounded curves of her breasts. 'I understand that the temp I arranged to cover my absence only lasted a week, and HR organised three more replacements but you dismissed them after a few days.'

'They were all useless,' he snapped. Glancing at his watch, Alekos discovered that he had wasted ten minutes ogling his PA, who normally did not warrant more than a five second glance. He felt unsettled by his awareness of Sara as an attractive woman and was annoyed with himself for his physical response to her. 'I hope you are prepared for the fact that we have a ton of work to catch up on.'

'I guessed you'd have me tied to my desk when I came back to work,' she said airily.

Alekos's eyes narrowed on her serene expression, and he was thrown by the idea that she knew the effect she was having on him. His mental vision of her tied, face down, across her desk made his blood sizzle. He felt confused by his inability to control his response to her.

This was dull, drab Sara—although, admittedly, he had never found her dull when she'd made it clear, soon after he'd promoted her from a secretary in the accounts department to his PA, that she wasn't going to worship him like most women did. But her frumpy appearance had been one reason why he had chosen her. His position as chairman of GE demanded his absolute focus and there was no risk of him being distracted by Miss Mouse.

Alekos had become chairman of the company, which specialised in building luxury superyachts, two years ago, following the death of his father, and he had decided that Sara's unexciting appearance, exemplary secretarial skills and excellent work ethic would make her his ideal PA.

He walked around his desk, lowered his long frame into his chair and took a sip of coffee before he glanced at her. 'I need to make a few phone calls and no doubt you will have plenty of stuff to catch up on, so come back in half an hour and bring the Viceroy file with you.'

'Aren't you forgetting something? The word *please*,' Sara reminded him crisply when he raised his brows questioningly. 'Honestly, Alekos, no wonder you frightened off four temps in as many weeks if you were as surly with them as you're behaving this morning. I suppose you've got woman trouble? That's the usual reason when you come to work with a face like thunder.'

'You must know by now that I never allow my relationships to last long enough for women to become troublesome,' Alekos said smoothly. He leaned back in his chair and gave her a hard stare. 'Remind me again, Sara, why I tolerate your insolence?'

Across the room he saw her eyes sparkle and her mouth curve into a smile that inexplicably made Alekos feel as if he'd been punched in his gut. 'Because I'm good at my job and you don't want to sleep with me. That's what you told me at my interview and I assume nothing has changed?'

She stepped out of his office and closed the door behind her before he could think of a suitably cutting retort. He glared at the space where she had been standing seconds earlier. *Theos*, sometimes she overstepped the mark. His nostrils flared with annoyance. He could not explain the odd sensation in the pit of his stomach when he caught the drift of her perfume that still lingered in the room.

He felt rattled by Sara's startling physical transformation from frump to sexpot. But he reminded himself that her honesty was one of the things he admired about her. He doubted that any of the three hundred employees at Gionakis Enterprises' London offices, and probably none of the three thousand staff employed by the company worldwide, would dream of speaking to him as bluntly as Sara did. It made a refreshing change to have someone challenge him when most people, especially women, always said yes to him.

He briefly wondered what she would say if he told her that he had changed his mind and wanted to take her to bed. Would she be willing to have sex with him, or would Sara be the only woman to refuse him? Alekos was almost tempted to find out. But practicality outweighed his inconvenient and, he confidently assumed, fleeting attraction to her, when he reminded himself that there were any number of women who would be happy to help him relieve his sexual frustration but a good PA was worth her weight in gold.

The day's schedule was packed. Alekos opened his laptop but, unusually for him, he could not summon any enthusiasm for work. He swivelled his chair round to the window and stared down at the busy street five floors below, where red London buses, black taxis and kamikaze cyclists competed for road space.

He liked living in England's capital city, although he much preferred the current June sunshine to the dank drizzle and short days of the winter. After his father's death it had been expected by the members of the board, and his family, that Alekos would move back to Greece permanently and run the company from GE's offices in Athens. His father, Kostas Gionakis, and before him Alekos's grandfather, the founder of the company, had both done so.

His decision to move the company's headquarters to London had been mainly for business reasons. London was closer to GE's growing client list in Florida and the Bahamas, and the cosmopolitan capital was ideally suited to entertain a clientele made up exclusively of millionaires and billionaires, who were prepared to spend eye-watering amounts of cash on a superyacht—the ultimate status symbol.

On a personal front, Alekos had been determined to establish himself as the new company chairman away from his father's power base in Greece. The grand building in Athens which had been GE's headquarters looked like a palace and Kostas Gionakis had been king. Alekos never forgot that he was the usurper to the throne.

His jaw clenched. Dimitri should have been chairman, not him. But his brother was dead—killed twenty years ago, supposedly in a tragic accident. Alekos's parents had been devastated and he had never told them of his suspicions about the nature of Dimitri's death.

Alekos had been fourteen at the time, the youngest in the family, born six years after Dimitri and after their three sisters. He had idolised his brother. Everyone had admired the Gionakis heir. Dimitri was handsome, athletic and clever and had been groomed from boyhood to take over running the family business. Alekos was the spare heir should the unthinkable happen to Dimitri.

But the unthinkable *had* happened. Dimitri had died and Alekos had suddenly become the future of the company—a fact that his father had never allowed him to forget.

Had Kostas believed that his youngest son would make as good a chairman of GE as his firstborn son?

Alekos doubted it. He had felt that he was second best in his father's eyes. He knew that was still the opinion of some of the board members who disapproved of his playboy lifestyle.

But he would prove those who doubted his abilities wrong. In the two years that he had been chairman the company's profits had increased and they were expanding into new markets around the globe. Perhaps his father would have been proud of him. Alekos would never know. But what he knew for sure was that he could not allow himself to be distracted by his PA simply because her sexy new look had stirred his desire.

Turning away from the window, he opened a document on his laptop and resolutely focused on work. He had inherited the company by default. He owed it to Dimitri's memory to ensure that Gionakis Enterprises continued to be as successful as it had been when his father was chairman, and as Alekos was sure it would have been under his brother's leadership.

Sara ignored a stab of guilt as she passed her desk, piled with paperwork that required her attention, and hurried into the bathroom. The mirror above the sink confirmed her fears. Her flushed cheeks and dilated pupils betrayed her reaction to Alekos that she had been unable to control.

She felt as though she had been holding her breath the entire time she had been in his office. Why was it that she'd managed to hide her awareness of him for two years but when she had set eyes on him this morning after she hadn't seen him for a month her pulse-rate had rocketed and her mouth had felt dry?

The sensation of her heart slamming against her rib-cage whenever she was in close proximity to Alekos wasn't new, but she had perfected the art of hiding her emotions behind a cool smile, aware that her job depended on it. When Alekos had elevated her to the role of his PA over several other suitably qualified candidates for the job, he had bluntly told her that he never mixed business with pleasure and there was no chance of a sexual relationship developing between them. His arrogance had irritated Sara and she'd almost told him that she had no intention of copying her mother's mistake by having an affair with her boss.

During the eighteen months that she had worked in the accounts department before her promotion, she'd heard that the company's board members disapproved of Alekos's playboy lifestyle, which attracted the wrong type of press interest, and she understood why he was determined to keep his relationship with his staff on a strictly professional footing. What Alekos wanted from his PA was efficiency, dedication and the ability to blend into the background—and plain, conservatively dressed Sara had fitted the bill perfectly.

In truth she would have worn a nun's habit to the office if Alekos had required her to because she was so keen to secure the job. Her promotion to personal assistant of the chairman of Gionakis Enterprises had finally won her mother's praise. For the first time in her life she had felt that she wasn't a disappointment to Joan Lovejoy. The surname was a misnomer if ever there was one because, as far as Sara could tell, there had been no love or joy in her mother's life.

She'd wondered if her mother had loved the man who'd abandoned her after he had made her pregnant. But Joan had refused to reveal Sara's father's identity and only ever made a few oblique references to him, notably that he had once been an Oxford don and it was a pity that Sara hadn't inherited his academic brilliance.

Sara had spent most of her life comparing herself to a nameless, faceless man who had helped to create her but she had never met—until six weeks ago. Now she knew that she had inherited her green eyes from her father. He was no longer faceless, or nameless. His name was Lionel Kingsley and he was a well-known politician. She'd been stunned when he had phoned her and revealed that there was a possibility she might be his daughter. She had agreed to a DNA test to see if he was really her father but she had been sure of the result before the test had proved it. When she looked into a mirror she saw her father's eyes looking back at her.

For the first time in her life she felt she was a whole person, and so many things about herself suddenly made sense, like her love of art and her creativity that she'd always suppressed because her mother had pushed her to concentrate on academic subjects.

Lionel was a widower and had two grown-up children. Her half-siblings! Sara felt excited and nervous at the thought of meeting her half-brother and half-sister. She understood Lionel's concern that his son and daughter from his marriage might be upset to learn that he had an illegitimate daughter, and she had told herself to be patient and wait until he was ready to acknowledge publicly that he was her father. Finally it was going to happen. Lionel had invited her to his home at the weekend so that he could introduce her to Freddie and Charlotte Kingsley.

Sara had seen pictures of them and discovered that she bore a striking resemblance to her half-siblings. But the physical similarities between her and her half-sister did not apply to their very different dress styles. Photographs of Charlotte wearing stylish, figure-hugging clothes had made Sara realise how frumpy she looked in comparison. The smart suits she wore to the office reflected the importance of her role as PA to the chairman of the company and she had reminded herself that if Alekos had wanted a decorative bimbo to be his PA he wouldn't have chosen her.

The new clothes she had bought while she had been on holiday did not make her look like a bimbo, Sara reassured herself. The skirt and blouse she was wearing were perfectly respectable for the office. Shopping in the chic boutiques on the French Riviera where her father owned a holiday villa had been a revelation. Remembering the photos she'd seen of her stylish half-sister had prompted Sara to try on colourful summery outfits. She had dropped a dress size from plenty of swimming and playing tennis and she loved being able to fit into skirts and dresses that showed off her more toned figure.

She ran her fingers through her new layered hairstyle. She still wasn't used to her hair swishing around her shoulders when she turned her head. It made her feel more feminine and, well...*sexy*. She'd had a few blonde highlights put through the front sections of her hair to complement the natural lighter streaks from where she had spent a month in the French sunshine.

Maybe it was true that blondes *did* have more fun. But the truth was that meeting her father had given her a new sense of self-confidence. The part of her that had been missing was now complete, and Sara didn't want to fade into the background any more. Travelling to work on the Tube this morning, she'd wondered if Alekos would notice her changed appearance.

She stared at her flushed face in the mirror and grimaced. All right, she had *hoped* he would notice her, instead of treating her like a piece of office furniture: functional, necessary but utterly uninteresting.

Well, she had got her wish. Alekos had stopped dead in his tracks when he'd seen her and his shocked expression had changed to a speculative gleam as his eyes had roamed over her. Heat had swept through her body when his gaze lingered on her breasts. She felt embarrassed thinking he might have noticed that her nipples had hardened in a telltale sign that he excited her more than any man had ever done.

Her decision to revamp her appearance suddenly seemed like a bad idea. When she'd dressed in dowdy clothes she hadn't had to worry that Alekos might catch her glancing at him a dozen times a day, because he rarely seemed to notice that she was a human being and not a robot. Remembering the hot, hard gleam in his eyes when she had been in his office just now sent a tremor through her, and a little part of her wished she could rush back home and change into her safe navy blue suit. But when she'd returned home from her holiday she'd found that all her old clothes were too big, and she'd packed them into black sacks and donated them to a charity shop.

There was no going back. The old Sara Lovejoy was gone for ever and the new Sara was here to stay. Alekos would just have to get used to it.

CHAPTER TWO

AT EXACTLY NINE THIRTY, Sara knocked on Alekos's door and took a deep breath before she stepped into his office. He was sitting behind his desk, leaning back in his chair that was half turned towards the window, and he was holding his phone to his ear. He spared her a brief glance and then swung his gaze back to the window while he continued his telephone conversation.

She ordered herself not to feel disappointed by his lack of interest. Obviously she must have imagined that earlier he had looked at her with a glint of desire in his eyes. Just because she had a new hairstyle and clothes did not mean that she had become Alekos's fantasy woman. She knew his type: elegant blondes with legs that went on for ever. In the past two years a steady stream of models and socialites had arrived in his life and exited it a few months later when Alekos had grown bored of his affair with them.

Sara had hoped she would be able to control her reaction to Alekos but her heart leapt wildly in her chest as she studied his profile. Slashing cheekbones, a square jaw shadowed with dark stubble and eyes that gleamed like polished jet all combined to give him a lethal magnetism that women invariably found irresistible. His thick black hair had a habit of falling forwards across her brow and she was tempted to run her fingers through it. As for his mouth… Her eyes were drawn to his beautiful mouth. Full-lipped and sensual when he was relaxed and utterly devastating when he smiled, his mouth could also curve into a cynical expression when he wished to convey his displeasure.

'Don't stand there wasting time, Sara.' Alekos's voice made her jump, and she flushed as she registered that he had finished his phone call and had caught her out staring at him. 'We have a lot to get through.'

'I was waiting for you to finish your call.' She was thankful that two years of practice at hiding her reaction to his smouldering sensuality allowed her to sound calm and composed even though her heart was racing. The way he growled her name in his sexy accent, drawing out the second syllable… Sa*raaa*…was curiously intimate—as if they were lovers. But of course they were not lovers and were never likely to be.

She forced herself to walk unhurriedly across the room, but with every step that took her closer to Alekos's desk she was conscious of his unswerving gaze. The unholy gleam in his eyes made her feel as if he were mentally undressing her. Every centimetre of her skin was on fire when she sat down on the chair in front of his desk.

It would be easy to be overwhelmed by him. But when she had been promoted to his PA she'd realised that Alekos was surrounded by people who always agreed with him, and she had decided that she could not allow herself to be intimidated by his powerful personality. She'd noted that he did not have much respect for the flunkeys and hangers-on who were so anxious to keep on the right side of him.

She had very quickly proved that she was good at her job, but the first time she had disagreed with Alekos over a work issue he'd clearly been astounded to discover that his mousy assistant had a backbone. After a tense stand-off, when Sara had refused to back down, he had narrowed his gaze on her determined expression and something like admiration had flickered in his dark eyes.

She valued his respect more than anything because she loved her job. Working for Alekos was like riding a roller coaster at a theme park: exciting, intense and fast-paced, and it was the knowledge that she would never find a job as rewarding as her current one that made Sara take a steadying breath. She could not deny it was flattering that Alekos had finally noticed her, but if she wanted to continue in her role as his PA she must ignore the predatory glint in his eyes.

She held her pencil poised over her notepad and gave him a cool smile. 'I'm ready to start when you are.'

Her breezy tone seemed to irritate him. 'I doubt you'll be so cheerful by the time we've finished today. I'll need you to work late this evening.'

'Sorry, but I can't stay late tonight. I've made other plans.'

He frowned. 'Well, change them. Do I need to remind you that a requirement of your job is for you to work whatever hours I dictate, within reason?'

'I'm sure I don't need to remind you that I have always worked extra when you've asked me to,' Sara said calmly. 'And I've worked *unreasonable* hours, such as when we stayed up until one a.m. to put together a sales

pitch for a sheikh before he flew back to Dubai. It paid
off too, because Sheikh Al Mansoor placed an order for
a one-hundred-million-pound yacht from GE.'

Alekos's scowl did not make him any less gorgeous;
in fact it gave him a dangerous, brooding look that
turned Sara's bones to liquid.

'I can stay late every other night this week if you
need me to,' she went on in an effort to appease him.
Alekos's bad mood threatened to spoil her excitement
about meeting her father after work. Lionel Kingsley's
high profile as an MP meant that he did not want to risk
being seen in public with Sara. As they couldn't go to
a restaurant, she had invited him to her home and was
planning to cook dinner for him before he attended an
evening engagement.

'Oh, I can't stay late on Friday either,' she said. 'And
actually I'd like to leave an hour early because I'm going
away for the weekend.' She remembered the plans she'd
made to visit her father at his house in Berkshire. 'I'll
work through my lunch hour to make up the time.'

'Well, well.' Alekos's sardonic drawl put Sara on
her guard. 'You go away for a month and return sport-
ing a new haircut, a new—and much improved, I have
to say—wardrobe, and now suddenly you have a busy
social life. It makes me wonder if a man is the reason
for the new-look Sara Lovejoy.'

'My personal life is none of your business,' she said
composedly. Technically, she supposed that a man was
the reason for the change in her, but she had not met a
lover, as Alekos had implied. She had enjoyed getting
to know her father when he had invited her to spend
her holiday at his villa in the south of France but she

had promised Lionel that she wouldn't tell anyone she was his daughter.

Deep down she felt disappointed that her father wished to keep their relationship secret. It was as if Lionel was ashamed of her. But she reminded herself that he had promised to introduce her to her half-siblings on Friday, and perhaps then he would openly welcome her as his daughter. She pulled her mind back to the present when she realised Alekos was speaking.

'It will be my business if your work is affected because you're mooning over some guy.'

Sara still refused to rise to Alekos's verbal baiting. She tapped the tip of her pencil on her pad and said with heavy emphasis, '*I'm* ready to start work when you are.'

Alekos picked up a client's folder from the pile on his desk, but he did not open it. Instead he leaned back in his chair, an unreadable expression on his handsome face as he surveyed her for long minutes while her tension grew and she was sure he must see the pulse beating erratically at the base of her throat.

'Why did you change your holiday plans and go to France rather than Spain?'

'The holiday company I'd booked with cancelled my trip, but a…friend invited me to stay at his villa in Antibes.'

'Would this friend be the man whose voice I heard in the background when I phoned you with a query from the Miami office a week ago?'

Sara tensed. Could Alekos possibly have recognised her famous father's voice?

'Why are you suddenly fascinated with my private life?'

'I'm merely concerned for your well-being and offering a timely reminder that holiday romances notoriously don't last.'

'For goodness' sake!' Sara told herself not to be fooled by Alekos's 'concern for her wellbeing'. His real concern was he did not want his PA moping about or unable to concentrate on her work because she'd suffered a broken heart. 'What makes you think I had a holiday romance?'

He trailed his eyes over her, subjecting her to a thorough appraisal that brought a flush to her cheeks. 'It's obvious. Before you went on holiday you wore frumpy clothes that camouflaged your figure. But after spending a month in France you have undergone a transformation into a frankly very attractive young woman. It doesn't take a detective to work out that a love affair is probably the cause of your new-found sensuality.'

'Well, of course *you* would assume that a *man* is the reason I've altered my appearance.' Sara's temper simmered. 'It couldn't be that I decided to update my wardrobe for *me*.' His cynical expression fuelled her anger but she also felt hurt. Had she really looked so awful in her navy blue suit with her hair secured in a neat bun, as Alekos had said? It was pathetic the way her heart had leapt when he'd complimented her new look and told her she was attractive.

'You are such a male chauvinist,' she snapped. Ignoring the warning glint in his eyes, she said furiously, 'I suppose you think I altered the way I dress in the hope of impressing you?'

The landline phone on his desk rang and Sara instinctively reached out to answer it. Simultaneously Alekos did the same and, as his fingers brushed against hers, she felt a sizzle of electricity shoot up her arm.

'Oh!' She tried to snatch her hand away, but he snaked his fingers around her wrist and stroked his thumb pad over her thudding pulse.

'When you dressed to come to work this morning, did you choose your outfit to please me?' His black eyes burned like hot coals into hers.

Sara flushed guiltily. 'Of course not.' She refused to admit to herself, let alone to Alekos, that for the past two years she had fantasised about him desiring her. She stared at his chiselled face and swallowed. 'Are you going to answer the call?' she said breathlessly.

To her relief, he let go of her wrist and picked up the phone. She resisted the urge to leap out of her seat and run out of his office. Instead she made herself stroll across the room to the coffee machine. The familiar routine of pouring water into the machine's reservoir and inserting a coffee capsule into the compartment gave her a few moments' breathing space to bring herself under control.

Why had she goaded Alekos like that? She had always been careful to hide her attraction to him but he must have noticed how the pulse in her wrist had almost jumped through her skin because it had been beating so hard, echoing the thudding beat of her heart.

She could not put off carrying their coffees over to his desk any longer, and she was thankful that Alekos did not glance at her when he finished his phone call and opened the file in front of him. He waited for her to sit down and pick up her notepad before he began to dictate at breakneck speed, making no allowances for the fact that she hadn't taken shorthand notes for a month.

It set the tone for the rest of the day as they worked

together to clear the backlog that had built up while Sara had been away. At five o'clock she rolled her aching shoulders and went to the bathroom to brush her hair and apply a fresh coat of rose-pink lip gloss that was her new must-have item of make-up.

In Alekos's office she found him standing by his desk. He was massaging the back of his neck as if he felt as tired from their busy day as she was. She had forgotten how tall he was. He had inherited his six-foot-four height from his maternal grandfather, who had been a Canadian, he'd once explained to Sara. But in every other aspect he was typically Greek, from his dark olive complexion and mass of black hair to his arrogant belief that he only had to click his fingers and women would flock to him. The trouble was that they did, Sara thought ruefully.

Alekos was used to having any woman he wanted. She told herself it was lucky that there had been no repeat of the breathless moments that had occurred earlier in the day, when rampant desire had blazed in his eyes as he'd trapped her wrist and felt the giveaway throb of her sexual awareness of him.

He must have heard his office door open, and turned his head in her direction. They had played out the same scene hundreds of times before, and most days when she came to check if he needed her to do anything else before she went home he did not bother looking up from his computer screen as he bid her goodnight. But he was looking at her now. She watched his hard features tauten and become almost wolf-like as he stared at her with a hungry gleam in his eyes that excited her and filled her with illicit longing.

Something tugged in the pit of her stomach, tugged

hard like a knot being pulled tighter and tighter, as if an invisible thread linked her body to Alekos. And then he blinked and the feral glitter in his eyes disappeared. Perhaps it had never been there and she had imagined that he'd stared at her as if he wanted to devour her?

'I'm just off now.' She was amazed that her voice sounded normal when her insides were in turmoil. 'I'll finish typing up the report for the shareholders first thing tomorrow.'

'Did you remember that we are attending the annual dinner for the board members on Thursday evening?'

She nodded. 'I'll bring the dress I'm going to wear for the dinner to work and get changed here at the office like I did for the Christmas party.'

'You had better check with the restaurant that they won't be serving seafood. Orestis Pagnotis is allergic to it and, much as I'd like to have the old man off my back, I'd better not allow him to risk suffering a possibly fatal reaction,' Alekos said drily.

'I've already given the restaurant a list of the dietary requirements of the guests.' She smiled sympathetically. 'Is Orestis still being a problem?'

He shrugged. 'He's one of the old school. He joined the board when my grandfather was chairman, and he was a close friend of my father.' Alekos gave a frustrated sigh. 'Orestis believes I take too many risks and he has the support of some of the other board members, who fail to understand that the company needs to move with the times rather than remain in the Stone Age. Orestis's latest gripe is that he thinks the chairman should be married.'

Alekos muttered something in Greek that Sara guessed was not complimentary about the influential board member. 'According to Orestis, if I take a wife it will prove that I have left my playboy days behind and I will be more focused on running GE.'

Her heart dipped. 'Are you considering getting married?'

Somehow she managed to inject the right amount of casual interest into her voice. She knew he had ended his affair with a stunning Swedish model called Danika shortly before her holiday, but in the month she had been away it was likely that he had met someone else. Alekos never stayed celibate for long.

Perhaps he had fallen in love with the woman of his dreams. It was possible that Alekos might ask her to organise his wedding. She would have to pin a smile on her face and hide her heartache while she made arrangements for him and his beautiful bride—she was certain to be beautiful—to spend their honeymoon at an exotic location. Sara pulled her mind away from her unwelcome thoughts when she realised Alekos was speaking.

'I'll have to marry eventually.' He sounded unenthusiastic at the prospect. 'I am the last male Gionakis and my mother and sisters remind me at every opportunity that it is my duty to produce an heir. Obviously I will first have to select a suitable wife.'

'How do you intend to *select a suitable wife*?' She could not hide her shock that he had such a cavalier attitude towards marriage. 'Will you hold interviews and ask the candidates, who are your potential brides, to fill out a detailed questionnaire about themselves?' She was aware that her voice had risen and Alekos's amused smile infuriated her further.

'Your suggestion is not a bad idea. Why are you so outraged?' he said smoothly.

'Because you make marriage sound like a...a cattle market where finding a wife is like choosing a prize heifer to breed from. What about love?'

'What about it?' He studied her flushed face speculatively. 'Statistically, somewhere between forty and fifty per cent of marriages end in divorce, and I bet that most of those marriages were so-called love matches. But with such a high failure rate it seems sensible to take emotion out of the equation and base marriage on social and financial compatibility, mutual respect and the pursuit of shared goals such as bringing up a family.'

Sara shook her head. 'Your arrogance is unbelievable. You accuse some of GE's board members of being stuck in the Stone Age, but your views on marriage are Neolithic. Women nowadays don't sit around twiddling their thumbs and hoping that a rich man will choose them to be his wife.'

'You'd be surprised,' Alekos murmured drily. 'When I decide to marry—in another ten years or so—I don't envisage I'll have a problem finding a woman who is willing to marry a multimillionaire.'

'Well, I wouldn't marry for money,' Sara said fiercely. Deep inside her she felt an ache of regret that Alekos had trampled on her silly dream that he would one day fall in love with her. Realistically, she knew it would never happen but hearing him state so emphatically that he did not aspire to a marriage built on love forced her to accept that she must get over her embarrassing crush on him.

'You would prefer to gamble your future happiness on a fickle emotion that poets try to convince us is love? But of course love is simply a sanitized word for lust.'

'If you're asking me whether I believe in love, then

the answer is yes, I do. Why are you so sceptical, Alekos? You once told me that your parents had been happily married for forty-five years before your father died.'

'And therein proves my point. My parents had an arranged marriage which was extremely successful. Love wasn't necessary, although I believe they grew to be very fond of each other over the course of their marriage.'

Sara gave up. 'You're just a cynic.'

'No, I'm a realist. There is a dark side to love and I have witnessed its destructive power.'

A memory slid into Alekos's mind of that fateful day twenty years ago when he'd found Dimitri walking along the beach. His brother's eyes had been red-rimmed and he'd wept as he'd told Alekos he had discovered that his girlfriend had been unfaithful. It was the last time Alekos had seen Dimitri alive.

'Love is an illusion,' he told Sara harshly, 'and you would do well to remember it before you rush to give away your heart to a man you only met a few weeks ago.'

After Sara had gone, Alekos walked over to the window and a few minutes later he saw her emerge from the GE building and walk along the pavement. Even from a distance he noted the sexy wiggle of her hips when she walked and a shaft of white-hot lust ripped through him.

He swore. Lusting after his PA was so unexpected and he assured himself that his reaction to Sara's transformation from dowdy to a very desirable woman was down to sexual frustration. He hadn't had sex since he'd split from his last mistress almost two months ago.

'What are you looking for?' Danika had asked him when he'd told her their affair was over. 'You say you don't want permanence in a relationship, but what do you want?'

Right now he wanted a woman under him, Alekos thought, conscious of his erection pressing uncomfortably against the zip of his trousers. A memory flashed into his mind of Sara leaning across his desk with her skirt pulled tight over her bottom. He imagined her without her skirt, her derrière presented for him to slide her panties down so that he could stroke his hands over her naked body. In his fantasy he had already removed her blouse and bra and he stood behind her and slid his arms round her to cup her firm breasts in his hands...

Theos! Alekos raked his hand through his hair and forced his mind away from his erotic thoughts. Sara was the best PA he'd ever had and he was determined not to damage their excellent working relationship. She was the only woman, apart from his mother and sisters, who he trusted. She was discreet, loyal and she made his life easier in countless ways that he had not fully appreciated until she had taken a month's holiday.

If he made her his mistress he would not be able to continue to employ her as his PA. Office affairs did not work, especially after the affair ended—and of course it would end after a few months at most. He had a low boredom threshold and there was no reason to think that his surprising attraction to Sara would last long once he'd taken her to bed.

Alekos turned his thoughts to the party he was due to attend that evening. Perhaps he would meet a woman who would hold his attention for more than an hour. He received many more invitations to social functions than he had the time or the inclination to attend, but he had a particular reason for accepting an invitation to a party being given by a wealthy city banker. Alekos knew that a Texan oil baron would be included on the guest list. Warren McCuskey was looking to buy a superyacht to keep his wife, who was twenty years younger than him, happy, and Alekos was determined to persuade the billionaire Texan to buy a yacht from GE.

From his vantage point at the window he continued to watch Sara standing in the street below. She seemed to be waiting for someone. A large black saloon car drew up alongside her, the rear door opened and she climbed into the car before it pulled away from the kerb.

He was intrigued. Why hadn't Sara's 'friend' got out of the car to greet her? Earlier, she had been oddly secretive about her boyfriend. And what was the real reason for her attractive new look? Alekos couldn't remember the last time a woman had aroused his curiosity and it was ironic that the woman who had fired his interest had been under his nose for the past two years.

CHAPTER THREE

On Thursday evening, Alekos checked the gold watch on his wrist and frowned when he saw that he and Sara needed to leave for the board members' dinner in the next five minutes. Usually when she accompanied him to work functions she was ready in plenty of time. He was annoyed that she had not been waiting for him when he'd walked out of the private bathroom next to his office, where he had showered and changed.

He wondered what she would wear to the dinner. He remembered that a few months ago it had been a particularly busy time at work and Sara had stayed at the office until late, only dashing off to change for the staff Christmas party ten minutes before it was due to start. She had emerged from the cloakroom wearing what he had supposed was a ball gown, but the long black dress had resembled a shroud and had the effect of draining all the colour from her face.

He had been tempted to order her to go and buy something more cheerful. The shop windows were full of mannequins displaying party dresses for the festive season. But then he'd remembered that Sara was grieving for her mother, who had recently died. For once he had studied her closely, and her pinched face and the shadows beneath her eyes had evoked a faint tug of sympathy for his PA, who reminded him of a drab sparrow.

Alekos turned his thoughts to the present. The board members' dinner was a prestigious event that called for him to wear a tuxedo, but he refused to be clean shaven. He glanced in the mirror and grimaced as he ran his hand over the trimmed black stubble on his jaw. No doubt his nemesis Orestis Pagnotis would accuse him of looking more like a pirate than the chairman of a billion-pound company.

Behind him the office door opened and Sara stepped into the room. His jaw dropped as he stared at her reflection in the mirror, and he was thankful he had his back to her so that she couldn't see the betraying bulge of his erection beneath his trousers.

The drab sparrow had metamorphosed into a peacock. Somewhere in Alekos's stunned brain he registered that the description was all the more apt because her dress was peacock-blue silk and the long skirt gave an iridescent shimmer when she walked. The top of the dress was high-necked and sleeveless, leaving her shoulders bare. A sparkling diamanté belt showed off her slender waist.

From the front, the dress was elegant and Alekos had no problem with it. But when Sara turned around to check that the espresso machine was switched off, he saw that her dress was backless to the base of her spine. A hot haze of desire made his blood pound through his veins.

'You can't wear that,' he rasped, shock and lust strangling his vocal cords. 'Half the board members are over sixty and I know for a fact that a couple of them have weak hearts. If they see you in that dress they're likely to suffer a cardiac arrest.'

She looked genuinely confused. 'What's wrong with my dress?'

'Half of it is missing.'

'Well, technically I suppose that's true. But I don't suppose the sight of my shoulder blades will evoke wild lust in anyone.'

Don't bet on it, Alekos thought grimly. He would not have believed that a woman's bare back could be so erotic. The expanse of Sara's skin revealed by the backless dress invited him to trace his fingertips down her spine and then spread his hand over her tempting nakedness.

Theos, what he actually wanted to do was stride over to her, sweep her into his arms and ravish her thoroughly and to their mutual satisfaction on top of his desk. That particular fantasy had been a common theme for the past four days, which had frankly been torturous. Sara had turned up for work each morning wearing outfits that had sent his blood pressure soaring. Her stylish skirts and blouses had hugged her curvy figure without being too revealing, and somehow the hint of her sexy figure beneath her clothes was much more exciting than if she had worn a miniskirt and boob tube.

He checked the time again and realised they would have to leave immediately or risk being late for the dinner. 'God knows what the board members will make of you dressed like a glamour model in a men-only magazine,' he growled as he held the door open and then followed Sara into the corridor. 'You know how conservative some of them are.' He shoved his hands into his pockets out of harm's way, but he could not control the hard thud of his heart, or the hard throb of another part of his anatomy, he acknowledged derisively.

'Nonsense, they'll think I'm wearing a perfectly nice dress,' she said serenely. 'The board members like me. They know I work hard and I would never do anything that might harm the company's image.'

Alekos had to admit she was right. Even his main critic Orestis Pagnotis approved of Sara and had remarked to Alekos that he should consider marrying someone as sensible and down-to-earth as his PA.

The trouble was that Sara no longer looked like his sensible PA. She looked gorgeous and unbelievably sexy, and while Alekos certainly had no thoughts of marrying her he couldn't deny that he wanted her— badly. He was not used to denying himself. But the rules he had made about not getting personally involved with any member of his staff meant that she was forbidden. To a born rebel like himself the word *forbidden* acted like a red rag to a bull. It was a fact of life that you wanted most what you couldn't have, Alekos brooded when they were in the car on the way to the dinner. It was also true that rules were made to be broken.

The restaurant was at a five-star hotel on Park Lane and a private dining room had been booked for the board members' dinner.

'Alekos!' A high-pitched voice assaulted Alekos's ears as he walked into the private function suite, and he swore silently when a young woman ran over to him and greeted him enthusiastically by kissing him on both his cheeks.

'Zelda,' he murmured as he politely but firmly unwound her arms from around his neck. Orestis Pagnotis's granddaughter was as exuberant as a young child but there was nothing childlike about the eighteen-year-old's physical attributes. Alekos was surprised that Orestis had allowed his granddaughter to wear a gold clingy dress with a plunging neckline. But he knew that Zelda was her grandfather's favourite grandchild—a fact she used shamelessly to get her own way.

Zelda had developed a crush on Alekos the previous year when he had spent a few days meeting with some of GE's senior board members aboard the company's flagship yacht, *Artemis*. One night, Alekos had found the teenager waiting for him in his bed. He had managed to persuade her to return to her own cabin and had done his best to avoid her since then.

But the gods were ganging up against him tonight, he decided as Zelda linked her arm possessively though his and he had no choice but to escort her into the salon, where champagne cocktails and canapés were being served. He looked around for Sara and his temper did not improve when he saw her chatting with the new whiz-kid CFO. Paul Eddis was in his early thirties, and Alekos supposed that women might consider his blond hair and rather delicate facial features attractive. Sara certainly looked happy in his company, and Eddis was staring at her with a stunned expression on his face as if he couldn't believe his luck that the most beautiful woman in the room was giving him all her attention.

The evening went from bad to worse when they were called to take their places for dinner and Alekos discovered he was seated next to Zelda. Sara had arranged the seating plan and he'd specifically asked her to put him on a different table from Zelda. Had Sara decided to have a joke at his expense? Alekos glared across the room to where she was sitting at another table. But she was facing away from him and white-hot fury swept through him when he noticed the waiter ogling her bare back.

He forced himself to eat a little of his cheese soufflé, which was as light as air but tasted like cardboard in his mouth. 'Shouldn't you be at school, studying for exams?' he muttered to Zelda as he firmly removed her hand from his thigh.

'I've left school.' She giggled. 'Well, the headmistress insisted I leave because she said I was a bad influence on the other girls. But I don't need to pass exams because I'm going to be a model. Pappoús is paying for me to have my portfolio done with a top photographer.'

'If you don't behave yourself, perhaps your grandfather will refuse to fund your modelling career.'

'Oh, Pappoús will give me anything I ask for.' Zelda leaned closer to Alekos. 'If I don't behave, will you punish me?' she said artfully.

He would like to punish his PA for putting him through an uncomfortable evening. Alekos's furious black gaze bored into Sara's shoulder blades. And yes, they could send a man wild with desire, he discovered. The hellish meal ended eventually but as the band started up and he strode away from the table—ignoring Zelda's plea to dance with her—he was waylaid by Orestis Pagnotis.

The older man glared at Alekos with his gimlet gaze. 'Keep away from my granddaughter. Zelda is an innocent young woman and I will not allow you to corrupt her, Alekos. I've always been concerned that your womanising ways would bring the company into disrepute. I'm sure I don't need to remind you that you need the support of *every* member of the board to implement the changes you want to make within GE.'

Alekos struggled to keep his temper under control. 'Are you threatening me?'

'I suggest you think hard about what I've said,' Orestis warned.

Sara stood up as Alekos approached her table. 'What's wrong? You don't look like you're enjoying the party.'

'I wonder why that is?' he snapped. 'Do you think it could be because you placed me next to Zelda Pagnotis at dinner, after I'd expressly asked you to seat her away from me? Or perhaps it's because Orestis believes that I have designs on his granddaughter, who he thinks is as innocent as a lamb, incidentally.'

'I didn't seat you next to her.' Sara looked puzzled. 'When we arrived I even popped into the dining room to check that the seating plan had been set out as I had organised it… Zelda must have switched the name cards around.'

Alekos's frustration with Orestis's manipulative granddaughter, and his anger with Orestis for threatening to withhold his support at the next board meeting, turned to a different kind of frustration as he stared into Sara's guileless green eyes. Across the room he saw Zelda heading purposefully in his direction. He caught hold of Sara's hand.

'Dance with me,' he ordered, pulling her towards him. She gave him a startled look, but Alekos was too stunned by the fire that ignited inside him when he felt her breasts pressed against his chest to care.

It was impossible to believe that this was the same Sara who had held herself stiffly and ensured that no part of her body touched his when he'd felt duty-bound to ask her to dance with him at the Christmas party. This Sara was soft and pliant in his arms and he was conscious of the hard points of her nipples through his shirt and the surprising firmness of her thighs beneath her silk dress as she moved with him in time to the music.

'I noted that you made sure you were sitting next to Paul Eddis at dinner,' he bit out. The memory of watching Sara leaning her head towards the CFO when they had sat together for the meal evoked an acidic sensation in his gut. *Theos*, was it *jealousy* that had made him want to walk over to Eddis and drag the guy out of his seat? Alekos had never been possessive of a woman in his life, but he felt a burning urge to drape his jacket around Sara's shoulders and hide her naked back from view. 'You are meant to be on duty this evening, not flirting with other members of GE staff, or the waiters.'

Twin spots of colour stained her cheeks and he could tell she was fighting to control her temper. The thought excited Alekos more than it should. He wanted to disturb her composure like she disturbed him.

'I haven't flirted with anyone. You're being ridiculous.'

'Am I?' Alekos succumbed to the demon called temptation and slid his hand up from her waist to her spine. The bare skin of her back was as smooth as silk but, unlike cool silk, her skin was warm and as he spread his fingers wide he felt the heat of her body scald him. 'You must be aware that every man in this room desires you,' he taunted her.

Her eyes widened and he thought he might drown in those mysterious deep green pools. 'Even you?' she taunted him right back.

Her refusal to be cowed by him had earned Alekos's

respect when she'd been his prim, plain secretary. But now her sassy tongue shattered the last vestiges of his restraint.

'What do you think?' he growled as he pressed his hand into the small of her back so that her pelvis came into contact with his. The hard ridge of his arousal could leave her in no doubt of the effect she had on him.

'Alekos…' Sara licked her dry lips. Her intention had been to remind him that they were on the dance floor in full view of GE's board members and senior executives. But, instead of sounding crisply efficient in her best PA manner, her voice emerged as a breathy whisper as if she were starring in a soft porn movie, she thought disgustedly.

'Sara,' he mocked, mimicking her husky tone. The way he said her name in his sexy accent, curling his tongue around each syllable, made her toes curl. When she had danced with him at the Christmas party she'd been so tense, terrified he would guess he was all of her fantasies rolled into one. But he'd caught her off guard when he'd pulled her into his arms just now. Dancing with him, her breasts crushed against his broad chest and her cheek resting on the lapel of his jacket, was divine. Beneath her palm she could feel the hard thud of his heart and recognised that its erratic beat echoed her own.

Every day at the office for the past four days had been a refined torture as she'd struggled to hide her awareness of him. It had been easier when he hadn't noticed her, but since she had returned to work after her holiday she'd been conscious of a simmering sexual chemistry between her and Alekos that she had tried to ignore. To be fair, he had seemed as if he was trying to ignore it too and a lot of the time they had been so stiff and polite with each other, as if they were strangers rather than two people who had built up a comfortable working relationship over two years.

But sometimes when she'd stolen a glance at Alekos she'd found him staring at her in a way that made her uncomfortably aware of the heaviness of her breasts and the molten heat that pooled between her thighs. That heat was inside her now, flooding through her veins and making each of her nerve endings ultra-sensitive. She was intensely conscious of his hand resting on her bare back. His touch scorched her skin as if he had branded her, and when she stumbled in her high-heeled shoes he increased the pressure of his fingers on her spine and held her so close that she could feel the muscles and sinews of his hard thighs pressed up against hers.

'Sara…look at me.' His voice was low and seductive, scraping across her sensitised nerves. Impossible to resist. She jerked her gaze upwards as if she were a marionette and he had pulled her strings. Her heart lurched as she was trapped by the dark intensity of his eyes. This had been building all week, she realised. Every searing glance they had shared had throbbed with sexual tension that was now threatening to erupt.

His face was so near to hers that she could feel his warm breath graze her lips. She had never been so close to his mouth before and, oh, God, its sensual curve compelled her to lean into him even closer and part her lips, inviting him to cover her mouth with his.

But she must not allow Alekos to kiss her. Certainly not in front of the board members of GE and the senior executives. Her sudden recollection of their situation shattered the spell he had cast on her. It was acceptable for Alekos to dance with his PA, but not to ravish her in public as the sultry gleam in his eyes warned her that he wanted to do.

The band finished playing and Sara took the opportunity to step away from him, murmuring an excuse that she needed to visit the ladies' room. She resisted the urge to glance back at him as she hurried across the dance floor but she felt his dark eyes burning between her shoulder blades, exposed by her backless dress. Luckily, the bathroom was empty and she stood at a basin and held her wrists under the cold tap to try and cool her heated blood. Thank goodness she had stopped him before he had actually kissed her.

The dull ache in the pit of her stomach mocked her for being a liar. She had wanted him to kiss her more than she'd wanted anything in her life. But her common sense reminded her that if he *had*, they would have crossed the line between employer and employee into dangerous territory.

She knew she couldn't put off returning to the party for much longer but she whiled away a few more minutes by checking her phone for messages. Her heart missed a beat when she saw that she had a text from her father.

Five minutes later, Sara stared at her white face in the mirror and willed herself not to cry. Not now, when she must go back and smile and chat to the party guests as her job demanded. She would have to wait until later, when she was alone, before she could allow her tears to fall. She read Lionel's text one more time.

After considerable thought I have decided that it would be unfair to tell Frederick and Charlotte that they have a half-sister at this time. They were very close to their mother and are still mourning her death. The news that many years ago I was unfaithful to my wife will, I fear, be a great shock to my son and daughter. I hope you will understand my decision. It is not my intention to upset you, Sara, but I must protect Freddie and Charlotte and allow them time and privacy to grieve for their mother. Unfortunately, my position as an MP and public figure means that any revelation that I have an illegitimate daughter would attract a great deal of press interest.

In other words, her father had decided that protecting the feelings of the children from his marriage was more important than publicly acknowledging that *she* was his daughter, Sara thought painfully.

Was it because she was as much of a disappointment to her father as she had been to her mother? All her feelings of self-doubt came flooding back. Maybe she wasn't clever enough, or pretty enough, for her famous father.

And maybe, Sara thought grimly, she should have worn the boring black ball gown to the dinner that she'd bought last year specifically to wear to work functions. The dress was a sensible classic style that did not draw attention to her. Instead tonight she'd worn a daring dress that she had secretly hoped would capture Alekos's attention. What had she been hoping for? Did she really want an affair with Alekos when she knew it would mean the end of her job? She'd felt the evidence of his desire for her when he had held her close while they were dancing. But she did not kid herself that his interest in her would last any longer than with his numerous other mistresses.

Alekos wasn't her knight in shining armour. And neither was her father, she acknowledged bleakly. Her mother had taught her that the only person she could rely on was herself. It was a lesson she was determined not to forget.

'Where the hell have you been hiding for the last twenty minutes?' Alekos demanded when Sara joined him at the bar. 'I looked everywhere for you.'

'Why, did you need me for some reason?'

'You should know I need my PA to be on hand at all times,' he growled. While Sara had done her disappearing act from the party he'd been forced to hide behind a pillar to avoid Zelda Pagnotis. Alekos feared no man, but an eighteen-year-old girl who was determined to get her claws into him spelled trouble. Sara sat down on a stool and he wondered if he had imagined that she seemed determined not to make eye contact with him.

'Do you want a drink?' He caught the barman's attention and ordered an orange juice, which he knew was Sara's usual choice of drink.

'Actually, I'd like a whisky and soda, please,' she told the barman. 'Make it a double.'

Alekos gave her a close look and noted her face was pale. Tension emanated from her and he wondered if she was in the grip of the same sexual tension that made his muscles feel tight and his blood thunder through his veins. He had tried to convince himself he'd imagined the chemistry that had simmered between them on the dance floor. But his body clenched as he breathed in her perfume. His reaction to her, the way his manhood jerked to attention beneath his trousers, mocked his assumption that his fascination with her was a temporary aberration.

He frowned when she picked up her glass and threw back her drink in a couple of gulps. 'Is something the matter? You seem on edge.'

'I've got a headache,' she muttered.

'If you didn't before, you soon will have after downing a double whisky,' he said drily.

She slid off the bar stool and picked up her purse. 'Seriously, I...I don't feel well and I need to go home.'

Out of the corner of his eye, Alekos spotted Zelda making her way over to the bar. 'I'll drive you,' he told Sara quickly.

She shook her head. 'I'll call a cab. You don't need to leave the party early on my account.'

'It's fine.' He didn't tell her he was glad of an excuse to leave. 'You are my responsibility and of course I'll take you home if you're not feeling well.'

Alekos had driven himself and Sara to the dinner party in his sports car, and so he hadn't had a drink. As soon as they had escaped the busy roads of central London and reached the motorway he opened up the powerful engine. Twenty minutes later, he turned off into a quiet suburb and drew up outside the nondescript bungalow where she lived.

'Thank you for the lift,' she said when he walked round the car and opened her door.

'No problem.'

On the few previous occasions when he had driven her home, she had asked him in for coffee but he had always declined. Tonight she did not issue an invitation but, perversely, Alekos was curious to see inside her home, thinking that he might learn more about the woman who had worked closely with him for two years but about whom, he realised, he knew very little.

'Goodnight.' Sara turned to walk away from him, but she caught her heel on an uneven paving slab and stumbled. *'Ouch.'*

'Are you all right? That's what comes of knocking back a double whisky when you're not used to drinking spirits,' he told her impatiently.

'I've just twisted my ankle a bit. *Alekos…*' her voice rose in protest when he scooped her up into his arms and strode down the garden path to the front door '…really, it's nothing. I'm fine.'

'Give me your key.'

He heard her mutter something beneath her breath but she obviously realised it was pointless to argue with him and dug inside her handbag and gave him a key. He shifted her in his arms so that he could open the front door and carried her into the narrow hallway.

'You can put me down now.' She wriggled in an attempt to make him set her on her feet. The friction of her breasts rubbing against his chest had a predictable effect on Alekos's body. The hunger he had tried to ignore since he had danced with her at the party ignited into an inexorable force that burned in his gut.

'You shouldn't walk in high heels if you've sprained your ankle.'

'I don't suppose it is sprained.' Tension edged into her voice. 'It was kind of you to bring me home but will you please go now?'

He ignored her request and continued walking down the hall, past the sitting room and a small functional kitchen. Both rooms were painted an insipid beige which matched the beige carpet. There were two doors on the opposite side of the hall. 'Which is your room?'

'The second door. I can manage now, thanks,' Sara said when he shouldered the door and carried her into her bedroom. She flicked the light switch and Alekos was surprised by the room's décor. The walls were covered with murals of exquisite, brightly coloured flowers and the floral theme extended to the curtains and bedspread. The single bed was piled with stuffed toy bears and a large pink rabbit, which he guessed were relics from her childhood. The room was a vibrant and startling contrast to the otherwise characterless house.

'You obviously like flowers,' he murmured. 'Who painted the murals?'

'I did.'

'Seriously?' He was amazed. 'You're very talented. Did you study art?'

'No,' she said shortly. 'My mother thought I would be wasting my time going to art school. It was her idea that I trained as a secretary because it's a more reliable career.'

Sara wished Alekos would leave. She considered struggling to force him to put her down, but his arms around her were like iron bands and she did not relish an undignified tussle. It was bad enough that he believed she had been affected by alcohol and it was the reason she had tripped and hurt her ankle. He had probably only carried her into the house because he'd felt it was his duty not to leave her sprawled in the gutter. But she did not want him in her bedroom. It was her personal space, and when her mother had been alive it had been the only place where she had been able to indulge the creative side of her nature that she'd recently discovered she had inherited from her father.

Her father who had refused to tell her half-siblings that she was his daughter.

Every word of the text her father had sent her was imprinted on her memory. She told herself it was understandable that Lionel Kingsley cared more about his children from his marriage than for the illegitimate daughter whose existence he had only been aware of for a few months. But it felt like a rejection and it hurt. She had no other family. Her mother had grown up in a children's home, and after Joan had died Sara had felt completely alone until she had met her father.

The tears she'd managed to hold back while she had been at the party filled her eyes and slid down her face. She brushed them away with her hand and swallowed a sob but she felt so empty inside, knowing that she would not now meet her half-brother and half-sister at the weekend. And maybe never, she thought bleakly. Perhaps her father regretted finding out about her.

'Sara, why are you crying? Does your ankle hurt?' Alekos sounded terse. Sara knew he hated displays of emotion as much as she hated displaying her emotions in front of anyone. Even when her mother had died she'd accepted Alekos's rather stilted words of sympathy with quiet dignity and had sensed his relief that she'd kept her emotions out of the office.

But she could not stop crying. Perhaps the whisky she'd drunk at the party had loosened her grip on her self-control. Her father's text had left her utterly bereft and the sense of loneliness that she'd always felt—because she'd never had a strong emotional bond with her mother—now overwhelmed her and she turned her face into Alekos's chest and wept.

Somewhere in her haze of misery she acknowledged that the situation was undoubtedly Alekos's worst nightmare. She remembered an occasion when one of his ex-lovers whom he'd recently dumped had stormed into his office in floods of tears and accused him of breaking her heart. Alekos had literally shuddered in disgust at his ex's undignified behaviour. What must he think of her? Sara wondered. But her tears kept coming. It was as though a dam inside her had burst and allowed her pent-up emotions to escape.

She expected Alekos to stand her on her feet before he beat a hasty retreat from the house. But he didn't. Instead he sat down on the edge of her bed and cradled her in his lap. She was aware of the muscled strength of his arms around her, and the steady beat of his heart that she could hear through his chest was oddly comforting. It was a novelty to feel cared for, even though she knew Alekos's show of tenderness wasn't real. He did not care about her. He'd reminded her when he'd offered to drive her home from the party that she was a member of his staff and therefore his responsibility.

But it was nice to pretend for a few minutes that he actually *meant* the gentle words of comfort he murmured. His voice was softer than she'd ever heard it, and she could almost fool herself that it was the intimate voice of a lover caressing her senses like the brush of velvet against her skin. Gradually her harsh sobs subsided and as she drew a shaky breath she inhaled the spicy musk of Alekos's aftershave mixed with an indefinable male scent that was uniquely him.

In that instant she became conscious of his hard

thighs beneath her bottom and the latent strength of
his arms around her. Heat flared inside her and she felt
a sensuous heaviness in her breasts and at the molten
heart of her femininity.

She could not have said exactly when she sensed
a change in him, only that she became aware that his
breathing became irregular and his heartbeat beneath
her ear quickened and thudded hard and fast. Desire
stole through her veins as she lifted her head away from
his chest. Her heart lurched when she saw the fierce
glitter in his eyes.

'Sara—' His voice throbbed with a raw hunger that
made her tremble as she watched him lower his face
closer to hers. She stared at his mouth. His sensual,
beautiful mouth. So often she had imagined him kissing her with his mouth that promised heaven. 'You're
driving me crazy,' he growled before he covered her lips
with his and the world went up in flames.

CHAPTER FOUR

HE HAD WANTED to kiss Sara all evening. All week, if he was honest, Alekos admitted to himself, remembering how he had barely been able to keep his hands off her at the office. By the end of each day his gut had felt as if it were tied in a knot, and punishing workouts at the gym after work had failed to relieve his sexual frustration.

There was only one way to assuage the carnal hunger that ignited inside him and made him shake with need. The ache in his groin intensified when Sara parted her lips beneath his and her warm breath filled his mouth. He kissed her the way he'd fantasised about kissing her when he'd first caught sight of her wearing her backless dress. At the party he'd struggled to concentrate on his conversations with the other guests, when all he could think about was running his hands over Sara's naked back. Now he indulged himself and stroked his fingertips up her spine before he clasped her bare shoulders and pulled her even closer to him.

If she had offered the slightest resistance, perhaps he would have come to his senses. But his heart slammed into his ribs when she wound her arms round his neck and threaded her fingers into his hair. Her eager response decimated the last vestiges of his control, and he groaned as he dipped his tongue into her mouth and tasted her. She was nectar, sweet and hot and utterly intoxicating. In the far recesses of his mind Alekos was aware that he should stop this madness. Sara was his secretary, which meant she was off-limits. But it was impossible to associate the beautiful, sensual woman who had driven him to distraction over the past few days with his plain PA who had never warranted a second glance.

She shifted her position on his lap and he groaned again as her bottom ground against his rock-hard erection. He couldn't remember the last time he had felt so turned on. He felt as if he was going to explode and the faint warning voice inside his head was drowned out by the drumbeat of his desire to feel Sara's soft curves beneath him.

He manoeuvred her so that she was lying on the bed and he stretched out on top of her before capturing her mouth once more and kissing her with a deepening hunger that demanded to be appeased. Trailing his lips down her throat, he slid his hand behind her neck into the heavy silk of her hair and discovered that three tiny buttons secured the top of her dress. Three tiny buttons were all that prevented him from pulling the top of her dress down and revealing her ripe breasts that had tantalised him when they had been pressed against his chest. Urgency made his fingers uncooperative. He swore beneath his breath as he struggled to unfasten the buttons and something soft fell across his face.

Lifting his head, Alekos found himself eye to eye with a large pink rabbit. The incongruousness of making love to a woman on a narrow single bed adorned with stuffed animals catapulted him back to reality.

This was not any woman. This was Sara, his efficient, unflappable PA, who apparently had an unexpected liking for cuddly toys. He was only here in her bedroom because she had shockingly burst into tears.

Usually, when faced with a weeping woman, Alekos's instinct was to extricate himself from the situation as quickly possible. But Sara's tears had had an odd effect on him and inexplicably he'd found himself trying to comfort her. He had no idea why she had been crying. But he remembered that in the car when he'd driven her home she had read a text message on her phone and had looked upset.

Memories pushed through the sexual haze that had clouded Alekos's mind. Sara had hurried out of the office at the beginning of the week to meet someone. She had admitted she'd spent her holiday with a male 'friend' at his villa, and she had returned from the French Riviera transformed from a frump into a gorgeous sexpot. At the start of this evening she had seemed happy, but something had happened that had caused her to act out of character and she'd gulped down a double whisky as if it was no stronger than milk.

The most likely explanation Alekos could think of for Sara's distress was that her holiday romance was over. So what the hell was he—*the consolation prize*? He rolled away from her and sat up, assuring himself he was glad he had come to his senses before any harm had been done. Before he'd made the mistake of having sex with her. A kiss was nothing and there was no reason why they couldn't put it behind them and continue with their good working relationship as they had done for the past two years.

He stared at her flushed face and her kiss-stung

mouth that tempted him to forget everything and allow the passion that had sizzled between them moments ago to soar to its natural conclusion. But apart from all the other considerations to them sleeping together— and there were many—Alekos did not relish the idea that Sara wanted someone else and he was second best. *Theos*, he'd spent much of his life feeling second best to his dead brother and believing that, in his father's opinion, he was inferior to Dimitri.

'Alekos.' Sara's soft voice made his gut clench. She sat up and pushed her hair back from her face. She looked as stunned as he felt, and oddly vulnerable. For a moment he had the ridiculous idea that having a man in her bedroom was a new experience for her. 'We...we shouldn't have done that,' she said huskily.

He was well aware of that fact, but he was irritated she had pointed it out. 'It was just a kiss.' He shrugged, as much to emphasise the unimportance of the kiss to himself as well as to her. 'Don't look so stricken, Sara. It won't happen again.' Anger with himself for being so damned weak made him say harshly, 'It wouldn't have happened at all if you hadn't practically begged me to kiss you.'

'I did no such thing.' Fiery colour flared on her cheeks. 'You kissed me. One minute you were comforting me because I was upset, and the next...'

Alekos did not want to think about what had happened next. Remembering how he had explored the moist interior of Sara's mouth with his tongue, and the little moans she had made when he had kissed her, caused his erection to press uncomfortably against the restriction of his trousers.

'Ah, yes, you were upset—' he focused on the first

part of her sentence '—I'm guessing that the reason you were crying was because your holiday lover has dumped you. Your eagerness to kiss me was because you're on the rebound from the guy in France who has rejected you.'

'There was no holiday lover,' she said tightly. 'The "guy in France" was my *father*. I spent my holiday at his villa.' Sara's bottom lip trembled. 'But you're right to think I feel rejected. I'm starting to believe my father regrets that he got in contact with me. Until recently I didn't know about him, or that I have a half-brother and half-sister.' Tears slid down her cheeks. She gave a choked sob and covered her face with her hands, and so did not see Alekos's grim expression.

He had never seen Sara cry until tonight and his abhorrence of emotional displays meant that he really didn't want to stick around. But the fact that she was crying in front of him suggested something serious had happened to upset her. Why, even when she had come to work one Monday morning just before Christmas and told him that her mother had died at the weekend she had kept her emotions in check.

He felt an odd tug in his chest as he watched Sara's body shudder as she tried to regain control of herself. Ignoring a strong temptation to leave her to it, he pulled the dressing table stool next to the bed and sat down on it before he handed her some tissues from the box on the bedside table.

'Thanks,' she said indistinctly. Her tears had washed away most of her make-up, and again Alekos was struck by her air of innocence that he told himself he must have imagined.

'What did you mean when you said you think your

father regrets contacting you? Had there been a rift between the two of you?'

She shook her head. 'It's complicated. I met my father for the first time six weeks ago. When my holiday
plans to Spain fell through he invited me to stay at his
villa in Antibes. He wasn't there for the whole time, but
he came to visit me and we began to get to know each
other. I pretended to anyone who asked that I was employed as a housekeeper at the villa because my father
was worried about the media.' Her voice broke. 'I'm a
scandal from his past, you see, and he doesn't want his
other children to find out about me.'

'But why would the media be interested in your father?'

'Because he's famous. I promised I would keep my
relationship to him secret until he is ready to publicly
acknowledge that I am his illegitimate daughter.'

She was her father's shameful secret, Sara thought miserably. And from the text that Lionel had sent her earlier, it seemed as though she would remain a secret and
never meet her half-siblings. She hadn't revealed her
father's identity to anyone, not even her closest friend,
Ruth, who she had known since they were at primary
school. But the truth about her father that at first had
been such a wonderful surprise had become a burden
she longed to share with someone.

She blinked away yet more tears. Her head ached
from crying and she wished she could rest it on the pillows. But if she did that, Alekos might think she was
inviting him to lie on the bed with her and kiss her
again. She darted a glance at him and heat ran through
her veins as she remembered the weight of him pressing

her into the mattress and the feel of his muscular thighs as he'd ground his hips against her pelvis.

Of course she hadn't 'practically begged him to kiss her', as he'd accused her, she assured herself. But she hadn't stopped him. She bit her lip. Alekos had been the one to draw back, and if he hadn't... The tugging sensation in the pit of her stomach became a sharp pull of need as her imagination ran riot and she pictured them both naked, their limbs entwined and his body joined with hers.

She flushed as her eyes crashed into his glittering dark gaze and she realised that he was aware she had been staring at him.

'Why did you only meet your father for the first time recently?'

'He wasn't part of my life when I was growing up.' She shrugged to show him it didn't hurt, even though it did. 'My mother was employed as my father's secretary when they had an affair. He was married with a family, but he decided that he wanted to try and save his marriage and ended his relationship with Mum. She moved away without telling him that she was pregnant. She refused to talk about him and I have no idea why, in the last week of her life, she wrote to him and told him about me.'

She sighed. 'My father found out about me six months ago, but his wife was ill and he waited until after she had died before he phoned and asked if we could meet. He said he was glad he had found me. He'd assumed that my mother had told me his identity. Now I'm wondering if his reason for finding me was because he feared I might sell the story about my famous father to the newspapers. If the press got hold of the story it could damage his relationship with his children from his marriage. And I imagine the scandal that he'd had an affair, even though it was years ago, might harm his political career.'

Alekos's brows rose. 'Your father is a politician?'

Sara felt torn between her promise to protect her father's identity and what she told herself was a selfish need to unburden her secret to *someone*. But to Alekos? Strangely, he was the one person she trusted above all others. The tabloids made much of his playboy reputation, but she knew another side to him. He was dedicated to GE and worked hard to make it a globally successful business. He was a tough but fair employer and he was intensely protective of his mother and sisters. He guarded his own privacy fiercely, but could she trust that he would guard hers?

'It's vital that the story isn't leaked to the media,' she cautioned.

'You know my feelings about the scum who are fondly known as the paparazzi,' he said sardonically. 'I'm not likely to divulge anything you tell me in confidence to the press.'

She snatched a breath. 'My father is Lionel Kingsley.' It was the first time she had ever said the words aloud and it felt strange. Alekos looked shocked and she wondered if she had been naïve to confide in him. Now he knew something about her that no one else knew, and for some reason that made her feel vulnerable.

He gave a low whistle. 'Do you mean the Right Honourable Lionel Kingsley, MP—the Minister for Culture and the Arts? I've met him on a few occasions, both socially and also in his capacity as Culture Secretary, when I sponsored an exhibition of Greek art at the British Museum. As a matter of fact he was a guest at a party I went to earlier this week.'

'It sounds as though you have a lot more in common with my father than I do,' Sara muttered. She didn't move in the exalted social circles that Alekos and Lionel did, and she would definitely never have the opportunity to meet her father or her half-siblings socially. She tried to focus on what Alekos was saying.

'What has happened to make you think your father regrets finding you?'

'I was supposed to go and stay at his home at the weekend so that I could meet my half-siblings. But Lionel has decided against telling Freddie and Charlotte about me. It's only two months since their mother died. They were very close to her, and he's worried about how they will react to the news that he had been unfaithful to his wife.'

She pressed her hand to her temple, which had started to throb. 'I get the impression that I'm a complication and Lionel wishes he hadn't told me he is my father. His name isn't on my birth certificate and there's no possibility I could have found out I'm his daughter.'

She swung her legs off the bed and stood up. Alekos also got to his feet and her small bedroom seemed to be dominated by his six-feet-plus of raw masculinity.

'You should go,' she said abruptly, feeling too strung out to play the role of polite hostess. 'What happened just now...when we kissed...' her face flamed when he said nothing but looked amused, damn him '...obviously it can never happen again. I mean, you have a strict rule about not sleeping with your staff. Not that I'm suggesting you want to sleep with me,' she added quickly, in case he thought she was hinting that she hoped he wanted to have an affair with her.

Hot with embarrassment, she ploughed on, 'It was an unfortunate episode and I blame my behaviour on the whisky I drank earlier.'

'Rubbish.' Alekos laughed softly. 'You're not drunk. And I haven't had a drink all night. Alcohol had nothing to do with why we kissed. It was chemistry that ignited between us and made us both act out of character.'

'Exactly.' Sara seized on his words. 'It was a mistake, and the best thing we can do is to forget it happened.'

He deliberately lowered his eyes to her breasts, and she fought the temptation to cross her arms over her chest and hide her nipples that she was aware had hardened and must be visible jutting beneath the silky material of her dress. Somehow she made herself look at him calmly.

'Do you think it will be possible to forget the passion that exploded between us?' he murmured.

'It has to be, if I am going to continue as your PA.' She sounded fiercer than she had intended as she fought a rising sense of panic that the memory of Alekos kissing her would stay in her mind for a very long time. 'And now I really would like you to leave. It's late, and I'm tired.'

He checked his watch and said in an amused voice, 'It's a quarter to ten, which is hardly late. We left the dinner early because you said you were feeling unwell.'

To her relief he said no more and walked over to the door. 'I'll see myself out. And Sara—' his gaze held hers and his tone was suddenly serious '—your secret is safe with me. For what it's worth, I think your father should feel very proud to have you as his daughter.'

Alekos's unexpected compliment was the last straw for Sara's battered emotions. She held on until she heard the front door bang as he closed it behind him before she gave in to the tears that had threatened her composure since he had *stopped* kissing her.

Yes, she was upset about her father, but she was horrified to admit that she was more hurt by Alekos's rejection. She couldn't forget that he had been the one who had come to his senses. But what did her tears say about her? Why was she crying over a man who hadn't paid her any attention for two years? He had only noticed her recently because she'd revamped her appearance.

Alekos's interest in her was a passing fancy, but he could very easily break her heart if she allowed him to. She wished she *had* been drunk tonight, she brooded. At least then she could forgive herself for responding to him the way she had. Instead she only had her foolish heart to blame.

It took all of Sara's willpower to make herself stroll into Alekos's office the next morning and give him a cheerful smile before she turned her attention to the espresso machine.

His eyes narrowed when she walked over to his desk and placed a cup of coffee in front of him. She had resisted the urge to wear the beige dress that still lurked in the back of her wardrobe—a remnant of her previous dreary style. Out of sheer bravado she had chosen a bright red skirt and a red-and-white polka-dot blouse. Red stilettos and a slick of scarlet lip gloss completed her outfit. Her layered hairstyle flicked the tops of her shoulders as she sat down composedly and waited for him to give her instructions for the day.

'You're looking very perky. I trust you are feeling better?'

The gleam in his dark eyes was almost her undoing, but she had promised herself that she wouldn't let him rattle her and so she smiled and said coolly, 'Much better, thank you. I'm just sorry that you had to leave the dinner early last night because of me.'

'I'm not,' he murmured. The gleam turned to something darker and hotter as he skimmed his gaze down from her pink cheeks to her dotty blouse, and Sara was sure he was remembering the passion that had exploded between them in her bedroom.

She was conscious of the pulse at the base of her throat beating erratically and said hurriedly, 'Shall we get on? I thought you wanted to go through the final details for the Monaco Yacht Show.'

Alekos's sardonic smile told her he had seen through her distraction ploy, but to her relief he opened the folder in front of him. 'As you know, GE is one of the top exhibitors at the show, and we will be using the company's show yacht to give tours and demonstrations to potential clients interested in buying a superyacht. I've heard from the captain of *Artemis* that she has docked in Monaco and the crew are preparing her for the show. You and I will fly out to meet the rest of the sales team, and we will stay on board the yacht.'

For the rest of the morning, work was the only topic of conversation and if Sara tried hard she could almost pretend that the events of the previous night hadn't happened. It helped if she didn't look directly at Alekos but on the occasions when she did make eye contact with him the glittering heat in his gaze caused her stomach to dip. Alekos had called it *chemistry*, and its tangible presence every time she stepped into his office simmered between them and filled the room with a prickling tension that seemed to drain the air from Sara's lungs.

She was relieved when he left for a lunch appointment and told her he did not expect to be back until later in the afternoon. But, perversely, once he had gone she missed him and couldn't settle down to her work because she kept picturing his ruggedly handsome face and reliving the feel of his lips on hers. It was just a kiss, she reminded herself. But deep down she knew that something fundamental had changed between her and Alekos. She had hidden her feelings for him for two years, but it was so much harder to hide her desire for him when he looked at her with a hungry gleam in his eyes that made her ache with longing.

He returned just before five o'clock and seemed surprised to find her still at her desk. 'I thought you wanted to leave early tonight.'

'I'm not going to visit my father at his home in Berkshire now, so I thought I might as well catch up on some filing,' she said in a carefully controlled voice. She was embarrassed that she had cried in front of Alekos last night and was determined to hide her devastation over her father's change of heart about introducing her to her half-siblings.

His speculative look gave her the unsettling notion that he could read her thoughts. 'I've been thinking about your situation and I have an idea of how to help. Come into my office. I'm sure you would rather not discuss a personal matter where anyone walking past could overhear us.'

Sara didn't want to have a personal discussion with him anywhere, but he held open his office door and she could not think of an excuse to refuse. Besides, she was intrigued that he had actually thought about her. 'What idea?' she said as soon as he had shut the door.

He walked around his desk and waited until she was seated opposite him before he replied. 'On Sunday evening I have been invited to the launch of a new art gallery in Soho.'

'I'm up to speed with your diary, Alekos.' She hid her disappointment that he had brought her in to discuss his busy social schedule. But why would he be interested in her problems?

He ignored her interruption. 'The gallery's owner, Jemima Wilding, represents several well-established artists, but she also wants to support new talent and the gallery's launch will include paintings by an up-and-coming artist, Freddie Kingsley.'

Sara's heart gave an odd thump. 'I didn't know that my half-brother was an artist.'

'I believe Freddie and Charlotte both studied art at Chelsea College of Art. Charlotte is establishing herself as a fashion designer. She will be at the gallery launch on Sunday to support her brother, along with Lionel Kingsley.'

'Why are you telling me this?' She could not keep the bitterness from her voice. Alekos was emphasising what she already knew—that she did not belong in the rarefied world that her father and half-siblings, and Alekos himself, occupied.

'Because my idea is that you could accompany me to

the gallery launch to meet your half-siblings. I realise you won't be able to say that you are related to them, but you might have a chance to talk to your father in private during the evening and persuade him to reveal your true identity.'

Her heart gave another lurch as she tried to imagine meeting Freddie and Charlotte. Would they notice the physical similarities she shared with them? Probably not, she reassured herself. They were unaware that they had an illegitimate half-sister. Alekos was offering her what might be her only opportunity to meet her blood relations. Common sense doused her excitement. 'It would look strange if you took your PA to a private engagement.'

'Possibly, but you wouldn't be there as my PA. You would accompany me as my date. My mistress,' he explained when she stared at him uncomprehendingly.

For a third time Sara's heart jolted against her ribs. 'We agreed to forget about the kiss we shared last night.' She flushed, hating how she sounded breathless when she had intended her voice to be cool and crisp.

His eyes gleamed like hot coals for a second before the fire in those dark depths was replaced by a faintly cynical expression that Sara was more used to seeing. 'I don't remember agreeing to forget about it,' he drawled. 'But I'm suggesting that we *pretend* to be in a relationship. If people believe you are my girlfriend it will seem perfectly reasonable for you to be with me.'

'I can see a flaw in your plan.' Several flaws, as it happened, but she focused on the main one. 'You have made it clear that you would never become personally involved with any member of your staff. If we are seen together in public it's likely that the board members of

GE will believe we are having an affair. They disapprove of your playboy reputation and might even decide to take a vote of no confidence against you.'

'That won't happen. As you said yourself, the board members approve of you. They think you are a good, stabilising influence on me,' he said drily.

Sara remembered the many glamorous blondes Alekos had dated in the past. 'I'm not sure your friends would be convinced that you and I are in a relationship,' she said doubtfully.

'They'd have been convinced if they had seen us together last night.' His wicked grin made her blush. 'The plan will work because of the sexual chemistry between us. There's no point in denying it.' He did not give her a chance to speak. 'It is an inconvenient attraction that we might as well use to our advantage.'

So she was an inconvenience! It was hardly a flattering description. 'Why are you willing to help me meet my half-siblings? You've never taken an interest in my personal life before.'

He shrugged. 'You're right to guess I am not being entirely altruistic. Zelda Pagnotis will also be at the gallery launch. She is a friend of Jemima Wilding's daughter, Leah. You saw how Zelda followed me around at the board members' dinner, how she changed the name cards around so that she was seated next to me.' Frustration clipped his voice. 'Her crush on me is becoming a problem, but if she believes that you are my girlfriend it might persuade her to move her attention onto another guy.'

'Are you saying you need me to protect you from Zelda?'

'Orestis thinks I want to corrupt his granddaughter,'

Alekos growled. 'Of course nothing could be further from the truth, but I guarantee Orestis won't disapprove of you being my mistress. He's more likely to be relieved.'

'But why don't you flaunt a genuine mistress in front of Zelda? There must be dozens of women who would jump at the chance to go on a date with you.'

'I don't happen to have a girlfriend at the moment. If I invite one of my exes to the gallery launch there's a risk they will read too much into it and believe I want to get back with them.'

'What it is to be Mr Popular,' Sara murmured wryly. Alekos's arrogance was infuriating, but he had a point. In the two years that she had been his PA she'd realised that women threw themselves at him without any encouragement from him.

He hadn't needed to encourage her to kiss him last night. She flushed as she remembered how eagerly she had responded to him. But he had called a halt to their passion even though he must have sensed that she wanted him to make love to her. Now he was asking her to pretend to be in love with him, and she was afraid she would be too convincing.

'What do you think of my idea, Sara? It seems to me that it will be an ideal solution for both of us.'

She looked into his dark eyes and her heart gave a familiar swoop. 'I need time to think about it.'

He frowned. 'How much time? I'll need to let Jemima know that I am bringing a guest.'

Sara refused to let him browbeat her into making a decision. Although she longed to meet her half-siblings she was worried about how her father might react to seeing her at a social event. 'Phone me in the morning and I'll give you my answer,' she said calmly. She stood up and walked over to the door, but then hesitated and turned to look at him.

'Thank you for offering to help me meet my half-siblings. I appreciate it.'

Alekos waited until Sara had closed the door behind her before he strode over to the drinks cabinet and poured himself a double measure of malt Scotch. Her smile had hit him like a punch in his gut. He'd always known he was a bastard, and Sara had confirmed it when she'd said that she appreciated his help.

He raked his hair off his brow. Sara had no idea that her revelation about her father's identity was a very useful piece of knowledge that he intended to use to his advantage. His keenness to attend the gallery launch had nothing to do with an interest in art and everything to do with business. Alekos knew that the Texan oil billionaire Warren McCuskey was on the guest list. He also knew that McCuskey and Lionel Kingsley were close friends.

The story went that many years ago both men had been amateur sailors competing in a transatlantic yacht race, but the American had nearly lost his life when his boat had capsized. Lionel Kingsley had been leading the race but had sacrificed his chance of winning when he'd gone to McCuskey's assistance. Three decades later, Warren McCuskey had become one of the richest men in the US and the person who had the most influence over him was his good friend, English politician Lionel Kingsley—who, astonishingly, happened to be Sara's father.

Alekos was aware that networking was a crucial part

of business, and the best deals were forged at social events where the champagne flowed freely. He'd heard that McCuskey was considering splashing out some of his huge fortune on a superyacht. At the party on Sunday evening, Sara would want to spend time with her father, and it would be an ideal opportunity for him to ingratiate himself with the Texan billionaire.

He took a swig of his Scotch and ignored the twinge of his conscience as he thought of Sara and how he planned to use a fake affair with her for his own purpose. All was fair in love and business, he thought sardonically. Not that he knew anything about love. GE was his top priority and he had a responsibility, a *duty*, to ensure that the company was as successful as it would undoubtedly have been under Dimitri's leadership. He secretly suspected that his brother had thrown his life away because of a woman. But Alekos would never allow any woman close to his heart and certainly not to influence his business strategy.

CHAPTER FIVE

THE LIMOUSINE CAME to a halt beside the kerb and Alekos prepared to step out of the car, when Sara's voice stopped him.

'I don't think I can go through with it.' Her voice shook. 'You didn't say the press would be here.'

He glanced out of the window at the group of journalists and cameramen gathered on the pavement outside the Wilding Gallery. 'There was bound to be some media interest. Jemima Wilding is well-known in the art world and naturally she wants exposure for her new gallery. I suspect she leaked the names on the guest list to the paparazzi,' he said drily.

The chauffeur opened the door but Sara did not move. 'Doesn't it bother you that photos of us arriving together might be published in the newspapers and give the impression that we are...a couple?'

'But that's the point.' Alekos stifled his impatience, realising he needed to reassure her. When he'd phoned Sara on Saturday morning, she had said she would pretend to be his mistress and accompany him to the gallery launch. Now she seemed to be having second thoughts. 'You want to meet your half-siblings, don't you?' he reminded her of the reason she had agreed to his plan.

'Of course I do. But I'm worried my father will be angry when he sees me. He might think I came here tonight to put pressure on him to tell Charlotte and Freddie about me.'

'Then we will have to put on a convincing act that you are my girlfriend and you are at the party with me.'

'I suppose so.' She still sounded unsure. Alekos watched her sink her teeth into her soft lower lip and was tempted to soothe the maligned flesh with his tongue. But such an action, although undoubtedly enjoyable, would be wasted here in the car where they couldn't be seen.

Glancing out of the window again, he noticed a young woman, wearing a skirt so short it was not much more than a belt, standing in the glass-fronted lobby of the gallery. He gritted his teeth. Zelda Pagnotis was an irritating thorn in his side, but unless he took drastic action to end her crush on him the teenager could become a more serious problem and cause a further rift between him and her grandfather.

'Thank you, Mike,' Alekos said to the chauffeur as he climbed out of the car and held out his hand to Sara. After a few seconds' hesitation she put her fingers in his and stepped onto the pavement. She stiffened when he slid his arm around her waist and escorted her over to the entrance of the art gallery. As Alekos had predicted, the paparazzi took pictures of him and Sara, and she pressed closer to him and put her head down as the flashbulbs went off around them when they walked into the building.

A doorman stepped forwards to take her coat. It had been raining earlier when the car had collected her from her house and Alekos hadn't seen what she was wearing beneath her raincoat until now.

Theos! He tore his eyes from her and glanced around him, thinking he had spoken out loud. But no one was looking at him. He returned his gaze to her and stared. 'Your dress...'

'Is it all right?' Her tongue darted out to moisten her lips. The gesture betrayed her nervousness and sent a shaft of white-hot desire through Alekos. 'Is my dress suitable?' she said in an undertone. 'Why are you staring at me?'

'It's more than suitable. You look incredible.' He ran his eyes over her bare shoulders, revealed by her emerald silk strapless dress, down to the rounded curves of her breasts that made him think of ripe peaches, firm and delicately flushed, tempting him to taste them. Lowering his gaze still further, he noted how the design of the dress drew attention to her slim waist before the skirt flared over her hips and fell to just above her knees.

Forcing his eyes back up her body, he noted how her layered hair swirled around her shoulders when she turned her head, and the hot ache in his groin intensified when he imagined her silky hair brushing across his naked chest as he lifted her on top of him and guided her down onto his hard shaft.

'Theos.' This time he spoke aloud in a rough voice as he curved his hand behind her neck and drew her towards him. He saw her eyes widen until they were huge green pools that pulled him in.

'Alekos,' she whispered warningly, as if to remind him that they were not alone in the lobby. But she didn't pull away as he lowered his face towards hers.

'Sara,' he mocked softly. And then he covered her mouth with his and kissed her, long and slow, and then deep and hard when she parted her lips and kissed him back with a sweet intensity that made his gut twist and made him want to sweep her up in his arms and carry her off to somewhere where they could be alone.

The low murmur of voices pushed into his consciousness and he reluctantly lifted his head and snatched oxygen into his lungs. Sara looked as stunned as he felt, but he had no intention of admitting that what had just happened was a first for him. He had *never* kissed a woman in public before. As he stepped away from her he caught sight of Zelda Pagnotis hurrying out of the lobby wearing a sulky expression on her face.

'First objective of the evening completed,' he told Sara smoothly, keen to hide the effect she had on him. 'Zelda can't doubt that we are having an affair. I've just spotted Lionel Kingsley and his son and daughter. Are you ready to meet your half-siblings?'

Sara could feel her heart hammering beneath her ribs as she walked with Alekos into the main gallery. She was excited that in a few moments she would meet her half-brother and half-sister for the first time, but she was still reeling from the sizzling kiss she had shared with Alekos.

While she'd been in his arms she had forgotten where they were, or why he had brought her to the art gallery. But when he had lifted his mouth from hers, she'd seen Zelda Pagnotis walk past them and realised that Alekos had deliberately kissed her in view of the teenager. *First objective completed.* She recalled his words ruefully. What an idiot she was to have believed that he'd kissed her because he desired her.

She looked ahead to the group of people Alekos was heading towards and her heart beat harder when she saw her father. Lionel was frowning as he watched her approach and her hesitant smile faltered. *She shouldn't have come.* The last thing she wanted to do was alienate her father. Her steps slowed and she felt a strong urge to run out of the gallery, but Alekos slipped his arm around her waist and propelled her forwards.

A tall woman with purple hair detached from the group and greeted them. 'Alekos, darling, I'm so glad you were able to come this evening. That was quite an entrance you made,' she said in an amused voice that made Sara blush. 'You must be Sara. I'm Jemima Wilding. I'm so pleased to meet you. Alekos, I think you and Lionel Kingsley have met before.'

'We have indeed.' Lionel shook Alekos's hand. 'Your financial support of the Greek art exhibition last year was much appreciated. But actually we met very recently at a party earlier this week.' He glanced at Alekos's hand resting on Sara's waist. 'You were unaccompanied on that occasion.'

'Yes, unfortunately Sara had another commitment,' Alekos said smoothly. He tightened his arm around Sara's waist as if he guessed that her heart was fluttering like a trapped bird in her chest. 'This is Sara Lovejoy.'

To Sara, the silence seemed to last for ever and stretched her nerves to the snapping point. But in reality Lionel Kingsley hesitated infinitesimally before he shook her hand. 'I am delighted to meet you... Miss Lovejoy.'

'Sara,' she said thickly. Her throat felt constricted and she smiled gratefully at Alekos when he handed her a flute of champagne from a passing waiter.

Lionel introduced the other people in the group, starting with a stockily built man with a rubicund face. 'This is my good friend Warren McCuskey, who flew to London from Texas especially so that he could attend the gallery launch and support my son Freddie's first exhibition.'

Sara greeted Warren with a polite smile, but her heart was thumping as Freddie Kingsley stretched his hand towards her. She prayed no one would notice her hand was trembling as she held it out to him.

Her half-brother smiled. 'Pleased to meet you, Sara.'

'I...' Emotion clogged her throat as Freddie closed his fingers around hers. His handshake was firm and his skin felt warm beneath her fingertips. Her secret drummed in her brain. Freddie was unaware that the blood running through his veins was partly the same as her blood. She swallowed and tried to speak but the lump in her throat prevented her.

Alekos moved imperceptibly closer, as if he understood that her emotions were balanced on a knife-edge. There was something comforting about his big-framed, solid presence at her side and, to her relief, she could suddenly breathe again.

'It's lovely to meet you,' she told Freddie softly. Her half-brother was taller than she had imagined, his brown hair curled over his collar and his smile was wide and welcoming. She looked into his green eyes and recognised herself.

He gave her a puzzled look. 'Have we met before? Your face seems familiar.'

'No, we've never met.' Sara was conscious of her father standing a few feet away and wondered if she was the only person in the group who could sense Lionel's tension.

Freddie shrugged. 'You definitely remind me of someone but I can't think who. Are you interested in art, Sara?'

'Very. I'd love to see your work.'

She followed Freddie over to where six of his paintings were displayed against a white wall. Even to her untrained eye she could tell that he was a gifted artist. His use of intense colour and light made his landscapes bold and exciting.

'My brother is very talented, isn't he?'

Sara turned her head towards the voice and discovered her half-sister standing next to her.

'I'm Charlotte Kingsley, by the way. I really like your dress.' Charlotte grinned and murmured, 'I really like your gorgeous boyfriend too. And he seems very keen on you. Even when he is talking to other people he can't keep his eyes off you. Have the two of you been together long?'

'Um…not that long.' Sara experienced the same difficulty speaking that had happened when she'd met Freddie. She felt an instant connection with Charlotte which made her think that maybe they could become friends. But perhaps her half-siblings would hate her if they learned that she was the result of Lionel Kingsley's affair with her mother.

She chatted for a few minutes and then slipped away to a quiet corner of the gallery, needing to be alone with her churning emotions. It was obvious that Charlotte and Freddie were deeply fond of each other. Sara felt a pang of envy as she watched them laughing together. Her childhood had been lonely because her mother hadn't encouraged her to invite school friends home. She had longed for a brother or sister to be a companion, unaware that growing up in Berkshire had been her half-sister, who was a year older than her, and her half-brother, three years her senior.

Tears gathered in her eyes and she quickly blinked them away when Lionel walked over to join her. She glanced around the gallery, searching for Alekos. Her instinctive need for his protection was a danger that she would have to deal with later. She saw him chatting with the Texan, Warren McCuskey, and her heart gave a silly skip as she realised that Alekos must have purposely given her and her father a few minutes of privacy.

'Sara, it's good to see you.' Lionel's smile allayed her concern that he was annoyed she had come to the party. 'I had no idea you were dating Alekos Gionakis. I thought you worked for him?'

'I'm his PA, but recently we…we've become close.' She felt her face grow warm. Lying did not come naturally to her. But she had to admit that Alekos's idea for her to pretend to be his girlfriend had allowed her to meet her half-siblings, and maybe she had a chance of persuading her father to reveal her identity to Freddie and Charlotte.

'Gionakis is an interesting man. He is knowledgeable of the arts but I've heard that he's a ruthless businessman.' Lionel lowered his voice so that he couldn't be overheard by anyone else. 'Sara, if Joan had told me she was pregnant I would have offered her financial support while you were a child. I regret that you did not grow up in a family.'

'I have a half-brother and half-sister who are my family, and I would love to get to know Charlotte and Freddie if only you would tell them I am your daughter,' Sara replied in a fierce whisper.

Her father looked uncomfortable. 'I will tell them when the time is right. Maybe if they got to know you first it would help when I break the news that I once cheated on their mother.' He looked round and saw Alekos approaching. 'Does Gionakis know of our relationship?'

Sara hesitated. 'Yes. But I know Alekos won't say a word to anyone,' she said hurriedly when Lionel frowned.

'You must love him to trust him so much.'

Love Alekos! Sara found she could not refute her father's comment. Her heart gave a familiar lurch as she watched Alekos walk towards her. He looked outrageously sexy, wearing a casual but impeccably tailored light grey suit and a black shirt, unbuttoned at the neck. His thick hair was ruffled as if he'd raked it off his brow several times during the evening, and the dark stubble shading his jaw added to his dangerous magnetism.

Of course she was in love with him; she finally admitted what she had tried to deny to herself for two years. She loved Alekos, but he'd told her he did not believe in love. Just because you loved someone didn't mean you could make them love you back. Her mother had discovered the truth of that when she had fallen in love with Lionel Kingsley.

'I told you my plan would work.' Alekos knew he sounded smug but he didn't care. He'd had a couple of drinks at the gallery launch and, although he was certainly not drunk, he felt relaxed and pleased with how the evening had gone. He leaned his head against the plush leather back seat of the limousine as they sped towards north London. His thoughts were on Warren McCuskey. The Texan billionaire was definitely interested in buying a superyacht and Alekos had used all his persuasive powers to convince him to commission a yacht from GE. He was confident he was close to finalising a deal with McCuskey. He could taste success, smell it.

He could also smell Sara's perfume. The blend of citrusy bergamot and sensual white musk, that had tantalised him every day at the office, filled the dark car and his senses. Suddenly he didn't feel relaxed any more. He felt wired up inside, the way Sara always made him feel lately. He was conscious of the hard thud of his heart and the even harder ache of his arousal that jerked to attention and pushed against the zip of his trousers.

'I don't think Zelda will continue to be a problem now that she believes you are my mistress,' he drawled, more to remind himself of the reason why he had spent most of the evening with his arm around Sara's waist. She'd fitted against his side as if she belonged there. He frowned as he remembered how, every time he'd leaned towards her, he'd inhaled a vanilla scent in her hair that he guessed was the shampoo she used.

'Good. That's one problem solved at least.' She sounded distracted.

Alekos glanced at her sitting beside him. She had put her coat on before they'd left the gallery, but it was undone and he could see the smooth upper slopes of her breasts above the top of her dress. 'Is there another problem?' he said abruptly.

'There might be.' She flicked her head round to look at him and her hair brushed against his shoulder, leaving a trail of vanilla scent. 'Alekos, we need to talk.'

Talking to Sara was not uppermost in his mind. But if he told her of his erotic thoughts about her she would probably slap his face. The car pulled up outside her house. 'Invite me in for coffee and you can tell me what's troubling you.'

'All right,' she said after a moment's hesitation. 'But I only have instant coffee. Will that do?'

As Alekos followed her into the house he regretted his suggestion. He detested the insipid brown liquid that the English insisted on calling coffee. But, more pertinently, he couldn't understand why he had suggested to Sara that she could confide in him what he assumed was a problem with her private life. He was about to tell her not to worry about the coffee but she showed him into the sitting room, saying, 'I'll go and put the kettle on.'

It was difficult to imagine a room more characterless than the one he was standing in. The neutral décor was joyless, as if whoever had chosen the beige furnishings had found no pleasure in life. It was a strangely oppressive room and Alekos retreated and walked down the bungalow's narrow hallway to the kitchen.

Sara had taken off her coat and she looked like a gaudy butterfly in her bright dress against the backdrop of sterile worktops and cupboards. She had also slipped off her shoes and he was struck by how petite she was without her high heels. The sight of her bare feet with her toenails varnished a flirty shade of pink had an odd effect on him and he felt his gut twist with desire. He searched for something to say while he struggled to control his rampant libido.

'How come your bedroom is so colourful, while the rest of the house is...' he swapped the word *drab* for '...plain?'

'My mother didn't like bright colours. Now Mum has gone I've decided to sell the house. The estate agent advised me not to redecorate because buyers prefer a blank canvas.' She placed a mug on the counter in front of him. 'I made your coffee extra strong so it should taste like freshly ground coffee.'

Alekos thought it was highly unlikely. But remembering Sara's brightly coloured bedroom brought back memories of his previous visit to her home when he had kissed her and passion had ignited between them. There was barely enough space for the two of them in the tiny kitchen but he didn't want to suggest they move into the sitting room, which was as welcoming as a morgue. He sipped his coffee and managed not to grimace. 'What did you want to talk about?'

'Lionel thinks it would be a good idea if I could mix with Charlotte and Freddie socially so they can get to know me before he tells them I am their half-sister. He intends to use his association with you— namely your support of art projects—to invite us both to his villa in Antibes, where he's planning to celebrate his birthday.' Sara tugged on her bottom lip with her small white teeth, sending Alekos quietly to distraction as he imagined covering her lush mouth with his.

'Go on,' he muttered.

'I couldn't tell my father that I had pretended to be your girlfriend tonight so I could meet my half-siblings. Lionel believes we are genuinely in a relationship and we would have to continue the pretence if you accept his invitation.'

'Who else has your father invited to his villa?'

'Charlotte and Freddie and my father's close friend Warren McCuskey. By the way, thanks for chatting to Warren at the gallery while I spoke to my father privately.'

'You're welcome.' Alekos ignored the irritating voice of his conscience, which reminded him he was an unprincipled bastard. It was a fact of life that you couldn't head a multimillion-pound business and have principles. He'd seized his chance to grab McCuskey's undivided attention while Sara was talking to Lionel. 'When is your father's birthday?'

'Next weekend. I'd mentioned that we will be in Monaco for the yacht show and he said that Antibes is only about an hour's drive away. But I did warn him that we will be busy with the show and might not have time to visit him.'

'Our schedule for the three days of the show is hectic. But how about if I arranged a birthday lunch for your father and his guests aboard *Artemis* for next Sunday? That way we can catch up on paperwork in the morning, and you'll be able to spend time with Lionel and your brother and sister in the afternoon.' It would also be an ideal opportunity to give Warren McCuskey a demonstration of GE's flagship superyacht, but Alekos kept that to himself.

'Would you really be prepared to do that on my behalf?' Her smile stole his breath and he shrugged off the niggling voice of his conscience. Sara caught her lower lip between her teeth again. 'But will you mind having to keep up the pretence that I am your girlfriend?'

Alekos dropped his gaze from her mouth to the delectable creamy curves of her breasts cupped in her silk dress, and he was surprised that the thud of his heart wasn't audible. 'I think I can put up with pretending that we are lovers,' he drawled.

He smiled when he heard her breath rush from her lungs as he wrapped his arm around her waist and drew her towards him so that she was pressed against his chest, against his heat and the hardness of his arousal that ached. *Theos,* he had never ached so badly for a woman before.

'Alekos,' she whispered. Her green eyes were very dark and he saw her uncertainty reflected in their depths as he lowered his head. 'What are you doing?'

'Rehearsing for when we meet your father,' he growled before he slanted his mouth over hers and kissed her like he'd wanted to do, like he'd been burning up to do since he had kissed her in the lobby of the art gallery. The difference was that that had been for Zelda Pagnotis's sake, or so Alekos had assured himself. But this time it was lust, pure and simple, that made him cup Sara's jaw in his palm and angle her head so that he could plunder her lips and slide his tongue into her mouth to taste her sweetness.

Without her high-heeled shoes she was much smaller than him and Alekos lifted her up and sat her on the kitchen worktop, nudging her thighs apart so that he could stand between them. The fact that she let him gave him the licence he needed to capture her mouth and kiss her again, hard this time, demanding her response as the fire inside him burned out of control.

Her shoulders were silky smooth beneath his hands. He traced his fingers along the delicate line of her collarbone before moving lower to explore the upper slopes of her breasts. Touching wasn't enough. He had to see her, had to cradle those firm mounds in his hands. With his lips still clinging to hers, he reached behind her and unzipped her dress. The green silk bodice slipped down and he helped it on its way, tugging the material until her breasts popped free. His breath hissed between his teeth as he feasted his eyes on her bare breasts, so pale against his tanned fingers, and at their centre her nipples, tight and dusky pink, just waiting for his tongue to caress them.

With a low growl Alekos lowered his mouth to her breast and drew wet circles around the areola before he closed his lips on her nipple and sucked. The soft cry she gave turned him on even more and he slid his arms around her back and encouraged her to arch her body and offer her breasts to his mouth. Every flick of his tongue across her nipple sent a shudder of response through her and when he transferred his attention to her other breast and sucked the tender peak she made a keening noise and dug her fingers into his hair as if to hold him to his task of pleasuring her.

He was so hard it hurt. His erection strained beneath his trousers as he shifted even closer to her, forcing her to spread her legs wider so that her dress rode up her thighs and he pressed his hardness against the panel of her knickers. Knowing that a fragile strip of lace was all that hid her feminine core from him shattered the last of his restraint and he groaned and cupped her face in his hands.

'Let's go to bed, Sara *mou*. This kitchen is not big enough for me to make love to you comfortably.' He doubted that her single bed would offer much more in the way of comfort and remembering her collection of child's soft toys strewn on her bed was a little off-putting. But the only other room was that soulless sitting room and he quickly dismissed the idea of having sex with her there.

He eased back from her and looked down at her naked breasts with their reddened, swollen nipples. 'Come with me,' he said urgently. If he did not have her soon he would explode.

Bed! Sara stiffened as Alekos's thick voice broke through the haze of sexual excitement he had created with his mouth and his wicked tongue. When he had sucked her nipples she'd felt an electrical current arc from her breasts down to the molten core of her femininity. She'd been spellbound by his magic, enthralled by the myriad new sensations induced by his increasingly bold caresses. But his words brought her back to reality with a thud.

On the opposite wall of the kitchen she could see her reflection in the stainless steel cooker splashback that her mother had religiously polished until it gleamed. Dear heaven, she looked like a slut, with her bare breasts hanging out of the top of her dress and the skirt rucked up around her thighs. She pictured Joan's disapproving expression and shame doused the heat in her blood like cold water thrown on a fire.

'Men only want one thing,' her mother had often told Sara. *'Once you give them your body they quickly lose interest in you.'*

Sara assumed that was how her father had treated her mother. It was certainly true of Alekos. She knew about all the gorgeous blondes who had come and gone in his life, because he'd given her the task of arranging an item of jewellery from a well-known jewellers to be sent to his mistresses when he ended his affair with them. Who would choose a pretty trinket to be sent to a mistress who was also his PA? She didn't know whether to laugh or cry.

'We can't go to bed,' she told him firmly. 'You know we can't, Alekos. We shouldn't have got carried away like we did.' She watched his expression turn from puzzlement to shock at her refusal before his eyes narrowed to black slits that gleamed with anger.

'Why not?' he demanded, his clipped tone betraying his frustration. 'We are both unattached, consenting adults.'

'I work for you.'

He dismissed her argument with a careless shrug of his shoulders. 'This evening we gave the impression that we are having an affair and tomorrow's papers will doubtless carry pictures of us arriving at the art gallery together.'

'But we were only pretending to have a relationship. You don't really want me.'

'It's patently obvious how much I want you,' Alekos said sardonically. 'And you want me, Sara. Don't bother to deny it. Your body doesn't lie.'

She followed his gaze down to her bare breasts and silently cursed the hard points of her nipples that betrayed her. Red-faced, she yanked the top of her dress back into place. 'We can't,' she repeated grittily. But her resolve was tested to its limit by the feral hunger in his eyes. 'If we had an affair, what would happen when it ended?'

'I see no reason why you couldn't carry on being my PA. We work well together and I wouldn't want to lose you.'

Alekos wouldn't want to lose her as his PA, but that was all. She could not risk succumbing to her desire for him because she would find it impossible to continue to work for him after they were no longer lovers. It would be torture to know he was dating other women after he'd finished with her. And she *would* know. In the two years she had been his PA she'd learned to recognise the signs that he was having regular sex.

She felt emotionally drained from the evening. Meeting her half-siblings had made her long to be part of a family. But she certainly wasn't going to sleep with Alekos to ease the loneliness she had felt all her life. 'I think you had better leave,' she told him huskily, praying he wouldn't guess she was close to tears.

'If you really want me to go, then of course I accept your decision,' he said coldly, sounding faintly incredulous that she had actually rejected him. 'But in future I suggest you do not respond to a man so fervently if you don't intend to follow it through.'

'Are you accusing me of leading you on?' Her temper flared. 'That's a foul thing to suggest and grossly unfair. You came on to me.'

'And you hated every moment when we were kissing, I suppose?' he mocked. 'It's a little too late to play the innocent victim, Sara.'

'I'm not trying to imply that I'm a victim.' But if he knew how innocent she really was he would run a mile, she thought grimly. She suddenly remembered that they had travelled from Soho to her house in Alekos's limousine. 'If I had invited you to stay the night, what would your chauffeur have done? Would he have slept in the car?'

Alekos shrugged. 'We have an arrangement. Mike

knows to wait for a while…' He did not add anything more but Sara understood that his driver had been instructed to leave after a couple of hours if Alekos went into a woman's house and did not reappear. No doubt it was an arrangement that had been used on many occasions. Sara got on well with Mike and she would have felt so embarrassed if she'd had to face him after Alekos had spent the night with her. It brought home to her that she could not sacrifice her job, her reputation and her self-respect for a sexual liaison with her boss.

But when she followed Alekos down the hall and he opened the front door she had to fight the temptation to tell him that she had changed her mind and wanted him to stay and make love to her. Love had nothing to do with it, she reminded herself. At least not for Alekos. And she had sworn she would not make her mother's mistake and fall in love with a man who could never love her.

'Goodnight,' she bid him in a low voice.

'Sleep well,' he mocked, as if he knew her body ached with longing and regret that would make sleep impossible. As she watched him stride down the path she thought that at least she would be able to face him in the office tomorrow morning with her pride intact.

But pride was a poor bedfellow she discovered later, as she tossed and turned in her single bed. Her nipples still tingled from Alekos's ministrations and the insistent throb between her legs was a shameful reminder of how close she had come to giving in to her desire for him.

CHAPTER SIX

MONACO WAS A playground for millionaires and billionaires, and for the last three days the tiny principality had hosted the iconic yacht show, which this year had taken place in June rather than its usual date in September. Some of the world's most impressive superyachts were moored in the harbour, the largest and most spectacular being the two-hundred-and-eighty-foot *Artemis* from leading yacht brokerage and shipyard, Gionakis Enterprises.

On Sunday morning, Alekos made his way through Port Hercules in the sunshine. Now that the show was over, the huge crowds that had packed the waterfront had gone and his route to where *Artemis* was moored was no longer blocked by yacht charter brokers, who had been keen to tour the vessel and discover the superlative luxury of her interior.

Gone too were the glamour models and hostesses who were synonymous with the prestigious show. Monaco surely boasted more beautiful women wearing minuscule bikinis that revealed their tanned, taut bodies than anywhere else in the world, Alekos thought cynically. He could have relieved his sexual frustration with any of the numerous women who had tried to catch his eye, but there was only one woman he wanted and she had studiously kept out of his way.

After the frenzy of the past three days, Alekos's preferred method to unwind had been to go for a fifteen-mile run along the coast. Now he felt relaxed as he boarded *Artemis* and walked along her deck, with nothing but the cry of gulls and the lap of water against the yacht's hull to break the silence. His sense of calm well-being was abruptly shattered when he entered the small saloon which he had been using as an office and found Sara sitting at a desk with her laptop open in front of her.

She was dressed in white shorts and a striped top and her hair was caught up in a ponytail with loose tendrils framing her face. Without make-up, the freckles on her nose were visible and she looked wholesome and utterly lovely. Alekos felt his gut twist.

'Why are you working already? I told you I was planning to go for a run and you could have a lie in this morning.'

'I woke early and decided to get the report about the show typed up,' she said, carefully not looking directly at him. 'I thought you wouldn't be back for another hour or so.'

'Is that why you started work at the crack of dawn, hoping to have finished the report before I came back, so that you could avoid me like you've done since you arrived on Wednesday?'

She flushed. 'I haven't avoided you. We've worked together constantly every day.'

'During the day we were surrounded by other people, and you took yourself off to bed immediately after dinner every evening. I can't believe you usually go to bed at nine p.m.,' he said drily.

The colour on her cheeks spread down her throat and Alekos wondered if the rosy blush stained her breasts. 'I was tired,' she muttered. 'The past few days have been incredibly busy.'

'I don't deny it. And because I came to Monaco a couple of days before you did, this is the first chance we have had to discuss what happened after we attended the art gallery launch last week.'

Now she did look at him, her eyes so wide and full of panic that she reminded him of a rabbit caught in car headlights. 'There's nothing to discuss. We...we got carried away, but it won't happen again.'

'Are you so sure of that?' Alekos deliberately lowered his gaze to the hard points of her nipples, outlined beneath her clingy T-shirt, and grinned when she crossed her arms over her chest and glared at him. He did not know why he took satisfaction from teasing her but he suspected it was to make him feel less bad about himself. He couldn't comprehend why he had come on to her so strong last Sunday evening. It was not his style. And she had rejected him! *Theos*—that was a first for him.

What was it about Sara that fired him up as if he were a hormone-fuelled youth instead of a jaded playboy who could take his pick of beautiful women? All week he had racked his brain for an answer while he'd been alone each night in the opulent master suite on *Artemis*, whereas at last year's show he'd enjoyed the company of two very attractive—not to mention inventive—blondes.

The only reason that made any sense—but did not make him feel good about himself, he acknowledged grimly—was simply that he wanted Sara so badly because she had turned him down. He wanted to see her sprawled on his bed, all wide-eyed and flushed with sexual heat, and he wanted to hear her beg him to make love to her because his ego couldn't deal with rejection.

She was watching him warily, and for some reason it angered him. She had been with him all the way the other night, right up until he'd suggested they go to bed. Even though she had said no, he'd sensed he could have persuaded her to change her mind. But he'd never pleaded with a woman to have sex with him before, and he had no intention of starting with his PA, who clearly had a hang-up about sex.

He leaned across the desk and tugged her arms open. Ignoring her yelp of protest, he drawled, 'It will help to make the pretence that we are lovers more convincing if you drop the outraged virgin act when your father and his guests arrive.'

Her eyes flashed with anger and she clamped her lips together as if to hold back a retort. Alekos wondered how much resistance she would offer if he attempted to probe her lips apart with his tongue. Lust swept like wildfire through him and he abruptly swung away and strode over to the door, conscious that his running shorts did not hide the evidence of his arousal.

'As you are so keen to work, you may as well type up the financial report for the shareholders. It will keep you busy until lunchtime, and as you are so averse to my company you won't want to join me for a swim in the pool, will you?' he murmured, and laughed softly at her fulminating look.

They had lunch on one of the yacht's four decks, sitting at a table set beneath a striped canopy that provided shade from the blazing Mediterranean sun. Lionel Kingsley, his son and daughter and Warren McCuskey had boarded *Artemis* at midday, and Alekos had instructed the captain to steer the yacht out of the harbour and drop anchor a couple of miles off the coast.

They were surrounded by blue, Sara thought as she looked around at the sparkling azure ocean which met a cornflower blue sky on the horizon. A gentle breeze carried the faint salt tang of the sea and lifted the voices and laughter of the people sitting around the table. She popped her last forkful of the light-as-air salmon mousse that the chef had prepared for a main course into her mouth and gave a sigh of pleasure.

After her run-in with Alekos earlier in the morning, her nerves had been on edge at the prospect of them having to act as though they were a couple. She'd fretted about the lunch, knowing that she had lied to her father about being Alekos's girlfriend and, even worse, not being truthful to Charlotte and Freddie that she was their half-sister.

But she need not have worried. Alekos had been at his most urbane and charming, although his eyes had glinted with amusement and something else that evoked a molten sensation inside her when he'd slipped his arm around her waist as they had walked along the deck to greet Lionel and his party. 'Showtime, Sara *mou*,' Alekos had murmured before he'd kissed her mouth, leaving her lips tingling and wanting more, even though she knew the kiss had been for the benefit of the interested onlookers.

Recalling that kiss now, she ran her tongue over her lips and glanced at Alekos sitting across the table from her. Heat swept through her when she discovered him watching her through narrowed eyes, and she knew that he was also remembering those few seconds when his lips had grazed hers. She tore her gaze from him when she realised that Charlotte was speaking.

'An office love affair is so romantic. When did you and Alekos realise that there was more to your relationship than you simply being his PA?'

'Um…' Sara felt her face grow warm as she struggled to think of a reply.

'It was a gradual process,' Alekos answered for her. 'Obviously, Sara and I work closely together and to begin with we were friends before our friendship developed into something deeper.'

He sounded so convincing that Sara almost believed him herself. It was true that friendship had grown between them over the last two years. But that was where fact ended and her fantasy that he would fall in love with her began, she reminded herself.

Keen to change the subject, she turned to Freddie. 'Tell me what it was like at art school. It must have been fun. I would have loved to study for an art degree.'

'Why didn't you, if it is a subject that you say you have always been interested in?'

She shrugged. 'My mother wanted me to find a job as soon as I'd finished my A levels. There was only the two of us, you see, and she struggled to pay the bills.'

'Couldn't your father have helped?'

Sara froze and was horribly aware that her father had broken off his conversation with McCuskey and was waiting tensely for her to respond to Freddie's innocent question.

'No…he…wasn't around.'

'Luckily for me, Sara joined GE,' Alekos said smoothly. 'I realised as soon as I met her that she would be an ideal person to organise my hectic life.' He rang the little bell on the table and almost instantly a steward appeared, pushing the dessert trolley. 'I see that my chef has excelled himself with a selection of desserts. My personal recommendation is the chocolate torte.'

Following his words, there was a buzz of interest around the table over the choice of dessert and the awkward moment passed. Sara gave Alekos a grateful look.

'After lunch I thought you might like to use the jet skis,' he said to Charlotte and Freddie. 'Or if you prefer an activity that involves less adrenalin there is snorkelling equipment, or the glass-bottomed dinghy is a fun way to view marine life.'

'You've got one heck of a boat here, Alekos,' McCuskey commented. 'Is it true there is a helipad somewhere on the yacht?'

'The helipad is on the bow and there is a hangar below the foredeck which is specially designed. I could give you a tour of *Artemis* if you'd like to see all of her many features.'

'I surely would,' the Texan said enthusiastically.

Sara had never had as much fun as she did that afternoon. The sea was warm to swim in and, with Charlotte and Freddie's help, she soon got the hang of snorkelling. Alekos joined them later in the day and when they took the jet skis out Sara rode pillion behind him and hung on tightly to him as they sped across the bay. With her arms wrapped around his waist and her cheek resting on his broad back, she allowed herself to daydream that it was all real—that she and Alekos were lovers and her half-siblings accepted her as their sister.

'Dad and Warren are driving back to Antibes. But

Charlotte and I are meeting up with some friends in Monte Carlo this evening,' Freddie said as they stood on deck and watched the glorious golden sunset. 'Why don't you and Alekos come with us?' He put his head on one side as he studied Sara's face. 'It's bugging me that you remind me of someone, but I can't think who.'

Alekos slid his arm around her waist. 'What do you say, *agapi mou*? Would you like to go to a nightclub?'

'Yes. But I don't mind if you'd rather not,' she said quickly, unaware of the wistful expression in her eyes.

'I want to do whatever makes you happy,' he assured her.

Sweet heaven, he was a brilliant actor, but it was all pretend, Sara reminded herself firmly. She must not allow herself to be seduced by the sultry gleam in Alekos's dark eyes and the velvet softness of his voice that made her wish for the moon even though she knew it was unreachable.

Monte Carlo at midnight was a blaze of golden lights against a backdrop of an ink-black sky. Sara followed Alekos out of a nightclub that apparently was *the* place to be seen and to see celebrities. She had spotted a famous American film star and a couple of members of a boy band, but she'd only had eyes for Alekos.

They had met up with Charlotte and Freddie's friends, and Alekos had arranged for their group to use a private booth in the nightclub. He had stayed close to her all evening, draping his arm around her shoulders when they had sat in the booth drinking cocktails, and drawing her into his arms on the dance floor so that her breasts were crushed to his chest and she was conscious of his hard thigh muscles pressed against her through the insubstantial black silk dress she had chosen to wear for a night out.

He led her over to a taxi and opened the door for her to climb inside. 'My feet are *killing* me,' she complained as she flopped onto the back seat.

Alekos slid in beside her and lifted her feet onto his lap. 'Your fault for wearing stilts for shoes,' he said, inspecting the five-inch heels on her strappy sandals. Sara caught her breath when he curled his fingers around her ankles and unfastened her shoes before sliding them off her feet. While they had been in the nightclub they had continued the pretence of being lovers in front of her half-siblings. But now it seemed way too intimate when he trailed his fingertips lightly up her calves. 'Did you enjoy yourself tonight?'

'It was the best night of my life,' she said softly. 'And the best day.' Her eyes were drawn to him. In the dark taxi his chiselled profile was shadowed and the sharp angles of his face were highlighted by the glow from the street lamps. 'Thank you for making it possible for me to spend time with Charlotte and Freddie, and with my father earlier today. I hope you weren't too bored showing Warren McCuskey around *Artemis*. I guessed you had offered to give him a tour of the yacht so that I could have time alone with Lionel.'

'Yeah, I'm all heart,' he drawled. His oddly cynical tone made Sara dart a look at him, but the taxi drew up to the jetty and he climbed out of the car. She couldn't face putting her shoes back on, and while she stood contemplating whether to walk the short distance along the jetty in bare feet Alekos scooped her up in his arms and carried her up the yacht's gangway.

'Thanks.' She silently cursed how breathless she

sounded and hoped he couldn't feel the erratic thud of her heart. 'You can put me down now.'

He continued walking into the main saloon before he lowered her down. She curled her toes into the soft carpet. Every sensory receptor on her body felt vitally alive and she was intensely aware of Alekos, of the spicy scent of his aftershave, the heat of his body and the smouldering gleam in his dark eyes. It all felt like a wonderful dream—staying on a luxurious yacht, spending time with her half-siblings and dancing the night away with a man who was so handsome it hurt her to look at him.

'I wish tonight didn't have to end.' She blurted out the words before she could stop herself and flushed, thinking how unsophisticated she sounded.

'It doesn't have to end yet. Will you join me for a nightcap?'

'Um…well, I shouldn't. It's late and we both have to be up early in the morning. You're flying to Dubai to visit Sheikh Al Mansoor, and my flight to London is at ten a.m.'

'I realise that it's three hours past your bedtime,' he said drily. 'But why not live dangerously for once?'

Alekos had simply invited her to have a drink with him. This was not a defining moment in her life, Sara told herself firmly. 'All right.' She ignored the warning in her head that sounded just like her mother's voice, and sided with the other voice that urged her to stop hiding from life and *live*. 'Just one drink.'

'Sure. You don't want to overdose on excitement.' He gave her a bland smile as he ushered her out of the main saloon and towards the stairs that led to the upper decks.

When she hesitated he murmured, 'There is champagne on ice in my suite.'

Sara had never been in the master suite before and its opulent splendour took her breath away. The décor of the sitting room and the bedroom she could see beyond it was sleek and ultra-stylish while the colour scheme of soft blue, grey and white was restful. Not that she felt relaxed. Quite the opposite as she watched Alekos slip off his jacket and throw it onto a chair before he strolled over to the bar. His white silk shirt was unbuttoned at the throat, showing his dark olive skin and a glimpse of black chest hairs. His hair fell across his brow and the dark stubble on his jaw gave him a rakish look that evoked a coiling sensation in the pit of her stomach.

The sliding glass doors were open and she stepped outside onto the private deck and took a deep breath. On this side of the yacht facing away from the port there was only dark sea and dark sky, lit by a bright white moon and stars like silver pins studding a black velvet pincushion.

Alekos's footfall was silent but she sensed he was near and turned to take the glass of pink fizz he handed her. 'Kir Royale, my favourite drink.'

'I know.' He held her gaze. 'Why were you looking sad?'

Sara sighed. 'Charlotte and Freddie both talked a lot about their happy childhoods, and how much their parents loved each other. Lionel's wife suffered from multiple sclerosis for several years and he cared for her devotedly until her death two months ago.' She bit her lip. 'If Lionel reveals that I am his daughter, all their memories of growing up in a happy family will be tainted by the knowledge that their father cheated on their mother.'

She placed her glass down on a nearby table and curled her hands around the deck rail, staring into the empty darkness beyond the boat. 'I'm afraid that my half-siblings will hate me,' she said in a low voice.

'I don't believe anyone could hate you, Sara *mou*.'

The gentleness in Alekos's voice was unexpected and it tore through her. 'I'm not *your* Sara.'

He smiled at her fierce tone. 'Aren't you?' He un-curled her fingers from the rail and turned her to face him. Sara trembled when he drew her unresisting body closer to his—so close that she could feel his heart thundering as fast as her own.

Of course she was his. The thought slipped quietly into her head. It wasn't complicated; it was really very simple. She had been his for two years and she could not fight her longing for him when he was looking at her with undisguised hunger in his eyes that made her tremble even more.

'I want you to be mine, and I think you want that too,' he murmured. She felt his lips on her hair, her brow, the tip of her nose. And then his mouth was there, so close to hers that she felt his warm breath whisper across her lips, and she couldn't deny it, couldn't deny him when it would mean denying herself of what she wanted more than anything in the world—Alekos.

Maybe it was because she had made him wait that ex-plained the wild rush of anticipation that swept through him, Alekos brooded. And perhaps it was the lost, al-most vulnerable expression on her lovely face moments ago that had elicited a peculiar tug on his heart.

The haunted look in her eyes should have warned him to back off while he still retained a little of his sanity. But it was too late. His desire for her was too strong for him to fight. Sara had driven him to the edge of reason for too long and the feel of her soft curves pressing against his whipcord body, and the little tremors that ran through her when he smoothed his hand down her back and over the taut contours of her bottom decimated his control.

He took possession of her mouth and gave a low growl of satisfaction when she parted her lips to allow his tongue access to her sweetness within. This time she would not reject him. He felt her desperation in the way she kissed him with utter abandon, and her response fuelled his urgency to feel her naked body beneath his.

He liked the little moan of protest she made when he ended the kiss and lifted his head to stare into her green eyes with their dilated pupils. She was so petite he could easily sweep her up in his arms, but he stepped back and held out his hand. 'Will you come and be mine, Sara?'

He liked that she did not hesitate. She put her fingers in his and he led her into the bedroom. His heart was pounding faster than when he'd gone for a fifteen-mile run that morning. And he was already hard—*Theos*, he was so hard; his body was taut with impatience to thrust between her slim thighs. The sight of her wearing a bikini when they had swum in the sea earlier in the day had driven him to distraction, and he had suggested using the jet skis to hide the embarrassing evidence of his arousal that his swim shorts couldn't disguise.

Most women would have played the temptress and given him artful looks as they performed a striptease for his benefit. Sara simply stood at the end of the bed and looked at him with her huge green eyes. Her faint uncertainty surprised him. She was, after all, a modern single woman in her mid-twenties and he assured himself that this could not be new for her. It was difficult to picture her as the drab sparrow who he had barely noticed in his office but, remembering the old style Sara, he thought it was likely that she hadn't had many lovers.

But he did not want her to be shy with him. He wanted her to be bold and as eager as he was. His hunger for her was so intense and he sensed that this first time would not last long. He needed her with him all the way, which meant that he must turn her on by using all his considerable skill as a lover.

'I want to see you,' he said roughly. The bedside lamps were switched off but the brilliant gleam from the moon silvered the room and gave her skin a pearlescent shimmer as he pulled the straps of her dress down, lower and lower until he had bared her breasts.

'*Eisai ómorfi.* You are beautiful,' he translated, realising he had spoken in Greek. His native tongue was the language of his blood, his passion, and he groaned as he cradled her breasts in his hands, testing their weight and exploring their firm swell before he was drawn inexorably to their dusky pink crests that jutted provocatively forwards, demanding his attention.

She shivered when he flicked his thumb pads over her nipples, back and forth before he rolled the tight nubs between his fingers until she gave a low cry that corkscrewed its way right into his gut. Giving her pleasure became his absolute focus but when he lowered his head to her breast and closed his mouth around her nipple, sucking hard, she bucked and shook and her undisguised enjoyment of what he was doing to her drove him to the brink.

'Sara, I have to have you now. I can't wait,' he muttered as he straightened up and sought her lips with his, thrusting his tongue into her mouth to tangle with hers. Next time he would take it slow, he promised himself. But he was fast losing control and the drumbeat of desire pounding in his veins demanded to be assuaged.

He would have liked her to undress him, maybe knelt in front of him to pull his trousers down and then taken him in her mouth. His body jerked at his erotic fantasy and he swore beneath his breath. There was no time for leisurely foreplay and he fought his way out of his clothes with none of his usual innate grace, while she stood watching him, her eyes widening when he stepped out of his boxers. She stared at his rock-hard arousal, and the way she swallowed audibly made him close his eyes and offer a brief prayer for his sanity.

'Alekos...' she whispered.

'If you have changed your mind. Go. Now,' he gritted.

'I haven't. It's just...' She broke off and ran her fingertips lightly, almost tentatively over his proud erection.

He grabbed her hand and lifted it up to his chest where his heart was thundering so hard he knew she could feel it. 'Playtime's over, angel.' He tugged her dress over her hips and it slithered to the floor. A pair of black lacy knickers were all that hid her femininity from him and he dealt with them with swift efficiency, sliding them down her legs before he lifted her and laid her on the bed.

The strip of soft brown curls between her thighs partially shielded her slick heat from his hungry gaze. He lifted her leg and hooked it over his shoulder, then did the same with her other leg, and his laughter was deep and dark when she gasped in protest.

'Beautiful,' he growled. She was splayed in front of him, open and exposed, and he had never seen anything as exquisite as he lowered his head and placed his mouth over her feminine heat.

'*Oh.*' She jerked her hips and clutched his hair. It crossed his mind that maybe she hadn't received pleasure this way before, and the possessive feeling that the thought elicited rang a faint alarm bell in his mind. He had never felt possessive of any woman and Sara was no different than any of the countless lovers he'd had since his first sexual experience when he was seventeen.

She squirmed beneath him. 'You can't...' She sounded scandalised, but there was something else in her guttural cry, a note of excitement that made Alekos smile.

'Oh, but I can,' he promised. And then he bent his head once more and probed his tongue into her slick heat, straight to the heart of her. Her hoarse moans filled his ears and her sweet feminine scent swamped his senses. She tasted of nectar and he licked deeper, sliding his hands beneath her bottom to angle her hips so that he could suck the tiny nub of her clitoris.

The effect was stunning. She gave a keening cry, bucking and writhing beneath him so that he gripped hold of her hips and held her fast while he used his tongue to drive her over the edge. She shattered. And watching her climax, her fingers clawing at the satin bedspread as her body shook, fired his blood and his need.

Theos, he had never *needed* a woman before. His

brother had been needy for the woman who had broken his heart, but Alekos had learned from Dimitri's
death that needing someone was a weakness that made
you vulnerable. Although he was loath to admit it, right
now he needed Sara the same way he needed to breathe
oxygen.

Somehow, Alekos retained enough of his sanity to
take a protective sheath from the bedside drawer and
slide it over his erection. And then he positioned himself between her spread thighs once more and his need
was so fierce and consuming that the flicker of appre-
hension in her eyes did not register in his mind. Not
until it was too late.

He could hear the sound of his ragged breaths and
his blood thundering in his ears. His fingers shook as
he stroked them over her moist opening and found her
hot and slick and ready for him. He was so close to his
goal and with a groan he thrust his way into her and
froze when he felt an unmistakable resistance.

She could not be a virgin.

But the evidence was there in the sudden tension of
her muscles and the way she went rigid beneath him.
His brain told him to halt and withdraw, but his body
was trapped in the web of his desire. A sense of urgency that was more primitive and pressing than logical thought overwhelmed him. His shock at discovering
her innocence was followed by an even greater shock
as he realised that he was out of control. His body was
driven by a fearsome need that drove him to move inside her and push deeper into her velvet heat.

Somewhere in the crazy confusion of his mind he
was aware that she had relaxed a little and she flattened her hands against his chest and slid them up to

his shoulders, not pushing him away but drawing him down onto her. She shifted her hips experimentally to allow her internal muscles to accommodate him, and just that small movement blew his mind. With a sense of disbelief Alekos felt his control being stretched and stretched. Everything was happening too fast. He closed his eyes and fought against the heat surging through his veins, but he couldn't stop it… He couldn't…

He let out a savage groan as his control snapped and he came hard, his body shuddering with the force of his climax. Even as the tremors still juddered through him, shame at his lack of restraint lashed his soul. How could he have been so weak? How could Sara have made him so desperate?

And what the hell was he going to do with her now?

CHAPTER SEVEN

'WHY DIDN'T YOU tell me it was your first time?'

Alekos's voice sounded…odd, not angry exactly, but not pleased either. And perhaps his gruff tone was to be expected, Sara acknowledged. He had been anticipating a night of passion with a sexually experienced mistress, but instead he'd found himself making love to a woman whose sexual experience could be documented on the back of a postage stamp.

'It was my business,' she said huskily, finding it hard to speak past the lump that inexplicably blocked her throat.

'But now you have made it my business too.' He said something in Greek that she thought it was best she did not understand. 'I'm sorry I hurt you.' He sounded remorseful and again there was that odd tone in his voice that was not quite anger but might have been regret.

'You didn't really. I mean, just a bit at first but then it was…okay.'

'You should have told me,' he said more harshly this time.

She sighed. 'I was curious.' Not the full truth but it would do. She wanted to cry—perhaps every woman felt emotional after her first sexual experience—but she was determined to wait until she was alone before she let her tears fall.

Alekos's weight was heavy on her, pressing her into the mattress and making her feel trapped. She didn't want to look at him, but there was nowhere else *to* look when his body was still joined with hers. His dark eyes that only moments ago had blazed with desire were now chips of obsidian and his beautiful mouth was compressed into a hard line. It was impossible to believe that his lips had ever curved into a smile of sensual promise.

She pushed against his chest. 'Can we talk about this some other time, and preferably not at all? We're done, aren't we?' She bit her lip. 'To be honest, I don't understand why people make sex such a big deal.'

She could not hide the disappointment in her voice. The discomfort she'd experienced when Alekos had pushed his powerful erection into her had only lasted a few moments. The stinging sensation had faded and been replaced with a sense of fullness that had begun as pleasant, and when he'd moved, and pushed deeper, had become a tantalising throb that she had wanted to continue.

But it had ended abruptly. Alekos's ragged breaths had grown hoarser before he'd made a feral growl that sounded as if it had been ripped from his throat as he had slumped forwards and she'd felt his hot breath on her neck.

He was still on top of her. Still *inside* her. There was too much of him for her fragile emotions to cope with, and now he was frowning, his heavy brows meeting above his aquiline nose.

'No, we are not done, Sara *mou*. Nowhere near.'

'I'm not your Sara.'

He laughed softly and the rich sound curled around her aching heart. Tenderness from Alekos was something she hadn't expected and it was too beguiling for her to bear right now.

'I have indisputable proof that you are mine. Am I hurting you now?' he murmured. He shifted his position very slightly and she felt something bloom inside her, filling her once more so that her internal muscles were stretched. While she was stunned by the realisation that he was hardening again, he bent his head and captured her mouth in a slow, sensual kiss that started out as gentle and, when she responded because she couldn't help herself, became deeper and more demanding.

She was breathless by the time he trailed his lips over her cheek to her ear and nipped her lobe with just enough pressure that she shivered with pleasure that was not quite pain. He moved lower, kissing his way down her throat and over the slopes of her breasts before he flicked his tongue across one nipple and rolled the other peak between his fingers, making her gasp at the sheer intensity of the sensations he was creating.

He played her body the way a skilled musician wrung exquisite notes from an instrument, his touch now light, now masterful, and always with the utmost dedication to giving her pleasure. And all the while he moved his hips unhurriedly, sometimes in a gentle rocking motion, sometimes circling his pelvis against hers.

Each movement resulted in his erection growing harder within her and stretching her a little more, filling her until she was only aware of Alekos—the warmth of his skin, the strength of his bunched shoulder muscles beneath her hands, the power of his manhood pushing into her, pulling back, pushing into her, pulling back, in a steady rhythm that made her want more of the same.

He looked down at her and his mouth curved into a slow smile as he slid his hands beneath her bottom and encouraged her to arch her hips to accept the thrust of his body.

'Does that feel good?'

'Yes.' It felt amazing but she was suddenly shy, which was ridiculous, she told herself, when she was joined with him in the most intimate way possible.

'Tell me if it hurts.'

'It doesn't.'

'Tell me what you want.'

Oh, God, how could she tell him that his relentless rhythm was driving her mad? How could she tell him what she wanted when she didn't know? She stared up at his handsome face and thought she would die of wanting him. 'I want you to move faster,' she whispered. 'And harder. Much harder.'

'*Theos*, Sara…' He gave a rough laugh. 'Like this?' He thrust deep and, before she had time to catch her breath, he thrust again. 'Like this?'

'Yes…*yes*.'

It was unbelievable, indescribable. And so beautiful. She learned his rhythm and moved with him, meeting each thrust eagerly as he took her higher, higher. He possessed her utterly, her body and her soul, and he held her at the edge, made her wait a heartbeat before he drove into her one final time and they exploded together, her cries mingled with his hoarse groan as they shattered in the ecstasy of their simultaneous release.

Sara came down slowly. A heavy lethargy stole through her body, making her muscles relax and blocking out the hundreds of thoughts that were waiting in the wings of her mind, preparing to lambast her with recriminations. Alekos moved away from her and moments later she heard a click that she guessed was the door of the en suite bathroom closing. She wondered if it was her cue to leave. What was the protocol when you had just lost your virginity to your boss?

Oh, God, it was better not to think of that. Better not to think at all, but to keep her eyes closed and that way she could pretend it had all been a dream. Hovering on the edge of sleep, she was aware that the mattress dipped and she breathed in the elixir that was Alekos— his aftershave, sweat, the heat of his body.

In her dream she turned towards his warmth and curled up against him, her face pressed to his chest so that she felt his rough chest hairs against her cheek. In her dream he muttered words in Greek that she didn't understand as he slid his arm beneath her shoulders and pulled her close to him.

Alekos knew he was in trouble before he opened his eyes. The brush of silk on his shoulder and a faint vanilla scent were unwelcome reminders of his stupidity. Lifting his lashes, he confirmed that the situation was as bad as it could get. Not only had he had sex with Sara, but she had slept all night in his bed. *Theos*, in his *arms*.

He hardly ever spent an entire night with a lover. Sharing a bed for sleeping suggested a level of intimacy he did not want and could lead to mistaken expectations from a woman that she had a chance of being more than his mistress. Last night he had intended to leave Sara in his bed and go and sleep in another cabin.

He could not explain to himself why he had climbed

back into bed after he'd visited the bathroom. Alarm bells had rung in his head when she'd snuggled up to him, all soft and warm and dangerously tempting. He'd been tired and had closed his eyes, promising himself he would get up in a couple of minutes, and the next he'd known it was morning.

He swore beneath his breath. Sara was still asleep and he carefully eased his arm from beneath her. The sunlight filtering through the blinds played in her hair and made the silky layers burnish myriad shades of golden brown. With her English rose complexion and her lips slightly parted she looked innocent, but of course she wasn't, thanks to him, he acknowledged grimly.

What had he been thinking when he'd made love to her, not just once but twice? But that was the trouble. *He hadn't been capable of rational thought.* His actions had been driven by desire, by his need for Sara that in the crystal clarity of the-day-after-the-night-before shamed him. Discovering that she was a virgin should have immediately prompted him to stop having sex with her. But he had been unable to resist the slick, sweet heat of her body, and he'd come—*hell*, he'd come so hard. Even now, remembering the savage intensity of his release caused his traitorous body to stir.

Failing to satisfy a lover was a new experience for him and Sara's obvious disappointment had piqued his pride. He grimaced. His damnable pride was not the only reason he'd set out to seduce her a second time. He'd convinced himself it was only fair that he should gift her with the pleasure of an orgasm. Despite her inexperience, she had been a willing pupil and he'd found her ardent response to his lovemaking irresistible.

It was that thought that compelled him to slide out

of bed and move noiselessly around the bedroom while he dressed. In his mind he replayed the last conversation he'd had with his brother when he was fourteen.

'Why are you so upset just because your girlfriend cheated? You can easily find another girlfriend. Women love you.'

'No other woman could ever replace Nia in my heart,' Dimitri had said. 'When you are older you'll understand, Alekos. One day you will meet a woman who gets under your skin and you'll be unable to resist her. It's called falling in love and it's hellish.'

He wouldn't visit hell for any woman, Alekos had vowed years ago as he'd watched his brother weeping. Love had brought Dimitri to his knees. Had it also been ultimately responsible for his death? The question had haunted Alekos for twenty years.

There was no danger he would fall in love with Sara. But his weakness last night served as a warning he could not ignore. He didn't know why she had chosen to lose her virginity with him, and he did not want to know what hopes she might be harbouring about them making their pretend affair a reality.

One thing he knew for sure was that he needed to get the hell off the yacht before she woke up. A short, sharp lesson might be brutal but it was best to make it clear that all he'd felt for her was lust. He still felt, he amended when she moved in her sleep and the sheet slipped down to reveal one perfect rose-tipped breast. She was peaches and cream and he wanted to feast on her again. The strength of his desire shocked him and he strode over to the door, resisting the urge to look back at her.

Sara would probably expect to find him gone when she woke up. She knew he was planning to fly to Dubai to take part in a charity polo match organised by his friend Sheikh Al Mansoor. Kalif had brought one of his cousins to Monaco to visit the yacht show, and the three of them would fly to Dubai on the Prince's private jet. There was no reason why he should feel guilty for abandoning Sara, Alekos assured himself. After all, she was his PA and she had arranged his diary around his ten-day trip to stay at Kalif's royal palace.

Deep down, Alekos acknowledged that he was running away, and the unedifying truth did not make him feel good about himself. He was running scared, his conscience taunted him. Sara had made him lose control and it had never happened before. No woman had ever got under his skin and he hoped—*no*, he was sure—that distance would allow him to put his fascination with her into perspective. He'd responded to the chemistry between them. That was all. When he returned to the London office in ten days' time she would no doubt be as keen as him to forget about their night of passion.

Sara was woken by a *thud-thud* noise that she recognised was a helicopter's rotor blades. She opened her eyes and frowned as she looked around her. This was not her cabin on *Artemis*. This was... *Dear, sweet heaven!* Memories of the previous night flooded her mind. Last night she'd had sex with Alekos and he had not been pleased when he'd discovered it was her first time.

She turned her head on the pillow and, finding she was alone in the bed, assumed he was in the bathroom. Her thoughts flew back to last night. It had been over fairly quickly and she'd felt underwhelmed by the experience. But then Alekos had made love to her a second time, and nothing she'd ever read about sexual pleasure came close to the incredible orgasm that had exploded through her body like an electrical storm and left her shaking in its aftermath.

It had been just as good for Alekos. His harsh groan before he'd slumped on top of her had told her he'd reached his own nirvana. But what would happen now? Where did they go from here?

It suddenly seemed a good idea to get dressed before she faced him. Muscles she'd been unaware of until this morning tugged as she slid out of bed and scooped up her dress and knickers from the floor where they had scattered. The memory of his hands on her body and his mouth on her breasts and— *dear God*—between her legs when he'd bestowed a shockingly intimate caress, caused heat to bloom on her cheeks and she felt even hotter inside.

When he'd realised she was inexperienced he had tempered his passion with tenderness that had captured her heart and made her hope— *No*, she must not go down that road, she told herself firmly. Just because Alekos had made love to her with exquisite care and made her feel beautiful and desirable, she must not hope he might fall in love with her. *But he might*, whispered a little voice in her head.

The sound of rotor blades was becoming fainter, as if the helicopter was flying away. Sara frowned. Who could have been delivered to the yacht by helicopter? As far as she was aware, no guests were expected. Alekos was taking a long time in the bathroom. Struck by a sudden sense of foreboding, she knocked on the bathroom door and when he didn't answer she tried the handle and found it unlocked and the room empty. She ran over to the sliding glass doors and out onto the deck.

Looking up, she saw that it was the *Artemis* helicopter flying away from the yacht and her heart dropped faster than a stone thrown into a pool as she realised that Alekos must be on board.

She remembered she'd arranged for the pilot to fly him to the airport at Nice, and from there he would travel to Dubai. Of course she wouldn't have expected him to change his plans, but why hadn't he at least woken her to say goodbye? Because he was reluctant to face her after last night, she thought bleakly. She felt sick to think that Alekos had used her for sex. She heard her mother's voice: *'Once you've given a man what he wants you won't see him for dust.'*

Choking back a sob, Sara hurried back to her own cabin on the deck below, praying she wouldn't bump into any of the yacht's crew. She had things to do: clothes to pack, paperwork to stow in her briefcase before she was due to leave *Artemis* and travel to the airport with members of GE's sales team. Keeping busy stopped her from brooding on the fact that Alekos had abandoned her.

Laden with her suitcase and laptop, she descended to the main deck and forced a smile when she saw her father's friend Warren McCuskey walking up the gangway onto the yacht.

'I'm afraid you have just missed Alekos. He left early for an appointment.'

'Not to worry. I'll call him with the news he's been wanting to hear.' The Texan laughed. 'I've gotta hand it to your guy—he's a damned good salesman. When I met him a couple of months back I happened to say that my wife, Charlene, fancied us having a boat, and since then Gionakis hasn't missed a chance to try and persuade me to buy a yacht from GE. The day after we met at the art gallery in London he invited me to visit *Artemis* while she was in Monaco. By lucky coincidence I'd arranged to stay at Lionel's place in Antibes.'

'Did you say you had met Alekos *before* the gallery launch?' Sara strove to sound casual while her brain reminded her that Alekos did not operate on 'lucky coincidences'. He'd known Warren would be staying at her father's villa because she'd told him.

'Sure. And, like I said, he used every opportunity to use his sales tactics on me. But what really sold me on the idea of buying a yacht from his company was when he said that you are Lionel's daughter.'

Warren mopped his sunburned brow with a handkerchief and so did not notice the colour drain from Sara's face. 'Lionel is my closest friend, and if Gionakis is going to be his son-in-law I'll be happy to buy a boat from him.'

'Alekos told you that he and I are getting married?' she said faintly.

'Not in so many words. But I can tell when a fella is in love. He couldn't keep his eyes off you at lunch yesterday. I was impressed with this yacht and I've decided to buy her.'

'You want to buy *Artemis*?' Sara was stunned. The superyacht's price was two hundred million dollars, making her one of the most expensive yachts ever built. Alekos had seen a business opportunity when she'd told him that Lionel Kingsley was her father. No wonder he had suggested they could pretend to be having an affair so that she could attend functions with him and socialise with her father. He had been aware that Warren McCuskey was Lionel Kingsley's close friend; it was fairly common knowledge.

Alekos had been *so* helpful talking to Warren to give her time alone with her father, she thought cynically. She had believed his offer to help her had been genuine, out of kindness. But Alekos wasn't *kind*. He was a ruthless businessman and, unforgivably, he had betrayed her secret and told Warren that Lionel was her father.

Idiot, she thought bitterly. Why had she given herself to Alekos, knowing he was a notorious womaniser and heartbreaker? The answer—that she was in love with him—filled her with self-disgust. Did she really have so little self-worth to love a man who only loved himself?

'If you speak to Alekos, will you pass on a message?' Warren said.

'Oh, I'll give him a message, don't you worry.' She disguised her sardonic tone with a bland smile. The Texan would be shocked if he knew she intended to tell Alekos he was an arrogant, manipulative bastard. Beneath her outwardly calm exterior she was seething. Alekos had played her for a fool but she would never give him the chance to humiliate her again.

After the cloudless blue skies and golden sunshine of Monaco, the typical British summer weather of rain and a chilly wind that whipped along Piccadilly did nothing to lift Sara's spirits. It was strange to be back in the office without Alekos and she felt annoyed with herself for missing him as she tried to focus on work.

'Sara, do you have a minute?' Robert Drummond, the CEO, stopped by her desk on Friday afternoon.

'Of course. What's up, Bob?' She noticed he seemed tense. 'Can I get you a coffee?'

'No, thanks. Remind me, when will Alekos be back?'

'He's due in the office next Wednesday. His trip to

Dubai is a private visit but I can contact him if necessary.' She hadn't heard from Alekos since they had left Monaco but she had not expected to, and luckily there had been no work issues that required her to phone him.

The CEO frowned. 'Keep this to yourself. There has been some unusual trading activity of the company's shares in recent days. It's probably nothing to be concerned about but I'll keep my ear to the ground and talk to Alekos when he's back.'

After Bob had gone, Sara drummed her fingertips on her desk, wondering if she should call Alekos. She was still his PA for now and it was her job to alert him of anything that might affect the company. Her phone rang and her heart leapt into her throat when she saw his name on the caller display.

'Sara, I need you to come over immediately.' Alekos's sexy Greek accent was more pronounced than usual, making the hairs on her body stand on end. Damn the effect he had on her, she thought bitterly.

'You want me to come to Dubai?' She was pleased that she sounded cool and composed.

'I returned to London earlier than planned,' he said tersely. 'I'm working from home. I've sent Mike to collect you, so go and wait in the car park for him.'

She stared at the envelope on her desk containing her letter of resignation. The sooner she gave it to Alekos the better.

'Sara—' he sounded impatient, and nothing like the sensual lover who had spoken to her tenderly when he'd made love to her '—did you hear me?'

'Yes.' She dropped the envelope into her handbag. 'I'm on my way.'

CHAPTER EIGHT

ALEKOS'S LONDON HOME was a penthouse apartment next to the river with stunning views of the Thames, Tower Bridge and the Shard.

His valet opened the door to admit Sara into the hallway and her tension racked up a notch when she heard a female voice from the sitting room. Did he have a woman here? Maybe someone he'd met in Dubai. It was only four nights ago that he had slept with *her*. She was tempted to hand the letter in her bag to the valet and ask him to deliver it, but just then the sitting room door opened and Alekos's mother came out to the hall. When she saw Sara she burst into tears.

'No, no, Sara,' she sobbed, 'you must not allow Alekos to work. The doctor said he has to rest.'

Sara had met Lina Gionakis a few times and had found her to be charming but excitable. She frowned. 'Doctor? Is Alekos unwell?'

'He could have died,' Lina said dramatically.

'Rubbish.' Alekos's gravelly voice made Sara's pulse race as she followed his mother into the sitting room and her gaze flew to him, sprawled on a sofa by the window. He was wearing faded denim jeans, a cream shirt undone to halfway down his chest and no shoes.

She dragged her eyes from the whorls of black hairs that grew thickly on his chest and stared at his bare feet. There was something curiously intimate about seeing his feet that reminded her of when he'd stripped in front of her before he had undressed her in his bedroom on *Artemis*.

Pink-cheeked, she jerked her gaze up to his face and did a double take when she saw he was wearing a black eye patch over his right eye.

'Polo,' he said drily, answering her unspoken query. 'I was hit in the eye with a mallet during a match.'

'The doctor said you are lucky you were not blinded in your eye.' Lina wrung her hands together. 'Promise me you will wear a helmet and faceguard in future. What if you had fallen from your horse? A head injury can be fatal. Polo is such a dangerous sport and you know I couldn't bear it if I lost another son.'

'Mana, I am not a child.' Alekos was clearly struggling to control his impatience with his mother and he looked relieved when the valet returned with a tea tray. 'Sit down and Giorgos will serve you tea and cakes while I go over a few things with Sara.'

He strode out of the room and Sara followed him into his study. 'Is your eye injury serious?'

'Not really. The blow from the mallet caused a blood vessel in my eye to rupture and my vision is blocked by a pool of blood covering the iris and pupil. The condition is called a hyphema and it shouldn't result in long-term harm.' He shrugged. 'It's fairly painful and I have to use eye drops and wear the patch for a few weeks. But I'll live,' he added sardonically.

'Your mother is very upset. What did she mean when she said she couldn't bear to lose another son?'

Alekos leaned his hip against the desk and folded his arms across his chest. But, despite his casual air, Sara sensed a sudden tension in him. 'I had an older brother,' he said abruptly. 'Dimitri died...in an accident when he was twenty-one. My mother still mourns him and, as you saw just now, she is terrified of losing me or one of my sisters.'

'I'm not surprised after such a tragic event. You've never mentioned your brother to me.'

'Why would I?'

Why, indeed? she thought painfully. Alekos was an intensely private man who guarded his personal life and his family. He would not choose to confide in his PA, not even one he'd had sex with. It was a timely reminder that she meant nothing to him and she opened her handbag and gave him the letter.

'What's this?'

'My formal notice of resignation. I can't continue to work for you after we...' Colour flooded her cheeks. 'After what happened a few nights ago.'

'We had sex,' he said bluntly. 'It's too late now to be embarrassed about it.'

'But I am embarrassed. We both behaved unprofessionally and that's why I have to leave my job.'

'*Theos*, Sara.' Impatience was etched onto his hard features. 'Why are you getting so worked up because we spent one night together? It didn't mean anything.'

She felt a knife blade pierce her heart. 'You made that very clear when you left the next morning without saying a word.'

Dark colour streaked along his cheekbones. 'You were asleep.'

'You made me feel like a whore.' She drew a shud-

dering breath and would have laughed at his astonished expression if she hadn't wanted to cry. 'It would have been less insulting if you'd left a cheque for my sexual services on the pillow.'

'You wanted me as much as I desired you,' he said grimly. 'Don't pretend you were the innocent one in this.'

Alekos's words hung in the air. He must have thought she was a freak when he'd discovered she was a twenty-four-year-old virgin, she thought painfully. She had been stupidly naïve to have fallen for the well-practised seduction routine of a playboy. 'When you read the letter, you will see that I have requested to leave earlier than the three months' notice my contract stipulates. It will be easier if I go as soon as possible.'

She turned and walked over to the door, but his harsh voice made her hesitate.

'Damn it, Sara. Where's your loyalty? You can't leave me now when I need you.'

'I'm sorry about your eye, but you said there will be no long-term damage.' She fought the insidious pull on her emotions. Alekos did not need her; he simply wanted to avoid the inconvenience of having to employ another PA. 'And how dare you throw my loyalty in my face after you showed me no loyalty at all?' She breathed hard as her anger with him exploded. 'I told you that Lionel Kingsley is my father in absolute confidence. How could you betray my secret to Warren McCuskey?'

'I didn't...'

She ignored him and continued. 'You were determined to sell a yacht to Warren and you knew that Lionel has a lot of influence over him. When you learned that I was Lionel's daughter you suggested we could pretend to be a couple so I could meet my half-siblings. But the real reason was to give you access to Warren, and your manipulation worked,' she said bitterly. 'One reason why Warren has decided to buy *Artemis* is because you let him think you are in love with me—his best friend's secret daughter.'

'I didn't tell him.' Alekos's voice was as sharp as a whiplash and made Sara flinch. 'Warren asked me if I knew you were Lionel's daughter, and I said yes because it would have looked odd if you hadn't told me when we were supposedly in a relationship.'

She looked at him uncertainly. 'Then how did Warren know?'

'It's likely that Lionel confided in his closest friend.'

Sara had to acknowledge the truth of what Alekos said but it didn't ease the hurt she felt. 'You still used my relationship with my father to your advantage to promote GE.'

He did not deny it. 'There is no room for sentiment in business. Which is why I need you to carry on being my PA, for now at least.' He straightened up and walked towards her, and his face was grimmer than Sara had ever seen it.

'GE is the target of a hostile takeover bid. In the past few months a large amount of company shares have been bought, seemingly by several smaller companies. I received a tip-off that these companies are all owned by one individual who has accumulated a significant number of GE's shares. In business, an unwanted takeover bidder is known as a black knight. If the black knight acquires fifty-one per cent of GE's shares he will be able to appoint a new management team and board of directors, and effectively take over the company.'

'Do you know how close the black knight is to acquiring fifty-one per cent?'

'Too damned close. It will be more difficult for him now he's out in the open. Instead of buying up shares stealthily through his various companies, he will have to try to persuade GE's shareholders to sell stock to him.'

'Are you saying that if this black knight does manage to buy enough shares, you could lose the company that your grandfather set up?' Looking closely at Alekos, Sara saw evidence of the strain he was under in his clenched jaw and the two grooves that had appeared on either side of his mouth. Despite his cavalier treatment of her, she felt a tug on her soft heart. 'There must be something you can do to stop him.'

'There are various strategies which I am already putting in place, but my best hope—only hope, to be brutally honest—is if I can convince the shareholders, many of whom are board members, not to sell their shares and remain loyal to me.' He raked his hair off his brow. 'As you are aware, I haven't always had the support of every member of the board. In fact, the black knight is a board member.'

'Orestis Pagnotis,' Sara guessed.

'Actually, no, it's Stelios Choutos. He doesn't like the new direction I am taking GE and his takeover bid is backed by an American hedge fund. Fortunately, Warren McCuskey's decision to buy *Artemis* will win me a lot of support from shareholders. An injection of two hundred million dollars into the company's coffers couldn't have come at a better time.'

'I'm sorry about your problems, but I still intend to

resign. I don't see what use I can be.' Sara's heart jolted when Alekos moved to stand between her and the door. The patch over his eye made him look even more like a pirate and his rugged good looks were a dangerous threat to her peace of mind.

'I need to have people around me who I can rely on and trust. If you are really determined to walk away from your job for no good reason I'll allow you to leave after you've served one month's notice. The future of GE will have been decided by then,' he said grimly. 'I'll pay you a full three months' salary. But in return I will expect you to be at my call constantly while I fight to save my company.'

Sara warned herself not to be swayed by his admission that he trusted her. But didn't she owe Alekos her loyalty while GE was under threat? She bit her lip, torn between feeling it was her duty to help him and the knowledge that if she stayed in her job and saw him every day it would be harder to fall out of love with him.

'All right,' she agreed before she could change her mind. 'I'll stay on for one month. But I want six months' salary.'

The extra money would pay for the college art course she wanted to do. Instead of having to wait until she had sold her mother's house, she would be able to start the art course in the new term in September. She had never made any demands on Alekos and had put him on a pedestal, always doing her best to please him. The result was that he'd treated her badly. He had made it clear that she did not matter to him, and she realised that she had wasted two years of her life loving him when he did not deserve her love. It was time she started to value herself, Sara decided.

'I guess I shouldn't be surprised that you are as mercenary as most other women,' Alekos said in a hard voice. 'I've admitted I need your help.'

'There is no room for sentiment in business,' she quoted his words back to him coolly. 'If you want me, you're going to have to pay for me.'

Alekos felt as if his head was going to explode. His eye injury had caused him to suffer severe headaches, but he hadn't taken any of the strong painkillers he had been prescribed because they made him feel drowsy and he'd needed to have all his wits about him at a crucial meeting with a group of shareholders.

He pinched the bridge of his nose to try and control the pain in his head. Behind him, the staccato click of stiletto heels on the marble-floored foyer of GE's offices in Athens sounded as loud as gunshots. He dropped his arm as Sara came to stand beside him and saw her frown when she darted a glance at his face.

He knew he did not look his best. For the past two weeks he'd survived on patchy meals, not enough sleep and too much whisky, while he'd criss-crossed the globe to meet with shareholders and tried to persuade them to back his leadership of GE. Since Stelios Choutos had issued GE with a formal notice of an intended takeover bid the battle lines had been drawn. Shareholders either supported the company's current chairman or the disgruntled board member Stelios. So far, Stelios was winning.

Now Alekos had brought the battle to GE's birthplace in Greece. He stared at the blown-up photographs on the wall of his grandfather and founder of the company, Theo Gionakis, his father, Kostas, and brother,

Dimitri. Failure was not an option he would consider. But maybe he *was* second best, as he was certain his father had thought. He wasn't the true Gionakis heir. Self-doubt congealed in the pit of his stomach.

'Why are there photos of your grandfather, your father and your brother above the reception desk, but not a picture of you?' Sara asked.

'They are all dead,' he said bluntly. 'The photo gallery is of past chairmen. Although my brother never actually became chairman, my father had his picture placed here after Dimitri died.' Alekos's jaw clenched. 'If my brother had lived to take over from my father, maybe GE would not be under threat.'

'Surely you don't believe that?'

'I have no way of knowing whether I am as good a chairman as I have no doubt Dimitri would have been.'

He felt Sara's eyes on him but he carefully avoided her gaze. It was easier, he'd found, if he did not look directly at her. That way his heart did not thump quite so hard and he could kid himself that the effect she had on him was a temporary aberration. For the past two weeks he had spent virtually every waking hour with her while they had worked together to save the company. When he was alone in bed at night it was his fantasies about making love to her, fuelled by erotic memories, rather than worry about GE that kept him awake.

He glanced at a message on his phone. 'The helicopter is waiting for us on the helipad. Let's go.'

'Go where?' she asked as they rode the lift up to the roof of the building. 'I know you have a home in Athens, and I assumed I would check in to a hotel.'

'You will stay with me. It'll be easier if you are on the same premises when we have to work late,' he countered the argument he could see brewing in her green eyes. *Theos*, she could be stubborn. But he was damned glad she was on his team.

Sara had impressed him with her dedication to GE. She'd accompanied him on his tour of cities around Europe, as well as to the US and the Far East. They had clocked up thousands of air miles to visit GE's shareholders and at every boardroom meeting, every dinner, every long evening spent in hotel bars Sara had invariably charmed the shareholders with her warmth and grace and personable nature.

She was an asset to the company and he did not want to lose her as his PA. He dismissed the thought that he did not want to lose her at all. She was not his, and perhaps this inexplicable possessive feeling was because he had been her first lover.

They boarded the helicopter and it took off, flying over Athens and out over the coast. 'I thought we were going to your house?' Sara said.

'We are. It's down there.' Alekos pointed to a small island just off the mainland. 'I own the island. Its name is Eiríni, which means *peace* in Greek.'

The helicopter hovered above the many trees that covered the island. From the air, Eiríni appeared like an emerald jewel set amid a sapphire-blue sea and some of his tension eased. This was home, his private sanctuary, and it occurred to him that Sara was the only woman, apart from his mother and sisters, who he had ever brought here. When they landed, he pulled in deep breaths of the fresh sea air mingled with the sweet scent of the yellow mimosa bushes that lined the path leading up to the house. But, as always, the scent that filled his senses was the evocative fragrance that was Sara.

He led her from the baking sun into the cool entrance hall of the house, where they were met by his housekeeper. 'Maria will show you to your room,' he told Sara. 'Feel free to explore or use the pool and we'll meet for dinner in an hour.'

She took a small bottle of pills out of her bag and gave it to him. 'You left your painkillers on your desk back in Athens. If I were you, I'd take the necessary dose and try to rest for a while.'

Her soft voice washed over him like a mountain stream soothing his throbbing head and her gentle smile made something twist deep inside him. He wanted to lie on a bed with her and pillow his head on her breasts. But that was too needy, he thought grimly. Needing someone made you vulnerable.

'Stop fussing—you sound like my mother.'

'If I had been your mother when you were growing up, I would have sent you to your room until you'd learned some manners.'

The softness had gone from her voice and Alekos heard a note of hurt that her cool tone couldn't hide. *Theos*, what the hell was wrong with him that he couldn't even be civil? As Sara turned to follow the housekeeper he caught hold of her arm.

'I'm sorry.' He raked his hair off his brow. 'I'm under a lot of strain, but that's no excuse for me to take my bad mood out on you.'

She held his gaze, and he had a feeling she knew his secret fear that his father had been right to doubt his abilities. 'You're a good chairman, Alekos, and I believe you will win the backing of the shareholders.'

'Let's hope you're right,' he said gruffly.

* * *

When Alekos woke it was dark, and a glance at the bedside clock showed it was ten p.m. *Ten!* He jerked upright and discovered that his headache had mercifully gone. After showering, he had taken Sara's advice and swallowed a couple of painkillers before he'd stretched out on the bed for twenty minutes. That had been three hours ago. She must have thought he'd abandoned her—again.

Leaving her on *Artemis* when he'd rushed off to Dubai had not been his finest hour, he acknowledged. He had been stunned to discover she was a virgin, but what had shaken him even more was the intensity of the emotional and physical connections he'd felt with her when they had made love.

He stood up, thinking he should get dressed and go and find her. Maybe it was the painkillers that had caused his sleep to be fractured with unsettling dreams about his brother, but a more likely reason was his ever-present dread that he could lose GE, which should have been Dimitri's by birthright.

His trousers were on the chair by the window. He was about to put them on when he happened to glance at the beach. The full moon shone brightly on the sand and on Sara. Alekos frowned as he watched her walk along the shoreline. She was wearing a long floaty dress, and when a bigger wave swirled around her ankles she stumbled and fell. *Theos*, what was she doing going into the sea alone at night? He stared across the beach and his heart crashed into his ribs when he could no longer see her.

Swearing, he tore out of his room and took the stairs

two at a time. The back door was open and he ran outside and sprinted across the sand. 'Sara, *Sara…*' His breath rattled from his lungs when he saw something in the shallows. It was her dress. *'Sara?'* He ploughed through the waves. 'Where are you?'

'I'm here.' She swam out from behind some rocks and stood up and waded towards him. 'What's the matter?'

Her calm tone turned his fear to fury. *'What the hell are you doing swimming on your own in the dark?'* he bellowed as he splashed through the water and grabbed hold of her arm. 'You bloody fool. Don't you have *any* common sense?'

'Ow! Alekos, you're hurting me. Why shouldn't I swim? It's not dark—there's a full moon.' She tried to pull free of him but he tightened his grip and dragged her behind him back to the shore. She kicked water at him. 'Let go of me. You're a control freak, do you know that?'

He tugged her closer to him so that her breasts, barely covered by her wet bra, were pressed against his heaving chest. Alekos's lungs burned as if he'd run a marathon. His dream about Dimitri was jumbled in his mind with the reality of seeing Sara disappear into the sea.

'I won't have another death by drowning on my conscience.'

She stopped struggling and stared at him, her green eyes huge and dark in the moon shadow. 'What do you mean?'

He silently cursed his emotional outburst. He knew he should shrug it off and walk back to the house, but inexplicably he found he wanted to tell Sara the terrible secret that had haunted him since he was a teenager. He trusted her implicitly, but he did not want to think of the implications of that right now.

He exhaled heavily. 'My brother drowned in the sea.' Sara drew a sharp breath as he continued. 'He'd gone swimming alone at night and his body was discovered washed up on the beach the next day.'

'Oh, God, how awful. Do you know how it happened? Maybe he had an attack of cramp.'

'Dimitri was a strong swimmer and a superb athlete.' Alekos released Sara's arm and dropped down onto the sand where the waves rippled onto the beach. He loved the sea but he hated it too for taking his brother from him. He hated himself more for his failure. 'It was my fault,' he said harshly. 'I could have saved Dimitri.'

She sat down on the sand next to him. 'Do you mean you were both swimming when your brother got into trouble? I know you would have done your best to save his life,' she said softly.

He shook his head. 'I wasn't with him. At the inquest his death was recorded as an accident. But...' he swallowed hard '...I believe Dimitri took his own life.'

Again she inhaled sharply. 'Why do you think that?'

'Because he told me he wanted to die. My brother was heartbroken when he found out his girlfriend had cheated on him, and he said to me that he didn't want to live without her.' Alekos raked his hair off his brow with an unsteady hand as his mind flew back to the past. Aged fourteen, he hadn't understood why Dimitri had cared so deeply for a woman.

'You'll understand when you fall in love,' Dimitri had told him. *'You'll find out how love catches you when you least expect it and eats away at you until you can't*

*think or sleep or eat for thinking about the woman you
love. And when you find out that she doesn't love you,
love destroys you.'*

Alekos had vowed when he was a teenager that love
would never have a chance to destroy him like it had
Dimitri. But for twenty years he'd felt guilty that he had
not taken his brother's threat to end his life seriously
and he hadn't sought help for Dimitri. His parents had
been devastated by their oldest son's death and Alekos
hadn't wanted to add to their grief by revealing that he
believed Dimitri had committed suicide.

'I had spoken to my brother earlier on the day that
he died, and he told me he felt like walking into the sea
and never coming back. But I didn't take him seriously.
I assumed he'd get over Nia and go back to being the
fun, happy guy my brother was—until he fell in love.'

Alekos's jaw clenched. 'Love destroyed him, and
I did nothing to save him.' He tensed when Sara put
her hand on his arm. Her fingers were pale against his
darkly tanned skin. She did not say anything but he
sensed compassion in her silence and it helped to ease
the raw feeling inside him.

'My memories are of him laughing, always laughing,' he said thickly. 'But on that day I found him crying. I was shocked but I still didn't do anything. I should
have told my parents that Dimitri had suicidal thoughts.
I didn't understand how my amazing brother, who everyone loved, could really mean to throw away his life
and hurt his family over a goddamned love affair.'

'I don't believe you could have done anything, if your
brother was determined to take his life,' Sara said gently. 'He may have had other problems you didn't know
about. Young men in particular often find it hard to talk

about things. But you don't know for certain that he did commit suicide. Presumably he didn't leave a note as the inquest recorded an accidental death.'

'He told me what he intended to do but I've never confided to anyone what I'm convinced was the real reason for Dimitri's death.'

'And so you have kept your guilt a secret for years, even though you don't know for sure that you have anything to feel guilty about. Dimitri's death *could* have been an accident. But even if it wasn't, you were in no way to blame, Alekos. You were young, and you were not responsible for your brother.'

Sara stood up. 'We should go back to the house. It must be late, and there is another meeting with shareholders tomorrow.' She brushed sand from her legs. 'I'm going for a quick swim to wash off the sand but I'll stay close to the shore.'

'I'll come with you.' He jumped up and followed her into the sea. The water was warm and its silken glide over his skin cleansed his body and his mind. The fact that Sara had not judged him and had tried to defend him helped him to view the past more rationally. *Could* it simply have been a terrible coincidence that Dimitri had died soon after confiding that he was depressed? Alekos had never considered the possibility before because he'd blamed himself when he was fourteen and he'd carried on blaming himself without questioning it.

He swam across the bay and back again, once, twice, he lost count of how many times as he sought to exorcise his demons, cutting through the water with powerful strokes until finally he was out of breath.

He watched Sara wading back to the beach. Her impromptu swim meant that she was in her underwear and her wet knickers were almost see-through so that he could make out the pale globes of her buttocks. When she turned to look for him, he saw in the moonlight her dark pink nipples through her wet, transparent bra.

Desire coiled through him, hardening him instantly so that he was glad he was standing waist-deep in the water. But he couldn't remain in the sea all night. He knew from her stifled gasp that she had noticed the bulge beneath his wet boxer shorts when he walked towards her. As he drew closer to her he watched her pupils dilate until they were dark pools, full of mystery and promise, and he asked the question that had been bugging him since the night they had spent together.

'Why did you choose me to be your first lover?'

CHAPTER NINE

SARA KNEW THAT telling Alekos the truth was not an option. Even if she was brave enough, or foolish enough, to admit she loved him, the revelation was not something he would want to hear. She understood him better now that he had told her about the nature of his brother's death. Living with the belief that Dimitri had taken his own life because of a failed love affair explained a lot about Alekos's opinion of love.

'Love is simply a sanitized word for lust,' he'd once sneered. The truth was that he blamed love for his brother's death as much as he blamed himself for not preventing Dimitri's suicide—if it *had* been suicide.

She frowned as she examined her own past that, like Alekos, she had allowed to influence her for far too long.

'I grew up being told by my mother that men only want women for one thing. Mum never revealed who my father was but she made it clear that she blamed him for abandoning her when she fell pregnant with me.'

She paused, remembering the brittle woman who she had called Mum and yet she'd never felt any kind of bond between them. Her mother's unplanned pregnancy had resulted in an unwanted child, Sara thought painfully. When she'd been old enough to start dating she had never allowed things to go too far, and when guys had dropped her because she refused to sleep with them it had reinforced her mother's warning that men only wanted sex. 'I'm sure she had loved my father and I think she continued to love him up until her death. I'm certain she never had another relationship after Lionel went back to his wife.'

She stirred the wet sand with her toes. Alekos was standing very close and she was agonisingly aware of him. The moonlight slanted over his broad shoulders and made the droplets of water clinging to his chest hairs sparkle. 'When I finally met my father I realised that he wasn't a bad person. He admitted he'd made a mistake when he'd had an affair with my mother. But she'd known he was married and so it was her mistake too.'

Sara made herself look directly at Alekos. He still had to wear the eye patch and, with a day's growth of dark stubble covering his jaw, he looked more like a pirate than ever. Dark, dangerous and devastatingly attractive. 'I had sex with you because I wanted to. You didn't coerce me or pretend that it meant anything to you—and that's fine because it didn't mean anything to me either.'

'But why me?' he persisted. 'Why not Paul Eddis, for instance? You seemed pretty friendly with him at the board members' dinner.'

She shrugged. 'Paul is a nice guy, but there was no spark between us like there was between you and me.'

'*Was?*' Alekos said softly. 'I would not use the past tense.' He curved his arm around her waist and tugged her into the heat of his body. The effect on her was electrifying and she was mortified, knowing he must feel the hard points of her nipples. Her brain urged her to step away from him but her body had other ideas and she was trapped by her longing for him when he lowered his head towards her.

'Is this the spark you referred to?' he growled. He kept her clamped against him while he ran his other hand down her spine and lower, sliding his fingers beneath the waistband of her knickers to caress her bare bottom. 'Sexual chemistry enslaves both of us, Sara *mou*.'

She couldn't deny it, not when her body shook, betraying her need for him as he covered her mouth with his and kissed her deeply, hungrily, making the spark ignite and burn. He'd called it *chemistry* and she told herself that was all it was. His story about his brother had touched her heart, but it had also shown her that Alekos would not fall in love with her because he despised love and maybe he was afraid of it.

She could end this now. But why deny herself what she so desperately wanted? Alekos was an incredible lover. True, she had no one to compare him to, but instinctively she knew that when they'd made love it had been magical for him too. She had already decided to leave her job and she had two weeks left to serve of the month's notice period they had agreed on.

Why shouldn't she make the most of the time she had with him and then walk away with her head held high? Her mother had spent her life loving a man she couldn't have. There was no way she was going to do the same, Sara vowed. Knowing that Alekos would never love her freed her from hope and expectation and allowed her to simply enjoy his skill as a wonderful lover.

And so she kissed him back with a fervour that revealed her desire and made him groan into her mouth when she traced her fingertips over his chest and abdomen, following the arrow of black hairs down to where his wet boxer shorts moulded the burgeoning length of his arousal.

His hands were equally busy as he unfastened her bra and peeled the sodden cups away from her breasts so that he could cradle their weight in his palms. 'Beautiful,' he muttered before he bent his head and took one nipple into his mouth, sucked hard until she cried out, and her cry echoed over the empty beach. Then he transferred his lips to her other nipple and flicked his tongue across the tender peak while simultaneously he slid his hand into the front of her knickers and pushed his finger into her molten heat.

Her legs buckled and he tightened his arm around her waist and lowered her onto the sand, coming down on top of her so that his body covered hers. She was aware of him tugging her panties off and her excitement grew when he jerked his boxers down and his erection pushed into her belly. His ragged breaths filled her ears and his male scent swamped her senses. She licked his shoulder and tasted sea salt.

'Open your legs,' he said hoarsely.

She wanted to feel his length inside her and she shared his impatience. But his voice broke through the sexual haze clouding her brain and she remembered something vital.

'We can't here. I'm not on the pill.' Not even her overwhelming desire for Alekos was worth risking an unplanned pregnancy.

He tensed and swore softly as he lifted himself off

her and pulled up his boxers before he held out his hand and drew her to her feet. 'I can't go back to the house naked,' she muttered as he began to lead her up the beach. 'One of the staff might see me.'

'None of them sleep here. There is a small fishing village on the island and all the staff return to their own homes every evening.' He scooped her up in his arms and strode across the sand. 'So, are you going to sleep with me, Sara *mou*?' His sensual smile did not disguise the serious tone of his voice.

'I hope not.' She grinned when he frowned. 'I'll be very disappointed if all we do is sleep.'

Laughter rumbled in his big chest. 'Do you know the punishment for being a tease?' He proceeded to tell her exactly how he intended to punish her, so that by the time he carried her into his bedroom and laid her on the bed Sara was shivering with anticipation and a wild hunger that grew fiercer when he slid a protective sheath over his erection and positioned himself between her thighs.

He drove into her with a powerful thrust that made her catch her breath as she discovered again his size and strength. He filled her, fitted her so perfectly as if he had been designed exclusively for her. She pushed away the dangerous thought and concentrated on learning every inch of his body, running her hands over his chest and shoulders, his long spine and smooth buttocks that rose and fell in a steady rhythm.

She arched her hips to meet each thrust as he plunged deeper, harder, faster, taking her higher with every measured stroke. He was her joy and her delight, her master and tutor. Her love.

Terrified she might say the words out loud, she

cupped his face between her hands and kissed his mouth.

'Ah, Sara.' His voice sounded oddly shaken, as if he too felt a connection between them that was more than simply the joining of their mouths and bodies. Don't look for things that are not there, Sara told herself. Enjoy this for what it is—fantastic sex.

Alekos showed her how fantastic, how unbelievably amazing sex could be when he slid his hands beneath her bottom and lifted her hips to meet his devastatingly powerful thrust that hurtled her over the edge and into ecstasy. It was beyond beautiful, and she sobbed his name as pulses of pleasure radiated out from deep in her pelvis. The fierce spasms of her orgasm kept shuddering through her while he continued to move inside her. His pace was urgent now as he neared his own release. And when he came, it was with a groan torn from his throat as his body shook so hard that she wrapped her arms around him and held him tight against her heart.

Another week passed, as tense and turbulent as the weeks preceding it, as Alekos fought to save the business his father had entrusted to him. In many ways it was the worst time of his life. Endless meetings with shareholders at GE's offices in Athens, strategy meetings with his management team and, hanging over him, the possibility he refused to consider—that he might fail. It *should* have been the worst time of his life and the fact that he could smile—*Theos,* that he could actually be happy—was totally down to Sara.

At work she was a calming presence, offering thoughtful and intelligent suggestions when he asked her advice—which he had found himself doing more and more often. She charmed the shareholders and the board members liked and trusted her. Sara was an asset in the office as his PA, and when they returned to Eiríni each evening she delighted him in her role as his mistress.

Often they walked down to the village and sat on the small harbour to watch the fishing boats unload the day's catch. Later they would return to the house and eat dinner served on the terrace by his housekeeper before they went to bed and made love for hours until exhaustion finally claimed them. Alekos was waiting to grow bored of Sara, but when he woke each morning and studied her lovely face on the pillow beside him he felt an indefinable tug in his chest and a rather more predictable tug of sexual hunger in his groin that he assuaged when he woke her and she was instantly aroused and ready for him.

'Why do you think your father would blame you for GE's problems when you yourself told me that hostile takeover bids are a common threat to businesses?' she asked him one day, after he'd confided that he felt he had let his father's memory down.

'He doubted my ability to run the company as successfully as he believed Dimitri would have done.' Alekos rubbed a towel over his chest after he'd swum in the pool. He sat down on a lounger next to where Sara was sunbathing in a tiny green bikini which his fingers itched to remove from her shapely body that drove him to distraction.

It was Sunday, and after six crazily busy days of working he had decreed that today they would not leave the island. In truth, he would have been happy not to leave the bedroom they now shared, but Sara had murmured that they couldn't spend *all* day having sex.

'Why do you think your father compared you to your brother?'

He shrugged. 'Dimitri was the firstborn son and my father groomed him for his future role as chairman of GE from when he was a young boy. My relationship with my father was much more distant. I was the youngest of his five children, the second son. When Dimitri died and I became my father's heir he made it obvious that I was second best. Sometimes,' he said slowly, 'I wondered if he wished that I had died and Dimitri had lived.'

Sara sat up and faced him, her green eyes bright and fierce. 'I'm sure that's not true. It must have been a difficult time for all the family, but particularly for your parents who were grieving for their son. It sounds like he was very popular.'

'Everyone loved Dimitri.'

'Especially you. I think you were very close to your brother,' she said softly.

'I idolised him.' Images flashed into Alekos's mind: Dimitri teaching him to sail, the two of them kicking a football around the garden, that time when he'd accidentally smashed the glass panes of the greenhouse with a misaimed kick and his brother had taken the blame. He had blocked out his memories of Dimitri because when he'd been fourteen it had hurt too much to think about him. It still hurt twenty years later. And he was still angry. If his brother hadn't fallen in love with some stupid girl he would still be here, still laughing, still Alekos's best friend.

He hadn't spoken about Dimitri in all those years

and he did not understand why he had told Sara things that he'd buried deep inside him. He didn't want her compassion, he didn't want to want her so badly that he found himself thinking about her all the time. His crazy obsession with her would pass, he assured himself. Desire never lasted and the more often he had sex with her, the quicker he would become sated with her and then he could move on with his life and forget about her.

He walked back over to the pool and dived in, swimming length after length while he brought his emotions under control. Of course he did not need Sara. She was simply a pleasant diversion from his work problems.

She came to sit at the edge of the pool and he swam up to her. 'How about we have some lunch, followed by an afternoon siesta?'

'Hmm...' She appeared to consider his suggestion. 'Or we could forget lunch and just go for a lie-down.'

'Aren't you hungry?'

'I'm very hungry.' Her impish smile made his gut twist and he pulled her into the water, ignoring her yelp that the water was cold.

He felt angry with himself for his weakness and angry with her for making him weak. 'In that case I'd better satisfy your appetite, hadn't I,' he mocked as he untied the strings of her bikini top and pulled it off, cupping her breasts in his hands and playing with her nipples until she moaned softly.

He was completely in control, and he proved it when he carried her up to the bedroom and placed her face down onto the bed. He made love to her using all his considerable skill until she climaxed once, and when she came down he took her up again and only when she buried her face in the pillows to muffle her cries as she had a second orgasm did he finally let go, and felt the drenching pleasure of his own release.

By the middle of their second week in Greece the situation with GE started to look more hopeful, as increasing numbers of shareholders pledged their alliance to Alekos and refused to sell their shares in the company to Stelios Choutos. Alekos was still tense and Sara knew he would not be able to relax while GE and his position as chairman were still threatened. But, although she continued to be supportive, she had a niggling worry of her own that made her pop to the chemist during her lunch break. Of course, having bought a pregnancy test, she felt the symptoms that her period was about to start and, although the dull pain low in her stomach was annoying, she felt relieved that she wouldn't need to use the test.

The news came on Friday afternoon. Alekos strode into Sara's office, which adjoined his, and found her standing by the window, gazing up at the iconic Acropolis. She pulled her mind from her thoughts and her heart leapt when she saw the grin on his face.

'We won.' He swept her into his arms. 'Stelios's financial backers have pulled out and I've just had a call confirming he has withdrawn his takeover bid.'

'So it's over? The company is safe and you will continue to be chairman?' She blocked out the realisation that the end of the battle for GE meant that her affair with Alekos would also be over.

'I have the unanimous backing of the board, including Orestis Pagnotis.'

His victory made him almost boyish and he swung her round before claiming her lips in a fierce kiss that deepened to a slow and achingly sweet exploration of her mouth with his tongue. Sara was trembling when he finally released her and she moved away from him while she struggled to regain her composure.

'Congratulations. I never doubted you.'

'I know.' He no longer needed to wear the eye patch now that his injury was completely healed, and his eyes gleamed as he held her gaze. 'Your support was invaluable. We work well together as a team. We'll fly to back to London tomorrow and start focusing on what GE is renowned for, which is to make the best yachts in the world.'

Sara did not say anything then, but when the helicopter flew them to the island and they walked up to the house Alekos slipped his hand into hers. 'You're very quiet.'

'I was thinking that this is our last night on Eiríni—and our last night together. Today was the final day of my notice period,' she reminded him when he frowned. 'I've arranged for a temporary PA to fill my place while you hold interviews and appoint a permanent member of staff.'

He looked shocked, and that surprised her until she told herself he'd been too busy fighting for his company to have been aware that her notice period had finished. She followed him into the sitting room and looked through the glass doors that opened onto the garden where the swimming pool was a brilliant turquoise beneath a cloudless blue sky. She had fallen in love with Alekos's island and it would have a special place in her heart for ever.

Alekos crossed to the bar and poured them both a drink, as he did every evening: a crisp white wine for her and a single malt Scotch with ice for him. Usually they carried their drinks out to the terrace, but this evening he drained his glass in a couple of gulps and poured himself another whisky.

'You could stay on,' he said gruffly. 'Why do you want to leave? I know you enjoy your job.'

'I do enjoy it, but actually I never wanted to be a secretary. I only did it because I needed to help my mother pay the mortgage. Now I'm selling the house and I have plans to do something different with my life.'

'I see.' Alekos did not try to persuade her to stay, nor did he ask about her future plans, Sara noted. She ignored the pang her heart gave and reminded herself that it was time she took control of her life. 'We both know that our affair…or whatever it is we've been having for the past few weeks…was temporary. I think it will be better to end our professional and personal association once we are back in London.'

Once again a flicker of surprise crossed his sculpted features. She was possibly the only woman who had ended a relationship with Alekos before he was ready for it to finish, Sara thought wryly. It was only the thought of her mother's empty life that kept her strong when her treacherous heart and traitorous body both implored her to be his mistress for as long as he wanted her.

'In that case we had better make the most of tonight,' he said in a cool voice that forced her to acknowledge that she really did mean nothing to him other than as a good PA and a good lay. Knowing it helped her to harden her heart when he drew her into his arms and kissed her with such aching tenderness that she could almost believe he was trying to persuade her to change her mind.

It was just great sex, she reminded herself as he undid the buttons on her blouse and slid his hand into her bra to caress her breast. He stripped her right there in the sitting room and shrugged out of his clothes, taking a condom from his trouser pocket before he pushed her back against the sofa cushions. He hooked her legs over her shoulders so that she was splayed open to him and used his tongue to such great effect that she gasped his name when he reared over her and thrust into her so hard that she came instantly.

It was the beginning of a sensual feast that lasted long into the night and Alekos's passion and his dedication to giving her pleasure tested Sara's resolve to leave him to its limits. She wished the night could last for ever, but with the pale light of dawn came a reality that stunned her.

She woke to the sound of the shower from his bathroom and the horrible lurch her stomach gave sent her running into her own bathroom. There could be a number of explanations of why she had been sick, but although she still had an uncomfortable cramping pain in her stomach her period was now over a week late. The pregnancy test took mere minutes to perform and the wait for the result seemed to last a lifetime.

Alekos knocked on the door while she was still clinging to the edge of the basin because her legs had turned to jelly. 'I'll meet you downstairs for breakfast.'

'Sure.' She was amazed that her voice sounded normal. 'See you in a minute.' She almost threw up again at the thought of food, and the much worse prospect of telling Alekos her news. But not telling him was not an option. She wasn't going to make *every* mistake her mother had made, Sara thought grimly.

He found her on the beach, standing on the wet sand where the waves rippled over her bare toes. Alekos remembered how he had seen Sara walk into the sea the night they had arrived on the island, and his body tightened at the memory of how she had come apart in his arms. Sex with her was better than he'd known with any other woman but, *Theos*, he wasn't going to beg her to stay with him. The idea of him pleading with a mistress was laughable but he didn't feel in the mood to laugh, even though he had won the battle to keep GE. Curiously, he hadn't given a thought to the company since Sara had announced her intention to leave him when they went back to London.

'Don't you want something to eat?' he said as he walked up to her. 'The helicopter will be here to collect us in a few minutes.'

'I'm not hungry.'

She was pale and he frowned when he saw her mouth tremble before she firmed her lips. The breeze stirred her hair and Alekos smelled the evocative scent of vanilla. 'What…?' he began, unable to rationalise his sudden sense of foreboding.

'I'm pregnant.'

She said the words in a rush, as if they might have less impact. But they left him reeling. He stared at her slender figure, which of course showed no signs yet that a new life was developing inside her. Was it possible she was expecting his baby? He had never thought about fatherhood, apart from in a vague way as an event that he supposed would happen at some point in his future. His family impressed on him the need for him to provide an heir. But this was real. If Sara was telling him the truth, and he had no reason to doubt her, he was going to be a father and he couldn't begin to assimilate the emotions churning inside him. Crazy though it was, he felt a flicker of excitement at the idea of holding his child in his arms. *Theos*, he hoped he would be a good father.

In the years since his brother had died Alekos had become adept at hiding his feelings and his coolly logical brain took charge. 'You're sure?'

'I did a test this morning and it…it was positive. My period is a week late, but I thought…' she bit her lip '… I hoped there was another explanation. We've always been careful.'

Alekos went cold as he recalled that he had been careless that first time when they had been on *Artemis*. His hunger for Sara had been so acute that he'd made love to her a second time immediately after they'd had sex.

He stared out across the sea—flat and calm today, it looked like a huge mirror reflecting the blue sky above, but the idyllic scene did not soothe his tumultuous thoughts. His irresponsible behaviour had resulted in Sara conceiving his child and the implications were huge. He should have taken more care. He should have fought his weakness for Sara. Anger with himself made his voice clipped and cold.

'In that case a damage limitation strategy is necessary.'

She frowned. 'What do you mean by damage limitation?'

'How do you think GE's board members will react to the news that I have fathered an illegitimate child?'

he said grimly. 'Once the press get hold of the story—as they undoubtedly will—I'll be accused of being an irresponsible playboy and that kind of reputation will not go down well with the board or the shareholders, especially now, so soon after the hostile takeover bid. There is only one solution. We will have to get married.'

He looked at her stunned expression and ignored the inexplicable urge to enfold her in his arms and promise her that everything would be all right. Instead he drawled, 'Congratulations, Sara *mou*. You've done what many other women dream of and secured yourself a rich husband.'

She flinched as if he had struck her, but then her chin came up. 'Firstly, I have never been *yours*, and secondly I am not any other woman—I'm me, and I would never marry for money. Your arrogance is astounding. I'm certainly not going to marry you to save your reputation.'

Sara spun round and walked up the beach towards the house. She heard the helicopter overhead and felt glad that soon she would be on it and leaving Eiríni. She wished she could leave Alekos behind. She hadn't expected him to be pleased about her pregnancy. Pleased had not been *her* first reaction when she'd stared at the blue line on the pregnancy test that confirmed a positive result. She felt stunned and scared and very alone, and Alekos's implication that she was a gold-digger who had somehow engineered falling pregnant to snare him was so unfair that tears choked her.

'Would you deny the child its father then, Sara?'

She stopped walking and turned to find he was right behind her, so close that she breathed in his aftershave, mingled with an indefinable scent that was uniquely Alekos. 'You don't want a child,' she muttered.

'It doesn't matter what I want or don't want. The child is my heir and if we marry he or she will inherit not only GE but the Gionakis fortune. If you refuse to marry me I will financially support my child, but in the future I will take a wife and any legitimate children born within the marriage will bear my name and be entitled to inherit my legacy.'

Alekos trapped her gaze with his eyes that were as black and hard as pieces of jet. 'Will you deny your child its birthright the way you were denied yours, Sara? You told me you wish you'd grown up knowing your father. Can you really deprive your child of the chance to grow up with both its parents?'

CHAPTER TEN

ALEKOS HAD HIT her with an emotional body blow. He had aimed his argument straight at her heart, aware that she would do anything to give her baby a father—even if it meant she had to marry him.

She had tried to dissuade him. During the helicopter flight from the island and when they'd boarded his private jet bound for London, she had offered various suggestions of how they could both have a role in their child's life. But his response had been unequivocal. They must marry before the baby was born so that it was legitimate.

She looked across the plane to where he was sitting in one of the plush leather armchairs and her heart predictably gave a jolt when she found him watching her. He was casually dressed in grey trousers and a white shirt open at the throat, showing his tanned skin that had turned a darker shade of olive-gold from two weeks in the hot Greek sun. His hair was longer, and the black stubble on his jaw reminded her of the faint abrasion marks on her breasts where his cheek had scraped her skin when he'd made love to her numerous times the previous night.

Their last night together, she had believed. Now she

wondered if he intended their marriage to include sex, and if—or perhaps that should be when—he tired of her would he have discreet affairs that did not attract the attention of the press or the board members?

'I will make a press statement on Monday announcing our engagement and forthcoming marriage.'

Sara's stomach lurched. 'Why so soon? We should at least wait until I've seen my doctor to confirm my pregnancy. The test showed that I am about five weeks, and I believe a first scan to determine when the baby is due is at around eight to ten weeks.'

'I can't risk the media finding out you are pregnant before I've put an engagement ring on your finger. The board members are jittery after the takeover bid. The news that I am going to marry my sensible secretary and leave my playboy days behind will bolster their confidence in me. For that reason I've made an appointment for us at a jewellers so that you can choose a ring.'

Everything was happening too fast, she thought frantically. Yesterday she'd believed she would never see Alekos again after they had returned to England, but now she was expecting his child and he was bulldozing her into marriage.

'I don't believe a loveless marriage will be good for anyone, including the baby.' She imagined a future where Alekos had mistresses and she became bitter like her mother, and said rather desperately, 'It can't possibly work.'

'My parents did not marry for love and had a very successful marriage.' Alekos opened his laptop, signalling that the conversation was over. It was convenient for him to marry her to keep GE's board members happy, Sara thought. And by becoming his wife she would be doing the best thing for the baby. But what about what was best for her? How could she marry Alekos when she loved him but he would never love her? But how could she deny her baby the Gionakis name? The stark answer was that she couldn't.

The jewellers was in Bond Street and the price tags on the engagement rings made Sara catch her breath. 'Choose whichever ring you want,' Alekos told her. 'I don't care how much it costs.'

But diamond solitaires the size of a rock were not her style, and she finally chose an oval-shaped emerald surrounded by white diamonds because Alekos commented that the emerald matched the colour of her eyes.

'I thought you were taking me home,' she said when the limousine drew up outside his apartment block.

'This will be your home from now on. I'll have your clothes and other belongings packed up and sent over from your house. But I want you here, where I can keep an eye on you.'

She looked at him suspiciously. 'You make it sound like I'm your prisoner. Are you worried I'll leak the story to the press that I am expecting the chairman of GE's baby?'

'*No.* You proved your loyalty to me and to the company when you helped me fight off the hostile takeover.' Alekos raked his hair off his brow and she was surprised to see colour flare on his cheekbones. 'I want you to stay with me because you are pregnant and you need looking after.'

'Of course I don't.' She tried to ignore the tug on her heart at the idea of him taking care of her as if she were a fragile creature instead of a healthy, independent woman.

'You're pale, and you fell asleep on the plane and in the car just now,' he persisted.

'I'm tired because I didn't get much sleep last night.' She blushed as memories of the many inventive ways he had made love to her for hours the previous night flooded her mind. The gleam in his eyes told her he was remembering their wild passion too. 'Alekos…?'

'Yes, it will be a real marriage in every way,' he drawled.

Her face burned. 'How did you know I was going to ask that?'

'Your eyes are very expressive and they reveal your secrets.'

Sara prayed they didn't, but she carefully did not look at him when he showed her to a guest room in his penthouse because she didn't want him to guess she was disappointed that she would not be sharing his bed until they were married.

The following week passed in a blur. News of their engagement was mentioned in most of the newspapers and Sara was glad to hide away in the penthouse to avoid the paparazzi, who were desperate to interview the woman who had tamed the notorious Greek playboy Alekos Gionakis.

Her father phoned to offer his congratulations, but when she asked him if he would attend her wedding with her half-siblings Lionel hesitated for so long that Sara's heart sank.

'Why don't you tell Charlotte and Freddie Kingsley you are their sister?' Alekos asked when he discovered her in tears. He had come home from the office unexpectedly in the afternoon and found her lying on the sofa.

She shook her head. 'I can't betray my father to his children. Perhaps it will be better if he never tells them about me and they won't know that he was once unfaithful to their mother.'

Alekos sat down on the edge of the sofa and studied her face intently. 'You're as white as a sheet. How many times have you been sick today?'

'Three or four.' She tried to shrug off his concern. 'Nausea and tiredness are normal in early pregnancy and I'll probably feel better soon.'

But she didn't. Over the next few days the sickness became more frequent and the dull ache on the right side of her abdomen that she'd had on and off for weeks turned into a stabbing pain. Sara had read that a miscarriage was fairly common in the first three months of pregnancy and nothing could be done to prevent nature taking its course.

For the first time since the shock of finding out that she was pregnant her baby became real in her mind. She pictured a little boy with black hair and dark eyes like his daddy and she felt an overwhelming sense of protectiveness for the new life inside her. 'Hang on, little one,' she whispered when she went to bed early that night, praying that if she rested her baby would make it through the crucial early weeks of her pregnancy.

The pain woke her some hours later. A sensation like a red-hot poker scourging her insides was so agonising that she struggled to breathe. Sadness swept through her as she realised that she was probably going to lose the baby and when she fumbled to switch on the bedside light the sight of blood on the sheets confirmed the worst. But the amount of blood shocked her and the pain in her stomach was excruciating. She felt faint, and her instincts told her something was seriously wrong.

'Alekos…' Dear God, what if he couldn't hear her and she bled to death, alone and terrified? She called on every last bit of her fading strength. '*Alekos*…help me…'

'Sara?' She heard the bedroom door open and the overhead light suddenly illuminated the room. She heard Alekos swear and she heard fear in his voice. 'I'm calling an ambulance.' His hand felt cool on her feverish brow. She tried to speak but she felt so weak. His face swam in front of her eyes as he leaned over her. 'Hang on, Sara *mou*,' he said hoarsely, repeating the plea she had made to her baby. But pain was tearing her apart and she slipped into blackness.

Someone, at some time—Alekos did not know who or when—had come up with the gem of wisdom, *You don't know what you've got till it's gone.* The quote had been painfully apt while he had paced up and down the waiting room while Sara had undergone emergency surgery to stop serious internal bleeding resulting from an ectopic pregnancy.

'An ectopic is when a fertilised egg implants in a fallopian tube instead of in the womb,' the obstetrician at the hospital where Sara had been rushed to by ambulance had explained to Alekos. 'The pregnancy cannot continue but the condition is not life-threatening unless the tube ruptures, which unfortunately occurred in Miss Lovejoy's case.'

An hour-long operation and two blood transfusions later, Sara was transferred to the intensive care ward and a nurse told Alekos she had been lucky to survive.

He'd known that, even without much medical knowledge. The sight of her lying pale and lifeless on the blood-soaked sheets was something he would never forget.

It had been much later, when he'd sat by her bed in ITU, steadfastly refusing the nurse's suggestion to go home and get some sleep, when he'd allowed himself to think about the baby they had lost, and the fact that he had very nearly lost Sara. He had spent his life since he was fourteen building a fortress around his heart so that nothing could hurt him like Dimitri's death had. So why were his eyes wet, and why did it feel as if a boulder had lodged in his throat making swallowing painful?

Five days later, he stepped into her room in the private wing of the hospital where she had been moved to after she was well enough to leave ITU and a ghost of a smile curved his lips when he found her dressed and sitting in a chair. He was relieved to see a faint tinge of colour on her cheeks, but she still looked as fragile as spun glass and his stomach twisted.

'You look better.' It was a lie but he suddenly didn't know what to say to her. The little scrap of life that neither he nor Sara had planned for her to conceive was gone. He did not know how she felt about the loss of their child, and he didn't want to face his own feelings. So he forced himself to smile as he picked up her holdall. 'Are you ready to come home?'

She avoided looking directly at him, and that was a bad sign. 'I'm not going to the penthouse with you.'

'I realise it holds bad memories. We can go somewhere else. I'll check with the doctor that you are okay to fly and we'll go to Eiríni.'

'No.' At last she did look at him and wiped away a

tear as it slid down her cheek. 'It's not the penthouse. I'm sad that I lost the baby, but we only knew I was pregnant for two weeks. I was just getting used to the idea of being a mother but now…that's not going to happen.' She took something out of her handbag and held out her hand to him. 'I need to give you this.'

He stared at her engagement ring sparkling in his palm and a nerve jumped in his cheek.

'Now there is no baby there is no reason for us to marry,' she said quietly.

Something roared inside Alekos. He felt unbalanced, as if the world had tilted on its axis and he was falling into a dark place. All he had thought about for the past days was Sara and the baby they had lost. *This* scenario had not occurred to him and he didn't know what to say or think or feel.

'There is no need for either of us to make hasty decisions. You've been through hell and need time to recuperate before we think about the future.'

She shook her head. '*We* don't have a future together. Your only reason for deciding to marry me was because I was pregnant with your child.'

'That's not strictly true. There were other reasons that are still valid even though there is no baby.'

'What reasons?' She stared at him and Alekos saw the sudden tension in her body and the faint betraying tremble of her lower lip. For a moment he almost gave in to the urge to put his arms around her and smell the vanilla scent of her hair. He was almost tempted to listen to the roaring inside him. But then he thought of Dimitri walking into the sea, throwing away his life for love, and the fortress walls closed around Alekos's heart.

'My position as chairman of GE will be strengthened

if I marry. The board members like and respect you—as I do. I value you, Sara. We are a good team and I am confident that if you were my wife you would run my home as efficiently as you ran my office.'

To his own ears his words sounded pompous and Sara gave an odd laugh. 'You make marriage sound like I would be your PA with a few extra perks.'

'Excellent perks,' he said drily. A lot of women would jump at the chance to live the wealthy lifestyle he was offering. 'You would not have to work and could study art or do whatever you want to do. And let's not forget sex.' He watched her pale cheeks flood with colour and was amazed she could blush when he knew her body as well as his own and had kissed every centimetre of her creamy skin. 'The sexual chemistry between us shows no sign of burning out.'

'And you resent it,' she said slowly. 'The marriage you described is not enough for me. I don't care about your money,' she said quickly before he could speak, 'and I agree the sex is great. But you would tire of me eventually. I was your PA for two years and I know the short lifespan of your interest in women.'

'What do you want, then?' he demanded, furious with her for reading him too well.

'The saddest thing is that you have to ask.' She stood up and gathered up her handbag. 'My friend Ruth is coming to pick me up and she's invited me to stay with her because my mother's house has now been sold.'

It hit Alekos then that she actually meant it and something akin to panic cramped in his gut. 'Sara, we can talk.'

'Until we're blue in the face,' she said flatly, 'but it won't change anything. I understand why you won't allow anyone too close. I know you feel guilty because you think you should have done more to help your brother. But you can't live in the past for ever, Alekos. Love isn't an enemy you have to fight and I don't believe Dimitri would have wanted you to live your life without love.'

'Even though loving someone cost him his life?' Alekos said savagely.

'You don't know for sure that he did mean to end his life. You told me you never talked about Dimitri's death with the rest of your family. Maybe you should. Because a life without love will make you as bitter and unhappy as my mother was, and how I would become if I married you.'

Her words stung him. 'I don't remember you being unhappy when we were on Eiríni.' He pulled her into his arms and sought her mouth. 'I made you happy,' he muttered against her lips. 'Do you think you'll find this passion with anyone else?'

He kissed her hard and his body jerked when he felt her respond. She was a golden light in his life, and he realised that almost from the first day she had started working for him he had looked forward to her cheerful smile every morning and he'd felt comfortable with her in a way he had never felt with other women. They had been friends before they were lovers but she was prepared to walk away from what they had because he refused to put a label on what he felt for her.

He knew how to seduce her. He knew how to kiss her with a deepening hunger so that she flattened out her bunched fists on his chest and slid her arms up around his neck. Her body melted into him and triumph surged through him, spiking his already heated blood. She couldn't deny *this*.

He couldn't believe it when she wrenched her mouth from beneath his and pushed against his chest. He was unprepared for her rejection and dropped his arms to his sides as she stepped away from him. 'You want me,' he said harshly. 'We're good together, Sara, but I won't beg. If I walk away I won't come back. Ever.'

He held his breath as she stood on tiptoe and brushed her lips gently on his cheek. 'I hope that one day you will find the happiness you deserve. And I hope I will too. I can't settle for second best, Alekos.'

He froze. *Second best.* Was that what she thought of him? The same as his father had thought. *Theos*, she might as well have stabbed him through his heart. The pain in his chest felt as if she had.

Sara watched Alekos stride out of her hospital room and nearly ran after him. She sank down onto the bed as the enormity of what she had done drained the little strength she had in her legs after her ordeal of the ectopic pregnancy. The sense of loss that swept over her was almost unbearable.

When she'd regained consciousness and discovered she was lying in a hospital bed she had known immediately that her baby hadn't survived. The grief she felt was greater than anything she'd experienced. It was true she had only known for a few weeks that she was pregnant but there was a hollow space inside her and she felt as though her hopes for her future as a mother had been ripped from her as savagely as her child had been ripped from her body.

Now she had lost Alekos too. She would never see

him again, never feel his strong arms around her or feel him move inside her in the timeless dance of love. Because it wasn't love, she reminded herself. What she'd had with Alekos was wonderful sex that for him had been meaningless.

Much as she hated to acknowledge it, she had been just another mistress. The only difference between her and all the other countless women he'd had affairs with was that the board members of GE approved of her, which was why he had wanted to marry her despite her no longer being pregnant.

She knew she had done the right thing to turn him down. Her close brush with death when her tube had ruptured had shown her that life was too precious to waste a moment of it. There had been a moment when she'd thought Alekos was going to admit that he cared for her and she'd held her breath and hoped with all her heart, only to hear him say that he valued her in the same way that he might have said he valued a priceless painting or one of the flash superyachts his company was famous for building.

Once she would have been grateful for any crumb he offered her. She had been so lacking in self-confidence that she would have married him because she had adored him and didn't believe that a handsome, charismatic and sophisticated man such as Alekos could fall in love with his plain, frumpy secretary.

Meeting her father had made her feel like a whole person. Casting her mind back over the past months, she could see that she had taken more interest in her appearance because she felt more worthwhile, and maybe it was her new confidence that had attracted Alekos as much as her new, sexier clothes and hairstyle. But crucially she had forgotten that he'd once said love was simply a word used by poets and romantics to describe lust.

The sound of a deep male voice outside the door made her heart leap into her throat. But when she stepped into the corridor it was not Alekos standing in front of the nurses' station, arguing with a nurse and drawing attention from a crowd of curious onlookers.

'I don't care if my name is not on the visitor list,' Lionel Kingsley said loudly. 'Sara Lovejoy is my daughter and I have come to visit her.' He glanced round and his expression became concerned when he saw her. 'Sara, my dear, you should be resting.' He spoke briefly on his mobile phone as he walked over to her and Sara hurriedly pulled him into her room and shut the door.

'What are you doing here? There must be a dozen people who heard you say that I am your daughter.' She bit her lip. 'It's probably already on social media and once the press get hold of the story it will be headline news, especially as there is speculation that you will be the new Home Secretary in the Cabinet reshuffle.'

'None of that is important.' Lionel swept her into a bear hug. 'What matters is that you are safe and as well as can be expected after you nearly lost your life. Alekos phoned and told me what had happened, and how you lost your baby.' He squeezed her so hard that she felt breathless. 'I'm so sorry, Sara. For your loss, and also for my behaviour. Alekos used some very colourful language when he pointed out that I had failed you as a father twice. The first time by not being around when you were a child, and the second by not publicly acknowledging you as my daughter.'

'He told you that?' she said faintly.

'And a lot more. He reminded me I was lucky to have a beautiful, compassionate and loyal daughter. When he told me how you had almost died I realised how stupid and selfish I had been. I should have welcomed you unreservedly, and I'm sorry I didn't before now.'

'But what about Charlotte and Freddie?' Sara was reeling from hearing how Alekos had stood up for her to her father. 'How do you think they will take the news that I am their sister?'

'Why don't you ask them? Or one of them, at least,' Charlotte Kingsley said as she walked into the room. 'Freddie is in America, but he said to tell you that he knows who you remind him of now.' She smiled at Sara's startled expression. 'You and I do look remarkably alike and not only because we both have green eyes. All three of dad's offspring take after his side of the family, and Freddie agrees with me that we can't think of a nicer person to have as our sister.'

'I thought you would hate me,' Sara said unsteadily.

Charlotte clasped her hand. 'Why would we hate you? Nothing that happened in the past is your fault. I'm sad that I didn't know about you for twenty-five years, but now I hope you will be part of our family for ever…if you want to be.'

Sara glanced at her father. 'Aren't you worried that the scandal will affect your political career?'

Lionel shrugged. 'These things often blow over. I behaved badly towards your mother and my wife many years ago and the person who suffered most was you. Far more important than my career is my determination to try and make amends and be the father I should have been to you when you were growing up. And I'd like to start by taking you to my home in Berkshire so that you can recuperate, but of course I'll understand if you want to go home with Alekos.'

Her father looked puzzled. 'Actually, I assumed Alekos would be here. I know he refused to leave your bedside while you were in intensive care. And when he came to see me yesterday to tell me what he thought of me for treating you badly, he looked like he'd been to hell and back. But it's not surprising after he lost his child and could have lost you too. It's obvious how much he cares for you.'

Sara sat down heavily on the chair and buried her face in her hands. She felt as if she was on an emotional roller coaster from her intense sadness at losing her baby and the shock of realising how close she had come to losing her own life. She had rejected Alekos without considering his feelings about the loss of their child. Although her pregnancy had been in the early stages, it was likely that the trauma had reminded him of losing his brother when he was a teenager.

A sob escaped her and she felt a hand patting her shoulder. Charlotte—her sister—she thought emotively, pushed some tissues into her hand. 'Cry it out, Sara. You've been through a terrible experience and you need time to grieve for the baby.'

As Alekos did. But she knew he would bottle up his feelings like he had when Dimitri died. 'I think I've made a terrible mistake,' she choked. Alekos needed her but she had sent him away and her tears were for the baby, for her, but mainly for the man she would always love.

CHAPTER ELEVEN

ALEKOS HAD SPENT his childhood at his parents' house just outside Athens. As a boy he had spent hours playing on the private beach but after Dimitri died he had stopped going there.

He moved away from the window, where he had been watching huge waves crash onto the shore. The recent storm had made the sea angry and the heavy sky echoed his mood. He picked up his brother's death certificate from the desk in his father's study and read it once more before he looked at his mother.

'Why didn't you tell me Dimitri suffered a heart attack when he went swimming and that was why he drowned?'

'You never wanted to talk about him. If his name was mentioned by anyone you would leave the room. Your father and I were advised not to push you to discuss the accident but to wait for you to bring up the subject.'

She sighed. 'Dimitri was born with a small hole in his heart but later tests showed that the defect had healed by itself and it was not expected to cause problems as he grew up. Your brother was such a strong, athletic boy and your father and I more or less forgot that there had been the early problem. When we learned that Dimitri had suffered heart failure we felt guilty that we should have persuaded him to have more health checks. The reason why Dimitri drowned was something we could not bear to discuss with you and your sisters. Why does your brother's cause of death matter now, so many years later?'

Alekos swallowed hard. 'I believed for all those years that Dimitri took his own life. He was heartbroken when he found out his girlfriend had cheated on him and he told me he did not want to live without Nia.'

His mother frowned. 'I remember he was upset over a girl. Your father had arranged for him to go and work in the Miami office for a few months to help him get over her. You were not at home on that last evening and so you did not see how excited Dimitri was about the trip to America.' She looked intently at her youngest son. 'I'm quite certain your brother knew he had everything to live for. He often went swimming at night and told me I worried too much when I asked him not to go into the sea alone.'

'I blamed myself for not getting help for Dimitri after he told me he felt depressed,' Alekos said gruffly. 'I felt guilty that I hadn't saved him. I missed him so much but I didn't want to cry in front of anyone because I was fourteen, not a baby. The only way I could cope was by not talking about him.'

'Dimitri's death was fate,' his mother said gently. 'I wish I had known how you felt, but I'm afraid you take after your father in the respect of not discussing your feelings. Kostas believed he must be strong for the rest of the family, but losing Dimitri made him withdraw emotionally. I think he found it hard to show how much he loved you because he was afraid of losing another child and suffering the same pain and grief he'd felt when Dimitri died.' She wiped away a tear. 'Your father was very proud of you, you know. He admired your drive and determination to take GE forward.'

'I wish I had known that Bampás approved of my ideas. I regret I didn't talk about Dimitri with him. It might have helped both of us.'

His mother nodded. 'Honesty and openness are important in a relationship and you should remember that when you marry Sara.'

Alekos's jaw clenched. 'Sara ended our engagement because I can't give her what she wants.'

'Sara does not strike me as someone who craves material possessions.'

'She says she will only marry for love.'

'Well, what other reason is there for marriage?'

He frowned. 'I thought that you and Bampás had an arranged marriage?'

His mother laughed. 'Our parents thought so too. But Kostas and I had met secretly and fallen in love, and we engineered our so-called arranged marriage. Love is the only reason to marry. Why is it a problem? You love Sara, don't you?'

Alekos could not reply to his mother's question, although he suspected the answer was somewhere in the mess of emotions that had replaced the cool logic which had served him perfectly well for two decades.

'I understand why my father was scared to love after he lost a son,' he said. His voice sounded as if it had scraped over rusty metal. He had a flashback to when he had been in the hospital waiting room, praying harder than he'd prayed in his life that Sara's life would be saved. 'Love can hurt,' he said roughly.

'But it can also bring the greatest joy,' his mother said softly. 'I am glad I was blessed with Dimitri and it was better to have him for twenty-one years than not to have known him and loved him. The pain I felt when he died was terrible, but the happiness he gave me in his short life was far greater.'

It was a wonderful party, and she was absolutely having a brilliant time, Sara told herself firmly. She looked around the ballroom of the five-star hotel in Mayfair and recognised numerous celebrities who, like her, had been invited to the birthday celebrations of a famous music producer.

Since the news that she was the daughter of Lionel Kingsley, MP, had made the headlines a month ago, she had been on the guest list at many top social events with her half-brother and half-sister. She loved being part of a family and while she was staying at her father's beautiful house in Berkshire she'd grown close to Lionel, Charlotte and Freddie. They and her father had encouraged her to follow a different career path after she'd resigned from her position as Alekos's PA. She had started an art foundation course at college and her plan to go to university to study for an art degree helped to take her mind off the trauma of the ectopic pregnancy.

Long walks in the countryside and the companionship of family mealtimes had gradually enabled her to come to terms with the loss of her baby, although there would always be a little ache in her heart for the child she would never know. Getting over Alekos had so far proved more difficult, especially when she had told her father and siblings that she had broken off her relationship with him and they had asked if she was sure she had done the right thing.

Well, she was sure now, she thought dismally. Photos of Alekos at a film premiere with a busty blonde wrapped around him had featured on the front pages of all the tabloids. She was furious with herself that she'd wasted time worrying about him. Why, she'd even phoned him to check if he was okay because it had been his baby too. He hadn't answered her call or replied to the message she'd left him, and seeing the picture of him with his latest bimbo had forced her to accept that he had moved on with his life and she should do the same.

She was jolted from her thoughts by a sharp pain in her foot. 'Sorry—again,' the man she was dancing with said ruefully when she winced. 'That must be the third time I've trodden on your toes.'

'Fourth, actually.'

She hid her irritation with a smile. He had introduced himself as Daniel, 'I'm doing a bit of modelling but I really want to be an actor,' and he was very good-looking, although it was lucky he wasn't hoping for a career as a dancer, she mused. Unfortunately, his good looks were wasted on her. She wished her heart did skip a beat when he pulled her closer, but she felt nothing. Although she managed to put on a cheerful front, she missed Alekos terribly and couldn't stop thinking about him.

'Is there a reason why the tall guy over there is staring at me as if he's planning to murder me?' Daniel murmured. 'He's coming this way and I get the feeling it's time I made myself scarce.'

'Which guy…?' Sara felt her heart slam into her ribs when Alekos materialised at her side.

'I advise you to find another woman to dance with,' he growled to Daniel, who immediately dropped his hands from Sara as if she were highly contagious. But her attention wasn't on Daniel. Alekos swamped all of her senses and he was the only man in the ballroom.

He looked utterly gorgeous dressed in slim black trousers and a black shirt open at the throat to reveal a sprinkling of curling chest hairs. His hair was ruffled as if he'd been running his fingers through it—or someone else had, Sara thought darkly, remembering the photos of him with the blonde who'd been stuck to him with superglue. Temper rescued her from the ignominy of drooling over him.

'How dare you barge in and spoil my evening?' she snapped.

'I dare, Sara *mou*, because if I hadn't persuaded your pretty boy dance partner to back off I would have throttled him with my bare hands.' His dark eyes burned like hot embers and the tight grip of his hands on her waist warned her that he was furious. Well, that made two of them, she thought, glaring at him when she tried to pull away and he jerked her against his body. The feel of his hard thighs pressed close to hers was almost enough to make her melt.

'I am definitely not *your* Sara. Will you let go of me? You're making an exhibition of us.'

'I haven't even started,' he warned. 'You can walk out of the ballroom with me or I'll carry you out.'

She snapped her teeth together as if she would like to bite him, but to safeguard her dignity she allowed him to steer her out of the ballroom and across the hotel foyer to the lifts. 'Won't your girlfriend mind? Don't pretend you don't know who I mean. You must have seen the picture on the front page of this morning's papers of you and Miss Breast Implants.'

His puzzled expression cleared. 'Oh, you mean Charlene.'

'I don't read gossip columns so I don't know her name.'

'Charlene McCuskey is the wife of Warren McCuskey, who I'm sure you recall is buying *Artemis*. They are in London so that Warren can finalise the purchase, but he has come down with a virus and so he asked me to escort Charlene to a film premiere, which I dutifully did before I took her back to their hotel. Unsurprisingly, she is devoted to her billionaire husband,' he said sardonically.

'Oh, I see,' Sara muttered. Without fully realising what she was doing she'd followed Alekos into a lift, and as the doors closed and she was alone with him in the small space she had a horrible feeling that he saw way too much of her thoughts. 'Where are you taking me?'

'I'm staying at the hotel and we are going to my suite.'

'I don't want...'

'We need to talk.' Something in his expression made her heart give another painful jolt. The lift had mirrored walls, and her reflection showed her breasts rising and falling jerkily beneath her scarlet silk dress that she'd worn thinking the bright colour might lift her spirits. 'You look beautiful,' Alekos told her brusquely.

Her eyes flew to his face and after weeks of feeling nothing every nerve ending on her body was suddenly fiercely alive. The lift stopped, and as she followed him along the corridor and into his suite she wondered why she was putting herself through this. Seeing him again was going to make it so much harder to get over him.

'Would you like a drink?'

It would give her something to do with her hands. When she nodded he walked over to the bar, poured a measure of cassis into two tall glasses and topped them up with champagne. Sara remembered they had drunk Kir Royale the night they had become lovers on the yacht in Monaco. It seemed a lifetime ago.

'How are you?'

'Good,' she said huskily. It wasn't true, but she was working on it. 'It's been great getting to know Charlotte and Freddie. I feel very lucky that they and my father are part of my life.'

'I'm sure they feel lucky to have found you.' There was an odd note in his voice and, like in the lift, the indefinable expression in his eyes stirred feelings inside her that she told herself she must not feel.

'How about you?' She hesitated. 'I phoned you...but you didn't call back.'

'I was in Greece. I visited my mother and we talked about my brother.' He indicated for Sara to sit down on a sofa but she felt too edgy to sit, and he remained standing too. 'Dimitri died of a heart attack while he was swimming,' he told her abruptly. 'I finally read the coroner's report. My parents had their reasons for not talking about the cause of his death and I never spoke about Dimitri because I tried to block out my grief.'

'I'm glad you found out the truth at last and can stop blaming yourself,' she said softly. 'I hope you can put the past behind you and move on with your life.'

'Do you include yourself in my past and hope I will forget about you?'

She swallowed. Alekos had moved without her being aware of him doing so and he was standing so close that she could see the tiny lines around his eyes that suggested he hadn't been sleeping well. There were deeper grooves on either side of his mouth and she sensed he was as tense as she felt.

'I guess we both need to move forwards,' she said, aiming for a light tone. 'Make a fresh start.'

'What if I asked you to come back to me?'

Her heart missed a beat, but she shook her head. 'I couldn't be your PA now that we...' she coloured '...now that we have had a personal association.'

'A *personal association*?' he said savagely. '*Theos*, Sara, we created a child together.'

'*A child you didn't want.* Any more than you wanted to marry me.' She spun away from him, determined not to break down in front of him.

'That's not true on both counts. I did want to marry you. I didn't respond to your phone call because when you went to stay with your father after you left hospital, I agreed with Lionel to give you some space. You needed to recover from the ectopic and spend time with your new family.'

Sara shrugged to show she didn't care, even though she did desperately. Alekos frowned but continued, 'I also did what every bridegroom is expected to do and asked your father if he would allow me to marry you.'

Sara choked on her mouthful of champagne. '*You did what?*' She was so angry she wanted to hit him and for about twenty seconds she forgot that she wanted to kiss him. 'There is no way I would agree to marry you to keep the board members of GE happy.'

'Good, because that's a terrible reason for us to

marry,' he said calmly, although his eyes blazed with a fierce heat that melded Sara to the floor and stopped her rushing towards the door.

'I'm being serious.' She put her hands flat on his chest to stop him coming closer but he clasped her wrists and pulled her arms down, at the same time as he tugged her against him with a force that expelled the air from her lungs.

'So am I.' He stared at her intently and his jaw clenched when he saw the tears she was struggling to hold back. 'Why were you jealous when you saw the photo of me with Charlene?'

She flushed. 'I wasn't jealous.'

'Did you feel like I did tonight when I saw you dancing with that guy and I wanted to tear his head off?'

'Definitely not.' She didn't know what game of refined torture Alekos was playing but it had to stop before the intoxicating warmth of his body pressed up against hers and ruined her for ever.

'Liar,' he taunted. 'Were you jealous because you love me?'

She could deny it but what would be the point? She couldn't fight him or herself any more, and Sara knew she would be his mistress if he asked her because she'd learned that life was too short to turn down the chance to be with him, even though he would break her heart when he ended their affair.

But she still had her pride and her eyes flashed with green fire. '*Yes*, I love you. I've loved you for ever, even though you are the most arrogant man I've ever known.'

'But I am the only man you have ever known intimately, arrogant or not,' he said softly, his mouth curving in a crooked smile that tugged on Sara's heart. He sounded strange, as if his throat was constricted, and her eyes widened in disbelief when she saw that his lashes were wet.

'Alekos?' she whispered.

'Sara *mou*...' He held her so tight that she felt the thunder of his heart. '*S'agapo*. I love you so much.' He framed her face with his hands that were shaking. 'When I watched your life ebbing away in the ambulance on the way to hospital I was terrified I would lose you. And I realised then that I had tried hard *not* to fall in love with you because of fear. I associated love with the loss and pain that I felt after Dimitri died.'

'That's not surprising,' she said shakily. 'You were at an impressionable age when he died, and your brother was your best friend.'

'We became friends when you worked for me, didn't we, Sara? I liked you and I respected you when you put me in my place. I felt closer to you than I'd ever felt with any of my mistresses. But one day I walked into my office and I was blown away by a gorgeous sexy brunette. You can imagine my shock when I discovered it was you.'

She flushed. 'Before that day you didn't notice your frumpy PA.'

'I did notice you. Often I would find myself thinking about a funny remark you'd made, and I appreciated your fierce intelligence and your advice on how to handle work issues. I almost resented you when you made me desire you too. I knew I was in danger of falling in love with you and I told myself that once we were lovers my interest in you would fade. Instead, it grew stronger every day and night that we were together. When you told me you were pregnant I seized the excuse to marry you without having to admit how I felt about you.'

How he felt about her. Sara bit her lip and told herself it was too good to be true. 'You said love is a word that poets use to describe lust. Are you sure you haven't got the two mixed up?'

'I don't blame you for doubting me, *kardia mou*. That means my heart, and I love you with all my heart.'

Sara's head advised caution but her heart was desperate to believe that, incredible as it seemed, Alekos was looking at her with adoration in his eyes. She caught her breath when he stroked his finger gently down her cheek.

'Will you marry me, my Sara, for no other reason than you are the love of my life?'

That was the moment she knew she should have listened to the warning that it was all too good to be true. Carefully she eased out of his arms and closed her eyes to blot out the sudden haggard look on his face. 'I can't.'

'*Theos*, Sara, I will do whatever it takes to prove to you that I love you.' His voice cracked. 'Please believe me.'

'I do. And I love you. But you need an heir to one day run GE, and there is a strong chance I won't be able to give you a child because I lost one tube and there is a higher risk I could have another ectopic pregnancy.'

He caught her to him and buried his face in her hair. 'Then we won't have children. There's no way I will risk your life. I need *you*,' he told her fiercely. 'Nothing else is important. Whatever the future holds, I want us to share it together, the ups and the downs, for the rest of our lives.'

He tightened his arms around her so that she was

aware of his hard thigh muscles pressed against her. 'My body knew the truth before I was ready to accept it,' he said roughly. 'When we made love it was so much more than great sex.'

Joy fizzed inside Sara like champagne bubbles exploding. Hearing Alekos say he loved her wiped away the pain and misery of the past weeks and the future shimmered on the horizon like a golden sun. 'Mmm, but it was great sex, wasn't it?' Her smile was wicked and adoring. 'I think you should remind me.'

His laughter rumbled through her and the unguarded expression in his eyes stole her breath even before his mouth did the same as he claimed her lips and kissed her so thoroughly, so *lovingly*, that she was trembling when he finally lifted his head.

'I'd better warn you that this is the honeymoon suite and the staff have really gone to town,' he murmured. 'There are rose petals everywhere in the bedroom.'

Alekos had been right about the rose petals, Sara discovered when he carried her into the bedroom and laid her on the bed, adorned with fragrant red petals. He undressed her slowly, kissing each part of her body that he revealed, and when he removed her knickers and pressed his mouth to her feminine heat she told him she loved him, loved him. She repeated the words when he thrust into her so deeply that he filled her and he made love to her with all the love in his heart.

It was as wonderful as she remembered and more beautiful than she could ever have dreamed because this time Alekos didn't just show her he loved her; he told her in a mixture of English and Greek.

'Will you let me love you for ever, and will you love

me?' he murmured as he drew her close and they relaxed in the sweet aftermath of loving.

'I will,' Sara promised him and she meant the words with her heart and soul.

They were married three months later on Christmas Eve, in a church decorated with holly and ivy and fragrant red roses, and filled with their families and friends. Sara wore a white satin and lace gown and carried a bouquet of white lilies. Alekos looked stunning in a dark grey suit, but it was the look in his eyes as he watched his bride walk down the aisle towards him that made his mother and sisters wipe away tears. Sara's father walked proudly beside her to meet her husband-to-be, and her half-sister was her maid of honour.

After the reception at Lionel Kingsley's home in Berkshire, the happy couple flew to South Africa for their honeymoon. 'Somewhere hot where you can wear less clothes,' Alekos had stated when Sara had asked him where he wanted to go.

As it turned out, neither of them got dressed very often during the three weeks they stayed in a private bungalow at a luxury beach resort, a fact that Sara later accounted for her pregnancy that was confirmed a month after they returned to London. It was an anxious time until an early scan showed that her pregnancy was normal and they watched the tiny beating heart of their baby with hope in their hearts.

Theodore Dimitri Gionakis, to be known as Theo, arrived in the world two weeks early with a minimum of fuss and instantly became the centre of his parents' world.

'Love changes everything,' Alekos said one evening

as he held his son in the crook of one arm and slid his other arm around his wife's waist. 'You changed me, Sara *mou*. You showed me how to let love into my heart and now it's there to stay for ever.'

'For ever sounds wonderful,' she told him, and then she kissed him and no further words were necessary.

* * * * *

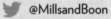

MILLS & BOON

THE HEART OF ROMANCE

A ROMANCE FOR EVERY KIND OF READER

MODERN

Prepare to be swept off your feet by sophisticated, sexy and seductive heroes, in some of the world's most glamourous and romantic locations, where power and passion collide.
8 stories per month.

HISTORICAL

Escape with historical heroes from time gone by. Whether your passion is for wicked Regency Rakes, muscled Vikings or rugged Highlanders, awaken the romance of the past.
6 stories per month.

MEDICAL

Set your pulse racing with dedicated, delectable doctors in the high-pressure world of medicine, where emotions run high and passion, comfort and love are the best medicine.
6 stories per month.

True Love

Celebrate true love with tender stories of heartfelt romance, from the rush of falling in love to the joy a new baby can bring, and a focus on the emotional heart of a relationship.
8 stories per month.

Desire

Indulge in secrets and scandal, intense drama and plenty of sizzling hot action with powerful and passionate heroes who have it all: wealth, status, good looks…everything but the right woman.
6 stories per month.

HEROES

Experience all the excitement of a gripping thriller, with an intense romance at its heart. Resourceful, true-to-life women and strong, fearless men face danger and desire - a killer combination!
8 stories per month.

DARE

Sensual love stories featuring smart, sassy heroines you'd want as a best friend, and compelling intense heroes who are worthy of them.
4 stories per month.

To see which titles are coming soon, please visit

millsandboon.co.uk/nextmonth